ore . . .

The pseudonymous **K. C. CONSTANTINE** is the author of thirteen crime novels set in Rocksburg, Pennsylvania. They include *Family Values, Cranks and Shadows, Bottom Liner Blues, The Rocksburg Railroad Murders, The Man Who Liked Slow Tomatoes, Sunshine Enemies, Upon Some Midnights Clear,* and *Joey's Case,* which was nominated for the Edgar Allan Poe Award for Best Mystery Novel.

By K.C. Constantine

K. C. CONSTANTINE

GOOD SONS

THE MYSTERIOUS PRESS

Published by Warner Books

A Time Warner Company

MYSTERIOUS PRESS EDITION

Cover design by Jackie Merri Meyer
Cover illustration by Douglas Fraser

The Mysterious Press name and logo are registered trademarks of Warner Books, Inc.

 Mysterious Press books are published by
Warner Books, Inc.
1271 Avenue of the Americas
New York, NY 10020

Visit our Web site at
http://pathfinder.com/twep

W A Time Warner Company

Printed in the United States of America

Originally published in hardcover by The Mysterious Press.
First Printed in Paperback: March, 1997

10 9 8 7 6 5 4 3 2 1

GOOD
SONS

ROCKSBURG DET. SGT. RUGGIERO CARLUCCI slumped into a chair at his desk in headquarters and pulled off his icy wet running shoes and socks. He blew on his hands and took hold of his numb toes and held them for a long moment. He yawned and shivered upright with a jolt out of the chair and tottered on his heels over to the heater vent and set his shoes and socks on top of it. Then he went downstairs to the locker room, still on his heels, and stripped off the rest of his clothes and took a shower, thinking all the while that he'd never again be caught without a pair of overshoes.

During his shower and on the way back upstairs, he kept wondering whether he'd let the cold prevent him from doing everything he should have. He worried most that his 35mm camera had been working. It had not failed him in twelve years, but he was never able to relax until he actually had the pictures in hand. Even though the camera had always worked, he invariably worried that *this time* it hadn't, *this time* when he went to pick up the photos he'd get an envelope full of blank negatives, and there would go his case.

He relied on the photos more than he relied on his notes and sketches because the photos held the details he always believed he'd overlooked and because he trusted nothing to memory. He had the nuns at Central Catholic to thank for that. The one thing they'd managed to drum into him over twelve years of schooling was that what was inside his skull was average at best, stupid at worst, unreliable most of the time.

This time, though, he really was worried about the camera. This time his fingers had been so stiff from the cold, he didn't know if his notes were legible, and if he had been that cold, maybe this time the camera had been affected as well. After he was back upstairs at his desk, he got a new pack of sheets for his loose-leaf notebook and transferred his original notes to it because he knew the longer he postponed that the more trouble he would have deciphering them. The notes were more scribbly than he feared, especially at the end, which made him worry even more about the camera.

The scene wouldn't have been any more of a problem than any other scene if it hadn't snowed and if a patrolman had secured it initially. But it had snowed—it was still snowing—and the two officers on patrol at the time he took the call from 911 had been occupied with a traffic accident and a domestic dispute, so before Carlucci could secure the scene, he'd had to interview the EMTs and the nurses and doctors in the emergency room in Conemaugh General and collect all the evidence they'd gathered. It was the worst order of working, but when there was nobody else to do it, it couldn't be helped.

He'd gotten the call from 911 on his pager at 7:05 P.M. but hadn't arrived at the Rocksburg Pre-Cast Concrete Company off West Washington Street until 9:10, so more than two hours had passed between when 911 got the call for help from the woman and when he finally arrived at the scene.

Once there, he'd tramped around the whole building in his running shoes in snow up to his ankles, taking pictures of the exterior windows and doors, trying not to be blinded by the flashbulb, all the while berating himself for his procrastination about buying boots. He was certain after his tramp around the perimeter that entry had been made through the outside door in the front. He wasn't sure exactly when it had started to snow, sometime after dinner, six maybe, maybe later, but no matter when it had started to snow, the fact was that no other door or window in the building showed any sign of having been forced open.

He'd thought that even if there hadn't been any snow on the ground when the incident had gone down, the ground under the snow was frozen anyway, so looking for footprints was a waste of time. Besides, if the perp had gone in and out the front door after it had begun to snow as he suspected, every footprint would have been obliterated by the EMTs anyway because that's the way they'd gone in and out. Instead of worrying any more about footprints, Carlucci had taken pictures of the front door to establish that there were no pry marks around the locks, that it had been opened by a simple turning of the knob. After he'd done that, he reminded himself again that the lights in the office had been on because the EMTs had told him they'd left them on.

Before he'd gone into the office, he'd taken out his compass and oriented himself to north. Then he'd put on his rubber gloves and gone inside, being careful where he stepped while he took almost ten minutes to look around before he started making sketches and taking pictures. After he'd finished his second sketch, he compared it with the one he'd made in the hospital after interviewing the EMTs about how the woman had been positioned when they'd found her.

When he saw that the sketches he'd just made compared fa-
vorably with the one he'd made after interviewing the EMTs,
he was satisfied that he'd made the right choice: staying in
the hospital and pumping the EMTs about what they'd found
instead of rushing to the scene to check it out himself. The
only thing that even slightly surprised him was how cramped
the office was, how jammed it was with desks, chairs, and
file cabinets. For some reason, he'd gotten the impression
from the EMTs that it would be bigger, not that that made
any difference.

The office was eighteen feet long and twelve wide, with a
chest-high counter about four feet from the front door running from the west wall to within three feet of the east wall.
Under the counter were five two-drawer file cabinets. There
were two metal desks, two straight-backed metal chairs, a
Rolodex on the desk next to the west wall, and a computer
on the desk against the east wall. Two phones were on the
floor: the connecting wire to one had been pulled out of a
box on the baseboard along the west wall; the other phone
was the one the woman had apparently used to call 911.
Lucky for her, and incredible as it seemed to Carlucci, the
perp hadn't smashed the connectors. All the desk drawers
had been pulled out and the contents thrown on the floor. Six
four-drawer file cabinets were lined up along the south wall.
Every file drawer had been opened and the floor was covered
with invoices or correspondence about invoices. Two of the
drawers were jammed open about a third of the way.

There was a door at the southeast corner of the office
which led to a small bathroom with only a toilet, sink, and a
medicine cabinet with a mirror on the door. The medicine
cabinet contained several boxes of bandages of different
sizes and a large bottle of aspirin. The bathroom had another
door that led onto the plant floor but that door was locked
from the inside. Carlucci thought that whoever managed the

business wasn't very interested in his customers' comfort. There wasn't another chair in the office, no magazines, no ashtrays, nothing except a small coffeemaker to show that management wanted the customers around any longer than necessary. And the coffee was probably for whoever worked in the office, because there was only one mug beside the coffeemaker and another one on the floor. Both were clean. A bottle of powdered cream was in a wastebasket, the lid still tight, probably knocked there during the rape or when the perp was throwing things around in his search.

Carlucci went out onto the floor of the plant through the door in the bathroom that had been locked from the inside and found the switches for the overhead fluorescents and kept them on until he was satisfied that nothing had been disturbed there. He knew he'd have to talk to the owners or employees to make certain of that, but he was almost positive when he turned off the overhead lights that whatever the perp had wanted had been in the office and not in the plant.

Which left the big questions: what had the perp wanted, who was the woman, and why had she been there at that time of day? The most obvious assumption was that the woman was an employee who stayed late to work—or had gone home and come back. Carlucci was thinking about that when he went back into the office and focused on the small pool of coagulating blood on the scattered invoices between the desks, which according to the EMTs was where they'd found the woman, her head to the north.

She'd been on her back, the phone inches from her left hand. She'd been conscious but just barely and the only thing she'd told them was that her mouth hurt and she couldn't close it. Her skirt had been pushed up around her hips, her panty hose shredded and tangled around her left ankle, her panties ripped into two pieces with one piece below her left knee and the other lying on the floor. Blood had been pooling in her mouth, and the EMTs, almost immediately on arrival, had turned her over to keep her from choking. The blood was smeared over a great scattering of invoices, obviously from where the EMTs had turned her over and then back and then lifted her onto the litter. Also, one of the litter's wheels had swirled a path through the blood, but nobody had stepped in it.

Carlucci's eye followed the path of the wheel and fell on something shiny at the edge of the blood. He photographed it from two different angles, then bent down and saw that it was a dental bridge, two false molars still connected to the bicuspid that had come out broken at the root. While he was bagging and tagging it, he thought that it must have been knocked out when the perp had hit the woman so hard he'd left black fibers embedded in her jaw and cheek. One of the doctors in the emergency room had told him about that, which made Carlucci assume it was going to be a waste of time dusting for fingerprints—not that he would've done that anyway, as incompetent as he felt about collecting print evidence. So if the perp had worn gloves, why hadn't he thrown the phones away? Why had he just disconnected them? Or why hadn't he smashed the connectors with his heel so they couldn't be reconnected? Did somebody surprise him before he was able to do that? Wasn't he smart enough to think that far ahead? Did he think the woman wasn't going to be able to use the phone? Did he think she was never going to get conscious enough to use it?

While Carlucci was shuffling on his haunches slowly around the floor, he kept thinking about what the doctor had said about the force of the blows and surmised that what had gone down was probably the work of a driven, hostile, woman-hating amateur, but it was an amateur who'd been through the system with enough awareness to know that gloves prevented the collection of one piece of evidence.

Carlucci was always surprised by how many burglars he'd encountered who'd taken two and three falls who still hadn't learned about gloves. Course if they were working Rocksburg, they didn't have to worry about gloves. He didn't know anybody who didn't know what a klutz he was about fingerprints.

This amateur, on the other hand, also knew that by taking the woman's purse he was going to cause the police to spend a lot of time and energy trying to identify her, time and energy they would otherwise have spent trying to find him, so maybe he wasn't an amateur. Or maybe he was a pro who'd gotten seriously pissed because he found a witness instead of what he thought was going to be there, which didn't explain why he raped her, but Carlucci knew you couldn't predict what any burglar—amateur or pro—would do when he encountered a witness. The ugliest homicide he'd ever seen was the result of a burglar encountering a witness. . . .

After Carlucci finished transferring his notes at his desk, he checked them over once again and then went to the radio console where Patrolman Larry Fischetti was swiveling nervously in his chair.

"Yo, Detective Rugseroo, what's up?"

"It's colder'n shit, that's what's up. What's the degrees out, you hear?"

"I heard twenty, wind chill minus five, but that was about two hours ago. Hospital didn't call by the way. You wanna know that, right?"

"Yeah, right. Do me a favor, okay? Call the county airport—not right now, whenever you get a chance—ask 'em when it started snowin' tonight, and what the degrees was around, say, between eighteen and nineteen hundred hours, okay?"

"Yeah, okay, you got it."

"What d'you get out of the crisscross, anything?"

"Here it is, right here, " Fischetti said, pushing a piece of notepaper at him. "Owner of Rocksburg Pre-Cast Concrete Company is, uh, Alfredo V. Picadio Jr., 12 Mercury Way, Rocksburg RD 9. Phone number's there too. Nowicki called him and I called him. Just got a machine."

"How many times you call?"

"Nowicki made the first call right after you called, lemme think, 'bout twenty-thirty I guess. I'm not sure about the second time, but I called right after I got squared away here. That would've been maybe twenty-three-thirty-five, give or take five minutes."

"Fish, you gotta start writin' things down, man, you can't do this 'give or take five minutes' shit anymore. You know better'n that and I'm gettin' tired tellin' ya."

"Ouu, he's talkin' the chief talk already. Pretty soon he'll be walkin' the chief walk. Look out Chief Rugseroo."

Carlucci sighed but said nothing, turning instead to go back to the heater vent to check on his shoes and socks.

Fischetti called after him, "Hey, Rugs, *paisan*, when you do get to be chief, you gotta get me away from this radio. It's makin' me crazy, I'm tellin' ya."

"Knock it off with the chief stuff, okay? I don't wanna hear it."

"C'mon, Rugs, somebody got to be it, why not you? They ain't gonna let this department run on memories forever. And Balzic's history. Time marches on'n all that shit."

Carlucci said nothing. Back at his desk, he picked up his phone and hit the buttons for Alfredo V. Picadio Jr.'s home phone again. He got a machine message directing the caller to leave his name and number, which he did.

When he hung up he called back to Fischetti, "You leave a message when you called before?"

"Certainly I left a message, I'm not stupid. I'm just not as smart as you think I oughta be."

"Fish, man, it don't have anything to do with smart. It has to do with careless. And one day it's gonna come back on ya—"

"And you're gonna remember what I said," Fischetti picked up the beat and mimicked him, "only it's gonna be too fuckin' late."

Carlucci shook his head at Fischetti but said nothing.

Fischetti also said nothing for a while, then he called out, "So what d'ya hear about who's gonna be chief, Rugs? Huh? You musta heard somethin', right?"

"I don't hear nothin' 'cause I don't listen to nothin'," Carlucci said. But he was lying and he knew that Fischetti knew it too. "I can't do anything about it anyway, so it doesn't make any difference what I hear."

"Gonna make a lotta difference, *paisan*," Fischetti said. "To you, to me, to everybody around here. You better start doin' more'n listenin', you ask me."

"I didn't."

"Yeah? Well whatever happens happens. Just remember what I said about gettin' me away from this fuckin' microphone duty, that's all I'm askin'. Feel like a goddamn disc jockey sometimes. Anyway, sergeants used to do this, you know? If I'm gonna do it, at least gimme the stripes. And the raise too, don't forget the raise. But I mean just doin' this? No stripes? No raise? Fuck this, man, get me on the street. Please!"

Carlucci, glumly feeling that his steaming running shoes were still very damp, put them back down near the vent, but said nothing. He couldn't afford to waste any more time arguing with Fischetti because he had a lot of work to do— starting the case file, getting all the evidence he'd collected at the hospital ready for the state police crime lab, getting his preliminary reports written and his film ready for the developer. It was the paperwork most police officers stereotypically complained about, but not Carlucci. His greatest satisfaction as a police officer came when his testimony resulted in a conviction—it didn't matter whether it came through a trial or a plea bargain. And every time a prosecutor thanked him for his testimony, Carlucci silently thanked Sister Mary Joseph, who'd told him the day before he'd graduated from Central Catholic that he should apply for a job at Kmart because they always needed people to stock the shelves and if he applied himself he might some day work up to be assistant manager in the garden department.

Carlucci remembered Sister Mary Joseph every time he worked a new crime scene, especially afterwards when he started the case file. He'd dredge her up out of a cranny of his mind, park her on his shoulder, and say, See, Sister? I don't have to be what you think is a good student. 'Cause every time I get tested it's an open-book test, and I'm who's writing the book. . . .

The last thing he did before going home was to gather up all the evidence he'd bagged and marked in the hospital, every piece of the woman's clothing, all the samples of blood, scalp hair and pubic hair, the vaginal, oral, and anal swabbings, the scrapings from under the woman's fingernails, and put them in boxes and hauled them to the state police crime lab at Troop A Barracks. He spent another forty minutes there filling out all the papers necessary to preserve the chain of custody. He was bone tired and fighting sleep the whole time, but he didn't leave until he'd checked everything twice and made a copy of the receipt for the evidence he was given by the crime lab clerk. Only then did he think about going home, but right before he left the building, something started to bother him. He didn't know what it was, but he found himself looking down at his shoes.

He stood by the front door of the lab, staring at his shoes and trying to figure out what he was doing standing there. He retraced his movements since he'd first been called to the hospital. He closed his eyes and visualized what he'd done, trying to re-create every step he'd taken—then it came to him. It was the word *step*. Every step he'd taken shuffling on his haunches around the office at Rocksburg Pre-Cast, he'd heard something. For a long time, he'd thought it was the invoices underfoot. But then he'd reached down and lifted some of those invoices and wiped the floor with the side of his hand. It was covered with a fine, grainy, gray dust. Sand and cement, that's what it was, he said to himself, as he hurried back into the lab.

"Hey," he called out to the lab tech who'd signed in all the evidence bags, "you got a sweeper I can borrow, huh? I need to go back and sweep the floor."

"Nothin' doin'," the lab tech said. "The sweeper never leaves unless I'm attached to it, and I'm not goin' anywhere."

"Aw c'mon, man, gimme a break, mine's in the shop, ain't gonna be ready till next week," Carlucci said.

"You were there, right? Where you wanna sweep?"

"Course I was there."

"Then take your shoes off, I'll sweep them."

"I been a lotta places since then."

"Won't matter. I'll get every place you've been. You bring a comparison sample, if it matches I'll match it. Or you can go do it yourself, I don't care, but my sweeper's not leavin' here without me, so it's up to you, I don't care how you do it."

Carlucci took his shoes off and handed them over. He was so tired, he almost fell over getting them off. Five minutes later, after he'd tagged and bagged the contents of the sweeper bag, he dragged himself out to his car and drove home.

He didn't even open his mother's bedroom door to see if

she was all right. He could hear her snoring, and that was good enough. Mrs. Viola would've left around eleven, but he didn't bother to go into the kitchen to read the note she usually left for him. He crept into his room and collapsed on the bed with his clothes on.

After waking up, showering, and changing clothes, he made coffee for his mother and made her swear she'd put her diaper on. Then he went next door and walked Mrs. Comito over because she was terrified of falling. She believed the purpose of snow was to prevent her from seeing ice whose purpose was to cause her to break her hip. As Mrs. Comito was taking her scarf and coat off by the front door, she crooked her finger at Carlucci to bend down so she could whisper to him.

"Hey, Rugsie, you been watchin' TV? Huh? You seen about all them people didn't pay their Social Security taxes for their cleanin' ladies and the people watch their kids'n stuff?"

"I didn't watch it. I been readin' about it, yeah, not a whole lot, but, Mrs. Comito, we already talked about this—"

"Rugsie, what're we gonna do?" she interrupted him. "You never paid any taxes for me, 'cause if you did you never said nothin' to me about it. I'm startin' to get worried, you know? All this stuff on TV, Jeez."

"Mrs. Comito, we talked about this twice now, you know?"

"Yeah but, Rugsie, what if somebody finds out how you pay me, huh? You sure I won't have to pay a fine or something? Or God forbid go to jail maybe? Rugsie, I'm just tryin' to be a good person'n help you out here, you know? And make a little something for myself, that's all I'm doin', I'm no criminal, they make it sound like you're a criminal on TV you do this."

Carlucci cleared his throat and said, "Uh, we don't have

anything to worry about, Mrs. Comito. Really. I mean, uh, nobody's callin' you up, are they? From Washington? Askin' you to be attorney general or somethin' like that, huh? Are they?"

"C'mon, Rugsie, don't be jokin', this ain't funny. My daughter-in-law, you know, Rickie's wife? The one's always dyein' her hair all the time, you know?"

"I met her a couple times, but I don't know her—"

"Well, she's always threatenin' to turn in this woman lives down the street from her 'cause the woman cleans houses and she's always makin' the people she cleans for, you know, she makes 'em pay her cash, she won't take their checks, so she brags sometimes she never pays no taxes, and my daughter-in-law can't stand it when she thinks somebody's gettin' away with somethin' she's not gettin' away with, you know? I mean, what if—God knows what for—but what if she gets mad at me for something? She got mad at me once 'cause I bought her a blouse the wrong color for her birthday. I'm worried about this, Rugsie, c'mon, you're a cop for cryin' out loud—"

"Mrs. Comito, I know you're worried about this—"

"Yeah but you don't know how bad I'm worried. You know how long I been watchin' your mother, Rugsie? Holy cow, twenty years, Jeez, come on. All this stuff on TV, it's really startin' to scare me, Jeez, last night I started to add up all the money you paid me, my God, Rugsie, I really got scared. It's like more'n a hundred and twenty thousand dollars. I mean, I had to quit, I couldn't add it all up, I looked at all those numbers, Jeez, that's a lotta money over twenty-some years, twenty-one I think exactly. I couldn't sleep. I feel terrible about this. We never paid no taxes. I know I never did and you told me twice now you never did—"

"Mrs. Comito, listen to me, you're gettin' carried away here, really, I'm tellin' ya. I know, I paid you a lotta money over the years, there's no question about that, but it's nowhere near—listen to me now, you listenin' to me?"

"Yes, I'm listening, I'm listening."

"All the money I paid you isn't nothing compared to the money I would've had to paid to a nursing home to take care of Ma, you hear? I need you. A lot. I need you and I need Mrs. Viola, and I've paid her a lotta money too. But believe me, what I've paid you both isn't anywhere near what it would've cost me to put my mother in a home. I mean, I can't afford that, Mrs. Comito. This is the third time you talked about this, you can't tell me you don't remember we've been over this twice before, I know you know that—"

"Yeah, sure I know that, Rugsie, but—"

"No buts, Mrs. Comito, listen. I'm not gonna turn you in. Why would I turn you in? I need you too much. Are you gonna turn me in? Huh? Are you?"

"Well, no. Course not."

"So then from what you're tellin' me, the only person you have to worry about is your daughter-in-law, right? Well now, think about it, she get along good with your son?"

"Oh yeah, he's still crazy about her. He takes all kinda crap from her, God I'd smack her one, but not him, oh boy, Jeez oh man, him, he follows her around like a puppy—"

"Well see, then all you have to do is be nice to her once in a while, that's all. And when she's around, if I'm around, you tell me, and I'll be nice to her too, that's all. And we're okay. Okay? You believe me?"

"What're youns two talkin' about behind my back?" Mrs. Carlucci growled from around the corner of the living room. "I'm sicka youns two always whisperin' behind my back."

"No, Ma, no no, it's not what you think, honest."

"You always say that. I don't believe you. If you got nothin' to hide from me, what're youns whisperin' about, huh?"

"Ma, we're not hidin' anything from you, honest to God we're not. Listen, I gotta go. Mrs. Comito, stop worryin' about this, really."

"What's she have to worry about? She don't have no son goes off every day leaves his mother. What the hell's she got to worry about? I'm gettin' sicka all this whisperin', I'm tellin' ya. Sick of it! Sick! Sick sick sick!"

Carlucci blew out a sigh, grabbed his parka, and left without another word.

He drove straight to Conemaugh General Hospital, parked in the public garage, and hurried to the intensive-care unit. He stopped at the nurses' station and held up his ID and told the three nurses bent over their paperwork that he was there to see about the woman who'd been brought in last night. They all looked up at once, their eyes bright with fear and anger and commiseration, mostly anger. Their looks lasted only a flicker of time, and then they had their work faces back on, but that flicker told Carlucci he had to watch himself. A wrong word, a wrong tone, and it wouldn't matter that he was a cop trying to find out who'd attacked the woman. He was a man before he was a cop. It wasn't something he'd ever heard directly in so many words; it was just something he'd come to recognize in the women who wound up caring for women who got beat up by men.

"How's she doin'?"

"Not good," said the one who seemed to be in charge. Carlucci didn't recognize any of the nurses.

"Can I talk to her?"

"You can try, but she's not conscious."

"Was she ever? I mean, last time I saw her was about seven-thirty last night. I mean she was conscious when the EMTs found her, but, uh, so she didn't wake up again, is that what you're sayin'?"

"No record of it."

"Anybody been in, askin' about her? Anybody call, lookin' for a woman. Any woman?"

"Main switchboard would know that. Nobody here would get a call unless somebody asked for her by name."

Before Carlucci could ask, she picked up the phone and handed it over the counter to him and said, "Just hit '0.'" Carlucci did and learned that nobody had called since last night trying to find a woman, or anybody for that matter.

"So much for that," he said to himself. He took out his Polaroid and said, "I have to get some pictures of her, so if there's something I could screw up or, uh, you know, disturb somebody you don't want disturbed, you wanna tell me about it? And you wanna show me which bed she's in?"

The nurse who'd handed him the phone got up and came around the end of the counter and nodded for him to follow. She pointed to the bed in the far right corner of the room. "You won't disturb anybody if you stay on this side of her, if that's possible. If it isn't, well, do what you have to do."

Carlucci thanked her, walked quietly to the woman's side, and took two shots of her left profile, then two of her right, and then held the camera over her face from above and took two more that way. Her eyelids never responded to the flashbulb. He looked at the Polaroids and shook his head. How the hell was anybody supposed to identify this woman with this much distortion of her face, caused by the respirator and feeding tubes and the swelling. He shrugged and told himself that what he had was what he had.

He bent close to her ear and said softly, "Uh, I'm detective Carlucci. If you can hear me, would you give me some sign? Would you move your fingers or maybe move your eyelids, huh?"

There was no response, just the raspy inhale and exhale of the respirator.

He said it again, two more times, and each time she didn't respond. He licked his lips and whispered, "I'll be checkin' on you. I want you to hang in there, hear? Don't give up. I need you to help me. 'Cause I wanna help you. Don't quit, you hear?"

As he straightened up, he thought he saw her right eyelid twitch. Her left eye was swollen to the size of half a small lemon, but her right eye was more or less normal, and he was not sure he'd seen anything. Maybe he was just wishing he'd seen something. He bent down and repeated what he'd said, watching her right eyelid intently, but it didn't move, so he turned away and left.

He walked past the nurses' station and held his card aloft and made sure all three nurses saw him put it on the counter and said, "Any change, call me, okay? Don't matter what time it is, okay? If I'm not at the station, you can always get me on the pager, okay? All the numbers're on my card here. I answer the pager no matter what, no matter when."

The nurses nodded and said they would do as he asked, and he left.

He drove out of the hospital garage and across town to the *Rocksburg Gazette* building. He went to the reception desk and asked to talk to the editor in charge in the newsroom. He also asked for an envelope, into which he put three of the Polaroids, one of each profile and one full face. Then he licked and sealed the envelope and printed on the back where and when the woman had been found and her approximate age. He wrote nothing about the rape.

In about five minutes, a paunchy balding man came through a set of doors and said, "Who wants to see me?" He wore very thick bifocals. He came straight for Carlucci even though there was another man waiting at the receptionist's counter.

Carlucci asked if he was in charge of the newsroom, and

when the man said he would be until five o'clock, Carlucci showed his ID and handed him the envelope and told him what was in it. The man said he recognized Carlucci and said they'd met several times before, but the last time had been many years ago.

Carlucci figured the man was just doing the normal public relations some people can't stop from doing to show what good guys they are. Instead of debating whether they'd ever met, he said, "All the information you need is on the back of the envelope there. I would appreciate it a lot if you'd run one of those pictures as close to the front of the paper as possible. Two would be better. If you can't, please run at least one of them somewhere, okay? 'Cause we don't know who she is."

"Well I'm not gonna promise anything."

"Thought you said you were in charge."

"Just until five. But I don't put the paper out. I'll give the information to the man who does, but if it's a hot news day and he comes up short on space, I'm not gonna make promises for him."

"Yeah. Well, do the best you can," Carlucci said, heading for the door. "I'd appreciate it. Oh, by the way, you know when the malls open? When Sears opens?"

"Probably around nine-thirty, ten. I do all my shopping at night." The paunchy balding man thought that was funny and was still laughing when Carlucci walked out of the lobby.

He figured he had at least an hour before the malls opened, so he headed for Rocksburg Pre-Cast Concrete Company. Once parked there, he saw that nobody had disturbed the building: the yellow tape he'd put across the front office door and the double garage doors was still in place and there were no fresh footprints around, so he began canvassing the nearby houses.

There were only three houses with windows that looked

out onto the plant, but none of the people who lived in them had seen or heard anything out of the ordinary yesterday afternoon or early evening. The first any of them knew anything unusual was happening was when they saw the reflections of the ambulance's light bar in their windows. The clearest impression Carlucci got from any of them was that to a person they wished either the plant wasn't there, had never been there, or was going to close immediately if not sooner. It was noisy, smelly, with tractor-trailers hauling in bags of cement, dump trucks hauling in sand and gravel, other trucks bringing barrels of oil, the cement mixer going on and off all day, tools clanging and banging, topped off by loud music, louder in the summertime. And every time anybody complained, the owner got his lawyer to go down to City Hall and remind everybody there how much taxes the owner and his employees paid.

The most important thing Carlucci learned was that the plant closed every year from the day before Christmas to probably the second week of January. None of the people in the three houses agreed on what week it reopened, but they all agreed it had been closed since the day before Christmas and that it was the owner's habit to close it around then each year and to keep it closed for at least two weeks, sometimes three, sometimes longer.

By nine-thirty he'd talked to everybody in the three houses who'd consented to talk to him. His running shoes were soaked again and his feet were going numb, so he headed back toward City Hall and stopped for coffee and a cheese omelet in one of the small restaurants off Penn Avenue that were always popping open and then going bust after a couple of years. Apparently there was no end to people who thought they could make a living in the restaurant business just because they'd found a location within a block of the Conemaugh County courthouse. So far, in Carlucci's memory at any rate, all of them had been wrong. Selling breakfast and lunch without a liquor license did not seem to be the happy highway to financial independence in Rocksburg.

Carlucci sat there sipping coffee and eavesdropping on the waitress and the cook bitching about their respective male spouses until he figured the malls would open. Then he paid his check and drove out to Rocksburg Mall and bought three pairs of wool socks and a pair of insulated waterproof boots in Sears. He knew the boots were insulated, but he didn't trust the advertised waterproofing, so on his way back to the station he stopped in Tommy's Shoe Repairs and bought a jar of beeswax leather protector.

He drove back to City Hall in a drizzle that looked at times like rain and at other times like snow. Before he parked, he checked to see that Mayor Angelo Bellotti's Chrysler New Yorker was parked in his slot on the southern side of the building. Carlucci circled the building and parked beside the animal shelter at the rear of the city lot and went in through the back door, hugging a wall and tiptoeing once he was inside. He had a lot of phone calls to make and he didn't want to get trapped by the mayor into a conversation about whatever the mayor had on his mind these days, mostly Carlucci's mother.

Carlucci nodded at Patrolman Fred Nowicki who was writing something while working as dispatcher. Nowicki looked up when he heard Carlucci and said, "Yo, Rugs, you wanna trade me? Huh?"

"Trade you what, jobs? I don't think so. Uh, anybody wants me—except the mayor—I'm gonna be behind door number one, you know? You follow me? Door number one?"

"Door number one?" Nowicki said, brows raised quizzically. "Door number one—you fuck, you, you're goin' in Balzic's office, huh?"

"Not his anymore, sad to say. Just don't tell Bellotti I'm in there, okay? I gotta make a lotta calls and he'll start buggin' the shit outta me—never mind."

"Hey, Rugs," Nowicki called after him, grinning wickedly. "You tryin' it on, huh? Seein' if it fits?"

"Get real."

"Fuck you get real, you're tryin' it on, you can't shit the Wickster." Nowicki jumped up and chased Carlucci into Balzic's office. "Hey, Rugs, Rugs, listen, man, you make chief, I'll do anything, I'm tellin' ya, I'll . . . I'll wash your car once a month for a year, just get me away from this radio, okay? Please?"

"At ease, for crissake, I'm just usin' the phone in here, that's all." He dropped into Balzic's chair and leaned back and said, "This is interesting, Nowicki. You think I can be had for twelve car washes? You actually think I care whether my car's dirty? I don't even know why I have a car. Fuckin' thing's seven years old, it don't have fifteen thousand miles on it. No. Sixteen. Three nights a week I'm takin' a city car home."

"Okay okay, so we'll work somethin' out. How about this. I'll fix you up with my cousin Franny. Huh? How about that? Third-place Miss Pennsylvania about ten, eleven years ago, and man, she's lookin' better now'n she looked then, I'm tellin' ya."

"Get outta here with your cousin, Christ."

"C'mon, Rugs, I'm tellin' ya, she's a dynamite chick. She wasn't my cousin I'd be shootin' at her myself. And sometimes, man, when I see her at the pool in the summertime? Huh? You listenin'? I don't even care she's my cousin, it's all I can do to keep my hands off her. Is first cousins incest?"

"Get outta here, Nowicki, go on, man, I got calls to make."

"Hey hey, you ain't usin' this place just to make calls.

Fuck you are. You know somethin'. I can smell it. Look at you." Nowicki splayed his hands smugly.

"Look at me what. What?"

"You're runnin' from Bellotti, man, and you run right in here and you sit in that chair like somebody made a cast of your ass." Nowicki snorted and smiled and licked his lips. "Oh man you're it, I can smell it. The Wickster's nose never lies. Promise, Rugs, please? Huh? Get me off the fuckin' radio, I'm goin' out of my mind, that's so fuckin' boring, Jesus. And you take care of me, I'll take care of you. You're gettin' old, man, you need a wife. I fix you up with Franny, who knows? Pretty soon, little Rugsters, you know?"

Carlucci put his hands behind his head and squinted and said, "You and Fischetti oughta start a support group or somethin', no shit. You two sound like you're in a twelve-stepper for kickin' a radio habit—which I didn't even know there was one of till now. C'mon man, get outta here, I got work to do."

"C'mon, Rugs, I never fucked you around, I always did everything you asked me to do," Nowicki whined.

"Hey. If you stop talkin' right now, and you leave, and you don't tell Bellotti I'm in here, then, maybe if your nose is right, who knows? If it is, maybe—maybe I'm sayin'—maybe I'll see what I can do. But forget your cousin. I'm not interested."

"Hey. Say no more, I'm outta here. Just think about my cousin, that's all. Did I show you her picture? Huh? I got it right here, lemme show ya—"

"You carry your cousin's picture around? You fuckin' pervert, get outta here."

"Hey, just give her a thought every once in a while, that's all I'm askin'. And lotsa guys carry their relatives' pictures around, what the fuck you talkin' about? Everybody in my family carries everybody's pictures around."

"Yeah yeah, get outta here."

Carlucci waited until Nowicki was gone before he opened the bottom drawer on the right side and brought up his Roledex file. He didn't want Nowicki to know this wasn't the first time he'd used Balzic's office to duck Bellotti and to make calls.

Carlucci called pawnbrokers, metal dealers, and coin dealers all over the county, telling them to call him if anybody turned up in the next couple of days trying to sell any pins, rings, watches, bracelets, or necklaces. He also called every fence and near-fence and fence-wannabe he'd developed over the years, and gave them the same message. Then he called everybody he knew with a history of dealing in plastic: major credit cards, department store cards, ATM cards, food market cards, gas cards, whatever.

After his last call, he closed his eyes and rubbed them with the heels of his hands. What the hell was the woman doing there if the place's been closed since Christmas Eve day? She had to be an employee. She couldn't have been just wandering by when it went down. That makes no sense at all. But none of the people living near the plant recognized her from the Polaroids, not that he expected them to, given the shape of her face with the swelling and the tubes.

Then, despite his best efforts to keep focused on the woman and what he should be doing about her case, he leaned back and rubbed the arms of what had been Balzic's chair and asked himself what he would be doing if he was no longer Detective Carlucci, if he was Chief Carlucci. Would he be thinking about this woman? Or would he be thinking about how much 9mm ammunition to requisition? Or how to get Nowicki away from the radio? Or how to settle beefs about vacation time and who was getting the overtime and who was calling in sick one day a month too many? Is that what he wanted?

You got to think about this stuff, Rugsie, he told himself, stuff you never in a million years thought you'd want to be thinking about. Going to council meetings. Getting on your feet in front of a room full of people and defending yourself and the members of your department. Explaining why your officers seemed to be ticketing certain vehicles in front of certain businesses and not others and why they seemed to respond more quickly to this address than to that one. Talking to the mayor every day just because the mayor had to feel like he was in charge, and one of the ways Bellotti did that was make it a point to have every department head give a report in person at least once a week—he was famous for that. Is that what you want, Rugs? Any of it? And what else is there? How much haven't I even started to think about? How much don't I have a clue about? Budgets. Mario was forever bitching about budgets. Man, what I don't know about budgets would fill this building.

And what am I missing about this woman? Probably just in the wrong place at the wrong time. Probably just an employee working late 'cause she took a long lunch hour to exchange Christmas presents. Aw bullshit. Why would she be working there if the place was closed?

And why does the name Picadio keep ringing bells for me? I got to ask Mario about this. Dummy! Is this what's going to happen to me, now? Huh? I let somebody open my nose about something I never thought was possible and all of a sudden I start fantasizing about a promotion and forget to ask the questions I should be asking and all I'm starting to think about is the promotion I'm maybe going to get? But even if I get it—a humongous if . . . how long do I think they'd let me keep it? Christ. I got to stop thinking like this. I got to call Mario.

He dialed Balzic's home phone, hoping that Balzic would answer and not his wife because if his wife answered she would ask about his mother and he didn't want to say how his mother was, he'd been doing that more than enough with the mayor.

"Yeah?" Balzic said after the second ring.

Carlucci identified himself with a grateful sigh and asked if the name Picadio meant anything to Balzic.

"Picadio, yeah, sure, Alfredo, yeah. Laid more sidewalks than all the other contractors combined. But he's dead."

"Yeah? How long?"

"Oh hell, twenty years. At least. I'll bet he died in the late sixties. Died real young. He was fifty maybe."

"Have any kids?"

"Aw, that I'm not sure about. Oh wait. Yeah, sure. Alfredo Junior, sure. He runs that company up off West Washington Street. Or he used to. Makes, uh, patio stones, stepping-stones, stuff like that. Uh, burial vaults too, I think. What's up?"

"How about Junior's mother? The old man's wife?"

"Aw, you got me there. See I never had anything to do with her. Now him, he'd call, he'd say he was gonna be layin' a sidewalk wherever, he was gonna be blockin' off a street 'cause he'd have to have the cement truck in there for twenty, thirty minutes, however long it was gonna take, and that was just to tell me if we had to reroute traffic maybe. He was always real good about that kinda stuff. But I never, uh, hell, I don't think I ever even met the woman, his wife. Why, what's up?"

Carlucci filled him in, as quickly and as fully as though Balzic were still chief.

"Jeez, Rugs, the only thing I can think is, probably, if Junior's still runnin' that business, and the city directory says he is, then the only thing I'd say is it's seasonal—"

"Yeah, that's what the neighbors say."

"Well, that's probably why you're not gettin' him. Probably went south or someplace. Wouldn't you? He's sure not gonna take his vacation in the summer. But shit, burial vaults, hell that can't be seasonal. You call the business association or the Chamber of Commerce?"

"I didn't get to them yet."

"Well, if they still make burial vaults, they gotta sell 'em to somebody, they gotta deliver 'em, they gotta put 'em in the ground. Call the funeral directors—not that any one of 'em's necessarily gonna remember the truck driver's name, but you never know."

"Right, okay. Didn't think of that."

"And if nothin' turns up there, call the garden shops, see in the Yellow Pages which ones sell patio stone, steppin'-stones, splash blocks, things like that. I used to see that truck all the time haulin' burial vaults around town, and there was always two guys in it. That can't be seasonal, that's ridiculous. People die every day, but, uh, maybe they build up an inventory, or, uh, maybe they do courtesy business with other companies, reciprocate, you know what I mean?"

"Right right," Carlucci said, "I'll get on it. Thanks, Mario, really, man, thanks a lot. Uh, one more thing. You gonna be home today? Huh? You free?"

"You kiddin'? I'm free for the rest of my life. Why?"

"'Cause I gotta talk to you and I don't wanna do it on the phone."

"Hey, I'm here. Just gimme a call, tell me when you're comin', that's all."

"Thanks, Mario. Appreciate it."

Carlucci hung up and then smacked himself in the forehead. Idiot! Fucking idiot! He's a junior, she gotta be missus senior, Jesus Christ, look up the mother's name in the phone book, you fuckin' idiot, what're you thinking about? Sittin' here daydreamin' about this fuckin' chair you're sittin' in, you're sittin' on your brains, for crissake.

He found the woman's name, address, and number in the White Pages right below her son's name, and sighed and berated himself again as he dialed her number. "How the fuck could you not think of this, Cheezus."

He got no answer and hung up after ten rings and went through Balzic's desk to see if there was a copy of the city directory, but there wasn't, so he went out to the radio console and asked Nowicki where the dispatcher's copy was. It was supposed to be chained to the console desk, but it wasn't in sight. Neither was the chain connected to where Carlucci expected to see it. The hook on the console was there but the chain was not.

Nowicki pointed with his thumb at the bottom drawer on his right. "Don't ask me what happened, I came in today, Fish told me the chain got snapped off somehow. I think he tripped over it, but he won't admit it, clumsy fuck."

"D'you tell somebody about it? This thing's never supposed to leave this desk, you know?"

"Man, Rugs, I'm tellin' ya, you're soundin' more and more chiefy every minute."

"Chiefy?"

"You know, when they say a guy looks presidential, you know, meanin' he looks like a president? Don't matter whether he knows shit. So I couldn't think of what the word would be for chief. Chiefial? That didn't sound right. So I thought chiefy—hey, what the fuck I know, I was never any good at English."

"Well, you know, since you are gonna be speakin' it the rest of your life, you probably oughta try to get better at it. Just a thought." Carlucci started to walk away, city directory in hand.

"Hey, oh no, uh-uh, where you goin' with that? Nothin' doin'. The chain got busted on Fischetti's watch, but that book ain't disappearin' on my watch, no way. You want somethin' to write on, here, here's some paper, but you stay here. And you put it back in the drawer when you're done. I'm not takin' my eyes offa you."

Carlucci bent over at the console and copied the names and addresses of the people listed as living on either side of Mrs. Alfredo Picadio Sr. and also across the street. He looked at the city map above the console and found Mrs. Picadio's address. It was appoximately four and a half blocks from the plant. He copied it and gave it to Nowicki, saying to himself, "She drove there. Had to. She didn't walk there, why the fuck didn't I think about a car?"

"You talkin' to me?" Nowicki said.

"Now I am. Run that name through DMV, see if she had a car. If she did, call around, see if anybody found it."

"Yes sir, Chiefy sir, at once, sir."

"I ain't your chiefy yet, bucky, but if I was I'd sure be on your ass to get this chain fixed, capeesh?" He put the directory back where he found it, then hustled into Balzic's office and started calling Mrs. Picadio Sr.'s neighbors, cradling the phone in the crook of his neck while he gave his new boots a heavy coat of beeswax.

He got no answer on the first two calls he made, to the residences on either side of Mrs. Picadio's house. On the third call, a woman answered.

"Is this the Raymond Evanowicz residence?"

"He's not here," the woman said, her voice thin and breathy.

"Are you Mrs. Evanowicz?"

"Who wants to know?"

"This is Detective Carlucci of the Rocksburg Police Department. Are you Mrs. Evanowicz?

"What do you want?"

"I'm trying to locate Mrs. Alfredo Picadio Senior. She

doesn't answer her phone and I'm wondering if maybe could you tell me where she is. Would she be on vacation or something? Out of town? Do you know? Does she tell you when she goes someplace?"

"Oh I don't know anything about that. Who did you say that was?"

"Detective Carlucci, ma'am."

"No. The person you want to call."

"Mrs. Picadio, ma'am."

"Well you have the wrong number."

"No, ma'am, I don't have the wrong number. I called the Evanowicz residence because, according to the city directory, you live right across the street from Mrs. Picadio Senior. Are you Mrs. Evanowicz?"

"Who are you again?"

"Detective Carlucci from the Rocksburg Police Department. You live across the street from Mrs. Picadio, right?"

"How do I know you're a policeman? How do I know you're not some thief calling to find out if I'm home or not?"

"Uh, Mrs. Evanowicz, I understand your caution, ma'am, and you're doin' the right thing, so how would it be if I came to your house and showed you my shield and my identification card, gave you the mayor's phone number so you could call him to verify what I'm tellin' you? I'll do whatever it takes to satisfy you that I'm who I am, would that be all right?"

"No. It wouldn't. Why do you want to come to my house? I'm not gonna let you in. Those things can be made up. Lotsa people make those things up. It's on television all the time, how people're tryin' to trick old people."

"Yes, ma'am I know, I know, you gotta be careful. Uh, I'm not gonna come to your house. I understand how you're feelin', and I don't wanna cause you any problems or make you upset—"

"I'm already upset—"

"Yes, ma'am, I can hear that. So, I'm sorry I disturbed you. You have a nice day now. Good-bye."

He dialed the numbers for the houses on either side of the Evanowicz residence, got a hang-up on the first and an answering machine on the second, and thought, the hell with it, the best way to do this is face-to-face. These people either don't want to answer their phones or they have a goddamn machine. Either way it's a waste of time.

He put on a pair of his new socks and his new boots and stopped to tell Nowicki where he was going and to see if the mayor had been around. "People are gettin' more fucking paranoid every day, you noticin' that?"

"You're askin' me if the mayor's been around and you're talkin' about bein' paranoid?"

"Yeah. Just talked to this woman, Christ, she wouldn't identify herself, wouldn't acknowledge her own name even though I kept askin' if that's who she was. Wouldn't believe me when I said who I was."

"So? You're hidin' from Bellotti all the time, you're bitchin' about this woman? *She's* paranoid?"

"That's not what I'm talkin' about. He's a specific guy, buggin' me with specific questions, and I don't wanna deal with it. This woman, she didn't wanna know anything."

"Hey, probably old, probably alone, probably doesn't do anything but watch TV all day, whatta ya expect? There been a lotta studies done about that."

"About what? What? You? *You're* gonna tell *me* about studies?"

"Yeah, me. You think I can't read? I read about how people who watch TV more than other people think the world's crazier than it is, more dangerous, more crime, more violent, more badder than it is, whatever. Hey, face it, TV puts us all on paranoid patrol. I been in the department ten years now, and not only have I never seen anybody get shot—I mean, I've seen guys *after* the shooting. I've seen people *after* the stabbing, *after* the wreck, whatever, but I've never been there when it was happening. I have never seen an accident—I'm not shittin' ya, I have never seen two cars crash into one another. I been there a hundred times afterwards, but I never saw it happen. And not one time have I ever used my piece, not one time. And I've never even had it outta my holster except on the range. Never. Have you?"

"Oh, yeah. To make collars. Sure. Anybody ever made me the least bit apprehensive, nervous, anything, I felt the least little bit wrong, hey, I had it out, man, had it in their face, put it behind their ear, you know. But you mean fire it?"

"Yeah."

"Aw no. Never. On the range, that's all. I don't even wanna think about that, that other thing. Shit no."

"Well that's what I mean. That woman probably sees ten shootings every night, half of 'em by cops. She probably don't know whether she's watchin' a show or the news or one of those live cop shows. They're gonna make it worse, those live cop shows. I mean Christ, can you imagine little kids tryin' to figure out which is real and which isn't? Huh? Or old ladies? It's gonna get worse, you ask me. But hey, I tell my mother the same thing. She lives alone. I bitch at her 'cause she still has her phone number listed. I tell her all the time if the guy's right, he's not gonna get pisssed you wanna check his ID before you let him in. Or call his company. And with all the meters outside the house now, there's no reason for anybody to wanna come in—anybody you didn't call. You don't tell your mother that?"

"Doesn't matter what I tell her, she doesn't listen to me anyway. Hey, I gotta go."

He managed to get out of City Hall without running into

the mayor and drove to Mrs. Alfredo V. Picadio Sr.'s house
on Baumann Street.

It was a three-story house situated on a sloping lot on the
east side of Baumann. It looked like most of the other houses
in the block, with more or less the same exterior design, except that it had shingles on the sides of the dormers and the
front door was red metal with a peephole in it. It was the
only house in the block with a red front door. The caulking
looked fresh around the door; the concrete porch and steps
had been painted in the last couple of years, and the painting
around the door and windows was sharply edged.

Carlucci rang the bell three times. Then he knocked three
times. Then he went around the house knocking on the side
and back doors and still got no answer. He couldn't see in
any of the doors because they were all solid, with peepholes,
and he couldn't see in the windows because of the drapes
and blinds.

He went to the houses on either side, but got no answer to
his knocks. He moved south and got an answer on the next
house, but the woman said she'd only lived there for a couple of months and didn't know anybody well enough to say
whether they ought to be home or not. Continuing south, he
got either no answer to his knock or no information when he
did.

He headed north on the other side of the street, but found
the same result: people either didn't respond to his knock or
didn't know anything about Mrs. Picadio or wouldn't say.

He hesitated about approaching the door of the Evanowicz
residence, but knew he had no choice. Before he could
knock, the curtain was pulled away from the corner of the
lowest of the three rectangular windows in the wooden front
door and one eye rose up out of that corner of the window.
This was hard to see because of the distortion from the glass
in the aluminum storm door.

He held up his shield and ID case, and tried his best to look harmless. "Mrs. Evanowicz? I'm Detective Carlucci. I talked to you on the phone, remember? About Mrs. Picadio?"

"What do you want? You said you wasn't gonna come."

He tried to tell himself to smile, even though he knew that wouldn't work, especially because he was forcing it. "I know I said that, but I have to talk to you about Mrs. Picadio. Mrs. Evanowicz, listen. I'm gonna give you the mayor's phone number and I want you to call him, okay?"

"I'm not gonna open this door."

"Well I'll write it on a piece of paper and hold it up to the window, you don't have to open the door."

"I'm not openin' this door."

Oh fuck. "Listen, you don't have to open the door. I'll hold everything up to the window, my shield, my ID, and you can call the mayor and ask him to describe me, and I promise to stay out here on the porch, I won't try to come in, we can talk through the door. How about that, will that make you feel more comfortable about talkin' to me?"

"No."

"Mrs. Evanowicz, please."

"I don't know anything anyway. Haven't seen her since the day before yesterday."

"You saw her the day before yesterday? What time?"

"She was goin' to work. Five to eight."

"She has a job? Where does she work, you know?"

"No, she don't have a job job. She got her own business."

"What kind of business?"

"I don't know. It's what her husband did, I don't know what it is, she never talks to me."

"You know where it is?"

"No."

"Did you see her after that? After you saw her leavin' for work?"

"No."

"You get up the same time every day? Approximately."

"No."

"Does it vary a lot, when you get up?"

"Sometimes."

"Does Mrs. Picadio have a car?"

"Yeah."

"There's no car parked in front of her house now. Do you see her car?"

The eyes moved from one corner of the window to the other as Carlucci stepped back so she could see. "No."

"You know what kind of car she has?"

"White."

White. Jesus. "Well, there aren't any white cars out here now, so do you know what make it is? Chevy, Ford, Plymouth, what?"

"They all look alike to me. I don't know what it is. Only has two doors, I know that. And it's white."

"Mrs. Evanowicz, does she go to work every day?"

"Yeah."

"You see her leavin' every day?"

"No. But I hear the car."

"What, you hear the door closin'? You hear the car start even if you don't see her, is that what you're sayin'?"

"Yeah."

"Did you hear her car start yesterday morning?"

"Yeah."

"Do you also hear when she comes home?"

"Sometimes. But she don't always come home the same time."

"Did you hear her come home last night?"

"Yeah."

"What time was that, do you remember?"

"It was right when Sally Wiggins was comin' on."

"Who?"

"Sally Wiggins, Sally Wiggins, WTAE news. Don Cannon. Joe DeNardo. Don't you watch the news on TV?"

"Uh, no. What time's that come on?"

"You don't know when the news comes on? Jeezo-peezo, you're a detective? You sure ain't no Columbo."

"Well that's why I'm talkin' to you. So I can get smarter. So you can tell me what you know. Like what time this Sally person comes on."

"Five o'clock."

"Every day?"

"Just Monday through Friday."

"Uh-huh. So Mrs. Picadio came home right after this Sally person came on TV, and she stayed home after that? She didn't go out again maybe?"

"Yes she did."

"She did? Oh. And what time was that?"

"Right after Pete come on I heard the car startin' up."

"Pete? What Pete?"

"Pete, Pete! Peter Jennings. ABC Evening News with Peter Jennings! Jeezo-peezo, you don't know anything!"

"Right, right, you're right, I don't. What time's he come on?"

"Six-thirty."

"And that's when you heard the car—her car—startin'."

"Yeah. Right."

"How do you know it was her car? Lotsa other cars out here right now. Gotta be more'n that after the other people come home from work, right?"

"The ones that're workin', sure."

"So how do you know it was her car?"

"I got up and looked. I seen her drivin' away."

"And this was right after this Pete came on, right?"

"Yeah."

"Could it've been six thirty-five maybe? Or later? Or earlier?"

"Couple minutes after."

"So it was between six-thirty and six thirty-five, approximately. So, uh, you seen her car since then?"

"No."

"Heard it?"

"No."

"You're sure now. A white two-door. You didn't see it this morning, or hear it this morning, you're sure about that?"

"Sure I'm sure."

"Did that disturb you or upset you?"

"Why should it, she don't talk to me. I don't care where she goes. Or when. Or who with."

"You have words with her or somethin'? You have a problem with her?"

"No I didn't have no words with her. She's just, you know, she's just . . . snooty, that's all. Thinks she got all this money, she don't need to talk to nobody."

"Mrs. Evanowicz, is it all right with you if I came in? I think we oughta keep the rest of this conversation quiet, you know? I'm talkin' real loud out here, and I don't feel right doin' that."

"I ain't lettin' you in! You could be anybody!"

Oh fuck. I could be anybody. I *am* anybody—I think. Ain't I? I could be. I could even be somebody. "Uh, Mrs. Evanowicz, thanks for your help, I appreciate it. Good-bye."

He started to turn away but then he remembered the Polaroids. He knocked again and held up the photos and when Mrs. Evanowicz's eyes reappeared, he said, "Is this her? Can you tell if this is her?"

"Holy Jesus, what happened to her?"

"Is this Mrs. Picadio?"

"I don't know. Looks sorta like her. That thing in her mouth, it makes it hard to tell. What is that thing?"

"It's a respirator tube. Try to imagine it without that bein' there, I know it's tough. Whatta ya think, is it her?"

"Hair's the same color. Same kinda nose, but I don't know. Jeezo-peezo. She's a mess. What happened to her?"

"Anybody around here friendly with her? Do you know?"

"Uh-uh, I don't know. I don't know lotsa people anymore. Most of the people I know, they moved. Or they passed away."

"Okay, Mrs. Evanowicz, thank you very much. I might have to talk to you again. Hope you remember me when you see me. Good-bye."

She said nothing, but he was sure she was watching him leave her porch.

He went back to his car and called Nowicki.

"DMV have anything on Mrs. Picadio?"

"Roger. Pontiac Grand Prix, 1990 two-door coupe, white, plate number AZS-2281—"

"I'll be damned, that goofy woman was right."

"What? Can't read you?"

"Never mind. You put it on the hot sheet?"

"Yeah. No word so far."

"Well, I'm gonna be canvassin' the neighbors for a little while longer, then I'm goin' to Balzic's. I'll check in then. Any word from the hospital on that woman?"

"That's a negative."

"Roger. Carlucci out."

He tried three more doors north of the Picadio house, but didn't get much at any of them. The people knew the Picadio woman, but didn't know as much about her comings and goings as Mrs. Evanowicz did. Two of them weren't aware that she still left her house to go to a job every day. They just knew they didn't see her very much. All three agreed she wasn't much for socializing, at least not with any of her neighbors. One man who wouldn't give his name thought she started keeping her distance after her husband died, but he couldn't be sure of that and his wife told him he didn't know what he was talking about, so he quit talking. Carlucci didn't get one solid confirmation from anybody that the woman in his Polaroids was Mrs. Picadio.

He gave up after he knocked on three more doors farther north in the block and got nothing at all. He walked back to his car as it started to snow again, his chin buried in his collar. Wasn't even the second week of January and already he was fed up with snow.

Carlucci had been a police officer in Rocksburg since 1971, since about three months after he'd come back from Vietnam. That was also how long he'd been caring for his mother because on the same day Carlucci had been flying back from the Philippines, his father had been driving south on Main Street about two blocks past City Hall, had hit some ice and then hit a utility pole and had died before the EMTs arrived. Carlucci's mother had been in the backseat—he'd never learned why she was there instead of the front seat—and had spent only a few hours in the hospital undergoing a routine examination because she had no visible injuries and didn't complain about any invisible ones. But even though she'd emerged without discernible wounds, she'd been walking wounded ever since, thoughtful and gentle one moment, outrageously spiteful and bitter the next, often vicious verbally, and sometimes violent, to herself as well as to anybody who might have the bad luck of being within her reach.

Two months after the funeral, while Carlucci was pouring

boiling water into a cup to make instant coffee, his mother had rushed at him from behind without warning and slapped him on the side of the head and screamed, "If you didn't go into that goddamn Army my husband would still be alive!"

Carlucci had never been able to get her to explain what one had to do with the other, but it was a connection that came raging up out of her every couple of months, her eyes bleary, nose red and runny, hands flailing at whoever was there, usually him. He also didn't have to look hard to make out the outline of the burn scar where the water had sloshed out of the pot onto the back of his left hand. It wasn't so much a scar as a discoloration, and while it apparently wasn't very noticeable to anybody else, occasionally Carlucci would catch himself staring at it and he'd have to shake himself and give himself a quick pep talk to focus on whatever he'd been doing.

Try as he might to understand his mother's twisted logic, he couldn't, and whenever it happened, whenever she went off on him, he would find himself hungry to be around people, the less familiar the better; so he would drive to one of the two malls situated on either side of Rocksburg and wander around until he found a place to stand where he could watch the people coming and going from at least two directions on two different levels. He would find a place on the corner of the second-floor mezzanine and think about who the people were and what they were doing and where they'd come from and where they were going when they left.

For some reason, this anonymous watching untied the knot in his gut. He didn't try to analyze it much beyond that, except that one day he thought he understood that peepers were motivated by a combination of fear and loneliness and a hunger to end both. But that was as far as he wanted to go with it; he decided it wouldn't be smart to conclude that what brought peepers to windows was the same thing that brought him to the malls.

The only thing that spoiled the watching was the canned music, always worst as far as he was concerned during November and December. He understood that the music at that time of year was supposed to put shoppers into a compliant holiday stupor, to make them feel generous and expansive and trusting and, most important, willing to spend money. But the music had just the opposite effect on him; it made him edgy, suspicious, and even more frugal than he normally was—all the years of caring for his mother with all her infirmities, understandable and not, had made his frugality a stone habit—and the holiday music fenced him out of the malls until the new year was at least a week old.

Actually, he had a problem with all background music. He couldn't watch a movie, couldn't watch television without feeling manipulated by the sound track. It had started one night at the end of March 1972, when the North Vietnamese Army attacked across the demilitarized zone, and the nightly news was showing an all-too-monotonous film of Army and Marine grunts milling around body bags waiting for the helicopters. When that film dissolved to a commercial, it was accompanied by the theme music of the news show which dissolved into an idiotic jingle from a commercial. Carlucci was transfixed by what struck him as an obscene and bizarre clash of sights and sounds and by the even more bizarre clash of music with his own memories of Vietnam. From then on he began to notice all the times that music faded in and out, in the movies in theaters, and during sports, sitcoms, dramas, and movies on TV, but especially on the news. Since he'd been hearing the music on the radio and in the movies and on TV all his life, he felt like a fish suddenly noticing water. Only instead of noticing that it was giving him life, it was choking him, the melodies winding around his throat, the rhythm hammering his chest like a howitzer's backblast sending shock waves into his diaphragm, the music insisting not only that he should feel something but what that something should be. In no time at all he began to notice how often somebody was pitching some emotion at him and in an even shorter time he came to hate the feeling of being pitched at by people he seemed unable to elude. The pitchmen were everywhere, the music was everywhere, more repulsive and obnoxious to him than laugh tracks on comedy shows.

The worst confrontation he'd ever had with his mother occurred about three years after his father's death, when she'd walked into the living room after she'd said she was going to bed and found him watching the news with the sound off.

"How come you ain't got the sound on?"

"I don't wanna hear it."

"You don't wanna hear it?! Know what I think? I think anybody don't wanna hear human voices ain't all there, anybody just wantsa look at pictures don't have all their marbles, that's what I think. I think you'da stayed home and never joined the goddamn Army, I think you'da ever showed your parents you really loved 'em the way the commandments say you oughta, I think your father would still be alive, that's what I think."

That last accusation, the stubborn wrongheadedness of it, cut him so deeply that the only thing he was able to do was vow never to have it repeated, so he quit watching TV by himself in the house. He would sit with his mother and pretend to watch to keep her company. But the moment she left the room to go to the bathroom, he'd turn the set off and keep it off until he heard her coming back. He stopped watching the news at home, not even to keep her company.

"Where you goin' now? Can't you ever sit still?"

"I gotta go to the bathroom."

"You always gotta go to the bathroom."

If he wanted news, he went to the library on his breaks and read newspapers and magazines. If he found himself in a bar when the TV news was on, he might pretend to watch, but he never watched TV news at home again, and never watched anything by himself . . . .

If problems with his mother weren't enough, he'd been sorely upset by how Chief Mario Balzic had been forced to retire. In all the years Carlucci had served with the Rocksburg PD, he'd known only one chief. But Balzic had not only been Carlucci's chief, he'd been his teacher, mentor, confessor, his "rabbi." Balzic had also persuaded Carlucci to become a detective despite Carlucci's doubts about his abilities, and then prepped him for the sergeant's test and goaded him to study for it and pass it.

Though not everything Balzic did had Carlucci's unqualified approval—especially Balzic's notorious attitude about his administrative duties—Carlucci had respected and admired Balzic's ability to seem to know just how far he could push superiors to get what he wanted while still remaining his own person, while still remaining apart from the politics of City Hall. It was also, Carlucci knew well, that very ability to remain apart from politics that had brought Balzic down. He'd said it himself in the one conversation they'd had about it, on New Year's Day when Carlucci found him cleaning out his desk.

"I tried my damnedest to keep politics out of it," Balzic had said. "I was wrong. You're a chief, you're a political animal whether you wanna be or not. I tried to act like I wasn't, and I let the bastards tunnel right under me."

So, while Balzic was still around for Carlucci, still living in Rocksburg, *being around* was a far distance from being in his office every day when Carlucci reported for duty. And even though the strangeness of not having Balzic in his office every day was only a couple of weeks old, Carlucci also couldn't shake the thought that if Balzic could be forced out, anybody could. It was a short slide from there to fretting about his own job security. And all his fretting and worrying were being topped off by the fact that the newly reelected mayor, Angelo Bellotti, had started sniffing around Carlucci the day after Balzic had cleaned out his office. So Carlucci had to deal with Bellotti on the one hand and listen to the rumors on the other about who was going to replace Balzic. Carlucci said nothing. Whenever anybody asked his opinion, he lied, as he had to Fischetti, and said he hadn't heard anything or was too busy to pay attention.

But he had heard the rumors—it was impossible not to—every one of them. And each one made him more edgy than the last. One had it that Balzic's replacement was coming from among the officers who'd done the most to support Mayor Angelo Bellotti in his campaign to reclaim the office from Kenny Strohn, though nobody seemed to know exactly which officers those were. Another had his replacement coming from among the three sergeants—Vic Stramsky, Joe Royer, and Bill Rascoli—who'd retired at the same time as Balzic; another that he was coming from a national search aided in part by the Fraternal Order of Police; another that he was going to be a she, a school crossing guard with no other police experience but who happened to be the daughter of City Councilman Egidio Figulli; another that he was going to be Bellotti's nephew, a patrolman in the Traffic Division in the Pittsburgh PD; still another that he was going to be the most senior ranking officer in the department, who was Carlucci.

It was the last rumor that had become background music for Carlucci, mainly because he seemed to be bumping into Mayor Bellotti almost every day in City Hall since Balzic had cleaned out his desk and office on New Year's Day.

"Hey, Rugsie, hi ya doin'? How's your mother?"

"Fine, Mr. Mayor. She's fine."

"That's great. Well you be sure and tell her I said hello."

When Bellotti had been mayor before, he'd still been in the home appliance business, which had required him to be in his store for most of the business day. But when he'd lost his bid for a fourth term to Kenny Strohn, he'd sold his business and moved to Florida. Now that he was mayor again and didn't have a business to go to, he was spending the entire day in City Hall doing mayorly things—or so he said to city employees who couldn't run or hide—doing the things a full-time mayor should be doing, keeping an eye on the day-to-day workings of the city, especially the police department. Mostly what he was being was a pain in everybody's ass.

Especially Carlucci's. Bellotti was being too friendly to Carlucci, too interested in Carlucci's mother's health and well-being. Carlucci found Bellotti's concern for his mother all the more annoying because it always came riding on questions about how much trouble it was for Carlucci to care for her, how much time it involved and how much money, and how it left so little time and money for him to have a life of his own. Not, Bellotti was quick to add, that Carlucci wasn't doing the absolutely right thing in caring for her; it was just that nobody would have thought less of him if he'd tried to lift the burden off himself any way he could.

Carlucci tried arriving at City Hall at different times of the day to duck Bellotti. That had worked for a week or so, but then Bellotti started to phone him at home. Carlucci had put up with those calls for another week. That was when he'd decided he had to call Balzic.

"You look like a worried man, Rugs," Balzic said, leading Carlucci into his kitchen and opening a beer for Carlucci and pouring wine for himself and pointing for Carlucci to have a seat.

"I am," Carlucci said, loosening his tie, unbuttoning his collar, and stretching his neck. "I think the bastard wants to make me chief."

Balzic stopped pulling out his chair, poised in thought. Then he turned down the corners of his mouth and nodded several times and said, "You mean Bellotti?"

Carlucci nodded and took a sip of beer.

"Well. He could do a lot worse." Balzic sat and took a long swallow of wine. Then he smiled and raised his glass. "I think he could do a hell of a lot worse. You gonna do it?"

"He hasn't asked me yet—I mean I might be way wrong. Maybe he's not goin' to. But he's been sniffin' around me ever since you got it in the back. Started practically the day after you cleaned out your desk, you know? All the time, it's how am I doin', how's it goin', how's my mother, all the time, how's my mother, you know?"

"Well, they interviewin' people, right? Is Bellotti doin' it himself, or they got a search committee, what?"

"I'm not sure who's doin' it. I'm not sure anybody's doin' it. But, hey, they could be interviewin' people anywhere, they wouldn't have to be doin' it in City Hall."

"Well whatta ya hear?"

"Oh man, everything. Everything from it's gonna be what's-his-face's daughter, you know, the asshole council-man's daughter? The crossin' guard? Can't even think of either one of their names now. He's such a goddamn jerk."

"Figulli. Hey. Don't be fooled. Egidio's smarter'n he looks. And don't ever forget how close he is with the fire chief. Never underestimate that. Figulli and old Eddie Sitko, hey, they got a lotta history. Same with Bellotti."

"I'm not forgettin' that. I just—I don't know, I feel like I'm bein' . . . I feel like I'm bein' set up."

"Set up? How?"

"I don't know. I know it sounds goofy. I just can't shake the feeling, you know?"

"Anybody else talk to you about it?"

"Nah, just Bellotti. So far. But I mean he's not even talkin' about it. He hasn't said one word about it officially, you know? But why else would he all the time be askin' about my mother, I don't get it. He never gave a rat's ass about her—or me—before now. Sonofabitch called me at home three times this week. About nothin'! Keeps makin' this lame excuse he got all this time on his hands now, so he gotta be a real hands-on kinda mayor, you know, to justify the faith of the people in electin' him. He actually says that stuff. Who's he tryin' to shit? He got elected 'cause Sitko told his guys they either vote for Bellotti or they're history. Does he actually think people don't know that?"

"C'mon, Rugs. Angelo knows exactly what's goin' on. So does Figulli. And so does the other new councilman, Joe Radosich."

"Yeah. Can't forget him. Good ol' Joe Radio. I haven't seen him around much though."

"Don't worry. He's the pipeline between the rest of them and Sitko. He may never show up down there for anything except council meetings, but he'll know more about what's goin' on down there than the other two."

"But he actually says that stuff. Bellotti. 'Justify the faith of the people'—you ever hear such shit in your life?"

"Many times."

"Yeah, guess you did. But still, it always comes down to how am I payin' for my mother—she must have a lotta prescriptions, and medicine costs money, and doctors, how much am I payin' them? And who watches her when I'm at work? And I must be real lucky to have a couple ladies do that kinda favor for me for all these years. That's what got to me. That last thing. 'Cause I never told him who watches my mother when I'm not there. So he must be callin' my house a lot to know that. He had to talk to them. Honest to God, Mario, it's givin' me the creeps."

"Why?"

"Aw come on, Mario, why do you think? I never paid any taxes for those women. Shit, I never even thought about it. One lady, Mrs. Comito, she asked me three times now, you know, hey, what happens if somebody turns her? She's watchin' all this shit about the attorney general on TV, she's scared her daughter-in-law's gonna turn us both."

"Rugsie, for crissake, you're not the only person didn't pay those kinda taxes."

"Hey, Mario, I'm payin' two women to watch my mother. One woman puts in a forty-hour week. The other one's there every time I'm on overtime and if I don't get the overtime? I'm fucked. I can't pay 'em. I mean, that's why I work the overtime—not that I have a choice about it most of the time, but what I'm sayin' is, if I didn't get the overtime, I couldn't pay 'em what I make on straight time. On top of which, I don't pay either one of 'em minimum wage. So if Bellotti wants to work a number on me, he got me three ways. He could say I'm paddin' my overtime—and he would have no trouble makin' that stick. I'm gonna try not to do it as much anymore—oh, man, listen to me, like I could control that. But what's done is done. And he could turn me to both Labor Departments, federal and state, 'cause I never paid minimum wage. I still don't. I can't afford to for crissake. And he could turn me to the IRS 'cause I never withheld their taxes and I never paid Uncle Sugar. I been payin' these women for more than twenty years, Mrs. Comito twenty-two years, Mrs. Viola since I been a detective. Twelve years. Mrs. Comito added it up. It's peanuts for crissake if you think about it as a hourly wage. But when you add it up over twenty years like she did? It comes to more'n a hundred and twenty grand. Scared the shit outta her. Scares the shit out of me—especially every time Bellotti mentions it."

"Rugs, they lock you up, they gotta lock up half the country."

"Whoa whoa, who says they can't? How many black males under the age of twenty-five we got locked up, you kiddin'? And for what? Most of 'em for conspiracy in a drug deal involvin' less than a hundred bucks, for crissake. You know that as well as I do. If somebody decides they wanna make an example of somebody—even though ten thousand other cops know that makin' examples out of a gazillion somebodies doesn't do shit—hey, they're gonna do it—"

"Rugs, Rugs, whoa, slow down, you're lettin' yourself get all outta joint here."

"Damn right I am. I know it! That's why I called you."

"Well, listen, let's just put this aside for a second, okay? Can you do that? I know that's what you wanna talk about, but whatta you say we give it a break, huh? Just for a little while."

Carlucci sighed and hung his head. "Yeah, sure. Okay."

"Good. Good. So, uh, what's some of the other noise goin' around?"

"Aw you can imagine. I mean if they're talkin' Figulli's daughter, Christ they could be talkin' anybody. Bellotti's got a nephew's a cop in Pittsburgh. So I call a guy down there, find out where he's workin', check him out. He's in Traffic but he just applied for a transfer to that drug task force. You familiar with that?"

Balzic nodded. "Yeah. They put about a hundred guys onto drugs, took 'em off everything else. They been catchin' all kindsa heat about that. But hey. Drugs is where the squeaks are. That's what's gettin' the grease. So, d'you talk to him?"

"Not to him personally, no. I didn't know how to approach him. I kept thinkin' how would it sound, you know—'Hey, you gonna be my boss?'"

"Well I can't call him, that's out."

"Oh no, right, I don't want you callin' anybody. But it sounds to me like, a guy who puts in for transfer doesn't have another job lined up, would you think? Least that's what I think. But, uh, I just wanna know what you think, that's all."

"About what exactly?"

Carlucci shrugged and hesitated, and shrugged again. He licked his upper lip. "You know. If . . . if it was offered to me . . . you, uh, think I could do it?"

Balzic grinned and then hunched forward, laughing. "Do I think you could do it? Be chief? Is that what you're askin' me?"

Carlucci shrugged again, his head bopping around. "Yeah. You know . . . could I?"

"Course you could do it, hell yeah, why not? Best thing you got goin' for you is what Bellotti thinks of you."

"Which is?"

"He thinks you're a dog. Always has. I could never convince him otherwise. He was always askin' me why I was always pushin' you along, you know, you, of all people. So I'd tell him why, but he wouldn't believe me. But now, hey, a dog is what he wants. Somebody to roll over and play dead and sit up and speak, you know, throw him a bone every once in a while, give him a good scratch on the belly and he follows you around waggin' his tail. Hey, Rugs, shit, you got the bastard right where you want him."

"*I* got *him*? Aw, Mario, I don't know, man."

"Oh, Rugs, absolutely. You got 'em all. They don't know you. Not like I do. They don't know what's behind those beady little eyes." Balzic threw back his head and laughed.

"Rugs, why you think I made you a detective, why you think I pushed you so hard for that, huh? And to pass the sergeant's test? Huh? You ever think about that, why I did that?"

"Sure I thought about it. In the beginning I thought it was 'cause I was such a lousy beat cop and you felt sorry for me."

"Aw bullshit, no no," Balzic said, chuckling and shaking his head. "I pushed you that way 'cause the best thing you had goin' for you—besides your brains—which you still think you don't have any of you're so sure the nuns were right—was you look like you don't have any."

"You're shittin' me." Carlucci almost looked hurt. "You're not shittin' me."

"C'mon, Rugs. Hey, look. Don't take this wrong, but, uh, you look like the average schmuck, you know? Like you couldn't ask a smart question if your life was ridin' on it. That's what I depended on. C'mon, man, you never figured that out?"

Rugs looked puzzled but he said nothing.

"Hey, how many perps did we double-team, huh? You and me. I'd piss 'em off and they'd tell you everything. And what'd you used to say all the time?"

"Right at this moment I don't know what you're talkin' about. I'm not bein' stupid, I just don't know what you want me to say."

"How many times did you come out of an interrogation and say the guy was laughin' at you? While he was tellin' you what a big bad ass he was and how smart he was and how stupid you were, what'd you used to say?"

"Oh that, yeah. Sure. The asshole was laughin' at me. Lotsa times."

"And it used to piss you off."

"Yeah. Still pisses me off—sometimes."

Balzic leaned forward and peered into Carlucci's eyes,

"Rugs, why you still pissed off about that? That's your strength. That's who you are, that's what makes you good at what you do. 'Cause all the wise guys and all the wise-guy wannabes, they love showin' other people up, laughin' at 'em, makin' 'em look like fools. Which is exactly why Bellotti wants you to be chief—if he does. Has the sonofabitch asked you anything about yourself yet? I'll bet he hasn't said a word about you, right? Just your mother."

"No. Right. Not a word just about me. It's always about my mother and me."

"See what I mean? His idea of doin' a background check is to read your personnel file—which he's already done. But that's as far as he's gonna go. He won't try to corroborate anything in there. And he thinks 'cause he reads that, he's got you covered. 'Cause all he's really doin' is workin' on the angle he thinks is gonna work on you. Which is your mother."

Balzic got up and poured himself another glass of wine. Carlucci had barely touched his beer.

"See, Rugs, Bellotti, he's always worryin' about what the people he respects think of him. He's like most people, he never worries what the people under him or around him are thinkin' about him. It's the asshole mistake. I don't know why it is, maybe they've seen too many pictures of Niagara Falls, I truly don't know what the fuck it is. Water goes down, power goes down I guess is what it is. From somewhere up there, from somebody up there. Assholes never understand what's goin' on around 'em 'cause they're all the time lookin' up, they're never lookin' around."

"Yeah. Well right now I'm not sure I'm any smarter'n they are."

"Aw sure you are, Rugs, Christ, come on, you're just not feelin' real confident now 'cause Bellotti got your nose open and you don't know whether you can do it. But your problem isn't gonna be the job. You'll handle that. Except budget time—and all the rest of the accounting crap. That'll make you as nuts as it made me. But you'll figure it out just like I did. And I'll help you, I'll tell you who to call. The problem's gonna be makin' Bellotti think he's always in charge while you know that everything he does, every single thing he does or is plannin' to do is based on him bein' sure he's never out of kissin' range of Eddie Sitko's ass. Same with Figulli. Same with Radosich. And that's not gonna be easy for you. For you to make him think he's always in charge— 'cause, hey, Bellotti, he's like all assholes about power. Assholes think power is nothin' but givin' orders and firin' the people who won't take 'em. But that's not what it's about, and you know it isn't. You just don't think you do right now."

"Yeah? Well right now I don't think I understand too much, so how about tellin' me what I understand," Carlucci said, slumping forward to rest his elbows on his knees and his chin on his hands.

"C'mon, Rugs, you tellin' me you don't understand where power comes from in a police department, huh? I watched you for what? Twenty years? Twenty-two?"

"Twenty-two, right."

"So what's the first question you ask yourself? Huh? What's the first question you always asked yourself? You know what I'm talkin' about."

Carlucci shrugged, then nodded. "If I gotta work with this guy, how do I get along with him?"

"Exactly," Balzic said, throwing his hands wide. "Exactly. Which is exactly the question assholes never ask. They're always askin', how do I get this jaboney to do what I want. Which is what Bellotti's askin' himself right now. 'Cause he's definitely on your trail, and he definitely thinks the road to you is through your mother, so he's gonna make you an offer built around some way he's gonna help you with your mother. Which is supposed to make you grateful. Rugsie, never forget—*quid pro quo*'s been around for a couple thousand years and it was Bellotti's ancestors who invented it. What you gotta remember is they were your ancestors too."

"So if he goes that way, what should I do?"

"Oh he's goin' that way, no doubt. But hey, Rugs, I'm not gonna answer that for you. That's for you to say."

"C'mon, Mario, I need all the help I can get here."

"Hey. You don't need my help. Not about this. You know exactly what to do. He offers you the job, take it. Just invite me when they swear you in. I wanna be there when they put the scrambled eggs on your cap."

"Yeah? And what if he throws this other shit in my face? About these women watch my mother, then what?"

"Aw, no, no way, uh-uh, he'll never do that," Balzic said, shaking his head.

"How can you be so sure?"

"C'mon, Rugs. You know how many people there are payin' other people to watch their kids, huh? While they go to work? Or their parents? Just like you? 'Cause they can't afford to put 'em in a home? You think any of them're payin' those fuckin' taxes. Get real. That's guys in Washington jaggin' each other off with that shit about who didn't pay their's maid's witholding or whatever.

"I don't know what the Clintons're gonna do with this health plan they're talkin' up, but, Christ, man, somebody gotta do somethin'. For exactly this reason. Nobody knows what to do about the people who can't afford to be left alone. Like your mother. But you can bet my ass—you hear? *My* ass, not *your* ass, *my* ass, *my* house, *my* car, everything I got, you can bet that nobody's gonna bust you for doin' what you're doin'. Never gonna happen, so quit worryin' about it. And if Bellotti even suggests anything like that, you hear me? If he even starts hintin' around at anything like that, you tell me, I'll give him a little call. I know some things about Angelo, you know, they wouldn't get him convicted. Wouldn't even get him indicted. But he'd sure be squirmin' for a coupla days watchin' the local news on TV, readin' the Pittsburgh paper. He'd look like he had a coupla hornets in his shorts. So don't forget. When he puts the eggs on your hat, I wanna be there, ya hear?"

"I hear. I just wish I had your confidence."

"You don't need mine, Rugs. You got your own. You just gotta remember where you put it. You keep losin' it all the time, I could never figure out why."

Carlucci was going to say, "That's because you don't know my mother," but he didn't. Instead, he stood up, shook Balzic's hand, and said thanks. Then he buttoned his collar, tightened his tie, and went back to work.

First thing he did after leaving Balzic's house was call the station and tell Nowicki that he was going to Sal Bruno's Funeral Home to talk to the owner.

"Uh, before I forget, you get the word out on that lady's Pontiac? Mrs. Picadio?"

"Course I did. You told me, didn't ya? Oh, I forgot. I'm supposed to say ten-four."

"You get anything back?"

"That's a negative."

"Well this is a roger and out." Carlucci replaced the speaker on the hook and licked his upper teeth. That woman's car could be in a thousand pieces by now. It could be in Ohio. It could be in the Ohio River. It could be in three states. It could be in the Ohio River in three states.

He pulled into Bruno's Funeral Home lot and parked as far away from the front door as possible to avoid interfering with visitor traffic. In the foyer, he saw two names on the small board to the right of the door to the main hall. He flashed his ID at one of the attendants and asked him to tell Sal Bruno that he wanted to talk to him for a few minutes.

The attendant disappeared down the hall and into one of the viewing rooms. In about a minute Sal Bruno, wearing a charcoal gray single-breasted suit, with a pewter gray shirt with a white collar and cuffs and a tie a shade darker than his silvery hair, strode down the hall. His brows went up and he bowed his head slightly as he recognized Carlucci, extending his hand, shaking Carlucci's hand and leading him into a small, square office off the foyer.

"Ruggiero, how are you, come in, come in, sit down."

"Fine, Mr. Bruno, how are you?" Carlucci took a seat beside Bruno's desk while Bruno held up a pot of coffee as a way of offering Carlucci some. Carlucci held up his hand and shook his head.

"You mind if I have some?" Bruno said. "This time, every day when it gets close to lunch, I get a little drowsy, you know?"

"Not at all," Carlucci said, admiring Bruno for his courtesy and poise, for always seeming to know how to put people at ease. It didn't matter to Carlucci that Bruno was in the business of putting people at ease. Carlucci had been around plenty of other funeral directors who'd no doubt had the same kind of training as Sal Bruno and who couldn't do it with half his style or class.

Bruno opened a small refrigerator beside the coffee pot, added some milk to his coffee and returned it to the refrigerator, stirred his coffee, and sat down before he took a sip, all the while saying, "Ruggerio, how's your mother? I haven't seen her for so long, I'm not sure I would recognize her."

"About the same, more or less. But I think you'd know her if you saw her."

"The same, huh? No sign of improvement? None at all?"

Carlucci shook his head.

"Ah well, grief is very necessary. I deal with it all the time. Mourning is something we all do eventually. But when it lasts too long?" Bruno shrugged and shook his head. "I can help people with their grief in the short term. But when it goes on and on? I wish I could help your mother. But I can't."

"I didn't come here for that, Mr. Bruno."

"Course you didn't. So. What can I do for you?"

"Uh, Mr. Bruno, do you do business with Rocksburg Pre-Cast Concrete? You get your burial vaults from them?"

"If I have to, yes. Why?"

"Uh, why do you say it like that?"

"I say it like that because if I have a choice, I call some-body else. I don't always have a choice."

"Well what's the problem?"

"Well, Ruggerio, uh, I'm not sure it's a good idea for me to be saying anything about my dealings with them until I know what you want to know. Why're you asking me about them?"

"Well actually what I wanted to know was if you could tell me who drives their truck for them, who installs the vaults. Do you know?"

"Oh if that's all, sure. Uh, Bill, uh, oh, it's right on the tip of my tongue. Bill, uh, oh God, I can't think of it. I have his phone number right here. Here, here it is," Bruno said, get-ting an address book out of his desk and opening it and slid-ing it around for Carlucci to see. "Well look at that. I don't even have his last name down there, do I? But he's who I call if we need a vault and they're closed—like they are now. They close every year at this time."

"But this guy's around? He's here? This Bill?"

"Oh, yes. That's a pager number. He'll call you right back. Yes, he's very reliable."

"Well if he is, who isn't? Reliable."

"Uh, Ruggerio, you, uh, you'll forgive me for saying this—you sound to me like you're fishing, is what I want to say. And I'm not sure I should be taking your bait—or let's say I'm not comfortable taking the bait. If you could be a little more specific . . . could you?"

Carlucci got out his Polaroids of the woman in intensive care. "You recognize her?"

Bruno looked at the pictures and shook his head sadly. "Oh my. No, I don't recognize her. Course in her condition it's very difficult to say. She's so swollen, and the tubes . . . what happened?"

Carlucci took the pictures back. "EMTs found her in the office of Rocksburg Pre-Cast Concrete last night. She called 911 around seven, five after, thereabouts. Then apparently she passed out right after the EMTs got there, didn't tell anybody anything, couldn't, and, uh, her purse is missing, probably stolen, so we don't know who she is. She's in pretty bad shape, I don't know how bad, but the thing that gets me is, uh, nobody's lookin' for her. Nobody called the hospital, nobody called us, I can't figure that out. The woman wasn't wearin' the fanciest clothes in the world, but they didn't come out of any thrift shop. Her fingernails were polished, her toenails were polished, she had a lot of expensive dental work, so how come nobody's lookin' for her, know what I'm sayin'?"

"Yes. And she was found in the office?"

Carlucci nodded.

"So if the place is closed—which it is—uh, you want to know what she was doing there, is that right?"

"Well that's second. First, who is she? I find out who she is, I'll probably know why she was there."

Bruno said, "Well, Alfredo's wife worked in the business, I know that, that's Alfredo Senior's wife I'm talking about. He was a good man, a very good man, died way too young, believe me. I liked him. A lot. Everybody did. But her, well, I have to say it right out. I couldn't stand her. Not many people could. She was just the opposite of him. Very hard woman. Very hard. She took care of the books, he did the labor. She used to collect the bills, and believe me, very unprofessional the way she did it. Very sarcastic, very sharp-tongued.

"Poor Alfredo, he was always going around smoothing things over, you know, telling people, take it easy, don't worry, he wasn't there to rip up their sidewalk or knock down their wall or whatever he'd just built, which was what she'd told them in order to get them to pay their bill. I don't think anybody could understand why he married her. So, of course, he's the one who dies young and she lives on—but I don't know if she's still living because she hasn't spoken to me ever since I took her to court."

"You took her to court? You sued her?"

"Yes. I had to. Believe me, I didn't want to. This woman, who was always hounding people to pay their bill, she refused to pay my bill. For his funeral. Yeah, how do you like that? I didn't have a choice. It was only the second time in my life I ever took anybody to court to collect my bill. And God, she put on such a performance, my God, it was revolting. She was crying, she was hollering, blowing her nose, I'll never forget it, she was swearing, 'He cheated me, he cheated me'—he meaning me—she kept saying it over and over, 'He played on my grief for my husband, I couldn't defend myself against his high-pressure tactics, he sold me the most expensive funeral he had, and the son of a bitch inflated all his costs because he knew I had money, because I just inherited the business.' She actually sat there and called me a son of a bitch. I thought I was going to have a heart attack.

"Because everything she was saying was a goddamned lie—not the most expensive funeral part, that part was true.

Because she insisted on it. She said she would have nothing less than the best for her husband, absolutely nothing less, top quality, everything had to be top quality, the best.

"But that I inflated the costs? That was the goddamned lie. And you won't believe how we defeated her. I'm going to tell you. We both testified in the morning, I testified first of course, because I brought the suit. My lawyer had depositions from a dozen other funeral directors about how they billed, and I had all the invoices from every item for his funeral, and she had no proof, not one shred of proof, about any of her claims about me inflating my bill. All she was doing, it was so obvious what she was doing, she was just playing on the judge's—oh what the hell was his name? I thought I'd never forget his name. Oh. Corcoran. Notorious skirt-chaser. Drinker, gambler, chasing women all the time. How he got to be a judge God only knows. And she was a good-looking woman, no question. So it was obvious their whole defense was for her to play up to him, play up to his appetites. She wore real short skirts, kept crossing and un-crossing her legs, my God, it was disgusting. Anyway, she was testifying for almost twenty minutes, all of a sudden she goes into this phony swoon, she fakes like she fainted, so naturally her attorney asks for a recess, she's too distraught, she can't continue, blah blah blah. So we recess for lunch.

"I'm having lunch with my attorney—he still can't under-stand how the thing got to trial in the first place and in the second place why the trial wasn't over in fifteen minutes—she'd been testifying, mind you, since ten after eleven. My attorney keeps saying the whole thing should've been over in fifteen minutes, and he was very worried because she'd been on the stand for twenty minutes herself and he's thinking that this skirt-chaser, this judge, this Corcoran, he's getting hornier by the minute and letting her and her attorney go on and on about nothing, and my attorney's starting to talk how if it keeps going the way it's going, we're not only going to lose, we're going to wind up paying court costs for bringing a frivolous suit, and I'm saying how can that be, and we're going round and round, and who do you think walks into the restaurant? We're eating in the Tea Room, which isn't there anymore, used to be almost directly across the street from the courthouse. We're paying our check, who do you think walks in?"

"No idea," Carlucci said, wondering where this was going and if any of it was going to help him.

"Mario Balzic's mother. Yeah. Somebody had called her up and told her what was going on—to this day I don't know who called her. I think it was the tipstaff, I can't remember his name, but I'm not sure it was him, except I don't know who else it could have been, there was nobody else there—thank God. It was humiliating enough for *me* to have to listen to that woman, thank God nobody else was there. Just the judge, that woman, her attorney, my attorney, the court stenographer, and the tipstaff, that's all. Me of course."

"So Mrs. Balzic comes in and what?"

"She comes up to me and volunteers to testify, be a character witness. My attorney, rest in peace, he was so sure the whole thing was going to be cut-and-dried, we didn't even talk about getting character witnesses. He said we didn't need any, the woman was just a deadbeat, she couldn't prove otherwise, and we had all these depositions from the other funeral directors that showed I had done nothing out of line and that was that. But for the last twenty minutes we both had to watch the judge, that Corcoran, practically drooling, and watch her looking up at him and crying and crossing her legs and licking her lips, my God, it was the most shameless thing I've ever seen.

"So we go back at one-thirty, two o'clock, whenever it

was, and her attorney says he's finished with her. So my attorney—"

"Who was that?"

"You know, honest to God, I can't remember his name right at this moment. Getting old I guess. Oh. Donatello. Francis. How could I forget. Wonderful man, I don't mean to give you the wrong impression, to make you think he wasn't competent. Believe me, he was very competent. In fact, when we got back in and he cross-examined Mrs. Picadio, he only asked her four questions. He showed her my bill. Was that my bill? Yes. Did you pay it? No. Did you take this bill to anyone else to try to determine whether the itemized charges were excessive—did you go to another funeral director or the association of funeral directors, or the Better Business Bureau, or the Chamber of Commerce? No. Then how can you claim you were overcharged? She got all flustered, didn't know what to say. My attorney says no more questions. The judge makes a great show of sympathy for her, like she's going to faint again or something. He tells the tipstaff to help her down, help her back to her chair, get her some water, all the while the lecherous bastard, he's painting her with his eyes.

"So then, my attorney calls Mrs. Balzic. Make a long story short, my attorney asks her what she's doing there, and she says she's there to swear before God that she knows at least sixteen families in Rocksburg who could not afford to pay for the funerals for some members of their families and for which I either charged them costs or else I charged them nothing at all. She says if the judge wants her to, if he could give her three days, she could collect three hundred signatures of people who would swear to my history of telling the truth and never cheating anybody. So that Corcoran, that bum, he made her do it. He said go ahead, if you come back in here with three hundred names on a petition, I'll rule in his favor. And that's what happened. That bastard, can you imagine, he wouldn't rule on the merits of the case? He insisted she go out and get the signatures! So three days later she's back. And she hands him a petition with more than four hundred names on it! My God I've never been prouder in my life.

"But naturally Mrs. Picadio, of course, she's never spoken a word to me since, and that's why, Rugs, you said you wanted to know, if I have a choice about getting vaults somewhere else, I will always go somewhere else. And since I'm telling you all this, I may as well tell you the rest. Their son—I think he's their only child, I don't think they have any more—he takes after his mother, not his father, and if anything, he's worse than she ever was. I don't know anybody who likes him. He's moody, surly, sullen, sarcastic, I don't know how anybody works for him. And *his* wife is worse than him. She's the worst of all. She used to keep the books for them—I don't think she does anymore—and she's a horrible person. Terrible. If the phone rings, and it's her, I hang up. I won't speak to her. I don't talk to any of them. Just Bill. The truck driver. The rest, I deal with only through the mail. I will not talk to them. Especially her. She's stupid, chews gum, cracks it, talks like she's in a whorehouse, filthy mouth, the only good thing I have to say about her is she married him so they didn't ruin two other marriages. Two people never deserved each other more."

"Uh-ha," Carlucci said. "Well that's some story."

"True. Every word of it true. Course the only one who can verify it would be Mrs. Picadio, all the rest of them have passed on. Except for the son of course. And his wife. And naturally none of them would see it the way I just told you."

"So, how do they do in that business, you know? You have any idea? They do okay? How much does a burial vault cost, for instance?"

"What can I say? They're in business. Been in business for years. Must do all right. As for the vaults, it depends what you want. A plain concrete box is not that expensive, but if you want adornment, a lot of ornamental work on the lid, gold paint and so forth, they can be very expensive."

"Would you be more specific, please? About the prices."

"Oh, they range from about five-fifty up to about three thousand. You can get cheaper ones, but I don't use them."

"And you mark 'em up about what, a hundred percent?"

"Roughly, yes."

"So they're chargin' you between what, two hundred seventy-five up to, say, fifteen hundred? Is that about right?"

"That's about right, yes."

"And you would never pay anybody in cash, right? You would never do that."

"Certainly not. I don't do that with anybody, but they would be the last people I would do that with. Every bill I send them, I send them return receipt requested. I only do that with one other business, but with some people you have to keep absolutely accurate records, because you just never know with them."

"Okay, Mr. Bruno," Carlucci said, standing and extending his hand. "I wanna thank you for takin' this time to talk to me, I know you're busy."

"Not at all, Rugs, anytime," Bruno said, shaking Carlucci's hand with both of his. "Say hello to your mother for me. Give her my best."

Carlucci said he would and hurried out to his cruiser and called the station.

"Nowicki? Carlucci here. Any word on that Pontiac yet?"

"Negative," Nowicki said, sounding more bored than usual.

"Hey, I'm goin' home get somethin' to eat, check on my mother, okay?"

"Ten-four. Mayor's lookin' for you."

"Tell him I'm workin' a case, can't talk to him now."

"Say's it's real important. You wanna tell him yourself? He's standin' right here."

Oh God, Carlucci winced. I almost said what I was thinking. "Ahhhh, sure. Put him on. Mr. Mayor, you there? What's up?"

"How do you work this?" the mayor said, talking to Nowicki.

"When you wanna talk, just hold that button down. You're holdin' it down, that's okay, he can hear you. Just talk, go 'head."

"Detective, I need to see you as soon as possible. We have something important to discuss."

"Yes, sir. But I haven't had anything to eat since this morning and I have to check on my mother. I'm on my way now, should be back at City Hall, thirty, thirty-five minutes. That all right?"

"Yes. Right. Fine. What do I say? Ten-four? Is that what you say?" He was again talking to Nowicki. "I always wanted to say that. Ten-four, Detective, ten-four."

"Roger and out," Carlucci said, hanging up and taking as many side streets up to Norwood Hill as he could, thinking, it's not enough you're hauntin' me at the station and at home, now you gotta start hauntin' me in the car. Ten-four my ass.

Carlucci was not comfortable driving and talking on the radio because he believed that anybody who tried to do two things at once could not possibly be paying full attention to either one of them. Now here he was, driving and thinking about the biggest career advancement of his life just because when he checked in the mayor happened to be standing by the radio. And the mayor was talking about "something important to discuss" and suddenly all kinds of thoughts and emotions were rolling around and up and down in his mind and body and—holy shit!

He jammed on the brakes with both feet. A bread truck, high and wide and white and as big as his mother's kitchen, had cut in front of him. And he'd never seen it. He knew it had to have come from in front of Oriolo's Confectionery.

"Stupid sonofabitch!" he shouted, leaning on the horn, as his front bumper stopped inches from the truck's left rear. The truck barely hesitated, then pulled away without a sign from the driver. Carlucci ballooned his cheeks with a sigh while he checked his mirrors for traffic behind him. Never fails, he thought. Let your mind wander and it never fails.

He turned right off McCoy Road and crawled around Mother of Sorrows Church and up Corliss Street to his mother's house and parked across the street and went inside, wondering why he persisted in trying to do two things at once since he knew in his heart it wasn't possible to pay attention to either one. No matter what you know, asshole, somebody opens your nose about a job and you forget everything. Like how to drive. And use your eyes. And you don't see little things like bread trucks. Like a two-and-a-half-ton bread truck painted solid white. Why can't I think and pay attention to what's goin' on around me? Lotsa people do that. Some of 'em gotta be able to pay attention. Jesus, what if it'd been a kid on a bike. God. . . .

"Ma? Mrs. Comito? Where you at?" he called out inside the front door, while hanging up his parka.

"We're out here, Rugsie," Mrs. Comito said. "Where you been at? I heated the soup up three times already." She came to the door of the kitchen, a metal ladle in her right hand, the other hand underneath it to catch drips.

"I got tied up." He untied his new boots and pulled them off and padded out to the kitchen, trying to give his mother a kiss on the top of her head, but she ducked down and threw up her right hand to ward him off.

"Don't do that!" she said, "Where you been? Don't that bastard Balzic even let you have lunch no more?"

"Balzic's not there anymore, Ma. Retired, you know? His last day was December thirty-first last year."

"Yeah, you said," Mrs. Comito said, dipping into an oval aluminum pan that doubled as soup pot and roaster. "You're gonna like this soup, Rugsie. It's really good."

"What kind of soup is it?"

"Oh, I don't know what to call it. I just put everything you had in the refrigerator in it. Or under the sink. There's white beans, onions, garlic, you know. And you still had some broccoli left from yesterday, so I put that in too. Gives it a real different taste. Ma liked it."

"You liked it, huh, Ma?"

"I ate it. Whatta you care? Soup's soup. Sicka soup. That's all we eat."

"You told me you liked it," Mrs. Comito said, gingerly setting a bowl brimming full in front of Carlucci. "I thought you liked it."

"Oh quit makin' such a big deal. It ain't steak."

"You're not supposed to have steak, Ma."

"You're not supposed to have steak, Ma," she mimicked him. "Who says? You? What makes you the expert all of a sudden about what I'm s'posed to eat?"

"Not me. Ma. Your doctors. Both of 'em."

"Oh what, you're mad now 'cause I got two doctors?"

"No I'm not mad you got two doctors—"

"Who the hell asked ya get me two doctors? I did, I guess. I woke up one day and I said, hey, one doctor ain't enough for me. I gotta have another one. Yeah, right. That's just what I said. Bullshit. They're both fulla shit'n so are you."

Carlucci sighed, swallowed, blew on his soup, and said, "Mrs. Comito, we got any bread?"

Mrs. Comito had just started to sit down opposite him but she lurched back up and went to the counter next to the sink. "I put it away already, I forgot."

"Wish you'd forget to come here once in a goddamn while. How come you never forget that?"

"Ma, cut it out."

"Ma," she said, mimicking him again, "cut it out. Ma, cut it out. Or what? What if I don't cut it out, huh? What're you gonna do? Shoot me? Go ahead. Take out your goddamn gun and shoot me. You got two guns. Use 'em! Do somethin' nice for me for a change!"

"Stop it, Ma, please? Huh?" He jumped up out of his chair and stood there straddling it, feeling hurt and foolish and frustrated.

"You could stop it. You. Not me. You. One bullet right here." She jabbed herself between the eyes with her right thumb. "Boom! Bang! Pow!" She lurched out of her chair and headed for the living room. "What time's *Wheel of Fortune*?"

"Seven-thirty, Ma. Right after *Jeopardy!*"

"Only five more hours," Mrs. Carlucci said, continuing to shuffle toward the couch in the living room. "All I have to do is get through the next five hours, and my life can start up again. *Jeopardy! Wheel of Fortune*. Alex Trebec. Pat Sajak. Alex Sajak, Pat Trebec. *Wheel of Jeopardy. Fortune*. Vanna Whiteski. I'd like to get my hands around her skinny throat, I'd show her how to turn those goddamn letters."

Carlucci hung his head and took a deep breath, exhaling loudly through his nose. He felt Mrs. Comito hovering beside him and he knew she was going to pat his head or his shoulder or touch his cheek or the top of his head or something and he wished she would just go back on the other side of the table and sit down.

She brushed his cheek with the back of her fingers and shook her head.

"It's okay," he whispered. "Really. Just sit down, okay? I'm okay. This isn't anything new. Except wantin' to choke Vanna White. That's new."

"I can hear youns whisperin' about me," Mrs. Carlucci sang out from the living room.

"Right, Ma, yeah. We hear ya." Carlucci wiped his mouth with one of the paper napkins Mrs. Comito brought because she thought they were so pretty. They had a terrible chemical smell that always nearly gagged him, but apparently neither Mrs. Comito nor his mother was bothered by them, so he didn't complain. He usually remembered how bad they smelled and didn't use them. This time he got miffed with himself for almost gagging and for not remembering how much their smell caused that.

"I gotta go," he said. "The mayor wants to talk to me. Uh, this morning, did you say somethin' about Mrs. Viola was sick or somethin', she wasn't gonna be able to make it tonight? Did you say that or did I just think you said that?"

"I didn't say nothin' about her," Mrs. Comito said, puzzled. "When? This morning? No. Last week she was sick one night, but I didn't say nothin' this morning."

Carlucci shook his head and shrugged. "I'm hearing things I guess. See ya, Ma. Gotta go."

"Not if I see you first," she said morosely. "Not if I go first."

"Rugsie, you didn't even touch your soup. What're you gonna eat? You gotta eat something," Mrs. Comito said.

Carlucci ducked his head around the corner to give his mother a smile and a wave. She smiled and waved back. Unlike him, she made no pretense of sincerity. Her wave was as exaggerated and phony as her smile. Then her eyes glinted and her lips pressed together and she said, "And tell that sonofabitch Balzic to give ya a raise, that cheap bastard. And if he says he don't have no money, tell him I said go on *Wheel of Fortune*. He could spin that wheel, he oughta know how to do that, you don't need any brains to do that."

Carlucci grabbed a slice of bread off the table then held it in his mouth while he put on his boots and parka and told Mrs. Comito that if he was going to be late, he'd call her. Then he hustled outside to his cruiser, feeling like he was going to choke, like the cold air was turning solid after it entered his nose and mouth and was damming up in his throat. He dropped into the seat of his cruiser and sat there and took the bread out of his mouth and looked at it. He finally put it on the seat beside him. He began to breathe from his belly, one long breath after another, exhaling fully and emptying his lungs before he began his next inhalation.

Balzic had taught him to do that, had told him it was the exact opposite of hyperventilation and it was something everybody who dealt with stress every day could not afford not to know. And at moments like this, when his mother said that doing something nice for her would be to shoot her, when he thought he was going to beat his forehead against the steering wheel until his brains dripped out of his nose, he was grateful to Balzic for that lesson in belly breathing. It was the only thing that seemed to make sense, forcing himself to inhale from the bottom of his belly until the top of his lungs burned and then to exhale until he was crunching his stomach backward against his spine.

If he did it long enough, he would regain his composure eventually. Some times took longer than others. Now he sat for almost five minutes before turning the key in the ignition, and he still wasn't composed. He wondered if he'd ever be composed again. Other people might dream of money when they thought about being rich, but Carlucci thought being rich was being composed, being cool and poised and not being afraid, not even letting the weakest part of him feel fear, that's what he thought being rich must feel like. . . .

When he finally pulled away from the curb and headed back toward City Hall, he felt so poor he thought he ought to be getting food stamps. Food stamps for his spirit. As though there was such a thing, as though anybody would understand that. He couldn't remember whether he'd even taken one spoonful of Mrs. Comito's soup. He finally picked the bread up and started chewing it, slowly. He stopped after the second mouthful. When he got to the parking lot at City Hall, he tore the bread into pieces and scattered it on the ground for the sparrows and starlings.

Carlucci knocked on the mayor's door, which was open. Angelo Bellotti looked up from something he was reading, smiled a campaigner's smile, and motioned with both hands for Carlucci to enter. "Come in, come in, Detective. And shut the door."

Carlucci shut the door, thinking, this is it. This is when he makes the pitch. Couldn't be anything else behind that smile. He's been doin' a lot of talkin' lately, but he's never given me his campaign smile. When Carlucci turned around from closing the door he almost bumped into Bellotti. The next thing he knew Bellotti was pumping his right hand with both of his and holding onto it all the way to a chair directly in front of Bellotti's highly polished walnut desk.

"Have a seat, Detective, have a seat. Hi ya doin' today?"

"Fine, Mr. Mayor. I'm fine. You?" He waited until Bellotti got around the desk and sat before he sat. One thing about Bellotti, Carlucci thought, the man likes fine furniture. Wonder what this desk cost. Wonder who paid for it. Wonder who polishes it.

Bellotti smiled professionally again and said he too was fine. He swiveled for a brief moment in his red leather chair and then his smile dissolved and he put his fingers together to form a steeple and drummed on the end of his nose with his index fingers before he spoke. "Detective, I don't have to tell you, because you know better than anybody else around here, you know we got a department but we don't have a chief, and we got problems and the problems never end. Things keep happenin', and no matter how much we might wanna say, hey, slow down, give us a chance to catch our breath here, they don't stop, they just keep on comin'. You know this, I don't have to tell you.

"And while, under the city code, as far as the police department, the buck stops with me—I mean I'm ultimately responsible for the department under the law, but the fact is, Detective, I'm not a policeman. Never been one. But on the other hand, see, as chairman of the Safety Committee of City Council, I'm also responsible for the fire department, but the difference there is, see, I've been a fireman for almost forty years now. Well I'm not anymore, I mean, I put on my bunker suit when I hear the siren, but it's not 'cause I'm gonna be layin' any hose. I got it on 'cause I'm there as chairman of the Safety Committee and I don't wanna ruin my clothes, you follow me?"

"Yes, sir."

"But the fact is, Detective, I'm not a policeman. I mean, I was in charge of the police for more than twelve years, not countin' the last four of course, but never been a police officer. Know a lot about the police, learned a lot about 'em. Had to. But I don't know what a cop knows. 'Cause I never saw it from the cop's side. Now you, on the other hand, you've seen it from your side a long time. You've been a police officer, civil servant, public-spirited citizen, huh? Huh?

Ever since you got out of the Army, am I right? That's correct, isn't it?"

"Right. Yes, sir. Well, I've been a police officer, which certainly makes me a civil servant. I don't know about the other thing there, the public-spirit thing."

"Don't be modest, Detective, don't be modest. Your record since 1971 is well known, you don't have to apologize for any compliment anybody pays you."

"Uh, yes, sir. Thank you, sir."

"Well, Detective, let me get to the point. No matter how much I had to learn about the department, the fact is I wouldn't know how to run it on a day-to-day basis if my life depended on it. But as I said, things don't stop happenin' just 'cause we need a breather, and while we've been goin' along like this, without a chief, for a coupla weeks now, everybody knows, and I'm sure I won't get any argument from you, we can't go on like this forever, no sir."

Carlucci was looking deeply into Bellotti's eyebrows—Balzic had taught him that, taught him how to fool another person into thinking you were sincerely focused on what they were saying—but he was worried that even though he had every reason to pay close attention to what Bellotti was saying, he knew that if he slipped and actually looked into Bellotti's eyes he would start to giggle. That had happened to him many times in his life, always at the worst possible times. The first time it happened, he'd giggled so uncontrollably during confession that Father Romanelli had dragged him by his wrist out of the confession box at Mother of Sorrows and out onto the sidewalk and told him to pray out there until God gave him composure. Carlucci was nine. He stayed on the sidewalk for about ten minutes. Then he went home and asked his father what *composure* meant. His father was helping him look it up in the dictionary when his mother came home from next door and wanted to know what they were doing and why. It was a terrible precedent.

Sitting here peering into Bellotti's eyebrows, worried that he might break into giggles for no reason at all, he started worrying more because Bellotti so far hadn't said what was going on here even though all his words sounded like what Carlucci had thought they were going to be as soon as the mayor had flashed his campaigner's smile. Carlucci's worries increased: maybe he was hearing what he wanted to be hearing and not what the mayor was saying; maybe he wasn't paying nearly as close attention as he'd thought.

"But the fact is, Detective—is it all right if I call you Rugs? I feel like I'm bein' too formal here. And as I recall, I always called you Rugs before, didn't I?"

"Yessir, you did."

"So it's okay I call you Rugs now?"

"Fine with me. Everybody does."

"Good. Rugs, I have to say it, I mean I will absolutely be the first to admit I miss our former chief as much as anyone does. Mario Balzic was an outstanding police officer, an outstanding chief. I don't think you'll find anybody in this town—or in this county for that matter—who would quibble about that. But the fact is, Rugs, no matter how much we all miss Balzic, no matter how much we admired him, respected him, and, yes, I have to say it, how much we revered him—because that man was revered, Rugs, no question about that. He was revered. But he's gone. And we have to move on."

"Yessir, we do."

"Absolutely. And I think he'd be the first one to agree with me."

"Oh, yessir. Absolutely. No question."

"So, uh, because I've never been a police officer myself and because that's all you've been—and I have to add this here and now—I can't leave this out because this is a fact—you are the senior officer in the department now. Yes. Oh yes. Both in terms of years of service and in rank and in years in rank.

"So, Rugs, since you have all this experience on the street and as a sergeant and as a detective, I was thinking, why am I not using this kind of experience? Why am I not asking you what you think? Who better to ask about who our next chief should be? Or what he should be—what qualities should he have, what attributes, what kind of personality, what kind of character? Because character's very important, Rugs. Extremely important.

"This last presidential election, Rugs, I'm tellin' you, I think the whole thing turned on character. Who had it, who didn't. Course now Perot, he screwed things up, gettin' involved. Turned it into a three-ring circus 'stead of a two-party race the way it should've been. So now, if you ask me, we have a man in there without a clear mandate, and I don't mind telling you I don't like that. Don't think it's good for the country. We would've been much better off if we'd just had the two men running. Would've been a lot easier, way easier to identify those things we want in a president, if there'd been just the two of them. Things would've been a lot clearer, more focused. You agree with that, Detective? Rugs?"

Carlucci had been thinking about snapping the middle finger of his right hand into the inside of his left wrist to keep from giggling. Carlucci had learned that from Balzic as well. It was the same principle smokers used when they wore rubber bands around their wrists and snapped them every time they wanted a cigarette. Sitting here now with his hands in his lap, right thumb cocking his middle finger and poised to snap, he sensed he was supposed to say something.

"Well, yessir, that's probably true, but, uh, a two-man race was not what happened, so, uh, I guess what I'm sayin' is, uh, I guess we have to deal with what happened, instead of, uh, what we wished would've happened."

"Very true, Rugs, very true. Good point. That's exactly what we have to do. Deal with what happened. Absolutely."

Carlucci sighed silently and as motionlessly as he could manage. Apparently he'd said something that made sense to the mayor.

"So, uh," Bellotti went on, "I guess I should be bringing this a little closer to home, right? I get the feeling you're gettin' a little impatient here—"

"Oh no sir. It's just I'm workin' on a case and, uh, I hate losin' time, you know. At the beginning. It's very important right at the beginning, you know, when everything's fresh?"

"Well of course it is. And I don't wanna keep you longer than necessary, so I'll just come right to the point. So, uh, tell me, what did you think of Balzic?"

Carlucci stiffened. What do I think of Balzic? Is that what he said? Is that what this is about? He got me in a pot with a fire under my ass and he wants to know what I think of Balzic? Jesus, does he actually think I'm gonna answer that?

"Now, Rugs, I can see by the look on your face, you're not sure about my intentions here, so let me put you at ease. I'm not here diggin' for dirt, Rugs, not at all, not about Balzic. The man's retired, I'd be the last man on earth to try to besmirch his reputation, that's not what I'm doin' at all. What I'm doing here—and I want to be very clear about this—I'm just trying to see how you thought he ran the department and what was good about what he did and what was maybe not so good. But what I'm really tryin' to get at is what *you* think we should be lookin' for in the next chief. Like, what were Balzic's flaws in runnin' the department— in your opinion. And this is strictly off the record here,

Rugs. What you say here doesn't go out of this room, you have my word on that."

Oh yeah, right, Carlucci thought. It doesn't *leave* this room, but everybody who comes *in* gets a bucketful of what I say. "Well, uh, Mr. Mayor, I don't think I, uh, should be talkin' about Mario's flaws—which isn't to say he didn't have any, but I'm not real sure this is the kind of thing I oughta be talkin' about—"

"Oh come on, Rugs, nobody's listening. It's you and me here. Mario, bless his heart, he's gone, I loved the man. Whatever loyalty you had—and I'm sure you were—and are—very loyal to him, hell, he was your rabbi, I understand that. That was well known, believe me. Especially by me. But Rugs, Rugsie, listen, the only marriages made in heaven, hey, they aren't made in heaven. They're made in Hollywood. The rest of us, once the bloom is off the rose, once the honeymoon is over, as they say, we wake up one morning and we find out we have to live with our spouse, with all her warts. And our spouse has to live with us, with all our warts. That's a fact. And Balzic, no matter how respected, revered—I've said the man was revered, I readily acknowledge that—but the man had warts. I don't think you would deny that. Am I wrong?"

Carlucci shrugged, but he said nothing.

"Look, Rugs, what I'm tryin' to do here is find a new chief. And Balzic himself told me, not once, but many times, right here in this office—you, Rugs. You—he said you were the sharpest investigator he ever trained, that's what he used to tell me. The teacher observes the student, Rugs. I know that, you know that, that's the way it goes, that's life. But we also know the student observes the teacher. That's also life. The teacher is observed by the student. That's a fact. And you were no different—you *are* no different from any student in that regard, am I right, Rugs?"

"No. No sir. No different. I mean, yessir you are right, that's what I meant to say." Carlucci's mouth suddenly felt very dry. "Okay if I have some water, Mr. Mayor?"

"Help yourself." Bellotti pushed a tray holding his gleaming stainless-steel carafe of water and two crystal tumblers toward Carlucci. "But, Rugs, I'm sensing stress here. You're feelin' stress here, and you don't need to feel that, really you don't. You get enough of that at home, you get enough on the streets, on the job. Relax, relax. What we have here, you and me, this is not an adversarial relationship here. We're both tryin' do do what's right. But I'm sensin' you think I'm tryin' in some way—I don't understand how—but you think I'm trying to get you to betray a friend, be disloyal in some way. Rugs, listen to me. What you're doin' is very admirable. I mean it. I admire that, I really do, and I understand it, completely. But you have to understand that I don't—that I'm not intending Balzic any harm here. That's not what this is about. I have no reason to want to hurt the man."

Carlucci drank almost a full tumbler of water and then put the tumbler back on the tray on the mayor's desk. "I understand what you're sayin', sir, but, uh, I just don't feel, uh, comfortable talkin' about Mario this way. I mean, I know what you're tryin' to do. You're tryin' to find out what I think a chief oughta be like—"

"Exactly."

"But what you got to understand is, even though the man had his, uh, flaws, his faults, I know that, I mean he could screw up, wow, big time, you know? Drank too much for one thing. Mario'd tell you that himself."

"Course he would. You don't drink, do you, Rugs?"

"Uh, no. I mean yes, I mean I drink. I love beer. It's just, I don't know, some guys can drink a lot, some guys can't, and, uh, I'm one of those. I can't hold it is what I mean. I fall asleep. Two beers, fine. Three beers, zonko, I'm history."

"Well, nothing to be ashamed of there, Rugs, that's good. Very good. More people should know when to quit."

Carlucci chewed his lower lip and looked at the floor for a long moment. "Mr. Mayor, I, uh, I have to know something. I mean I think I know where this conversation's goin', but I don't wanna—what do I wanna say? I don't wanna presume anything, you know? And I don't wanna be wrong either. Cause if I'm wrong, I'm gonna look like a jagoff here, but, uh . . . "

"But what?"

Carlucci took a deep breath and let half of it out. "Mr. Mayor, am I, uh, am I bein' considered? Am I a candidate— for the job I mean. Is this conversation, uh, is this a preliminary interview what we're doin' here? For the job of chief? I mean I would really like to know that, sir. I think it would make all the difference in the world how I'm gonna answer your questions. And I think, uh, in all fairness to me, I think you should tell me what's goin' on here."

"Rugs, I've told you several times what's goin' on. I'm askin' your opinion about what you think the next chief ought to be, his qualities and so on—"

"Yes sir, I know you said that. But, Mr. Mayor, this department is flyin' on rumors now, which I'm sure you know. I mean, I know that nobody can stop rumors, it's the situation that's causin' 'em, but one of these rumors, Mr. Mayor, is that because I'm the senior ranking officer—which you yourself referred to earlier—I mean, I'm included in the rumors. People're askin' me about this all the time, not just in the department. I took a couple boxes of evidence up to the state police crime lab, and, hey, first thing guys up there said to me, you know, was they heard I was gonna get scrambled eggs on my cap. Maybe.

"Mr. Mayor, what I'm sayin' is, uh, is that true or not? Because either way, see, either way, it's gonna make a big difference in what I do from now on. Oh, wait. I didn't mean that the way it sounded. I didn't mean, like as if, you know, if I wasn't bein' considered, I'd start screwin' off or somethin', or start lookin' for another job, that's not what I meant, no. It's just . . . " He didn't know what to say next because he suddenly had the overpowering feeling he'd just said way too much.

Bellotti had steepled his fingers again while Carlucci was talking and there was a faint trace of a smile behind his fingers. Carlucci could barely make it out, but it was there. No mistaking it. Aw shit, Carlucci thought, why didn't I just get a tattoo across my forehead that says APPLICANT?

Bellotti cleared his throat and tapped his fingers together for a moment before he put his elbows on the desk and leaned forward over them.

"I think it's fair, Rugs, to say that your name has come up, uh, in our search. Prominently. It's fair to say you are a candidate for the job. Or, what's more, to say you're on the short list. So, uh, if you wanna consider this a preliminary interview for the job, I'm not gonna argue with that. So, uh, now that that's out in the open, tell me about Balzic."

Okay, hotshot. Is that what you wanted to hear? Then think fast, 'cause you just pulled your zipper down and showed him your hard-on. So say what you wanna say. Just watch who you trash.

"Mr. Mayor, I thank you for bein' honest with me. I really appreciate that."

"You're welcome."

"Well, uh, the department, uh, it can't continue to operate with one detective, Mr. Mayor, and I don't want to make any presumptions here, but if I'm bein' considered for the job, if I'm on the short list as you just said, well, if you decide to promote me—I know that's a pretty big if—but if that happens, then you gotta promote two other men to detective. You, uh, we can't function with no detectives.

"On top of which, we're wastin' three officers workin' dispatcher duty. I think it's way past time this department got hooked up with 911. I think we should've been hooked up with the county 911 years ago. The county would have no problem with that. I've talked to those people several times. They could take us on in less than twenty-four hours. All somebody has to do is say the word—you, Council, whoever. And then, I guess, you know, you or somebody's gonna have to sell it to the taxpayers, 'cause they're who's gonna pay for it. But I think they will, sir. I never hear anything to the contrary."

"Very interesting, Rugs. Go on."

"Well, sir, mostly what I have to say is pretty much what Balzic used to say. We don't have enough people. It's that simple. I mean look at the TO—"

"Beg pardon? The what?"

"TO. Table of organization. How the department's set up. Or how it oughta be set up. We should have a captain, who should be the training officer, who should be findin' out what the rest of us need to know. We haven't had a training officer since I made detective. That's twelve years. Our training was, Balzic would hear somethin' or he'd read somethin', then he'd tell me, and I'd go see if there was anything on it at the community college. That's how we always did it."

"And that's not the way to do it, is that your opinion?"

"Uh, Mr. Mayor, the only reason that ever worked at all was because we had to make it work 'cause our hands were tied otherwise. I don't mind tellin' ya, I beat more'n a couple dead horses 'cause I wasn't up on the latest rulings on admissibility of evidence. I mean, if I'd've known about those rulings at the time, I wouldn't've been wastin' the DA's time. If I work a case and I think I got a righteous one and I go see him, and he says, hey, it ain't gonna fly, I mean, I feel pretty stupid.

"And, I don't know whether this is inevitable or not, but it happens that if there's nobody around whose job it is to be tellin' you how it's supposed to be workin'? Pretty soon you start thinkin' ignorance is bliss, and you get careless. Sloppy. But ignorance ain't bliss. Reality's bliss. I mean, what I don't know about investigative techniques would fill a library, and, believe me, I'm not feelin' very blissful.

"Mr. Mayor, lemme give you a real glaring example. I, uh, I don't wanna say this 'cause, uh, this is embarrassing. But I have to say it, 'cause it's, uh, it's what I'm talkin' about. Okay. So I'm just gonna say it. And I hope you won't hold this against me because, uh—well lemme just say it."

Carlucci swallowed hard and sighed and his shoulders drooped and then he pulled himself up and tried to sit tall. "I don't know how to use fingerprint evidence," he said. "I don't know how to collect it, I don't know how to record it, I don't know how to identify it. When it comes to fingerprints, I'm a mess." Carlucci threw his hands wide and giggled nervously. Oh God, please don't let me start. He snapped his left wrist with his right middle finger. "What I'm sayin' is, here's an investigative tool that's been around for God knows how long, and we don't use it here. 'Cause we don't have anybody here who's been trained in it except me—and I'm lousy at it. I mean, if, by some miracle, I do manage to get a print without smudgin' it or screwin' it up in some way, I can't testify about it 'cause if I tried, man, the dumbest lawyer anybody knows'd eat me alive."

Bellotti's brow furrowed. "Are you serious? Wait a minute. I remember one time talkin' to Balzic about this and he said we didn't even have a fingerprint kit. Now you're telling me this? Somethin's screwed up here, I don't get it."

Carlucci felt himself flushing. He swallowed hard and cleared his throat. "Well, see, what he, Balzic, what he was probably tryin' to do was make me, you know, not look bad."

"Not look bad? Not look bad? Does—my God, does anybody else know about this?" Bellotti was suddenly sitting at attention.

"Anybody? Which anybody you talkin' about? Balzic knew it. Everybody in the department knows it. I'm a joke."

"Well, I mean, is this, uh, common knowledge otherwise? Does the district attorney know, for example? The judges, do they know?"

"Well the DA knows. Course he knows. He has to."

"Well has he ever threatened to make it public?"

"Uh, threatened to make it public? Why would he do that?"

"Hell I don't know, to, uh, embarrass us, to use it against us. For some reason. For whatever reason he might have. Who knows what reasons he might have."

"Uh, Mr. Mayor, I don't take a case—lemme rephrase that. I try never to take a case to the DA unless it's solid otherwise. It has to be solid, 'cause, otherwise, hell, this is what I'm sayin'. If I got to rely on print evidence, I'm dead, I got no case."

"Well have we lost cases because of this?"

"Well sure we have. That's what I'm tellin' you."

"Well how did we lose 'em? And how come I never heard about 'em? I never heard about 'em. Why didn't anybody ever tell me about 'em?"

"How did we lose 'em? Well, we lost 'em—I mean, I would lose 'em. Me. We didn't lose 'em. I mean, when I was interrogatin' the perp, and I had him—in my mind I had him—but I didn't have him, you followin' me? And I was tryin' to get him to confess, but he wouldn't confess, because he wouldn't fall for the lie—that's how I would lose 'em."

"What lie?"

"That I had his prints. All over the scene."

"You just told me you don't know how to get anybody's prints."

"I don't. I just said, that's the lie. That's what I would be lyin' about. 'Cause what I'd be countin' on is, most perps wouldn't know that, see? The ones I lost were the ones that were, uh, they'd been through the system once or twice and, uh, somehow they figured out I was bullshittin'. Or else they wore gloves and they knew I was bullshittin'. I mean I didn't go around braggin' about it. But what I'm sayin' is, that's the only way I can use print evidence. To lie. That I have it, I mean." Oh man, Carlucci, how deep you wanna dig this hole? This is the way you go about gettin' the job?

"Well, Rugs, this is all—what do I wanna say? Very, very interesting, I guess. No it isn't. It's disturbing. That's what it is. But I don't know what to say about it. I mean, I have to think about this. I have to give this some thought, Jesus Christ." The mayor cleared his throat, and his mouth and jaw worked around as though he had a large number of things he wanted to say, but he said nothing for almost a minute, which in the silence of the office was very long. Finally, he said, "Shit, let's move on, let's not belabor the point, can't do anything about it now anyway. So, uh, what else would you do if you were in charge? I mean besides train somebody—or get somebody trained— in finger-prints, or fingerprinting."

"Well, Mr. Mayor, it's not just prints. There's all kinds of stuff we don't know very much about. But it isn't 'cause we have people who don't wanna learn. Who aren't willing. It's what Balzic used to complain about all the time. No money.

No money to get the people to where they need to be or to bring the instructors here. But the real problem is, uh, we don't have anybody around who knows how to use the federal government, to get the money and equipment and training they have available. I mean, in the big city departments I've visited, hell, they got one guy assigned, usually at least one, I mean, that's his job, that's all he does all day—he reads the federal laws about what money's available, what programs, what instructors, what equipment, and he applies for it. That's his whole job, that's all he does. We've never had anybody doin' that."

"Well maybe Balzic should've spent a little less time in Muscotti's and a little more time behind his desk, what do you think? Maybe he could've found out about those things himself."

"That's not it, Mr. Mayor. I'm not gonna defend Mario about that, what he should've done or what he shouldn't've. One time I tried to go through the, uh, oh what the hell was the name of that, the, uh, oh man I forget. Oh. Yeah. The Law Enforcement Assistance Act. LEAA, remember that one? Man, I tried to go through that one down the community college, man, Mr. Mayor, I'm tellin' ya, you really gotta know what you're lookin' for. I mean, you gotta understand the lingo, the legalese."

Belotti grunted and began to swivel in his chair again. "Well, Rugs, so far what you're talkin' about is a change in the whole way we're organized, the whole TO as you call it. A captain, right? A training officer, who would of course be the captain. Somebody trained in fingerprinting. And then a federal liaison officer, I guess is what you're talkin' about, for want of a better term. But hell, we already buy a lot of our equipment through the state. Cars, uniforms, weapons, ammunition, et cetera, et cetera, we get that stuff through the state's group purchasing plan, don't we?"

"Yessir, yessir, we do, but that's not what I'm talkin' about though. What I'm talkin' about is what we could be gettin' from the feds. Training, you know, and money for it."

Bellotti was already ignoring him. "Switching over to 911—which I wholeheartedly agree with, 'cause I tried pushin' that years ago, talked that up with everybody, couldn't get anybody to go along with me about sellin' that one to the taxpayers. But I think you're absolutely right, I think that's more'n just doable now. I could make a lot of, uh, never mind. But you said something about two detectives. Tell me that again. Why two detectives? Explain that."

"Caseload, Mr. Mayor. It's as simple as that. I don't think—I mean there's a lotta work to do and it's my job and I'm not bitchin' about it, believe me, but the fact is, it takes a lotta time, just doin' what needs to be done. Lemme give you an example. I have an evidence kit in my car at all times. Every case I work, I gotta make sure I replaced the things I used in the previous case, the boxes, the envelopes, the paper bags, the plastic bags, the tags, everything. I'm also who orders that stuff. I gotta type out the requisitions. And then when it arrives, I gotta unpack it, and then I gotta find a place to store it, you know, so nothin' gets contaminated. Now this is no big deal. This is part of my job. I'm not bitchin' about it. I'm just tryin' to tell ya it takes time to do these things, and every minute I spend doin' these things, that's one less minute I have to spend workin' the cases. You see what I'm sayin'?"

"Course I do. I understand exactly what you're saying. What else?"

"What else. Whatta you mean what else?"

"Why do we need two detectives?"

"Oh. Well. I'm in charge of the property room. All the evidence that, uh, once it's been worked by the state police lab techs, they gotta get it outta there, they got more stuff comin' in every day, so I gotta go get it. And make room for it here. Balzic and I used to split that job, you know, dependin' on who was doin' what. But now, hey, now it's just me.

"And, uh, another job I used to split with him was records. When we weren't doin' anything else, that's what we were doin', workin' records, we were forever workin' records, tryin' to keep everything current, you know? And, Mr. Mayor, I don't mind tellin' ya, we're like—excuse my language here, but we're like in the fuckin' dark ages with these records."

"I beg your pardon? What do you mean, dark ages?"

"Well, we should've had our records on computers, like, ten years ago. We're still workin' typewriters and file cabinets here. Coupla years ago, when I had to go to Florida, pick up a prisoner, I was down there for three days, I talked to people in a couple different departments down there? And Mr. Mayor, in some of those departments I seen, departments not a whole lot bigger'n ours, I'm tellin' ya, they had computers in their cars! Yeah! Right there next to the steering wheel. That patrolman right there in his car, he could punch up anything right there on that computer in his car, man, it'd take me like, three hours goin' through the paper here, to find what it takes him, like, seconds. Seconds!

"We don't even have a computer here, Mr. Mayor. And if we did, we don't have anybody to transfer the records we got in the file cabinets into the computer—and that's assumin' we had somebody who knew how. I'm talkin' basic stuff here, Mr. Mayor. This is what I mean by dark ages. Christ, the only new piece of equipment we got around here in the last five years is a fax machine. Otherwise, man, we're like fuckin' cavemen here."

"Uh-ha," Bellotti grumbled. "Well, computers are here to stay, there's nobody gonna argue with you about that, but you have any idea how much all this would cost, Detective?"

"Oh, nosir, no idea. But I've never had the time to make any inquiries about what it would cost. 'Cause I'm doin' about five jobs here, Mr. Mayor. But I'm not bitchin' about it, believe me. Doin' all these jobs keeps me interested, keeps me movin', keeps me hoppin', I like doin' 'em, I like stayin' busy. It's just not very efficient is what I'm sayin'. And Balzic didn't have any control over it. So it doesn't matter who you get to be chief. Lotsa times Mario was doin' those jobs himself. Believe me, he did a lotta stuff nobody ever knew he was doin'. And if you promote me? You make me chief and you don't hire anybody else? Hey, I'm gonna be doin' just what Balzic did. 'Cause there's no other way. 'Cause with Metikosh gone, we're down to twenty-five people."

"How many?"

"Twenty-five."

"We had thirty, where do you get twenty-five?"

"Thirty? Uh, excuse me, sir, but that was before Balzic and Stramsky and Royer and Rascoli retired. And then Metikosh, he took a job in Florida. And so that leaves us with one sergeant and one detective, which is me. So that's twenty-four patrolmen. Twenty-three men and one woman. With no captain, no lieutenants, no other sergeants, no training officer, no juvenile officer—which we used to have—and nobody doin' PR work with the schools, with the crime watch groups or nothin' like that. So, uh, if you don't mind my sayin' so, Mr. Mayor, you don't need just a chief. 'Cause whoever you hire is gonna need a lotta help from you, and from Council. What you need, what everybody needs around here is a commitment that you're gonna be willin' to spend some money."

"Ah. Well. Commitment, huh? There's the problem, Detective. I mean commitment's not the problem. It's easy to be committed when you have the money. Money's the problem. Where do we get it? Ain't no revenue sharing anymore, remember?"

Carlucci shrugged. "That, sir, I don't think is my problem."

"Uh-ha. Anything else you wanna add, Detective?"

"No sir."

"Well, I wanna thank you for comin' in, for talkin' to me." Bellotti wasn't smiling anymore. And he didn't stand up, or shake Carlucci's hand, or wish him well, and he hadn't said one word about Carlucci's mother.

Carlucci stood and shuffled around and finally backed out of the mayor's office, thinking, That's it? Thanks for comin' in? Thanks for talkin' to me? No I'll get back to you, no we'll talk again, no let me set up another interview, no let me tell you what the next step is? And what happened to "Rugs"? One minute it's Rugs this, Rugs that. Then it's "Detective" again. What the fuck. I'm fucked. Oh man, I'm fucked. I'm fucked and I don't even know how I did it. Just told the truth, what'd he want from me? Balzic said he was lookin' for a dog. What was I supposed to do—roll over and let him scratch my chest? Hey, look down, it's me, I'm on the floor here, the cartoon dog, McGruff Carlucci, I'm gonna show you how to take a bite outta crime. Fuckin' Bellotti. Fuckin' politicians. All the time talkin' about pass this fuckin' law, make this a felony, make that a felony, make this a fuckin' capital crime, make that a fuckin' capital crime, pass all these fuckin' laws, that's all you gotta do to show the voters how tough you are on crime. Man, you want tough? I'll show ya tough. I'll write you so many fuckin' laws nobody can read 'em all. I can make every-fuck-ing-thing you do a fuck-ing capital felony, how you like that, shitheads? You wanna take a bite outta crime, huh? Take a bite outta this. . . .

"Hey, Rugs," somebody called out to him as he was on his way to his desk. It was Nowicki.

"What?" he growled, taking his parka off the back of his chair and putting one arm into a sleeve before stopping to glare at Nowicki.

"Ouu, wow. What, you didn't get the job?"

"You got somethin' you wanna tell me?"

"Yeah, whoa, take it easy. Christ. Pittsburgh PD got your Pontiac."

"Got my what?"

"Your Pontiac. Remember? White two-door Pontiac, 1990? Registered to a Mrs. Picadio?"

"Oh, right, yeah. What's the number?"

"Here," Nowicki said, balling up a slip of yellow paper and tossing it at Carlucci. It landed on the floor in front of Carlucci's desk. "I don't know what his name is. He was eatin' when he was talkin'. Tapari, Tafari, Tasari, Safari, I couldn't understand him and he wouldn't spell it, said he was in a hurry."

Carlucci looked at the wadded-up notepaper and looked at Nowicki and looked at the paper again. He felt his adrenaline starting to rush up in him. He slipped out of his parka and went around his desk and retrieved the paper. "You couldn't hand this to me? Huh? Balzic was here you wouldn't be throwin' no paper around."

"Yeah? Is that a fact? So, uh, you still in the competition or what?"

Carlucci was back at his desk, unwadding the paper. "Iluh? Still in the what?"

"You still in the game or what?"

"What game? What're you talkin' about?"

"What game," Nowicki said disgustedly. "What game you think?"

"I don't know what the fuck you're talkin' about," Carlucci said. "I gotta make this call here." He punched the buttons for the number Nowicki had just tossed at him.

"This is Detective Carlucci, Rocksburg PD. I'm returning a call about a Pontiac, white, two-door, plate number, aw shit, I'll find it here in a second. Somebody called—hey, Nowicki, when'd this call come in?"

"I don't know. Twenty minutes ago. Twenty-five maybe."

Carlucci glared at Nowicki, but he said nothing. "Somebody called me twenty minutes ago, Detective Tapari, Tafari—"

"Tesari. He's here. Hold it. TESARI! PHONE!"

A minute later, a voice, shredded by years of smoking, came on and identified himself. Or tried to. Carlucci asked him to spell it.

"Tesari, Tesari, that's T as in terrific, E as in excellent, S as in superior, A as in avouchment, R as in righteous, I as in idiosyncratic. You got it? Think you can say it now?"

"Tesari. Yeah, I got it. But what's that avouch-what? Avouch, what was that again?"

"Avouchment."

"What's that mean?"

"That means good as fucking gold. A guaran-fucking-tee in other words."

"Okay. Avouchment. I'll remember that. So you got my Pontiac, huh?"

"If you're lookin' for a white, two-door, 1990 Grand Prix, yeah, I got your Pontiac."

"Plate number Alpha Zebra Sugar-2281?"

"That's it, you got it. Now you come up with the VIN and we're in business."

"Uh, I don't have that right now. It's gotta be the same one. But I'll confirm the VIN. Where'd you find the car?"

"In an alley off Larimer Avenue, East Liberty."

"What else you got?"

"What else I got? I got one black male, Wandoe Evon Best—"

"Wandoe what?"

"Wandoe Evon, I said. As in Wandoe, W-A-N-D-O-E, Evon, E-V-O-N, last name Best, spelled just the way it sounds, you think you can spell that? Huh? Best?"

"I think I can do that."

"These fuckin' people with their names, they kill me, no shit. My partner, he's a black guy, but he got a real name. He ain't got no stupid fuckin' name like Wandoe, what kinda name is 'at, Wandoe. Anyway, we got Wandoe in the front seat, passenger side, two nines in his chest, maybe more, there was so much fuckin' blood I couldn't tell. He's upstairs now."

"Upstairs? Where's upstairs? Where you at?"

"Allegheny General."

"The hospital?"

"Yeah, the hospital. What other Allegheny General you know? Where you from again?"

"Rocksburg. What else you have?"

"Rocksburg. Where the fuck is Rocksburg, where'sat? Never mind. I don't wanna know. What else? Whoo, what else I got here. Well I got three screamin' Bahama mommas in here, all weepin' and wailin' and chewin' their teeth over Wandoe Evon 'cause apparently they were all in contention to become his main number one boss fox, doncha know. HEY! YOU DON'T SHUDDUP I'M GONNA TAKE YOUNS ALL IN. WANNA GO TO GRANT STREET, YOU WANT THAT? THEN SHUDDUP!

"These people, I'm tellin' ya. I'd like to know whoever the asshole was who thought it was a good idea to let black people get around white powder. Cheezus Christ, this is all I do anymore—"

"Wait, wait, this was a dope shooting, is that what you're sayin'?"

"What the fuck give you that idea? Huh? I'm talkin' 'bout these whores screamin' here. Nobody would act like 'at wasn't flyin' on somethin'. Normal people don't act like 'at. I don't know what the fuck Wandoe got shot over. 'At's what I'm tellin' ya, 'at's all I do anymore, ask somebody named Wandoe Evon who shot him, or, or, last week it was Moreese. Get that one. Mo-reese, M-O-R-E-E-S-E, Moreese Abdul Johnson. He wouldn't tell me who shot him either. And this fuck, this, uh, Wandoe, he ain't gonna tell me either. SHUDDUP! I AIN'T GONNA TELL YOUNS AGAIN! Hey, I gotta go shut these whores up, they're makin' everybody crazy here."

"Hey wait wait wait. Did this Wandoe say what he was doin' in the Pontiac?"

"Did Wandoe say what he was doin'? Believe me, pal, Wandoe was not talkin' when we arrived. I'm not a doctor, understand, I just wish I was playin' one on TV, but in my opinion Wandoe ain't gonna be talkin' to anybody ever again. But if you wanna come on in and try to talk to him, you be my guest. You wanna talk to me, call Homicide. What's your name again?"

"Carlucci. Detective, Rocksburg PD. Listen, I really wanna know about this guy. Owner of the Pontiac's in real bad shape. I don't know if she's gonna make it—"

"Sorry to hear that. I'm not real familiar with Wandoe, but my partner says Wandoe's been a bad boy for a long time, so you can start with Records downtown. Hey I gotta shut these broads up, they're goin' nuts here. Bye."

Carlucci said, "Hey, wait. Tell those doctors do a rape workup on him," but Detective Tesari had hung up. Carlucci immediately dialed the Records Section of the Pittsburgh

PD, identified himself, and asked for Wandoe Evon Best's record to be faxed to him.

When the fax arrived fifteen minutes later, Carlucci shook his head when he read it. Wandoe had indeed been a bad boy for a long time. No telling what a lovely child he'd been, but since age eighteen, he'd had five busts in four years, all for some degree of felony assault. Two had been dismissed because witnesses failed to appear. One had been pleaded down to a third-degree misdemeanor and three months time served. One had got him a sentence of three months plus six months time served awaiting trial in Allegheny County Jail for assault aggravated with weapon, sock filled with gravel. The other one got him sentenced to seven months plus five months time served awaiting trial for attempted murder, assault aggravated with weapon, sock filled with sand.

Aw shit, Carlucci groaned. He wasn't wearin' gloves. He hit her with a sock full of something. A black sock. Son of a bitch, he probably left his fingerprints all over that office. Oh man, never assume anything, how many times did Balzic tell me that, never fuckin' assume anything. Some doctor tells me she got black fibers in her jaw and I assume it was a glove. Son of a bitch. I gotta talk to this guy. Gotta get his clothes, gotta get a rape workup or I got nothin'.

Carlucci quickly called home and when Mrs. Comito answered, he said, "Mrs. Comito, call Mrs. Viola and tell her she gotta work tonight, okay? I gotta go to Pittsburgh. I'll call you when I get there, okay? And I'll let her know when I'm comin' back, okay? Tell Ma I said hi. Bye."

On his way out, he told Nowicki where he was going and that he'd check in as soon as he got a chance. He started out the door, then felt a rush of adrenaline over the wadded-up phone number and ducked back in and said, "Next time somebody calls me, Patrolman, you put the exact time and date on that slip and you get the name of whoever's callin', you got that? I don't care who's in charge here, I don't care if nobody's in charge here, I don't ever wanna hear you say again you're not sure when a call came in. And the next time you got information for me? And you put it on paper? And you throw it at me? I'll have you up in front of whoever's in charge I don't care who it is. For insubordination. And for conduct unbecoming. And before you ask, who I am is Detective Sergeant Carlucci, that's who. And I don't *think* that. I *know* it. You hear that, Patrolman? Huh?"

"Yessir, Detective. Every word. And duly noted."

"Yeah? Duly noted. Well you remember you said that the next time you get the urge to tell me how much you wanna get outta that chair, get on some other kinda duty. You just remember that."

Nowicki shrugged but had no retort. What bothered Carlucci was that while Nowicki may have had the sense to shut up, he didn't look the least bit apologetic. Man, Carlucci thought, whoever Bellotti picks for chief, he better pick somebody fast. Balzic's gone not even three weeks, and this place's falling apart.

By the time Carlucci got to Pittsburgh's North Side, the rush-hour traffic leaving the city for the North Hills and beyond was creeping along in a sticky snow that made the roads feel greasy. He was almost to the Perrysville Avenue exit before he realized that while he could see Allegheny General Hospital from the Crosstown Boulevard, there seemed to be no exit off it that would get him to the hospital. By the time he'd decided he should get off at Perrysville Avenue and got turned around and headed back into the North Side, it was almost five o'clock, the day shift in the emergency room had long gone, and so had Detective Tesari and his partner. So between phone calls back to his station and to his mother's house letting everybody know where he was, Carlucci was asking everybody in white or green clothes if they knew whether Wandoe Evon Best was even in the hospital. That the two Pittsburgh homicide detectives had left should have tipped him off, but because he was so intent on his own purpose for being there, their leaving didn't register.

"Hey, miss? Ho, Nurse? You gotta help me out here," he said, clutching at a nurse's arm as she hurried past him. She never broke stride and didn't try to pull her arm away. He thrust his ID case and shield in front of her as they walked.

"What's the problem, Officer?"

"A gunshot victim was brought in here this afternoon. I know he was here 'cause I talked to the detective that came in with him—from Pittsburgh Homicide? I know he was in surgery while I was talkin' to that detective, okay? On the phone I was talkin' to him."

"And so you want to know where he is and how he's doing, right?"

"Right, yes. Thank you. His name is Best. Wandoe Evon Best. Black, male, young. I'm assumin' that, I don't know. I would really appreciate it if you could help me out here."

She veered off toward a counter, reached over it, and found a beat-up metal clipboard. She glanced over a couple of pages, then picked up a phone and punched some buttons. "Still snowing?" she said.

"Beg your pardon."

"Is it still snowing I said."

"Oh. Oh yeah. Least it was when I was tryin' to get here. Hey, is there some way to get off that Crosstown Boulevard? I mean, I'm comin' over the bridge there and I can see the hospital, you know, it's right there bigger'n shit—sorry, I didn't mean to say that. I mean you can see it, but I don't know where I'm supposed to get off and I end up on Perrysville Avenue someplace and I'm drivin' around like a jaboney through these side streets tryin' to get back to here."

She looked at him quizzically and shook her head no. "It's crazy. Everybody complains about it. Somebody forgot to look at the plans I guess . . .Yeah, you have a gunshot up there? Black male, young. Came in around three?" She turned back to Carlucci and said, "You really a detective?"

"Yeah. Why?"

She shrugged. "All the detectives that come in here don't apologize for sayin' *shit*. It just threw me a little bit. Course you don't look like any of them either."

Carlucci shrugged and looked at the floor. Before he could ask her how she thought a detective looks, she was talking into the phone again.

"Sorry," she said, hanging up.

"Whatta ya mean, sorry, what's that mean?"

"Means he didn't make it." She started to walk in the direction she was going when Carlucci had first grabbed her arm.

"Hey wait wait. He died? Where is he? I need somebody to do some work on him. He still up there? Where is that? Up there, where is that?"

"You can use that phone," she said over her shoulder. "Tell the operator you want O-R Four."

Carlucci rushed to the phone and did as she'd said. A woman identifying herself as a supervisor answered, and at that moment it occurred to him why the two homicide detectives were no longer around. As soon as they'd been told they weren't going to get a statement from Wandoe Evon Best, what was left of him was no longer their immediate problem. It was the coroner's.

"This is Detective Carlucci. Rocksburg, PD. I'm calling about Wandoe Evon Best—"

"Sorry, Detective, Mr. Best, uh, apparently died, that's the information I have here."

"Yes, ma'am, I know that. But he's—he was—he is, my primary suspect in an assault and rape. I need somebody to do a rape workup on him, ma'am, you know? Blood, semen, pubic hair, check his underwear, his clothes, you know?"

"I know, Detective, I know, but I'm sure he's on his way to the morgue by now."

"Well d'you know that for sure? He's on the way I mean?"

He heard ruffling and scraping of paper. "Well I don't know it for a hundred percent certain, Detective, but we'd have no reason to keep him around here. We wouldn't do that unless a physician ordered it specifically. But even then, the coroner would have to give his approval for that. We get them ready for the coroner as soon as possible. I'm almost positive I saw some of the coroner's people getting on the elevator with a body. I don't know who else it would've been. That was around four, give or take five minutes. But call the coroner's office, I'm sure they'll be able to help you."

"Yes, ma'am. Thank you." Shit, Carlucci thought. Double shit. Double dog shit with cat piss for a halo.

He called the coroner's office at the Allegheny County morgue and got an answer on the fifth ring.

"Coroner's office, Deputy Coroner Walter Hendrik speakin'."

Carlucci identified himself and asked the deputy coroner to spell his name so he could write it down along with the date and time of his call. Then he said, "I'm callin' about a gunshot from Allegheny General, a Wandoe Evon Best? He been delivered there yet?"

"Yes he has. Brought him in myself."

"Oh good. Then you're the man I wanna talk to."

"So talk to me."

"What I need is a rape workup on him. You want me to put this in writing? Huh? 'Cause I'll be glad to."

"No, no, that's not necessary. Just give me your ID, including shield number, department zip code, and so on. I don't know you, do I?"

"I don't think so. I haven't been over to your place in a long time. You sure you don't want me to put this in writing? 'Cause I can go back to my station and get you a fax in there in about two hours tops—course that depends how bad the Parkway's gettin' to be."

"I'm tellin' you, Detective, if you wanna do it, fine, but it's not necessary."

"Yeah, well one time I made a telephone request—admittedly, hey, you know, this was years ago, but man, did I get fucked around that time. I called you guys up—not you, understand—but somebody down there said yeah, yeah, don't worry, and I call back three days later, I say where's my report. And you know what I get? I get, daaaa, what report, nobody told me you wanted no report."

"Hey, Detective, as I said, if it would make you feel better to put your request in writing, be my guest, I'm not gonna argue with you. I don't know who it was who screwed you around, but it wasn't me. I have written your request down here and I will hand-carry it downstairs. It will be attached to the deceased's chart. I guarantee this. I don't guarantee the results you're lookin' for, but I do guarantee your request will be seen by whoever does the post. And it will be acted upon, of that I'm sure."

"Oh, okay, good. So how long you think before I get a copy of the results?"

"Now that I can't guarantee. That depends on the traffic, and right at this moment I don't know where your Mr. Best stands in line down there. He could be next, he could be fifth, but it's very doubtful he's next because up till this moment I have not received word that I have to notify City Homicide to get somebody down here."

"Well say he was next."

"Well then, you could possibly have what you want in three days. Then again, it could be three weeks—listen, I don't like makin' promises about when paper starts to flow, understand? Mr. Best looked to me like a fairly straightforward gunshot post, but I don't know what City Homicide is gonna want. I haven't talked to them yet. They might think Mr. Best was involved with some, uh, maybe some very strange designer drugs, and want some complicated tox work done. As I said, I haven't talked to them yet. I think maybe you oughta talk to them. You know whose case it is?"

"Uh, Detective Tesari."

"Oh sure. I know him very well. You got his number? Homicide's 255-2883. I think you should give him a call. Anything else?"

"Yeah. What about his clothes? D'you pick up his clothes? Pants, underwear especially? Did those city guys take 'em maybe?"

"I didn't pick up any clothes. Had to be Tesari took 'em. Give him a call. He'll help you out. He's a good man."

Carlucci thanked him, promised over the deputy's protest to fax his request as soon as he got back to his station, hung up, and looked around until he found the end of a counter that nobody seemed to be using. He leaned against it and made a note of everything he'd done since he'd arrived in the hospital, down to the number of quarters he'd spent so far in the phones.

Then, since nobody seemed to be objecting to his using the hospital phone, he immediately punched the number the deputy had given him for Pittsburgh Homicide and asked for Detective Tesari.

"He just stepped out for a moment. Can I help you?"

Carlucci identified himself and said, "Who's this?"

"Detective Walls. I'm Tesari's partner. What's this about, Detective?"

"This is about, uh, a guy got shot? You guys found him in a white Pontiac Grand Prix? In an alley—East Liberty someplace."

"Off Larimer Avenue. Yeah. Wandoe Evon Best. So what's your interest?"

"Uh, my interest is he's, uh, he's my best suspect in a rape and assault. Victim's in real bad shape—"

"Sorry to hear that, but, uh, I don't think Wandoe's your boy."

"Beg pardon?"

"I said I don't think Wandoe's your boy."

"Why not?"

"Wandoe's been a bad boy for a long time, ain't no question about that, but, uh—where'd you say you were from again? Rocksburg? What's 'at, thirty miles from here? Thirty-five?"

"About that, yeah, Why?"

"Oh I remember you now. You the one talked to Tesari at AG."

"AG? Oh. Allegheny General. Yeah, that's where I called him."

"Yeah, I remember now."

"Yeah. That's me. So what happened? What went down?"

"Don't know yet. Shots fired, you know, black-and-whites rolled, there was Wandoe, bleedin' and hollerin' for his mommas. I guess that's who he was hollerin' for, 'cause three of 'em showed up almost when we did. Still breathin' when we got there, so EMS took him to AG. My partner went with him, and I stayed and worked the scene. Found three nine cases, all of 'em in the front seat. Lab guys found a whole lotta prints, but, uh, nobody found the nine. Patrolmen still out there lookin'—they better be lookin'. And the mommas jus' wanted to get in each other's faces, you know, wouldn't tell me shit.

"Next thing I hear, they're carryin' on in the hospital, and my partner put their fat asses in Grant Street, but they ain't goin' say nothin' 'cause they don't know nothin'. They weren't there. I got two witnesses said Wandoe and the shooter are in the car by themselves, no females present, so whatever Wandoe was doin' with them, I don't think it had nothin' to do with him takin' the nines. Course I could be wrong. Wandoe has fooled me before."

"Before? Oh that's right, your partner said you were familiar with him, but you threw me a little bit when you said you don't think he's my perp. You did say that, right? Was that what you said? So, uh, what, you familiar with him?"

"Familiar? Shit, I know Wandoe since he was born. I know his momma, his daddy. *He* don't know his daddy, *I* know his daddy. Knew his daddy. Busted his ass at least three times myself. Followed him to the damn morgue, just like I'm doin' now with his kid. Imagine that. I can't believe this shit. Sometimes I wonder, I mean sometimes I truly wonder why the fuck some people get put here. No shit. And if I knew why some women let themselves be fucked by some men? Man, I could rule the world I knew that. Wandoe's momma's a fine woman, no lie. But why she ever let that piece a shit crawl up between her legs is somethin' Jesus couldn't tell you."

Carlucci said nothing.

Walls went on. "I said to her one time—we all went to Westinghouse High School together, man. Me and her was sophomores, and that piece a shit, Wandoe's daddy—he dropped out right after football season his junior year—and I said, more than once I said to her, Girl, you followin' him around, leavin' notes in his locker, rollin' your eyes at him, givin' him your lunch, what's wrong with you? What the fuck is wrong with you? You know? And she'd just say, Go on with your jealous self. I said, Shit, jealous don't have nothin' to do with it. What it is, is how can you be so smart about everything else and be so dumb about him?"

Walls stopped talking for so long Carlucci had to ask if he was still there.

"Yeah I'm still here. I don't know why I'm carryin' on. Wastin' my breath. She's a nurse. His momma's an operatin' room nurse at Shadyside Hospital. Raised Wandoe by herself—tried to. Never got married, that I know of. And Wandoe, I mean where is he now, huh? Inside the same motherfuckin' buildin' where his old man wound up. You wanna hear some shit? His old man was the second case I ever worked in Homicide, you believe that? It's true. And here I am, eight years later, and what am I workin' on? His kid. Ain't that some shit? I could not go face-to-face with his momma. Sent another detective out there to tell her. He come back and said all she could say was, Oh Lord."

Carlucci shook his head and chewed his thumbnail. "Uh, so whatta you think mighta happened?"

"To be honest with you, Detective, I don't know. Coulda been anything. I have to ask around, see who's tradin' for time. We're gonna have to wait'n see what the coroner says, see if maybe there's some surprise there, though I don't know what that could be. But it coulda been about the Pontiac, coulda been about somebody's dope, coulda been about his three mommas. Wandoe wasn't lazy. He just didn't like to work and he loved money. Which is the wrongest combination there is. I just thank God all my children are girls. I don't know what the fuck I'd do if I had a boy-child these days, I really don't. Course my girls could all do just like Wandoe's momma did—spread their legs for some piece a shit and what could I do about that? Nothin'. That shit wakes me up. Just thinkin' 'bout that shit wakes me up at night, I'm tellin' ya."

Carlucci shuffled around for a moment, pondering why this detective was telling him all this over the phone. It sounded like a conversation they might be having in a bar somewhere, some day, but not now, and not over the phone.

"So, uh, would you do me a favor?"

"Hey, Harvey John Walls at your service, my man, whatchu need?"

"I called the coroner's office, talked to a deputy named Walter Hendrik. He guaranteed me they'd do a rape workup on Best, but, uh, you guys have his clothes? Did you take 'em, you have 'em? This Hendrik said he didn't have 'em, I just need to know where they are. Includin' his shoes."

"Yeah, we got 'em."

"His shoes too?"

"Yeah we got them."

"Oh, okay, good. Well I need that—all that stuff—to go to the state police crime lab, you know? I need to know if this is my guy, and since he's no longer talkin', I need all the evidence I can get, which you understand, so what am I tellin' you for. Uh, also, you happen to find a weapon on him?"

"Wandoe didn't carry no guns or blades. He was strictly a sap man. These days, that's hard to believe, but it's true."

"Really? He have one on him?"

"Oh yeah. Always. Sock fulla somethin', I didn't even look yet. Sand or gravel probably, I don't know what."

"Remember what color it was? The sock?"

"Believe it was black, but I'm not sure. Somethin' dark."

"Well would you make sure that gets to the crime lab too, okay?"

"Hey man, you know I can't promise when any of that's goin' get there, you know that, right? And if we get a shooter? We make a case? I'm not goin' lie and tell you we're ever gonna give it up."

"Yeah, right, I understand you wouldn't wanna give up your evidence, I mean, I wouldn't either, but, uh, what interest would you guys have in his underwear? I mean you got no interest in his underwear, right?"

"No. Right."

"Or his pants? Or shoes? I mean, if you wanna keep his pants, I don't care, but couldn't you just cut the crotch out, you know, like the whole fly up to the button, like four, five inches all around the fly and mail that out, okay? With his shoes? I need to know what's on the bottom of his shoes."

"I hear ya, my man, I hear ya. I'll do my best, but sometimes, you know, things don't move the way we want 'em to move. They don't always move the way we think they oughta be movin'."

"I know, I know. But, uh, if it should work out, you know, do what you can do, is all I'm sayin'. But please, fax me all the reports or call me'n everything, okay? You gotta keep me in touch here. You will fax me the reports, right?"

"I'm makin' a note of it right now, Detective, but I can't promise when we gonna get the reports from the lab. Could be two weeks, could be a month. They run their own thing, and I learned a long time ago, man, some people you try to hurry 'em up? They just get slower, you know?"

"Yeah, okay. I hear ya. Listen, I'm gonna take off now. Oh. Lemme give you my numbers. And I answer all calls. May take a while, but I answer, okay?"

Carlucci gave Walls the numbers for the station, the fax, his pager, and his home, and said, "And please, if you have any influence at all, don't let those guys forget the rape thing, okay? I mean I know I told him and I'm gonna fax it in to him soon as I get back to my station, but it never hurts to have a little backup. I feel real bad about this woman, and

I really wanna clear the case—especially if she doesn't make it, you know?"

"Hey, just remember, I ain't Jesus. You want water I'll point ya toward the cooler, but don't expect no wine when you get there, hear? Meanwhile, you need somethin', gimme a call, I'll try to get it for ya. You can get Tesari with this number too, don't forget. My partner?"

"Oh, right. Nice to meet ya, Detective. And thanks."

Carlucci started to hang up but Walls called out to him. "Hold it, bro, hold it. Somethin' botherin' me here."

"What's that?"

"This rape you talkin' 'bout. More I think about that, I mean, Wandoe's done a lotta bad shit, but I don't recall that bein' part of his act. Course now, he was known to do a whole lotta coke, I'm not sayin' he couldn'ta got coke crazy on some woman, but what I'm thinkin' is, what the fuck was he doin' in Rocksburg."

"Why?"

"Didn't you say that was like, thirty, thirty-five miles from here?"

"About that, yeah."

"See, Wandoe, he was a homeboy. Thirty miles, see, Wandoe woulda had to get with a travel agent do that distance. East Liberty, Downtown, Wilkinsburg, Penn Hills, that was the world for him. And this Pontiac? This Pontiac ain't his style either. You get a fax of his sheet?"

"Yeah. Now that you mention it, I didn't see any auto theft on there either."

"See that's what I mean. Him goin' outta his 'hood like that? And doin' a rape? And boostin' a car? A *white* car? Man, the brothers don't deal with *white* cars, not unless it's a special order. But Wandoe wasn't in that business."

"Well that may be, but I still got this woman in intensive

care—I'm not even sure who she is yet, not a hundred percent, and—"

"Well whether it's that woman's car or not, it's still *somebody's* car, and you got a female owner for that car, right?"

"Right. Which isn't sayin' she's who I think she is, if
she's the woman in the hospital, you know."

"Yeah, right. And so what it was, bro—burglary, robbery,
what?"

"Hey, all I know for sure is, it wasn't a B and E. The door
was open. Who was there first is an unknown, is what I'm
sayin'."

"Well see, this don't sound right to me. I mean Wandoe's in your Pontiac, ain't no doubt about that. But this
other shit, I don't know, man, somethin' else goin' on
there. Wandoe, he was just your basic street hustler. Live
in his 'hood off his mommas, sell dope, count his money,
get high, and then hit his crib and wake up and do it all
over again. Career advancement to him was just more of
the same. This other shit, I can't see Wandoe in this all by
himself, uh-uh. Well hell, it ain't my problem anyways.
It's yours. Meantime, I gotta get movin' on this, been sittin' here too long as it is. Call me. Or Tesari. We ain't
here, they'll get us. Somebody will. Later."

"Yeah, right. You're right, it is my problem. And thanks
again."

Carlucci hung up and summarized the conversation in his
notebook. Then he made his way out to the parking garage,
found his cruiser, and started the slippery drive through
Downtown Pittsburgh, hunting for the entrance to the Parkway East. He got stopped only once, by a city black-and-
white, for driving the wrong way in a bus lane. Two city
patrolmen had a good laugh on him before they showed him
where to go. "Hey, Sarge, you gotta look at those things on

the poles every once in a while, you know? The signs? One Way? Do Not Enter? Bus Lane?"

Yeah, right, Carlucci thought. Dumb-ass dago from Rocksburg comes to the city, gets lost, provides moment of merriment for city police, that's me. Jeez, I hope the rest of these guys don't jag me off. Hope they do what they said they're gonna do, all of 'em.

It was almost nine o'clock when he finally pulled into the parking lot beside Rocksburg City Hall. He'd spent nearly forty minutes getting from Bates Street in Oakland through the Squirrel Hill Tunnels, a distance of less than three miles, and thereafter his top speed never exceeded twenty-five miles an hour. It took him an hour and forty-two minutes to go thirty-two miles. He was hungry, tired, and had to urinate so badly he ran into the station and downstairs, ignoring Nowicki who was hollering, whistling, and waving call slips at him as he ran by.

Back upstairs, he continued to ignore Nowicki until after he'd called Gino's Pizza and ordered a vegetarian six-cut. "What kinda vegetables I want? Everything, yeah, tomatoes, olives, green and black both, onions, mushrooms, sweet peppers, broccoli, cauliflower, and banana peppers, you got them tonight? . . . Last time, you didn't have any. Lotsa them. And thin crust. I don't want the thick. And a boss of Diet Pepsi too . . . Right, police station, Detective Carlucci. Don't call back, this ain't no gag . . . Right, right, just come inside to where the dispatcher's sittin', he'll call me, I'll have the money . . . Right. Bye."

He was steaming when he left his desk and went up to Nowicki. "Hey Patrolman, you whistlin' at me? You hollerin' at me? I look like a fuckin' dog to you?"

"'Patrolman'? C'mon, Rugs—"

"No *Rugs*, Patrolman. Detective. Detective Carlucci—"

"Okay, Detective. Detective Carlucci. Jesus. So I was an asshole for five seconds, what, you gonna hold it against me forever? Jesus Christ, I never thought we were bosom buddies or nothin', but I thought we were friends, you know, what the fuck. Fellow officers, that kinda friends. I fuck up and throw a piece a paper at ya? It ain't like I raped your sister, what the fuck."

Carlucci felt his eyes narrowing. "You wanna know what the fuck? Okay, I'll tell ya what the fuck. What the fuck is you thinkin' you can just forget everything you ever learned or everything you have to do just because Balzic's gone, that's what the fuck. Meanwhile, I wanna know somethin'. And I want a straight answer."

"Yeah? Before you do that, you gonna take your messages or not?"

"Just hold 'em for a second, just hold 'em. 'Cause before you hand 'em to me, I wanna know somethin'. I wanna know what the fuck would possess you to take a phone message and not put down the exact time the call came in? I mean, if you can take a message like that, and then wad it up and throw it at me, I'm wonderin' what the fuck you're puttin' in the phone log these days, huh? And I'm wonderin' how the fuck you could go from the kinda squared-away police professional you used to be—hey, less than three weeks ago— three weeks ago you were a professional officer in every respect. How'd you get from that kinda officer to the kind that wads up fuckin' phone messages and throws 'em at me? How the fuck'd that happen? Can you explain that to me?"

Nowicki said nothing. He looked away and started grinding his molars.

"Hey, Patrolman," Carlucci said, moving close to Nowicki and lowering his voice, "you listen up here for a second. You *know* what needs to be done, you can't shit me you don't. But when you forget to do what you know needs to be done? And when I call you on it, you start talkin' to me about how we were friends? You think 'cause we're friends you can stop doin' your job? You think 'cause we're friends you can throw paper on the floor and make me pick it up? That's what you think? Hey, I don't know what the fuck we were with each other, but friends was not it. And you thinkin' that way? Man, I can't believe you. All I know is you better take this home with you tonight 'cause you got a major problem with it. Not me. You."

Nowicki canted his head to the left. There was a pronounced pop, a crack in his neck, like somebody cracking his knuckles. "Uh, these phone messages here, Detective, uh, I think you'll see the information is all there."

"Oh. Okay. Good. Thank you," Carlucci said, reaching to take the slips of paper from Nowicki's extended hand. His mouth was very dry and he saw that his hand was shaking. He swallowed hard and felt his heart hammering and turned away and swallowed several times more and licked his lips. He started walking back to his desk. Once there, he said, "Oh. I forgot. I ordered a pizza from Gino's. I would appreciate it if, uh, you give me a call when it gets here."

"You don't want me to pay for it? Why don't I just pay for it? You can pay me whenever."

"Uh, no, uh-uh, that's all right. I wanna make sure it's what I ordered. 'Cause if it ain't, he doesn't get a tip, and uh—just gimme a call."

"Yes, sir, Detective. Oh. Coupla those calls were urgent. 'Bout your mother. And one of 'em was from your mother."

He looked at the slips Nowicki had given him. "Mrs. Viola. Call home. Says urgent. 1922." "Mrs. Viola. Call home. 1929." There were more, all from Mrs. Viola.

He punched the numbers for his home phone, thinking, My mother? Urgent? Wait a minute. 1914? 1922? 1929? Aw man. Awwwww man no. He started to hang up, but too late.

Mrs. Viola had picked up the phone and then he couldn't hang up.

"It's me, Mrs. Viola, what's up?"

"Oh Rugsie, I'm real sorry to bother you like this, but she's all worked up—"

"Just tell me," he interrupted her, "is this about *Jeopardy!*? Is this about what kinda tie he's wearin'? Huh? Or how stupid they are, which?"

Mrs. Viola cleared her throat and tried to answer, but there came a scuffling and scraping and his mother growling, "Gimme that. Gimme that, goddammit! Gimme the goddamn phone! I'm tellin' you, gimme that . . . Ruggiero? You there? You hear me? I know that's you. Answer me! Goddammit answer me!"

"It's me, Ma, I'm here, whatsamatter?"

"He wore that goddamn blue tie again. Every time he wears that goddamn tie, he gets these stupid people on there, it never fails, every goddamn time he wears that tie they ruin it, I'm sick of it, I'm sicka this crap, I musta wrote him a hundred letters already, I told him don't wear that goddamn blue tie no more, I'm gonna kill him, I'm tellin' you. Ruggiero, you listenin' to me? Huh? Him, him and that goddamn Vanna White, I'm tellin' you I'm gonna choke her, I'm gonna put my hands around her goddamn skinny neck'n I'm gonna choke her! Say somethin'! Answer me!"

A hundred letters? When did she write him a hundred letters? To that Alex guy? No. Never happen. "Ma, you writin' letters to that guy? Huh? When'd you start doin' that? You doin' that, Ma, or you just pullin' my chain, what?"

"Goddamn right I'm writin' him letters."

"You wrote him a hundred letters? A hundred?!"

"Yes I did. No. Maybe not that many. Fifty for sure."

"Ma, did you write to this guy or not? A hundred letters or fifty? Which?"

"What difference does it make how many? I wrote him, I told him quit wearin' that goddamn tie, he's ruinin' the program."

"D'you actually mail these letters, Ma? Huh? Answer me! You put 'em in envelopes and put stamps on 'em and actually put 'em in the box? C'mon, Ma, I'm not jaggin' around here."

"Goddamn right I did, somebody had to tell him, nobody else was tellin' him, you think I was just gonna sit around here and watch it get ruined? They took Richard—you remember, don't say you don't—they took Richard Dawson off *Family Feud* and look what happened to that. They ruined it, you know who I mean, don't say you don't. Richard Dawson. He used to be on *Hogan's Heroes*, I used to love 'at *Family Feud*'n they took him off'n I don't even watch it anymore, can't stand that guy they got on there now, he's so stupid."

"Ma, you actually put 'em in the mailbox? You tellin' me the truth, Ma, or you just jaggin' me, which?"

"I just said I did, didn't I? Whatta you want from me?"

"Well what'd you say in these letters? What'd you say? What'd you tell this Alec guy—"

"Alex Alex, not Alec!"

"Alec, Alex, whatever, d'you just ask him to please stop wearin' the blue ties or what?"

No answer.

"Ma? Hey, Ma, I know you're still there. C'mon, Ma, what'd you tell him? Did you tell him he didn't stop wearin' it you were gonna do somethin'? Or d'you just tell him please stop, which way did you tell him? C'mon, no jaggin' around, I'm serious now, what'd you say?"

"I told him he didn't stop wearin' that goddamn blue tie I was gonna choke him with it—"

"Aw Jesus, you didn't threaten him, please say you didn't

do that. You wrote this? You put this on paper? C'mon, Ma, what exactly d'you write down there?"

"I told him I had it all down on paper—what threat? Whatta you talkin' about, threat? That wasn't no threat, that's the way I talk, you know that. Ain't no threat, don't be stupid, I got facts. I got it all down on paper. I told him I got it all down in black and white and blue and red. All the good programs when he's wearin' the red tie, I got them marked down on one side, and all the lousy ones, with the blue tie, I got them marked down on the other side. I told him he didn't stop wearin' that goddamn blue tie I was gonna send 'em everything I got, all my charts, I was gonna send 'em to his bosses at the station—after you made me copies, so I would have proof, you know."

"At the station? Which station you talkin' about, where'd you mail it to?"

"Channel Eleven. Where you think?"

"You mailed it to Pittsburgh? For sure? You sent it to them down there, that's what you're tellin' me?"

"What're you, stupid? Ain't that what I just said? Sometimes I wonder, honest to God, Ruggiero, I wonder how the hell you ever got to be a detective, sometimes you're so stupid I can't believe it." Then her tone changed abruptly. Suddenly she was breathy, frightened. "When're you comin' home? I didn't see you all day, you know how I can't stand it if I don't see you all day. You tryin' to make me sick? You know I get sick if I don't see you all day."

He started to tell her that he'd seen her at lunch, but she was already starting to sob, and then she dropped the phone.

He heard the phone falling off the counter in the kitchen, and then Mrs. Viola telling his mother, "There there, honey, it'll be okay, Rugsie'll be home in a little while, he will. He just has to work a little bit late, that's all. He'll be here, you just go sit down over there, I'll make you some tea."

"I don't want no goddamn tea I want him to come home now!" his mother shrieked. "He's s'posed to come home now! He's never home when he's s'posed to be!"

Carlucci sighed until his cheeks ballooned and then flattened. He held the receiver to his ear for another half minute or so waiting to see if Mrs. Viola would come back on, but she didn't. He hung up and closed his eyes and rubbed them with the heel of his palms and did some neck rolls and closed his eyes and breathed very slowly.

He debated whether he should call station WPXI to talk to whoever handled crank mail, but he decided there probably wouldn't be anybody there at this time of night, so he put it out of his mind as best he could and instead typed up his request for a rape workup on Wandoe Evon Best and faxed it to Allegheny County Deputy Coroner Walter Hendrik.

Then he sat and debated some more about whether he should wait until tomorrow to call WPXI, and again he tried to put it out of his mind. Instead, he went rooting through his notebook for the phone and pager number that Sal Bruno had given him for Bill, the truck driver who delivered and installed burial vaults for Rocksburg Pre-Cast Concrete. There was no answer on Bill's home phone, so Carlucci tried his pager.

While he was waiting for Bill's return call, he kept wondering why his mother would believe this Alex guy would have only two ties, one red and one blue, and whether she'd actually written letters, and whether she'd actually mailed them and where. God, before, all she used to do was talk to the TV, talk to what's-his-face, this Trebek. Trebek, how could I forget *that* name, she's been talkin' about him like he's her brother-in-law, Jesus, for years now, for crissake. What am I gonna do if she actually threatened him? In writing? Over what fucking color ties he wears? What if she mailed 'em, Jesus, what am I gonna do with her? Man. Like there's something I can do with her. . . .

The phone rang. He picked it up and heard, "This is Bill. From Rocksburg Pre-Cast Concrete? I'm returnin' your call. Who're you again? Detective who?" He was talking over very loud country music.

"Carlucci. Thanks for returnin' my call. Appreciate it."

"What's this about?"

"Just wanna talk to you."

"I do somethin'? Couldn'ta been too much, whatever it was, I ain't been outta the house in three days. Not till tonight. Had the flu. Still got it a little bit."

"No, it's not about somethin' you did. I just need some information. Your place is closed, right, where you work?"

"The Pre-Cast?"

"Yeah, right."

"Oh sure. Yeah. Closes up every year from, uh, day before Christmas till whenever."

"Till whenever? You be a little more specific than that?"

"Aw hell, till whenever Junior and his old lady run outta money and decide they gotta come back to work I guess."

"Uh, by Junior you mean Alfredo Picadio Junior, right? And his wife?"

"Yeah. Guess that didn't sound too good the way I said it. Well fuck it, I don't care how it sounds, I'm about one-quarter shitface anyway."

"Uh, Bill, how much you had to drink? And what's your last name?"

"Aw hell, I was just exaggeratin'. This is only my second beer here. It's just I didn't eat anything much for the last two, three days, and this beer's gettin' to me kinda quick. Uh, before I tell ya my last name, am I gonna need a lawyer?"

"You done somethin' wrong, Bill?"

"Nah, no, fuck no I ain't done nothin' wrong. Well not for a while anyway. Can't put me in jail for not goin' to college, can ya?"

"For not goin' to college? Is that what you said?"

"Yeah. You asked me if I done anything wrong and I said not for a while. Last thing I done wrong was not go to college when I come back from Korea. Had the fuckin' G.I. Bill right there, four years a college I coulda got, but did I go? Huh? Fuuuuuuck no, not me. I was too fuckin' smart already, I didn't needa go to no fuckin' college. Now here I am, sittin' in the fuckin' VFW, fifty-eight-fuckin' years old, makin' eight dollars and fifty fuckin' cents an hour stickin' concrete boxes in the mud, freezin' my ass off, talkin' to women so dumb they actually believe me when I tell 'em I'm a doctor just 'cause I got this here pager on my belt. On second thought, maybe you oughta come down here and arrest me—or up here or whichever direction it is."

"Uh-ha. Hey, Bill, how 'bout you givin' me a call tomorrow morning, okay?"

"Why'sat? Oh, you think I'm drunk. I ain't drunk. I'm just buzzed up 'cause I ain't had nothin' to eat and I'm feelin' sorry for myself, that's all. I can tell ya whatever you wanna know. Whatta ya wanna know, go 'head and ask me."

"Okay. What's your last name?"

"Oh. Didn't I say? Guess not. Teslovich. William, F. for Frank, Teslovich."

"And how long you worked for Rocksburg Pre-Cast?"

"Oh man, ever since I come back from Korea. Yeah. Jesus Christ, ain't those the saddest words you ever heard. Holy shit, that's nineteen, gawwwwd damn, that was nineteen fifty-four. Holy fuck, it's worse'n I thought."

"You do anything besides drive a truck there?"

"You mean now?"

"Yeah, you ever work in the office?"

"Well I ain't supposed to."

"What's that mean?"

"Means I don't get paid extra for doin' it. It ain't my job but I do it. Don't have any choice. Every year at this time I gotta do office stuff, mostly just puttin' bills away, bankin' the checks if somebody gives me one. But when I first got hired, I didn't do any of that. I just worked with the old man, and we did all kinda concrete work. Sidewalks, patios, pointin', any masonry job, walls, houses, foundations, brick, block, shit, everything. Nah, that was okay, back then. We had a union shop, you know. The old man, shit, he even belonged to the union, that's the kinda guy he was. And he'd work right there alongside ya, you know? He wasn't 'fraid to get his hands dirty like his son, sonofabitch—oh man, his son didn't get murdered or nothin', did he? That'd sound real bad, what I just said."

"I don't know where his son is," Carlucci said. "I was hopin' you could tell me. Sounds like, uh, you don't like him a whole lot."

"That showed, huh? Man, why you think I'm sittin' here feelin' so sorry for myself? You oughta come'n arrest me for not goin' to college when I had the chance, I oughta be locked up. Might as well be. You know the first thing they did, huh? After the old man died? First thing they did, his old lady and his kid, wasn't two days after the funeral, they laid us all off. No fuckin' warnin', no nothin', bingo, said they was goin' outta business, that's all, adios. Then the pricks sat down with their lawyers, wrote 'em up a new corporation, changed the name from Picadio's Masonry to Rocksburg Pre-Cast. Then the fuckers called us all up, they said, hey, you want a job? Huh? You wanna come back to work for us? Sure, fine, come on back, suckers. But if you do, you dumb shits, you gotta start all over again. No seniority, no benefits for the first ninety days, no vacation the first year, brand-new. Yes sir, that's what they did. And no union neither. Busted the fuckin' union. Rigged the fuckin' election, union sued 'em, shit, they run the union through the courts for about six years, wasn't shit the union could do about it. And that's hows come I'm makin' eight-fifty an hour, today—today!—in nineteen-fuckin'-ninety-three, when I was makin' eight-fifty an hour when the old man died in nineteen-fuckin'-seventy-five. Yeah. Same exact pay damn near twenty years later. Ain't that some shit, huh? What's your name again?"

"Carlucci. Listen, where is, uh, where's Junior now, you know?"

"Down in the fuckin' Bahamas someplace. Same place he goes every year—wherever that is. Wherever there's wide, white beaches and warm blue water and slot machines everywhere you turn around, that's what his old lady says. Fuckin' jerk."

"And what, they go there every year? Same time?"

"Yeah. Every year, samey same. Work our asses off all through November and December, ten hours every day, all straight time, no time and a half, buildin' up fuckin' inventory. Then they lay everybody off 'cept me and another guy, whoever wantsa help me go plant 'em. Everybody's pissed off, all the grunts and the funeral directors, and I'm like, not only do I have to drive the truck and do the installations, I'm like the public relations guy and the clerk too. And you think they pay me for that? Fuuuuuuck no. They're down there layin' on the beach, gettin' all tanned up and every night they're partyin' and gamblin' their fuckin' money away. And then they come back here, and they laugh about it. Right in our faces. They think it's funnier'n hell how much money he loses playin' blackjack and how much she pumps in the goddamn slots. Stupid fuckers. Ain't that some way to run a business, huh? Man

I'm tellin' you, if somethin' did happen to him, you'd have one hell of a job figurin' out who done it, 'cause I don't think there's anybody in the world likes him. He could piss Mother Teresa off. Her too—his old lady."

"Uh, you keep sayin' 'his old lady,'" Carlucci said. "You talkin' about his mother or his wife?"

"His wife, his wife, no, fuck no, not his mother. I mean, she ain't no bowl a peaches neither, but least she's around. Least she'll pick up the goddamn phone, you know, if I run into any problems or anything. But then too, she's at work every day."

"She is?"

"Oh yeah. She's in there doin' the books, you know, gettin' ready for tax time. Yeah, the whole last week from right after Christmas till New Year's, that's when she's workin' on the books. And then, when she gets done with 'em, she takes 'em out to their accountant and they go over 'em together. I guess. Although I guess I shouldn't say, 'cause I don't know anymore how that works exactly since they got the computer in there, last year. Or maybe it was two years ago. I don't know how that works anymore, I shouldn't be talkin'. 'Bout the books, I mean. 'Cause of the computer. I just know she ain't down in the Bahamas pissin' her money away. She's here takin' care of business, you know?

"Shit, last year—listen to this," Teslovich sputtered, "last year they stayed gone six weeks, man, can you imagine that? How could you have a business and stay gone six fuckin' weeks. His old lady was so pissed off when they come back, 'at's all we heard for about a month was her bitchin' at 'em. Her and his old lady, they don't talk no more. Not good mornin', not go to hell, not kiss my ass, nothin'.

"Hey, I gotta get another beer, I been talkin' so much, my mouth's all dried out. Just a second here. Hey, Pop, you wanna gimme another one, okay? Okay, now, what's this about again? What'd you call me for?"

"Uh, you in the VFW, is that what you said?"

"Yeah. Why?"

"I'm gonna come get you—"

"Oh man I thought you said I didn't do nothin', whatchu comin' to get me for?"

"Just listen, okay? I'm gonna come get you, and take you someplace, show you somebody, see if you can tell me who it is, okay? Won't take fifteen minutes, I'll take you right back there, and if your beer gets warm I'll buy you another one, all right? Don't go anywhere, I'm gonna be right there, ya hear?"

"Yeah yeah, I hear. Damn." Before he hung up, Carlucci heard him say, "Whoa, you back, darlin', huh? Listen, I gotta leave ya for little while, don't you go 'way, hear? That's what happens when ya answer the damn pager, patients just won't let ya alone. Here ya go, Pop, you can hang it up now, thanks."

Carlucci was hanging up as Nowicki bent down and slid a pizza box onto his desk. "This just came, and, uh, I know what you said, but, uh, you looked busy, so, uh, I just went ahead and paid for it. It was eight somethin'. I gave him a ten and told him to keep it. Okay?"

"Yeah. Sure. Wait, here's the money," Carlucci said, reaching into his pocket and fishing out two fives. "You want some? No sausage or pepperoni on it, it's vegetarian, but go 'head, help yourself. I gotta take a witness up the hospital, see if he can ID that woman. I'll be back in a little while. Go 'head, go 'head, *mangia*. Hey wait a second, where's the Pepsi?"

"There was no Pepsi."

"Fuck there wasn't. I told 'em bring a boss of Diet Pepsi."

"Uh-uh, they didn't bring one."

"See, those fuckers, I'm tellin' ya. That's why I asked ya to call me. See now, they got the tip—you gave him a tip, right, and they didn't bring what they're supposed to. I hate that shit, when that happens."

"So next time I'll call ya. Jesus, Carlucci, you really got a hair up your ass, ya know it? Excuse me. Detective."

Carlucci led Bill Teslovich into the ICU ward at Conemaugh General and back to the corner bed where the woman was.

Teslovich sucked in his breath. "Holeeee fuck. What happened to her?"

"You know her?"

"Yeah, hell yeah, that's Mrs. Picadio."

"Junior or Senior?"

"Senior, Senior. What happened? Holy fuck, look at her eye, Jesus Christ. I didn't know you could swell up that much and not split. Damn."

"You sure that's her? No question?"

"Hell, man, I see her every day—damn near. Seen her practically every day for the last thirty-nine years, 'cept for weekends and vacations. Seen her on a lotta Saturdays too."

"When was the last time you saw her?"

"Well I told ya I been sick for the last coupla days. Ain't been outta the house till tonight. So I guess, probably three days ago was the last time. Yeah, she was there. What was that, Tuesday? What's this, Friday? Yeah, Tuesday."

"Anything out of the ordinary goin' on?"

"Tuesday you mean? No. Lemme think, I had one for the Catholic Cemetery out in the township, and then I had another one for St. James Lutheran, you know, and then I told her I was feelin' real lousy and if she had any more she was gonna have to get Jimmy to get somebody to help him, 'cause I was goin' home'n go to bed, and she said okay, and that was that."

"Jimmy?"

"Yeah, Jimmy. Aw shit, can't remember his last name. He's the guy workin' with me this year. His old lady just had a kid, and I guess he needs all the money he can get."

"She call you since then? You call her?"

"No. She didn't call me. But I called her, yeah. Told her I was still sick, and she just said, you know, okay, call me'n tell me when you're comin' in. I didn't call her today though. Yesterday I talked to her. I told her I'd call her at home Sunday night, you know, whether I was gonna make it in on Monday. Man, I never knew you could get that swelled up without bustin' open. She in a wreck? What?"

"Nah, it wasn't a wreck. C'mon, let's go."

"Whoa, you mean if it wasn't a wreck you mean somebody beat her up? I didn't see nothin' in the paper about it. What happened? When'd it happen? How come it wasn't in the paper?"

"C'mon, you wanna go back to the VFW?"

"Jesus, I don't know, my stomach's startin' to go all fluey on me again. Oh man . . . I'm gonna be sick. Hey, Nurse, where's the can, huh? The john?"

A nurse who'd been checking another patient took him by the arm and led him out of sight on the trot.

Carlucci went back out to the desk and asked the other two nurses on duty if anybody had been calling about the woman. They both shook their heads no.

"How's she doin'? Any change? Better, worse, anything?"

"I think you should ask the doctor," the older one said.

"What's his name?"

"Here's his card."

"You're givin' me his card? What, he leaves 'em around?"

"He's new. I guess he thinks that's the way to do it."

"Vijay Jwaharla? Did I say that right? Vijay, rhymes with deejay? Jwa-har-la?"

"That's it, you got it," the younger one sang.

"Okay, I'll talk to him maybe."

The nurse who'd escorted Teslovich to the john returned, shaking her head. "That guy better stop drinking and go home and go to bed. He's dehydrated. Beer's the last thing he needs."

"Hey, he's a big boy," Carlucci said, shrugging.

"He's a big boy who's gonna be in a bed up here soon he doesn't get some water in him, some clear broth, some weak tea, fruit juice, but lotsa water. Beer's the absolute last thing he needs. You better tell him, maybe he'll believe you. He didn't believe me."

"Why would he believe me? I'm not a doctor."

"Aren't you his friend?"

"Nah, he's a witness."

"Well if he was my witness I'd make him go home and go to bed and drink a lotta liquids—and that doesn't mean beer."

Teslovich came shuffling around a corner, looking raw-eyed and paler than when Carlucci had picked him up in the VFW. "Man, I don't feel so good," he said, wiping the corners of his mouth. "Anybody got any gum or Life Savers or somethin'?"

"C'mon, I'm takin' you home. We'll get whatever you want on the way if somethin's open."

"Aw I ain't goin' in no stop'n rob, they're a buncha thieves. I was in one last week, they wanted forty-five cents for a pack a gum."

"Whatever," Carlucci said, leading him out of the ICU but slowing down to let Teslovich catch up. "Hey, take a break here, grab ahold of some wall there, I'll be right with ya, I forgot to tell the nurses somethin'. Losin' my mind, I swear."

Carlucci hurried back to the nurses' station and wrote the woman's name on a piece of paper and pushed it toward them and said, "You get anybody makin' any inquiries about her, I don't care when it is, you hear me? You call me. You got my card, I can see it from here, it's up on your corkboard there. Any change in her, anybody calls askin' about her, I wanna know about it, you got me?"

The nurses said they heard him very clearly, so he left them and went hustling back to Teslovich and started to lead him out again.

Teslovich was just shuffling along, complaining about feeling dizzy. They were almost to the door of the elevator for the parking garage when Teslovich said, "That nurse said I didn't go home I was gonna be sorry. I think I already am. I'm dizzier'n shit."

"You ain't gonna pass out on me, are ya?"

"Just lemme lean up against the wall here for a second, I'll be okay. Goddamn, everything started spinnin' around there for a minute, thought me and the floor was gonna make love. Guess we ain't."

"Well go 'head'n lean on me. We'll be in the car here shortly. You okay?"

"Yeah. I guess. Can't lean on you, I gotta bend over to lean on you, you're too short. That just makes me dizzier worse. How could that nurse tell that fast what was wrong with me? I didn't tell her nothin'. I just ast her to show me where the can was. Next thing, she's feelin' my head and givin' me this speech 'bout how I better stop drinkin' or I'm gonna be in deep shit."

"That's her job, that's what she does."

"Oh. Yeah."

"She's right though."

"Huh?"

"She said the last thing you need is more beer. Alcohol dries you out'n you're already all dried out from the flu. Said you oughta be drinkin' fruit juice and weak tea and lotsa water, stuff like that, but definitely no more beer. Watch your step."

"Shit I was only startin' on my third draft. And I was sippin' 'em. Wasn't like I was makin' a hog outta myself."

"Well get in and I'm gonna take ya home."

"Shit I don't wanna go home. I been home for three days. I left a woman sittin' at the bar there thinks I'm a doctor, and, hoss, I'm tellin' ya, she looked like she had almost all her teeth. You know how long that's been? Since I been with a woman had almost all her teeth? Shit, I can't tell ya how long that's been—what's your name again?"

"Carlucci."

"Yeah, that's right. She was clean too, hoss. Didn't stink from old deodorant or nothin'. God, I can't stand the smell a old deodorant, can you? All perfumey'n everything and it gets all mixed up with sweat?"

"Uh, you in? You buckled up?"

"Yeah, I'm in. Course your old lady probably washes under her arms every day, right?"

"If you mean my wife I'm not married. Where you live?"

"Aw c'mon, hoss, I don't wanna go home, no shit. Home ain't nothin' but two rooms and a stinky bed and a busted tape player. I won't drink no more beer, I promise. Just water and Coke or somethin'. But I gotta go back the VFW and at least try to dance with that woman. Shit, I don't get back there, she'll be gone. Somebody'll snap her right up. Listen, hoss, I'm tellin' ya, she smelled good. You know how hard it is to hold your nose when you're doin' the thing and not let on that's what you're doin'?"

"You sittin' there talkin' about dancin'? Or screwin'? You

kiddin'? You try dancin' you're gonna fall on that woman and break her arm or somethin' and wind up gettin' sued insteada screwed."

Carlucci could feel Teslovich staring at him. He turned and saw Teslovich's mouth hanging open in admiration. "God, hoss, that was almost like a country song. 'I wound up sued insteada screwed.' I don't think you could say that on a record though, 'cause nobody'd be allowed to play it on the radio, you think?"

"You gotta be kiddin' me. Not that I listen to the radio that much, but, man, there's a lot of weird shit on there. And gettin' weirder. D'you have a car, or d'you walk, or what?"

"Nah, my car's at the VFW, around the back. Almost forgot about it. I'm glad you brung me back, hoss. You'da took me home, I'da woke up tomorrow and thought, now where the fuck's my car. I'd be thinkin' somebody stole it or somethin'. Hey, you don't have to pull around back, you can let me out right here."

"You sure this is what you wanna do?" Carlucci pulled over to the curb in front of the VFW.

"Oh fuckin'-A. Absolutely. I'd kick myself in the ass for a week I didn't find out if her teeth're for real. Gotta smell her again too, hoss. I gotta do that."

"Well maybe you better get some breath mints yourself. I can smell you from here."

"You can? Oh shit. Oh. Weren't we s'posed to stop and buy somethin'?"

"You said you didn't wanna go in any stop'n rob."

"Well, that's okay, they got a machine in here. I'm okay. See ya, hoss."

"Hey. I might have to talk to you some more, don't go anywhere."

"You got my numbers, hoss. I answer eventually, I do. No shit. See ya."

Teslovich turned and started up the sidewalk toward the side door of the VFW but stopped as a woman, leaving by the same door, approached him. Carlucci had to pull into the VFW's lot behind the building to turn around. By the time he got headed back toward the street, he could see Teslovich trailing the woman as she made her way down to the street, slightly behind her, arms outstretched trying hard to make some point with her and then throwing up his hands and letting them fall against his thighs as the woman continued to walk on without another look back. Teslovich staggered backward a step and a half, then turned and almost walked into the left front fender of Carlucci's cruiser.

Carlucci eased alongside Teslovich and wound down the window. "You okay?"

"Fuck no I ain't okay. She ain't buyin' it no more. Won't even dance one dance. Her teeth were real too, goddammit. They were too uneven to be fakes, you know? And damn, she smelled good."

"Get her number?"

"Nah, fuck, she spotted me gettin' outta your car. She says, 'Musta been some emergency, Doc, ya gotta get the cops to bring ya back.' Shit, and all I could think to say was, 'Hey, sayin' who ya ain't, what's wrong with that? It's practically the national pastime, you know? Sure ain't baseball. That's for goddamn millionaires.' I trieda tell her, 'Hell, tryin' to be who ya ain't is the American dream, ain't it? So what's wrong with sayin' it out loud?' She just laughed, hoss, and kept on walkin'. All I wanted to do was dance one dance with her. The way I feel, hell, I couldn't do nothin' else. Aw fuck. When they start laughin' at ya, it's time to go home. See ya, hoss."

Carlucci said good night and started to pull away, but heard Teslovich yelling and saw him waving in the mirror after he'd traveled only a few yards.

"What now?"

"I just thought of somethin'. Don't know what made me think of it, it just popped into my head. Mrs. Picadio had a colored cook. You know, you were askin' before 'bout when I talked to her last'n everything? Betcha she could tell ya somethin'. Her cook."

"Oh yeah? What's her name?"

"Oh now, see, you got me there. Lemme think for a second here. Nope. Can't think of it. But I'll tell ya what. Her number gotta be somewhere. She was always on the phone with that woman, what the hell was her name. Shit. Can't think of it. Real simple name. Lemme go home'n sleep on it'n I'll give ya a call tomorrow. But if I can't think of it, I'll bet I can find it in one of the books up the office."

"You can't go in that office yet."

"I can't? Why not? What if I gotta plant a box?"

"Don't worry about it, you're not gonna be doin' anything for a coupla days. You keep doin' what you're doin', you're gonna need a box."

"Hey that ain't funny, hoss. Bad enough the women're laughin' at me, I don't need cops tellin' me I'm gonna croak."

"I'm not tellin' ya you're gonna croak. I'm tellin' ya forget about work for a coupla days, you look like hell. And anyway, I don't want you in there, I'm not done with that place yet. You can call anybody else you work with and tell 'em to stay outta there too, ya hear me?"

"How long's 'at gonna last? I'm gonna have to go back to work sooner or later."

"You can't go in there as long as the tape's up, not without me or some other police officer with ya, and I don't know when I'm gonna be done. You go in there without an officer and I hear about it, you're gonna get arrested. Messin' with a crime scene's serious, I'm not jokin'."

"Well hell. Guess I'm gonna be takin' a vacation then. Brown. Brown! That's her name. Told ya it was real simple. Brown, oh what the hell's her first name. Valentine. No. Starts with a V, I know that. Vanessa. No that ain't it neither. Valeri. Velma. No. Valetta! No. Yes! Valetta. That's it! Valetta Brown. That's her name. Been cookin' for Mrs. Picadio, shit, ever since the old man died. She said one time, I heard her, she said she was never gonna cook again long as she lives. 'At's when she hired that colored woman. Valetta Brown, I'll be damned, my brain's sure workin' in funny ways tonight."

"Uh, Mr. Teslovich, I wanna thank you—"

"Mister? Is 'at what you said? Did you just call me Mister? Mister! Haw! That's funny."

"Yeah, uh, listen. Go home. Take care of yourself. Thanks again. I really appreciate your help."

"Sure, sure. Mister. Damn."

Back at the station, Carlucci looked at his watch while skimming down the list of Browns in the phone book, wondering whether he should take a chance to call Valetta Brown at this time of night. It was almost ten-thirty. If she was a cook, she was probably used to getting up early. Of course, on a Friday night, she could be out, having a little fun, instead of going to bed early. There were only five Browns with a first name beginning with V, none of them Valetta, and only one Brown with just the initial. He dialed that and took what was left of the pizza to the microwave oven and heated it up. She answered on the eleventh ring.

"Valetta Brown?"

"Who's this?" The woman sounded sleepy. And annoyed.

"Detective Sergeant Carlucci, ma'am. Rocksburg police." There was a long pause. "What do you want?"

"Are you Valetta Brown?"

"What's this about?"

"If you're Valetta Brown, I'll tell you in a minute. I have to know I'm talking to the person I wanna be talkin' to, okay? Are you Valetta Brown? You live at 103 Franklin Avenue?"

"I don't like the police callin' me up at ten-thirty at night. Yes I'm Valetta Brown. And that's my address. What's this about? If it's about Luther, he don't live here no more."

"Luther? Who's that? Your husband?"

"No he ain't my husband. I don't have a husband. What do you want? You don't tell me, I'm goin' hang up, I don't care if you are the police."

"Do you work for Mrs. Picadio? Alfredo Picadio Senior? Do you cook for her?"

"Why you want to know that? Oh Lord. Oh my. I knew it. Somethin' wrong with her, what's wrong with her, somethin' wrong with her, ain't it? She ain't been home since yesterday supper, she always turn the coffee on, coffee wasn't turned on this morning. I *knew* somethin' wrong, soon as I seen that pot, I knew somethin'. Went upstairs, her bed wasn't even mussed up, she didn't even sleep in her bed. Didn't leave me no note neither, she *always* leave me a note."

Carlucci cleared his throat. Valetta Brown's words had come in a rush, her breathing getting faster and shallower the longer she talked.

"Mrs. Brown? Is it Mrs. Brown or Miss? You have a preference?"

"Miss. I haven't been missus for thirty years. No. Thirty-one in June. You goin' tell me what's wrong or not? She all right?"

"Do you work for her, ma'am? As a cook? Do you cook for her?"

"Why do you want to know that? What difference does that make?"

"Ma'am, listen to me. From what I've already heard you say, I know you work for Mrs. Picadio—"

"You don't know that! I didn't say that!"

"Ma'am? Miss Brown? Listen to me. I'm not callin' about the conditions of your employment with Mrs. Picadio—"

"The conditions?! What you talkin' about, conditions of my employment? What that mean?"

"Ma'am, I don't care how you get paid, okay? I don't care whether you get paid cash, or whether you pay your taxes or what. Unless you give me a hard time. Then I'm gonna care a lot, you understand me now? Huh? Those are the conditions I'm talkin' about. I just wanna know about Mrs. Picadio, okay?"

She thought that over for a long moment. At last she said, "Oh. Okay. What do you want to know—but you better not be a lie."

"Do you cook for her? What I'm askin' is, if you cooked for her, that would mean you would have to see her all the time, right? Five days a week? Six? How many?"

"Six."

"Breakfast, lunch, and supper?"

"No, just lunch and supper. She just have coffee for breakfast. I fix the pot 'fore I leave at night. She turn it on when she get up."

"She eat the same time every day? All the time?"

"Miz Picadio won't eat no casserole and she won't eat no stew, and if you won't eat no casserole and no stew, you better eat the same time every day or you goin' get you another cook. If I'm goin' prepare everything fresh? And hot? The way she want it? She better eat the same time. Ten minutes after twelve o'clock noon and forty minutes after five at night. Ten minutes after she walk in the house, she be sittin' down at the table and the food be there. Been that way for fifteen years—no, uh-uh. Fourteen

years 'leven months. First month, she think she can eat
when she want to. I said no ma'am, you may wants to eat
like that, anytime you wants, but Valetta Brown don't
work that way, honey, uh-uh. And once I said that, we be
straight ever since. Now c'mon, po-liceman, c'mon, I be
talkin' to you till my mouth hurt and you ain't told me
nothin'! C'mon now, what's goin' on?! You wake me up
and makin' me real upset here. My blood pressure already
high—"

"Miss Brown, why didn't you call somebody, huh? You
were there today, and she wasn't, and you didn't call anybody? How long'd you stay there today? I was there today,
where were you? I knocked. On every door. You tellin' me
you were in there? And didn't answer the door?"

"That was you? I didn't know you. How was I s'posed to
know you? That crazy woman 'cross the street wouldn't let
you in. You were on her porch for a long time. I seen you
talkin'. If she don't let you in, I sure ain't goin' let you in.
You look like a bum to me."

"A bum?"

"Well you sure wasn't wearin' no cop uniform. You didn't
have no suit on or no tie or nothin'. Look scruffy to me.
I'm scared in there by myself. I don't open no door to no
strange man. How am I 'posed to know you was a policeman?"

"If you'd come to the door, ma'am, I would've showed
you my shield and my identification card with my photo-
graph on it, that's how you would've known. Man. I wasted
so much time 'cause you didn't answer—never mind."

"Hey that's not my problem. What I care, you wastin'
time. I'm not goin' open the door to no strange man I don't
care what you say, not when I'm in the house by myself,
nossir."

"You're right, ma'am, you're right, I shouldn't've said

that, I apologize. You did the right thing, absolutely. I understand. I'm sorry I tried to make it sound like it was your problem. It isn't. It's mine. But now I need you to help me with it, okay? Please?"

"Okay, okay, let's just go on here, am I goin' work tomorrow—can you tell me that much at least? Do I still have a job? Please say I still have a job."

"Uh, well not for a while anyway, you don't. She's in intensive care up at Conemaugh Hospital."

"Oh Lord. Is she bad? Is she goin' get better? At least she ain't dead. She goin' pull through? What happen? Why won't you tell me that?"

"Uh, ma'am, this Luther you mentioned earlier, is he a friend of yours? Or is he a relative? What is he?"

"I told you. Luther don't live here no more."

"Yeah, I know you said that, ma'am. Is he your boyfriend, ma'am?"

"Lord no! Boyfriend! He my sister's boy."

"Uh-huh. How old is Luther?"

"Luther be thirty this comin' April."

"And you say he's not livin' with you anymore, is that right?"

"That's right."

"Well where's he living now, you know?"

"I don't know where he gone."

"Uh, when did he move out, ma'am? Can you tell me that?"

Long pause. "Yesterday."

"Yesterday? What time yesterday, ma'am, do you know?"

"He be gone 'fore I get back."

"Get back from work? When you came home from work, he was gone?"

"Yes."

"What time was that, ma'am? When did you come home?"

"'Bout seven-thirty. Had to call a cab."

"Is that how you usually get home? You usually take a cab?"

"No. Luther be drivin' me since he be livin' here."

"So he took you in the morning and then he didn't show up, is that what you're sayin'?"

"No he did not. And I called him. And didn't nobody answer."

"So then you called a cab."

"Yes I did."

"And when you got home, he was gone."

"That's right."

"How do you know he was moving, ma'am? How do you know he didn't just take a ride someplace, somethin' like that? Did he take his belongings, his personal stuff?"

"He took everything. Clothes, box, tapes, everything." Her voice was getting slower and fainter while her breathing was getting louder and faster.

"His box, ma'am? What box is that?"

"His boom box. His tape player, you know?"

"Oh yes, ma'am, I know what you mean. Uh, did Luther have a job, ma'am?"

"Luther have lotsa jobs. Used to."

"Used to? Laid off is he?"

"Uh-huh."

"Where was he laid off from, ma'am, do you know? You know the name of the company or the people he worked for? You have any of his old paychecks, anything like that?"

"Cleveland, that's all I know. I don't know where."

"You never saw any of his paychecks?"

"Uh-uh."

"You happen to know his Social Security number, ma'am?"

"Oh you crazy. Don't know nothin' 'bout no Social Security."

"Uh-ha. Well was that job he worked, was that very recent, Miss Brown? Like in the last six months or so?"

"I'm not sure. I don't know . . . oh Lord, somebody hurt her, didn't they?"

"Uh, how long's Luther been livin' with you, ma'am?"

"This time? Since my birthday."

"Can you be a little more specific than that, ma'am, when's your birthday?"

"He come here the last day of September. That night. That's my birthday. He brought me some things. A purse. Real nice black leather purse. And a little ice cream cake from the Dairy Queen. In a cup. And some herb tea he know I like. Ginseng."

"Uh, ma'am, Luther ever had any problems with the law before, do you know?"

"Yes," she said. He could barely hear her.

"Did you say yes, ma'am? I can hardly hear you."

"Yes," she said, coughing and clearing her throat and trying to speak up. "Yes."

"Could you tell me where and when he had this trouble, ma'am?"

"No, uh-uh. It was in Ohio's all I know. He live with my sister's husband. In Cleveland. 'Bout ten years ago. I really don't believe he been in no kinda trouble since, I honestly don't believe that."

"I'm sure you don't, ma'am. Uh, did you tell me already and I just forgot—what's his last name?"

"No I didn't tell you. Givins. He was, uh, his father was my sister's first husband. Thomas Givins. He passed on. But her second husband, he didn't adopt Luther. He was name

Wilshire. Then he divorce my sister. But they stay close, Luther and him. Luther be livin' with him when he got in that trouble that time. Maybe he ain't s'posed to live with him, I don't know, I never did like that man myself. Uh, Mr. Detective, you goin' keep on much longer? 'Cause I'm havin' a terrible time catchin' up my breath here."

"Oh. You all right, ma'am? You havin' any pain anywhere? Is it just your breathing, ma'am?"

"No, no, it's no pain. It's just . . . I'm so all upset'n everything . . . and I really need to go to the kitchen and get a pill I take. Could we keep on tomorrow or somethin'? I really gots to stop now."

"Fine, ma'am, fine, you do what you have to do. You want me to send somebody around to look in on you? Make sure everything's all right? I could have Mutual Aid Emergency Service over there in three, four minutes. Less. You want me to do that, huh? Whatta ya say, ma'am, I could call 'em, it's up to you."

"I just need to get my pill, thank you."

"Okay, Miss Brown. And thanks for your time and your cooperation, ma'am. I'm sorry you're upset. I'll call you tomorrow, see how you're doin', okay?"

"Okay. Bye."

Carlucci printed the name Luther Givins on a piece of paper and took it to Nowicki and said, "This guy ring any bells with you?"

Nowicki shook his head no and handed the paper back.

"Know anybody in the Cleveland PD?"

"Nope."

"How about in the Ohio corrections department—I don't know what they call it over there, it's been so long since I had to do anything with them—you know anybody there?"

"Nope. What's the problem with this guy?"

"Problem is, he's a relative of the woman who cooks for

the woman who's in intensive care, and the cook can't give me any numbers, no addresses, no Social Security. I thought maybe you might have a friend in Ohio someplace so I wouldn't have to try to chase down his Social Security number."

"You check our records?"

"Hey. *I'm* the Records Department, you know? Me? This name doesn't go with anything. I'll go look, but I don't remember any Luther Givins. Before I do that, I'm goin' downstairs, get a Pepsi. You want anything from the machines?"

"No, uh-uh. Thanks anyway."

Carlucci came back up with a can of caffeine-free, sugar-free Pepsi and took it back to the file cabinets where he and Balzic had maintained department records. He set the Pepsi on top of the first file cabinet, the one indexed by last names, and started through the G's. And there it was. He called out to Nowicki. "Listen to this, I was wrong. Givins, Luther Alonzo, date of birth 16 April 1963, male, black, brown, brown, five-eleven, one-eighty, blah blah, residence 103 Franklin Avenue, Rocksburg, livin' with his aunt, Mrs. Valetta Brown, on the date of arrest 4 July 1984, drunk and disorderly, resisting arrest, hot damn, Nowicki, way to go, I woulda swore we didn't have nothin'. Social Security number, FBI fingerprint ID number, hey, do me a favor, okay, and run this guy through NCIC?" Given the fatigue he was feeling, he moved as fast as he could to hand Nowicki the information.

Then he found a chair by the fax machine and waited, sipping his Pepsi. The next thing he knew, Nowicki was shaking his shoulder and saying, "Fax comin' in from NCIC on Givins."

Carlucci shook himself and stretched. His mouth tasted awful. He looked around for the can of Pepsi, found it by his feet, and sloshed some around his mouth, thinking the bubbling might help to wake him up.

When the fax was done printing, he squinted at it. He was so tired, his vision was starting to blur, his eyes were burning. He knew he had to get home, get into bed and sleep, but he couldn't stop reading. "Luther Alonzo Givins, date of birth 16 April 1963, Social Security number blah blah, fingerprint ID blah blah, convicted 7 May 1983 Cuyahoga County, Ohio, felony assault, six months, two years pro, blah blah, convicted 8 January 1986 Cuyahoga County, Ohio, armed robbery, felony with a firearm, seven to fifteen, served forty months, parole ended 31 July 1992." Oh man, Luther, we need to talk. Do we ever. And I need to go home, Jesus, I'm gonna fall down I don't get some sleep.

The next morning, Saturday, Carlucci called Mrs. Comito as soon as he awoke at seven and told her she had to watch his mother because a case had come up and he had to work, he'd probably be gone all day, he didn't know how long, but she had to come, he hoped she didn't mind, he knew she never liked to work weekends, he was sorry, he couldn't help it. She came in puffing her cheeks out and complaining about the cold. He helped her off with her coat, and as he was hanging it up, he whispered to her, "Uh, Mrs. Comito, you ever see my mother writin' letters to anybody?"

"Oh yeah, sure. All the time."

"All the time? *All the time?*"

"Oh sure, she's always writin' to the TV stations, oh yeah. Every day. Two or three letters every day, at least, yeah."

Oh God. "Does she mail 'em?"

"No no, she gives 'em to me. I'm s'posed to mail 'em."

"You're supposed to? You mean you don't?"

"Oh my God no, Rugsie, no, I don't mail 'em. They're, uh—don't take this wrong, okay? I don't wanna sound like

I'm pickin' on your mother, Rugsie, 'cause I'm not, but they're a little bit, uh, you know, cuckoo. Anyway, she don't have any stamps. So I just take 'em home with me and—I don't know whether I'm doin' the right thing or not, Rugsie, please don't be mad with me, but, Jeez, I can't keep 'em all. I throw 'em out. I used to keep 'em. My God, I had paper bags full of 'em in my cellar, and I thought, this is crazy. So I threw 'em all out one day. And now, when she gives 'em to me, I just take 'em home, and you know, right away, pfffft, in the garbage. Please don't be mad with me that I do that, okay? I didn't know what else to do. And she works on 'em so hard, you know, with the dictionary and everything. I hope I'm doin' the right thing, huh, Rugsie? You ain't mad?"

"Mad? God, I could kiss you. God no, I'm not mad. You're doin' exactly the right thing, believe me. You're sure she don't have stamps?"

"Oh no. I know she don't. She don't have writin' paper or envelopes neither. I bring her all that stuff."

"Aw Mrs. Comito, you're a sweetheart, honest to God. You buyin' that stuff, really? Hey, from now on, whenever you buy it, you give me the bill. And I'll get straight with you, okay—for what you already bought before? You don't have to pay for that stuff, Jesus, you do enough already. I didn't know she was writin' letters, how long's she been doin' that, really?"

"Oh, she started that, I guess, it was March or April last year. I don't remember exactly. But right around then. She been keepin' her papers and charts about what color ties Alec wears, you know, for a long time—"

"Is his name Alec or Alex?" he interrupted her. "Every time I say it I get in trouble with her—"

"Well now you got me. I thought it was Alec, but maybe it's Alex. Oh and I know it makes her mad, but ain't this something. I don't know which one it is now. But I don't know why she started writin' the letters. She just got so mad one day, remember? The day she broke the lamp, remember that? You come home and I was tryin' to glue it back together? It was the next day she started, I think. Or maybe not, I can't remember—oh oh, she's comin', I gotta go, she'll be real mad I don't get the water goin' for her tea."

"Yeah yeah, okay, me too, I gotta go. And please don't ever let her get her hands on any stamps, okay?"

"Oh I won't, I promise, I know."

Carlucci left the house shaking his head. He arrived at the station at about seven thirty-five and checked in with Patrolman Larry Fischetti, who was working the radio. Fischetti told him the mayor hadn't showed up or called, so Carlucci locked himself in Balzic's office and started making calls. He learned from the ICU nursing supervisor at Conemaugh General that Mrs. Picadio seemed to be holding steady; he left a message on Dr. Vijay Jwaharla's answering machine; finally, he called Pittsburgh Homicide and learned that neither of the two detectives, Tesari or Walls, he'd talked to yesterday was available, so he didn't know how their work was going. That left Miss Valetta Brown. Or Mrs. Valetta Givins. He had the phone in his hand and had punched her first three numbers when he decided this name business, this required a face-to-face.

He told Fischetti where he was going and drove west across Rocksburg to Franklin Street, which ran parallel to the westbound entrance to Route 30. He drove to the dead end of Franklin and found the second house, 103, on the eastern side. It was a small, two-story frame house, with dingy white aluminum siding and four concrete steps leading from the sidewalk to a rectangular front porch covered by an aluminum awning so faded it was hard to say what color it had been originally. The aluminum storm door had no handle.

He pushed the doorbell three times before he guessed that

it might be broken, so he knocked. Shortly, he heard some-body coming, but the door didn't open.

"What you want?" a woman called out. "I ain't dressed, what you want?"

"Detective Carlucci, Miss Brown. Are you Miss Brown? I talked to you last night, remember? I just stopped by to see how you're doin', see if you need anything." That was only partly true, but he was hoping it was true enough to get him inside.

She opened the door just enough to frame her face. She was short and her graying hair was cut very short, like a man's. She clearly had not had a good night. Her eyes were bloodshot and puffy.

"You got a badge or somethin'? How I'm s'posed to know you a detective?"

"Yes, ma'am." He had his ID case in his right hand and pulled open the storm door enough to hold the case where she could see it without distortion.

"I need my glasses," she said, closing the door and padding away. In a moment she'd padded back. This time she opened the door only wide enough to get her hand through it, and she took the ID case from Carlucci.

About a minute later, after many glances back and forth from him to his photo, she opened the door and said, "Come on in. I guess you is who you say, but if you ain't, I got a .25 right here in my pocket, and it's loaded, and I knows how to shoot it." She patted something that was causing the right pocket of her pink chenille robe to sag. Then she handed his ID case back with her left hand, keep-ing her right hand near that pocket, and stepped back and nodded for him to come in.

The front door opened directly into the living room. It was full of unmatched furniture: a wooden rocking chair with a couple of spindles missing, a yellowish stuffed chair with the arms and seat threadbare, a bluish sofa covered by a faded brown throw with a tiger on it, unmatching end tables, a coffee table with a glass top crisscrossed with duct tape, a round wooden table with two wooden chairs all painted flat brown, and a TV and a stereo system on a series of shelves attached precariously to the wall opposite the sofa. The TV was turned on to some talk show, but it was showing a MUTE sign. The paint on the ceiling was cracked and blistered, and the greenish wallpaper was held up in places with masking tape.

"Mind if I sit down, ma'am? I didn't have a real good night myself."

She ignored his question and backed against the seat of the yellowish stuffed chair and eased down onto it. "You goin' ask me if I got a permit?"

Carlucci had sidled over to the couch and started to sit, but caught himself because she hadn't said whether she minded and he thought he'd better wait to find out if she did.

"You can go 'head and sit down," she said, "and I'm goin' tell you even if you ain't goin' ask. I ain't got no permit."

He sat and cleared his throat. "Miss Brown—you are Miss Brown, right?"

"If you say so," she said stonily.

"Uh-ha. Well, Miss Brown, I don't really care if you have a permit or not. I'm not here to talk about that."

"Well if you here to talk 'bout Luther, I told you last night, Luther gone, and I don't know where he is at."

"Yes, ma'am, I know that's what you said. But last night, see, I got the impression you thought Luther didn't have any serious problems with the law, and I checked that out, and I know that's not true. Maybe you don't know that's not true, but the fact is, Luther's had some bad problems. He did six months for felony assault and he did three and a half years for armed robbery, felony with a firearm. I also know that we arrested him for drunk and disorderly and he was livin' here, with his mother. You know anything about that?"

"I didn't lie to you."

"I didn't say you did, ma'am. Probably, it was just you didn't understand how much trouble Luther's been in, that's all I'm sayin'. Listen, how you feelin', you doin' all right? Last night you were, uh, you know, not doin' too good."

"How you think I feel? Miz Picadio be bad as you say, I'm goin' lose my job. And everything. I'm goin' lose everything." Her jaws grew tight, her eyes glistened with tears.

Carlucci tried to shrug that off. "I don't wanna say how old you are, ma'am, but I'm guessin' you qualify for Social Security."

"Social Security! Is that what you guess? Well I'm goin' tell you somethin', no I don't! I do not qualify for no Social Security."

"Uh, I don't understand, ma'am, why wouldn't you qualify?"

"I don't qualify, Mr. Detective, because I ain't never qualified. I ain't never been signed up for it."

"Excuse me? Ma'am, you qualify just by bein' born. You know, after you get your card—you get 'em when you're a baby now, I mean your parents get 'em—but in my time, which I'm guessin' is your time since you're obviously older'n me—you got it when you turned eighteen, that's when I got mine. And as soon as you got the card, that's when you were signed up—"

"You ain't listenin' to me. I said, I ain't never signed up for it. I don't have no card. Ain't nobody ever told me nothin' 'bout gettin' signed up. I ain't even sure when I was born. I don't have no birth certificate. I went down the Social Security two years ago when my knees started to hurt me real bad. Miz Picadio say, go down there and talk to 'em, and so I went, and they tell me, girl, you can't be, we ain't got no record of you, you jus' can't be. They look me straight in the eye and tell me, far as we know, you never was. I never was! I say to them, I'm standin' right here in front of y'all, what the hell you mean I never was?! And after they got through tellin' me all their because of thises and because of thats, I said, damn, they're right. 'Cordin' to them, I never was. 'Cordin' to them, I ain't never been!"

"Oh man, there's somethin' really screwed up here," Carlucci said, shaking his head and laughing nervously. "Somewhere along the line, somebody you worked for had to ask you for your Social Security card, or your number. You couldn't get a job for all these years and—"

"Oh, is that right? Well why don't you go tell all these people I be cookin' for all my life, why don't you go tell them they was 'posed to ask me my number. Why don't you go 'head on and do that. You go 'head on, I'll just stay right here."

"You mean nobody ever asked to see your card? Nobody ever asked you to fill out an application where there was a box on it that said Social Security number? How'd you get a loan for this house? Nobody'd loan you money for a house without a Social Security number—"

"This ain't my house. Where you get that idea from? This house belong Miz Picadio. She own this house, I don't. She just let me live in it. That part a how she pay me."

"Mrs. Picadio owns this house?"

"Ain't that what I just say? Why you think I'm havin' so much trouble catchin' up my breath? If somethin' happen with her, I ain't goin' just lose my job. 'Cause her son don't know nothin' 'bout this house. But when he find out, whatchu think he goin' do? You think he goin' just let me keep on keepin' on here, is that whatchu think? Let me tell you. Not that man. Not with his wife. That man by his own self maybe, but not with that woman, oh no. That woman evil. Terriblist woman I ever seen. Terrible woman. I got this here .25 on account of her." She took a small automatic pistol out of her robe pocket and held it up in her palm for Carlucci to see.

"She's why you got that? Why's that, ma'am?"

"She hit me! Come in the house one day and 'cuse me a stealin' from Miz Picadio—"

"This house? Or Mrs. Picadio's?"

"Miz Picadio's. Come in the kitchen, sneak up on me, I don't even know which door she come in the house, didn't hear nothin'. Grab me by the shoulder, spin me 'round, I'm washin' up 'sparagus gettin' ready for lunch. She call me a lie, call me a thief, say I be stealin' Miz Picadio's clothes, say she seen me comin' out the house with paper bags fulla Miz Picadio's blouses and underwear. I say, woman, you crazy, don't nobody give nobody ol' used-up underwear and I ain't dumb enough to wear it even if somebody dumb enough to give it to me. And Miz Picadio always give me her old clothes that I could fit. But she ain't never give me no underwear. This her robe I got on right now. She always give me her old clothes. 'Cept her pants and skirts. She too small in the hips. I can't wear them. They ain't big enough to let out.

"That bitch slap me 'cross my face, bust my glasses, call me out my name, I had to run 'round the counter, catch me up a knife, I tol' her I'll cut you, I ain't afraid to cut you, you hit me again I'll cut you. Next day I bought this pistol and I been carryin' it ever since. I showed it to her. One night I be walkin' home, she come drivin' up 'longside me, drivin' real slow for almost a whole block, lookin' over at me, lookin' real evil. I took it out. I held it up. I showed her. I didn't aim it, I just showed her. And she drove on. She crazy.

"But if Miz Picadio don't need me cookin', and them two find out 'bout this house, I'm gone. And you know they goin' find out 'bout it sooner or later, 'cause the tax bill be comin' Miz Picadio's house. It don't be comin' here. And you know the tax bill goin' keep on comin'. He might let me keep on here if he was by hisself, but not with her. She be so happy to put me out, she be dancin'. She crazy. Any woman put herself in a hospital many times she put herself in and let them doctors be cuttin' on her, makin' her a new face and new titties and a new belly—"

"Excuse me? She put herself in the hospital and did what?"

"Whatchu call that, that plastic surgery, that's what I'm talkin' 'bout. That woman put herself in the hospital four times in the last two years. First time she got a face uplift. She come out lookin' like she be made up by some funeral director. Then she go in, have her belly, all the fat in her belly get sucked out. Let somebody put some kinda vacuum cleaner up under her skin or somethin', God knows what all 'cause I don't. Then she go in and get some kinda silly titties, somethin' I don't know what kind—"

"Silicone?"

"Yeah, that's it. Silly cone. And one of them done shift around, wind up half under her armpit somewhere, and she got to get that one out and a new one in, and then the other one done the same thing on the other side. So that's five times she be lettin' doctors cut on her. You a po-liceman. How much evidence you want? That woman crazy!"

Carlucci mulled this information over for a few moments and then said, "How do you know all this? Mrs. Picadio tell you all this, is that what you're sayin'?"

"Well you know the bitch ain't goin' tell me her own self."

"And so what'd Mrs. Picadio say about it?"

"What did she say? What do you think she say? She say they crazy!"

"She ever tell them that?"

"Course she tol' 'em. They had a terrible fight when she said she was goin' get them silly cone plants. Miz Picadio pitch a fit right there in the kitchen. Tol' her, don't you know that silly cone is nasty? Don't you know it be causin' all kindsa problems? She say don't you watch Oprah? Don't you watch Phil? Don't you watch Jenny Jones? What's wrong wit'chu? And anyway, she say, who goin' be payin' for all this? Ain't no insurance goin' pay for it. And she say you know I ain't goin' pay for it. Who goin' pay for it? You ain't got that kinda money. Where that money be comin' from? Oh she mad. She smokin'. I run down the cellar I got so scared, 'cause Miz Picadio, she be terrible her own self when she wanna be. 'Cause she mad, see, 'cause that only be the half of it."

"The half of what?"

"The half of what Miz Picadio be mad about. With them."

"What was the other half?"

"'Cause they be doin' the same thing to their house what that bitch be doin' to her own self."

"Excuse me? Same thing to the house?"

"Yeah. Redecoratin'. Rebuildin'. Remodelin'. Got a whole new kitchen, cost 'em twelve hundred dollars just for the refrigerator! Twelve hundred dollars! Threw out all their furniture—didn't give none to me. Give it to the Good Will. And I mean the whole house too, every piece a furniture, out, gone, and all new in. And they don't have no little-bitty bungalow, uh-uh nossir. Listen to this—they ain't got no kids, and they got four bedrooms and three bathrooms—and ain't got no kids! They got one of them whirled pools right in the bathroom. Right there in the bathroom, big enough for two people! Miz Picadio so mad, she tol' me that whirled pool cost more'n three thousand dollars, she keep sayin', where'd they get that money from, where'd they get that, they ain't got that kinda money. She mad. And stay mad too, don't you think she didn't."

"Well, uh, besides that, did she ever say to you where she thought they might be gettin' the money from?"

"Oh no. Uh-uh. Miz Picadio keep her business to her own self."

"Yeah but you just said she told you how much some of that stuff was costin', so whatta ya mean she kept her business to herself?"

"I mean she might tell me how mad she be, but she didn't never tell me nothin' else. If she ever found out where them two gettin' their money from, she never told me, that's what I be tellin' you. Anyway, she only talk 'bout that two or three times with me—besides the time they had that terrible fight in the kitchen made me run to the cellar. Besides that."

"Uh-huh. Did you ever hear any of the doctors' names? The ones who operated on her? Or do you know which hospital she went in?"

"Uh-uh. 'Cept one time, she went to this hospital right here. In town here. When she want to get them silly cone plants, I heard Miz Picadio say she be so happy 'cause some doctor here, he wouldn't do it. Uh-uh. Wouldn't operate on her. Tol' her she wanted them, she was goin' have to go to Pittsburgh, he wasn't goin' do it, that's what Miz Picadio say, and she be so happy. That's all I know. But I don't know his name."

"How about the remodelers and the redecorators? You ever hear their names?"

"If I did, I didn't pay no attention, or I forgot." She looked at the floor suddenly, then took off her glasses and covered her face with her hands and started to sob softly and say, "Oh what is goin' happen with me?" She kept repeating it and rocking on the front edge of the stuffed chair until Carlucci got up and went over and put his hand on her shoulder. He couldn't think of anything to say, except, "It's all right."

After the third time he said it, she brushed his hand away and struggled to her feet and said, "Stop talkin' that. It ain't all right. Ain't goin' be all right. I ain't got nobody but my Luther and God knows what he gone and done this time!"

Carlucci backed up a step and swallowed. "Excuse me, but what about Luther's mother? Your sister. Couldn't she help you?"

"Oh, man, she ain't Luther's momma. I don't even know where she live anymore anyway. Luther don't neither. He ain't seen her since he went to Cleveland. Miz Picadio don't need me, they'll put me out faster'n I can say the words. And even if she get better I ain't goin' have no job till she get better, you just say so. And if she take a long time to get better, they goin' find out 'bout this house. This ain't no palace, I don't have to tell you that, you can see that for your own self, just look around. But the roof don't leak and the toilet work and so do the furnace and the hot water tank and all the rest of the plumbin'.

"And where you think a old black woman like me goin' get 'nother job? My knees hurt so bad I can hardly stand up sometimes. Where I'm goin' get 'nother place to live? And what I'm goin' live on? I got three hundred and fifty-one dollars in my can—oh God! My can! Oh my God, say not so, Lord, please, Lord, don't let him take my can! Please God don't let him take my can!" She whirled away from Carlucci and scurried, limping, into the kitchen and threw open the cupboard over the sink and grabbed a coffee can. As soon as she lifted it, she screamed, "Oh God he took my money! Oh God he took my money, he took my money, he took my money . . . son of a bitch . . . you son of a bitch . . ." She sank onto a chair, peering into the empty can and cursing Luther and shaking her head, until the can slipped out of her fingers to the floor and clattered between her feet, and she began to sob.

Carlucci started to move toward her, but thought better of it. He cleared his throat and waited for her to compose herself. It took what seemed like a very long time. It was hardly a minute. Finally he said, "Miss Brown, I don't know if you wanna hear this right now, but there are some people who can help you, I think, if you wanna know about 'em. I can leave you some phone numbers if you want."

"You mean welfare and stuff like that? No thank you, no thank you at all. I tried to deal with those people once. Made me think it was money comin' out their own damn pocket, no thank you very much."

"I'm sure they did that to you, ma'am, that used to be a very common complaint. But I really don't think that's what you're gonna find if you talk to 'em now. I'm gonna leave some numbers here for ya, I think you oughta give 'em a call, really."

"And what happens when they aks me for my Social Security number? What I do then? 'Cause that's what they done aks me last time. What I do then when I say I ain't got it? Come on, you so smart, what I'm goin' do then?"

Carlucci shrugged. "I don't know, ma'am, I'm not that smart. All I can tell you is, uh, let me write this down. And, uh, if we find Luther, if we get him in a corner where he has to help us, maybe, uh, maybe you can ask the DA to include restitution in the sentence."

"Rest-a-what?"

"Restitution, ma'am. If Luther gets in front of a judge on this charge, it's very likely that he will have bargained the charges against him down to, uh, you know, maybe simple theft, in exchange for him paying you back what he took."

She got slowly to her feet and pulled a paper towel off a roll under one of the cupboards and wiped her eyes and blew her nose. "And how long you think that goin' take? You think I'm goin' still be livin' then, huh?"

"I can't say, ma'am. But that's the only chance you have for gettin' your money back, unless Luther brings it back himself, which, uh, I wouldn't expect that."

"Why don't you jus' go on and go, Mr. Detective. More you talks, sadder I gets. But that damn Luther, he show up here and don't give me back my money? I'm gonna shoot him in his heart. I don't care he is my boy, I'm goin' shoot him—"

"Oh Miss Brown, uh, Miss Givins, don't even start thinkin' like that. Honest, I would hate to see you go to prison—"

"Why? Why would you hate that? Least I have a place to live. Least I be gettin' food three times every day. Least I could maybe get some doctor look at my knees once in a while, give me some asp'rin. I got four more asp'rins left and no money to buy no more! Miz Picadio would give me some I aks her, but how I'm goin' aks her now? And that damn Luther, I let him stay here six months'n clean up his dirty laundry'n fix his bed'n make his supper'n make his breakfast, and how he pay me back? Huh? He done took my money, every damn cent I got. Three hundred and fifty-one dollars and one cent, don't even leave me the cent!"

Carlucci sighed and shook his head. "Ma'am, I'm gonna need just a little bit more information before I can write up a report, and you won't be able to do anything without a police report. You wanna do that?"

She shrugged and clapped her hands disgustedly. "What else can I do. I don't know what else I can do. Whatchu wanna know?"

He took all the information he needed from her to fill out a theft report and then said, "Would it be okay with you if I took a look at his room? Luther's?"

"You can look if you want, but he didn't leave nothin'. Go 'head on up, I ain't goin' come on up, I don't go on up steps 'less I has to. The room on the right-hand side, you'll see. Took every damn thing 'cept the sheets and blanket."

He went upstairs and saw that what she'd said was true. The only thing left in the room besides the furniture was the sheets and blanket on the bed. He found nothing else on the bed, nothing under the mattress, and nothing under the bed. Both the single closet and the wobbly chest of drawers were empty. Carlucci pulled out all the drawers and looked on their bottoms and then pulled the chest away from the wall and checked its back and bottom and then the inside before putting the drawers back in. Either Luther had been traveling light when he'd arrived or else he was thorough.

Carlucci went back downstairs and found her still in the kitchen, rocking slightly on the chair where he'd left her.

"Uh, ma'am, you ever talk to Luther about his friends, people he hung with? Can you tell me any of their names?"

"Luther never talk about that. Luther all the time be talkin' 'bout music, do I hear this song, do I know that song. Luther all the time be listenin' to his box—when he ain't watchin' TV. He don't tell me where do he hang, or who do he hang with."

"Does he smoke?"

"You mean reg'lar or dope?"

"Either one. He's got to light 'em with somethin'. He ever leave any matchbooks around?"

"If he did, I ain't got 'em."

"Ma'am, you gotta help me out here. You say he was here for six months, right?"

"Right, yes."

"He didn't stay inside here for six months, did he? He had to leave once in a while, go someplace, right? Please try to remember. One of those times when he was walkin' out the door, he had to tell you where he was goin' or who he was goin' with, please try to recall."

"I done tol' you. He ain't never talk about that with me."

"Well, you said he took you back and forth to work, what kind of car did he have?"

"Oldsmobile. Black. All black, black seats'n everything."

"Did he have Ohio license plates, or Pennsylvania?"

"They was white. With blue numbers, that's all I know."

"That's Ohio. You know what year car it was? Or what model?"

"Uh-uh. Cars, they all look the same to me, and he didn't never say nothin' 'bout it. It was old, that's all I know."

"Old? You're not sayin' 'Olds' now, you're sayin' 'old,' is that right?"

"Yeah, it was all rusty and funky, he didn't never clean it or wash it or nothin'. And when he open the doors, they be squeakin' real bad. Why did he have to take all my money? Why did he have to do me like that?" She took off her glasses and buried her face in her hands and started to sob again.

"Uh, ma'am, did Luther ever ask you about Mrs. Picadio's schedule, when she was home, when she was at work?"

"Well he have to know when I be done work so he could come get me, carry me home."

"Yeah, right. Sure he would. But I mean, did he ever ask you specifically about when Mrs. Picadio was at home or at work? When she'd be there, when she wouldn't be there? You remember him sayin' anything like that?"

"If he did I don't remember. But sure we talk about that. He know when she be at work. She be gone 'fore I get there in the mornin'. He know that."

"But how about at night? Did he ask you about whether she worked late or not?"

"Whatchu tryin' say? Luther done done somethin' to her?

Huh? That what you tryin' say? I don't b'lieve that. I ain't never goin' b'lieve that. Luther a fool sometimes, but he ain't never goin' mess with me in my job."

"Uh, ma'am, somebody took your money. You don't have any trouble believin' it was him that did that—"

"That's diff'rent! He might take my money from me but he ain't goin' mess me up so I can't get no more money. Luther a fool, but he ain't that big a fool."

Carlucci sighed. "Okay, ma'am, okay. Listen, I'm gonna leave now. I'm gonna leave my card right here, I'm gonna put it on the table by your elbow here, okay? And it's got three phone numbers on it. If you wanna talk to me about anything, you hear? Anything at all, you call anytime, you hear me? If I'm not at one number, I'll be at another one, just keep callin', you hear?"

"I hear," she said, her voice cracking.

"And you remember that I gave you another number for the welfare office, you remember that?"

She nodded, but said nothing.

"Well, ma'am, you call 'em, I'm tellin' ya, you call that number. And if they give you any trouble, you tell 'em call me, you hear? I mean it. I know everything looks real bad to you right now, but you can get some help, I know you can. And if Luther should come back, you hear me? I want you to call me, okay? Don't you do anything. Okay? Don't you do anything, you hear me? Just call me and tell me you have to talk to me right away, right now, you don't have to mention his name, just say come right now, and I'll know what it's about and I'll be here, I promise you."

She dropped her hands and glared up at him. "Luther come back'n he don't have my money? I'm goin' shoot him in his heart."

Carlucci tilted his head back and threw up his hands and then let them fall to his face. He rubbed his jaws hard. "Miss

Brown, Mrs. Brown, I don't know what to call you, but please, don't even think that. He comes back, just pick up the phone and call me, okay? Please don't do anything else, okay? I know you're real real mad right now, but please don't do that, okay? I have to go now, ma'am. Thank you for talkin' to me. Oh, wait. You got a picture of Luther? A recent one?"

"No I do not."

"Well does he look the same as he used to look? I mean we're all gettin' older and we all change, but I mean did he do anything to change the way he looks? Did he grow a beard? Did he get fat? Did he shave his head, anything like that?"

She shook her head no. "He look about the same as he always look. He didn't do nothin' to hisself."

"Uh-ha. One more thing and then I'll let you go. Does he have a gun? Or a knife? Does he usually carry somethin'? Or does he keep it in his car?"

"He have a gun."

"A gun. You know what kind? Is it like yours?"

"Make a lotta noise, I know that."

"Lotta noise? He shoot it here?"

"Yeah. One day he in the cellar and I hear this terrible noise, I'm up in the bathroom, and come down here and Luther be holdin' his ears and his face be all twisted up and he be talkin' 'bout shootin' a rat down in the cellar. Didn't even clean it up. I had to go down there'n clean it up. I say, good for you, fool, I hope your ears hurt for a week."

"But you never saw the gun yourself?"

"No, but he say it be like mine, just bigger."

Carlucci thanked her again and hurried out to his car and called his station as he started to drive back there. He asked Fischetti to call Ohio Motor Vehicles and run Luther Alonzo Givins through their records to see if he matched up with a black Oldsmobile. He also asked Fischetti to put out the word to the Pittsburgh PD and the state police as well as to their own black-and-whites to look for a black Oldsmobile with Ohio plates driven by a black male in his late twenties, early thirties, and to detain the driver if he identified himself as Givins.

"Why don't I wait and see what Ohio says first?" Fischetti said.

"Do it whatever order you want, but put the word out even if Ohio comes back negative, okay?"

Carlucci signed off, but Fischetti called him right back. "You didn't gimme a chance to say, Rugs, but the hospital called, you know, Conemaugh ICU? Said you wanted to know if there was any change in a, Mrs. Picadio, is that her name?"

"Roger, what's up?"

"She died."

"Aw man, c'mon, don't tell me that. I just talked to them up there, they said no change, what the fuck, I just talked to 'em, hey, less than an hour ago. Two at the most. When'd they call?"

"'Bout five minutes before you did. I was just gettin' ready to call the coroner when you called. You goin' there, right?"

"Aw fuck. Yeah, I'm goin'. You talk to the coroner, tell him I'll meet him there. You call the state guys yet?"

"Yeah, I just did that."

"They say who they were sendin'? Anybody I know?"

"Nope. Didn't give me a name."

"Okay. I'm goin' the ICU first, I wanna talk to the nurses. Son of a bitch. Hey, this Givins? It's for questioning in connection with a homicide now. Get on Ohio's ass and stay on it till they give you somethin', okay?"

He drove to the hospital and went directly to the ICU, but

there was still the kind of glum confusion the death of a patient always seems to leave in the air, nurses from the cardiac team talking tight-lipped to the ICU nurses, so Carlucci went back out into the waiting room and found a pay phone and called Bill Teslovich at home. When Teslovich answered, Carlucci asked him if he could be more specific than he'd been last night about where Mr. and Mrs. Alfredo Picadio Jr. might be in the Bahamas. Teslovich said all he knew was that Junior didn't want to be bothered and so he never told anybody where he went specifically. "It was always just, you know, the Bahamas."

"C'mon man, guy owns a business, goes on vacation, he doesn't tell anybody where he's goin'? He gotta tell *somebody*. Think."

"I am thinkin', but why's he gotta tell somebody? His mother's there. She could run it just as good as he could. Anything happen, she'd know what to do just as much as he would, he knows that. And it's closed anyways, so what's he got to worry about?"

"Well for one thing, somebody could come in and beat the shit out of his mother, which is what happened." Carlucci didn't tell Teslovich that she'd just died.

"Well what'm I s'posed to say, huh? Junior's idea of plannin' ahead was to work our asses off in November and December so him and his old lady could take off. Other than that I don't know nothin'."

"Well forget the Bahamas. When he was here, he had to go someplace. He didn't just go to work and go home every day. If he's gamblin' in the Bahamas, he's gamblin' here, you don't turn that off and on. You remember him talkin' about it?"

"Oh, you mean that? Well, sure, he used to brag every once in a while, you know, 'bout how his bookie used to hate to see him comin', but mostly I figured that was just him bein' a blowhard. But now that you mention it, I did hear him talkin' a lot about football. But mostly it was horses. Yeah, he used to go to the Meadows a lot, now that I think about it. For the horses with the buggies behind 'em, I don't know what you call 'em."

"Trotters and pacers."

"Yeah, them. And, uh, yeah, they used to go down to Waterford Park a lot. For the regular horses, yeah. But I never heard him talkin' about goin' with anybody else, you know, just him and the old lady that's all I ever heard him say."

"He ever mention his bookie's name?"

"Not to me he didn't."

"Ever talk about losin'?"

"To his bookie, you mean?"

"Yeah."

"If he did, I can't remember. What always used to piss me off is when him and his old lady'd come back from the Bahamas braggin' about how much they lost, but, hey, maybe he knew somethin' about horses, maybe she did, I don't know."

"How about eatin'? He ever talk about where he went out? Restaurants? Ever mention any to you?"

"Nah, not to me—hey, I think you're gettin' the wrong idea here. You're askin' these questions like—hey, we were buddies or somethin'. He's the boss and I drive the truck, among other things, and that's all there is to it. It ain't like it was with his old man. Christ, the old man, he was like, you know, a human being. He used to have a picnic every summer for everybody, everybody who worked for him, bring the wives, bring the kids, the whole thing. He cooked, the old man. Nothin' fancy, you know, hot dogs, hamburgers, kolbassi, hot sausage, but all the beer you could drink, man, and he ate and drank right along with us. And had little toys there for the kids, you know, and goofy races, egg tosses'n shit like 'at. The kid, man, fuck, twelve o'clock comes, you get out your lunch, he looks at you like you're stealin' 'cause you wanna eat lunch. We ain't never been in his backyard and we ain't never gonna be. And the day we get a turkey for Christmas, shit, that's the day I know he sold the fuckin' joint—or else I'm workin' someplace else. As if anybody even does 'at good shit anymore, which I doubt."

"Well lemme ask you somethin' else," Carlucci said. "You ever hear him or anybody else, his mother maybe, his wife, anybody, you ever hear any conversation about his wife gettin' operated on? Anything like that?"

"His wife? Oh yeah, sure. We could hear that. Yeah, him and the old lady, they'd be pissin' and moanin' about that, yeah, how much it was gonna cost him. Oh yeah."

"What was what gonna cost him?"

"His old lady. Not his mother, his wife. Pullin' a Hollywood, you know, new face, new teeth, new tits, that lipo whatever, that suction job, whatever they call that, you know, on all the fat in her back and her belly, whatever. Yeah, I heard them talkin' about that a lot."

"And you heard him and his mother—you personally heard this yourself, not other guys in the plant told you about it—what'd you say? You heard them pissin' and moanin' about this?"

"Oh yeah. Everybody did. Last coupla years, yeah, Christ I don't know how many times she was in some hospital in Pittsburgh. And then somethin' got fucked up, I don't know whether it was the doctors or, uh, I guess it was probably what they put in, the implants I guess. They shifted around on her, and she got real real sick, had to go back in, fuck, I don't know how many times. I'll bet in the last two years, lemme see, I'll bet she was in the hospital, man, at least five times, easy."

"And you heard him and his mother arguin' about this? You could hear them?"

"Oh sure. Yeah. When the mixer wasn't runnin', yeah sure you could hear 'em. She kept raggin' him 'bout where was he gettin' the money, and he'd keep on sayin', 'Hey, long as I ain't askin' you for it, whatta you care where I'm gettin' it. And I ain't askin' you, so get off me.' Oh yeah, they went round and round lotsa times. Or what I mean is, she went round and round. He'd just take it for a while, then he'd tell her to get off his ass and walk away."

"He ever threaten her?"

"Him? Him threaten her? Aw no, fuck no, no way, he's an asshole, but he'd never do nothin' to her, uh-uh, no fuckin' way. I wouldn't believe that in a million years. All I ever heard him say, you know, he'd tell her to get offa his ass, but that was it. That's as far as he'd go. Nah, he wouldn't say nothin' else, nothin' more'n 'at to her, uh-uh. Now, the other way around? Now you ask me that, I'd have to say yeah."

"You heard the mother threaten the son?"

"Lotsa times, yeah. Lotsa times."

"Like what kinda threat? What'd she say?"

"Well one day she smacked him. I seen her. Jimmy seen her too. He was with me, you can ask him. We just come back from the Catholic Cemetery, just parked the truck, we're goin' in the office, Jimmy was right behind me, and whamo! She lets him have one in the chops. Man, you could hear it through the windows, oh yeah, she really let him have it."

"Slapped him, punched him, what?"

"Slapped him, definitely a slapperoo. Made a real loud noise, you know? Caught him flush. Me and Jimmy stop, we look at each other, we didn't know what the fuck to do, you know, go inside, get back in the truck, what. We're standin' there like a coupla jagoffs. Finally, you know, I said to

Jimmy, I said, hey, we gotta find out what we're doin' next, we can't stand out here like fuckin' jagoffs all day, so we went in, you know, tryin' to be real cool like we didn't see nothin'. Which turned out to be a fuckin' joke 'cause soon as we get inside, Jimmy gets the giggles. You know how some people get nervous, they start gigglin'?"

"I know exactly what you're talkin' about," Carlucci said.

"Yeah, well he starts gigglin', Jimmy, and asshole me, I start gigglin' too. I'm gigglin' at him gigglin', and they're so fuckin' pissed off, both of 'em, man, I mean, she was fuckin' smokin' she was so hot. And he's got this big red splotch all over his face, you know, it's spreadin', and I can't help lookin' at it, and finally I get straight enough to say, hey, here's the paper for that one, where we goin' now? And Junior, that's when he sees an out and he says he gotta show us somethin' in the shop, and he practically runs outta the office. And when we get in the shop, the asshole goes off on Jimmy. You know, blah blah blah, you think that's funny, huh? You think it's fuckin' funny my mother slaps me in my face, blah blah blah, man, he goes on like 'at for about two minutes. You know how long two minutes is when you're standin' there and somebody's gettin' his ass chewed? It's embarrassing, you know? I was real embarrassed for Jimmy, and the goofy thing was, I seen it too and I was gigglin' too and he never says a fuckin' word to me. Nothin'. Doesn't even look at me. He just chews Jimmy's ass right in front of me. Man, it was real . . . shit, I felt real bad for Jimmy, you know, the kid, he hadn't been workin' there that long at that time, he didn't know how to take that fuckin' asshole, so I just told him finally, I said, hey, knock it off, the kid didn't have nothin' to do with it, give him a fuckin' break, you know? He gives me this look, you know, like fuck you, who asked you? But he shut up. He didn't say no more. So I went back in the office and the old lady hands me the paper for the next job, and we load up, and away we go, and that was that."

Carlucci mulled that over for a moment and said, "But did you hear anything before you saw the slap? You don't know what came before that, right? You don't know what they were arguin' about is what I'm sayin'."

"No, right. I don't. I just assumed, you know, 'cause mostly that's what they'd be arguin' about—"

"But you don't know that, is what I'm sayin', right?"

"Yeah, right."

"Well can you remember any other times? Specifically now, times you actually heard them arguing about money and what he was spendin' it on. His wife's operations or anything else. You ever hear them arguin' about anything else?"

"Well now that you mention it, one time I heard 'em goin' around about, uh, somebody's house. His, I guess— oh wait I remember now. 'Bout ten years ago, maybe longer, he put in a patio in back of his house. Not me, I didn't go out there. He took some other guys from the shop. And last year—no, two summers ago, he did it again. That's what they were arguin' about that time. She says what the fuck you need a new patio for—she didn't say 'fuck.' Me, I said 'fuck,' she didn't say 'fuck.' She swore, but she never said 'fuck,' least not around me. Anyways, she says, concrete don't wear out in ten years, and he says it was a bad mix, all the top flaked off, and she said he was fulla shit—she did say 'shit,' I remember that—"

"Was it true? Could that've happened?"

"What, that it was flakin'? Oh yeah, that happens once in a while. You get too much sand in there sometimes. But whether that was true at his place, with the stones he had, hey, I have no way of knowin' that. I'm just sayin' that's what they was arguin' about, that's all."

"So she was sayin' she didn't think it was necessary,

right? To replace the patio stones that were already there, is that what you're sayin'?"

"Yeah. More or less."

"Uh-ha. Well did you ever hear anything else?"

"Nah, that was about it. Which was enough. I mean, man, sometimes, hey, they'd really be goin' at it. But never in front of his wife, I'll say that much for the old lady. In front of all the guys in the shop, you know, everybody who could hear 'em, yeah, she'd do that, but she never said nothin' to him in front of his wife. Now why, I don't know."

"Okay, Mr. Teslovich, thank you very much for your help. If I think of anything else, I'll give ya a call. You sound like you're feelin' a little better."

"Yeah, you know, I'll live. How's the old lady, she all right?"

"Uh, I don't know yet. I'm in the hospital, I was gonna check on her and I thought of these things I wanted to ask you about, so I'm gonna go find out about how she's doin' right now. Take it easy. Oh. Wait a second, one more thing. You said Mrs. Picadio was doin' the books, right? Gettin' ready to take 'em out to the accountant? Isn't that what you said?"

"Yeah."

"So who's the accountant, you know?"

"Oh, uh, lemme think. Oh. De-somethin', De, De, De—oh. DeFelice. Yeah. He used to be in town, then coupla years ago, he moved out on 30 East. Right out there by that GM dealer, Roscoe's. Same side."

Carlucci thanked him and hung up and added to the notes he'd taken while he was talking. Then he went over to the nurses' station and was told that nobody from the coroner's office had showed up yet. He glanced around and didn't see anybody with a state police uniform on either, so he turned back to the nurse he'd been talking to and asked if she had a roster of all the doctors and surgeons on staff.

She told him she didn't but that the operator on the main switchboard could give him whatever information he needed, so he called and found that there were only three plastic surgeons on staff. He got lucky on his first call. The receptionist who answered in Dr. Joshua Freeman's office remembered Mrs. Alfredo Picadio Jr. very well.

"Doctor was very upset with her. Very upset."

"Why?"

"Because he's a very cautious man, and very professional, which I'm sure you're well aware all doctors have to be these days. Well, most. But she tried to get him to do an implant procedure on her and he examined her and told her she didn't need one and not only would he not do one he wouldn't even refer her to anyone who would do one, not even if she'd had a full mastectomy which she most certainly had not. She hadn't even had any lumps removed, or cysts."

"And you remember this?"

"Well there was a lot more to it than that."

"Oh yeah? So what more was there?"

"Well, after he examined her, he told her both her breasts were healthy, they were just sagging. He told her, he said to her, you're in your fifties, what do you expect, they all sag eventually. Well she didn't want them to sag. She wanted them the way she wanted them and she knew exactly what she wanted. But he told her the companies that made the kind of implants she wanted had been involved in huge litigation, they were being sued for hundreds of millions of dollars. But she didn't care, she wanted what she wanted and she wanted it right now and she got very angry with him when he said he wouldn't do it. And so finally the only way he could get her out of the office was he said if she didn't leave he was going to call the police. So, yes, I remember Mrs. Picadio very well, believe me. And so does Doctor."

"So, uh, in other words, you can't give me the names of any surgeon who might've done it for her, is that what you're sayin'? He didn't give her a referral?"

"That's right. He most definitely did not."

"Well, just for my information here, say he would've done it, you know? Like how much would he've charged for that, just sayin' hypothetically."

"Well, in the first place he wouldn't have done it, and he doesn't do it, and he's not ever going to do it, so I wouldn't even begin to speculate about that. Besides which, I'm not permitted to discuss his fee schedule. You want to know his fees, you'll have to talk to him."

"Yeah, but off the record here, what I'm tryin' to do is find out about the extent of somebody else's debt here, not what your boss charges, you followin' me? I don't care what he charges. Say somebody else. Not your boss. You got any idea what maybe they would charge for that?"

"Off the record? You're never going to come back on me about this?"

"Absolutely not, ma'am. I don't even know your name, I haven't even asked you what your name is, have I? So how could I come back on you?"

"Well, okay," she sang hesitantly. "If somebody were having a silicone implant, in both breasts, I'd say a minimum of three thousand."

"For each or both?"

"Both, my God, both. Three thousand apiece? My God, nobody's that greedy. Listen, I have to go. Bye."

She hung up before Carlucci could thank her.

He leaned against the wall and mulled those figures over. Three large for a new chest? And she also got a new belly and back and face and teeth, man, I'll bet we're talkin' twenty-five, thirty big ones here. Easy. Probably a lot more. Teeth, Jesus, what'd that cap cost me that time? Christ, root canal and all, that was almost seven hundred. For one cap! And the house? Kitchen's got anything like the twelve-hundred-buck fridge, I'll bet that was another twelve, fifteen easy. Bathroom's another six, seven maybe. And they had three bathrooms. And they shut their place down and go to the Bahamas and gamble? Do any of these people know what they're talking about? I'm talkin' to a cook, a truck driver, and now this receptionist, and they give me all this information, all these impressions, these recollections, but this receptionist, she's the first one to maybe confirm that this woman ever actually did anything about wantin' to get a major overhaul. *Maybe confirm*, those are the key words here, Carlucci, don't forget. But all this receptionist is really sayin' is the woman *wanted* to have something done, she didn't know whether the woman ever actually had it done.

All I know is I got a lot of phone calls to make. A lotta calls. So what am I standin' around here for? Coroner's not gonna tell me anything for at least three days, state guy shows up, he's gonna want to take over, run the whole show, I'm gonna be flunkyin' for him, and I don't even know who he is.

"Excuse me?" somebody said, tapping him lightly on the shoulder. The state police had arrived. Tall, thick through the shoulders and neck, small in the waist, pink in the face, he looked like he wasn't old enough to drink. Carlucci's crest fell.

"Nurse says you're the local PD, is that correct?"

"That's me," Carlucci said, extending his hand. "Detective Sergeant Ruggiero Carlucci. Everybody calls me Rugs. At your service."

"Uh, Trooper Milliron. Troop A CID. We have a homicide, is that correct?"

Ouu boy, Trooper. No first name. Is this gonna be fun. "Why don't we go downstairs, whatta ya say? We can probably find us a desk in the coroner's office, and I'll tell ya what we have so far, okay? You wanna do that? Lot easier'n try to write on your lap we stay here."

"Fine. Fine with me. Lead the way."

Carlucci nodded, and hurried downstairs to the first basement where the county coroner, Dr. Wallace Grimes, maintained an office and morgue near the hospital's pathology labs. Carlucci knocked on the coroner's office door, which was slightly ajar, and then went in when he got no answer. Grimes obviously wasn't around, so Carlucci sat at the long table opposite Grimes's desk. Trooper Milliron pulled a chair around the corner of the table and opened his clipboard and got out his pen and looked expectantly at Carlucci.

"Before we do anything," Carlucci said, "I think maybe you oughta call your lab guys and get 'em over to the scene 'cause I didn't do a real good job there, you wanna do that, huh? Here's the address right here. Tell 'em that's my tape on the door, if it's still there, so why don't you go 'head and do that while I hunt us up some coffee. How you want it?"

"Just cream's fine."

"Okay. Go 'head'n use the coroner's phone."

Trooper Milliron was still poised to start writing, but he shrugged and got up immediately and was heading for the phone as Carlucci went next door to the pathology lab to scrounge some coffee. He came back with two paper cups full of coffee and set them on the table just as Milliron was resuming his seat.

Carlucci took a long sip of coffee and said, "They gonna do it?"

"They're on their way," Milliron said.

Carlucci took another long, slow sip of coffee, studying Milliron over the rim. Finally he put the cup down and said,

"Look, I may as well tell ya somethin' right now. You're gonna hear it sooner or later so you may as well hear it from me. I don't know fuck about fingerprints. I've read all the books you're supposed to read, I've taken all the courses you guys give, and, uh, nothin'. That stuff goes right over the top. I look at those swirls and loops, I might as well be lookin' at Chinese writing, you know? So I don't even bother tryin' to lift 'em anymore. I know I can't testify about 'em, I can't identify 'em, my fuckin' hands shake when I try to lift 'em, so I don't even fuck with them anymore. So I'm pretty much a joke about them, is what I'm sayin'. I'm used to it, I can take it, but that's really why I told you you had to get your lab guys up there, okay? I also didn't sweep the place. Otherwise, I generally know what I'm doin'."

"Well," Trooper Milliron said, smiling wanly and clearing his throat. "Since I guess you'll find it out soon enough yourself, I guess I ought to tell you this is my first homicide. Not the first first. I mean I've seen my share, but, uh, this is my first in CID."

"Your first as an investigator in other words."

"Right. Yes."

"Uh-huh. Uh, you got a first name, besides Trooper?"

"Sorry. Claude. My father's people came from France. And, uh, I was pretty much sick of people spelling it C-L-O-D by the time I got to the third grade."

"Well how'd you like to have 'Ruggiero'? I get it with one G, two G's, IE, EI, two E's, no E's, sometimes I forget how to spell it myself. Everybody calls me Rugs anyway. I already said that, didn't I?"

"Yes you did. What do you think they call me—as if Claude's not bad enough. Pinky. 'Cause of my complexion, naturally. And then my middle name, I was named after my mother's father. Clement. Claude Clement Pinky Milliron. And then people look at my name and they say, Mill-iron—

is that how you pronounce it? I say, no. Mill-i-ron, not Mill-iron, Mill-i-ron. And they go, Ohhhh. Names, boy, they're somethin'. So, uh, what do we have here?"

"Well, Claude—is that okay? Claude?"

"Sure. That's fine."

"Okay. What we have here, Claude, is probably what started out as a burglary that turned into a rape and an assault, which has now turned into a homicide, robbery, and car theft, not necessarily in that order, but all I really know is it was a rape and an aggravated assault and a car theft. I'm guessin' it started out as a burglary, and the coroner's gonna say whether it's a homicide or not, although I don't have any doubts about that. I'm also pretty sure the car thief is dead, but I'm guessin' about that—I mean I'm not guessin' he's dead. Somebody that was found in this woman's car—the rape victim's car—is dead. What I'm guessin' about, but what I'm pretty sure about, is he was the burglar and the rapist, but we gotta wait for Allegheny County to tell us whether he's the rapist or not, 'cause he's in their morgue and if they did the post on him yet I haven't heard about it. And your lab's gonna say for sure whether he was on the scene and whether he was the rapist whenever they get the rape workup from Allegheny County to match up with what the ER people here took from the woman . . . who just died. You followin' me so far?"

"I think so."

"Well, it gets better—or worse, dependin' how you wanna look at it. So here goes, you ready?"

Milliron nodded, and Carlucci, referring to his notes repeatedly, filled in as much as he had. It took almost forty-five minutes of Carlucci's steady talking and Milliron's steady writing before he finally had to stop and shake out the cramps in his fingers.

"The problems, as I see them," Carlucci said, standing and

stretching, "not to mention locating the NOK, are these. Since there were no signs of forced entry, that means that either the door was unlocked, which I find hard to believe, since she was workin' there alone, after dark, that she would not lock the door. It's possible she *forgot,* but that just strikes me as not too probable. A woman, her age, workin' alone, used to livin' alone, I don't think she would forget that. But then maybe she did forget, I don't know.

"What complicates this for me," Carlucci went on, "is the Pittsburgh detective sayin' to me—stressin' it really—that the shootee found in her car was not a travelin' man. He made a very strong point of sayin' that to me. He said almost exactly these words: the shootee was a true homeboy, the shootee did not habitually leave his 'hood. So now, that, coupled with the disappearance of the cook's nephew—with all the cook's money coincidentally—gives me very strange feelings about this."

"Strange in what way, I don't understand. I also don't understand some of the words you're using. Like 'homeboy' and, uh, 'hood,' what's that?"

"Where you from, Claude? Where were you born, raised?"

"Mercer. Well not in Mercer exactly. My parents have a farm—had, they don't have it anymore—about four miles out of town. It was pretty remote. You could only see four other farms, so I'd guess you'd say it was real remote."

"Where is 'at, Mercer? I mean I've heard of it, I just can't place it right offhand."

"It's on U.S. 19 about, oh, seventy miles north of Pittsburgh. Nineteen cuts right through town, it's the main street. It's about sixteen, seventeen miles north of New Castle, about fifteen northwest of Grove City, about twenty-five south of Meadville. It's about a lot of miles from a lot of places I guess," Milliron said, grinning sheepishly.

"Any black people there?"

"No, not really. You want to see black people, you'd have to go to New Castle or Meadville. Now if you want to know about Amish people, there's a lot of them around there. I know a lot about them."

"Yeah, well, ain't too many of them around here, that's for sure. Anyway, 'homeboy' is black slang, usually affectionate, for what one young black guy calls another. 'He's my homeboy,' or, 'He's my homey,' like that."

"I thought they didn't like the word 'boy.' I was told never to use that term in a potentially volatile situation, like if I was surrounded by them at an accident scene."

"They don't. I don't know why 'homeboy's' okay, but it is—if they're sayin' it. I don't know how they'd take it if you or I was sayin' it. And 'hood,' that's just short for neighborhood, that's all."

Milliron chewed his lower lip and made a note of this, and while he was writing, he said, "So why is this a problem again?"

"Because this detective, who is also black—I did say that, didn't I—he's black?"

"Yes, you did."

"Well, he's had a lot of dealings with this homeboy. Knew his mother and father, went to school with 'em, knew his mother very well, I guess maybe he had eyes for her at one time. The point is, when he said the shootee would not have come out of his 'hood without great cause, I took that to mean that either somebody scared the shit out of him or else somebody hung a great big carrot in front of him. Somethin' had to make him wanna move his butt to Rocksburg, no matter how temporarily, you get what I'm sayin'?"

"Yes, I think I do."

"Well that's the problem—what would make him leave his 'hood and come to that place, of all places in the world? It's a big world, man, why would he come to that place? I mean, he wasn't on some kinda rape rampage. We don't have any reports about a one-man crime wave, or even a two-man crime wave, you know? Him or anybody else cuttin' a path from Pittsburgh to Rocksburg. No other car thefts reported at approximately the same time. No other assaults, no other robberies involving a single black male or even two black males that remotely correspond to this guy, so what the fuck was he doin' there, is my problem. Why, of all places in the world, does he go to Rocksburg Pre-Cast Concrete Company, you follow me?"

"Yes, I follow you, but aren't you assuming some things? I mean, you just said yourself, the only admissible piece of evidence you have so far, if I heard you right, the only way you can connect him to the woman is the fact that he was found shot in her—what was it? Pontiac? Yes, Pontiac."

"Yep, you got it. That's it—until the lab guys tell us otherwise. But I think they will. I think they're gonna connect the fibers in her jaw and cheek and head with the sap they found on him, and I think they're gonna match up hair and semen with him and her, and I think they're gonna find sand and cement on his shoes which came from that office. I don't think there's gonna be any doubt he's our guy. But that still doesn't answer the question, Claude. There's six billion people on the planet, man—why'd he leave his 'hood to come to that place to rape that woman? 'Cause don't forget the cook's nephew, he's no cherry. All that hard time in Ohio? What I'm sayin' is, your guys find him, we're gonna know a whole lot we don't know now."

"So you're saying this started with the cook's nephew?"

"Not necessarily."

"Well then are you saying the cook started it? The old woman? With the bad knees? Who carries a .25?"

Carlucci shrugged. "Nah. Maybe, but I don't think so, nah. Course, you might get a whole different impression when you talk to her, I don't know. You should talk to everybody I talked to. Cause you shouldn't be takin' my word for any of this. I think you should be double-checkin' every step I made. I just think it would help us a whole lot more if we could talk to her nephew. Uh, speakin' of which, why don't you go put a bigger bug in your guys' ears, you know? I already did that, but I think it might be better if it came from you, you know?"

Milliron stood without hesitation and went back to Grimes's desk and picked up the phone. Carlucci watched him, his movements full of a youthful, eager sense of purpose, and couldn't help smiling. Maybe this wasn't going to be as bad as he'd thought. He'd worked with some state troopers who'd busted his balls from beginning to end, but this kid might turn out to be all right. So far, all he'd been was curious, courteous, and cooperative, the three best qualities an investigator from another department could have, as far as Carlucci was concerned. Still, it was early, and Milliron might be showing the three C's because this was his cherry, his first homicide investigation. Carlucci took another sip of coffee, screwed up his face, and went looking for a place to dump it. He went back to the pathology lab where he'd scrounged it in the first place and poured it into a sink. When he came back, he found Milliron leaning back in his chair and smiling.

"You're lookin' happy, what's up?"

"The Pennsylvania State Police get their man again."

"Givins? You're shittin' me."

"Black male, late twenties, in a black Oldsmobile with Ohio plates tried to get away without paying for a tank of gas in Sharon. Sharon PD patrol unit was a block away when the attendant called. Booked him, ID'd him, and then they saw your detainer, so now all we have to do is get a warrant and go get him. How 'bout that?"

"No shit," Carlucci said. "That's beautiful. Where's Sharon?"

"Oh that's up in my country. Sharon's about twenty miles from Mercer, about fifteen miles from the Ohio line. You want me to go get him?"

"They got the car too, right? We want the car too. You arrange that? Have it towed back?"

"Well, I don't think we could do it until Monday or Tuesday, but why not? I clear it with the lieutenant, he authorizes a search warrant for it, I get it, and then we hire a tow truck and we're ready to roll. In fact, I'm ready to roll right now, you?"

"Wait a minute. Anybody say anything about a gun? They find a nine?"

Milliron shook his head and shrugged. "Nobody said anything about a gun."

"Oh man they gotta find a gun. You get back to your station? Before you get the warrant? You call 'em, okay? And tell 'em toss that car, man, they gotta find that gun."

"Okay. I'll tell them. What're you gonna do?"

"Huh? Oh. I gotta make a lotta phone calls," Carlucci said. "I wanna know some other things before I get with Luther. I wanna be real prepared before I start talkin' to him."

Milliron shrugged and frowned. "Why? Seems to me like if you're going fishing with him, you have the best bait in the world. His aunt's boss was raped, robbed, and beaten up so bad she died. That's homicide in the commission of at least two other felonies. And he has two felony convictions. Seems to me like all you have to do is lay it out for him."

"Yeah yeah, I know. Oughta be that simple, but, uh, I don't think it's gonna be. In the meantime, uh, lemme think here, how do I wanna say this? I don't want you to take this the wrong way, Claude, okay? But you gotta promise me something."

"What's that?"

"Don't get upset now, okay? Don't get uptight on me, I'm just thinkin' about the case here, not you, not me, not anything else, okay?"

"Yeah," Milliron said, perplexed. "Just go ahead and say it, Detective. Rugs. I'm not upset."

"Okay. When you're bringin' him back? In the car? From the time you pick him up, till the time you get him booked? Don't say one word to him about this, okay? I know you're gonna want to, that's just natural, you're gonna want to try to get anything out of him you can, but you can't, man. You can't. You gotta promise me."

"Well I wasn't intending to anyway, but why're you so intense about this?"

"Well hell, if you weren't—if you didn't have any intentions yourself," Carlucci said, shrugging, "you don't need to know why. Why weren't you goin' to?"

"Well, I might be new at this, but I have been trained. I think I know enough not to say anything to him."

"Well, right. Sure you have. But you know what I do? Huh? You wanna know what I do? Maybe you don't care what I do, but in case you do, you know? Just to make sure the shysters don't try to scam me? Huh? I carry a tape recorder, man. Voice-activated. I get every word. I had a fuckin' shyster screw a case for me once about what I said when I was bringin' a suspect back in the car, and I said I'd never let that shit happen to me again, no matter what. Man, you just watch'n see how fast they shut up when you play the tape. I say, here, fuckhead, this is what I said, and this is what your client said, and you will notice there is not one word about me tryin' to scam a confession out of him."

Milliron smiled appreciatively. "Pretty neat. Your department provide you with that?"

"Oh fuck no, man, I had to buy it myself. I can let ya use

it. I'm not gonna need it. I got it right out in my car, c'mon, let's go get it. Just put fresh batteries in it. Fits right in your shirt pocket. Saved my ass a coupla times, I'm tellin' ya. I also use it sometimes when I'm takin' notes, you know? When people look like they're gettin' uptight when they see me writin'? I use it a lot. You oughta get yourself one, I'm tellin' ya."

They were heading for the door when Coroner Grimes walked in. He grunted a greeting at Carlucci and went to his desk and put some manila folders in the bottom left drawer. "Something I can do for you gentlemen?"

"No, sir," Carlucci said. "Hope you don't mind we were usin' your office. How long you think before you get to the post on that woman?"

"If you're referring to Mrs. Picadio Senior, that's why I'm here. Would've been here sooner, got hung up in traffic out on 30. Must've been an accident. I'm beginning to think automobile traffic wasn't what God had in mind."

"You know her, Doc? Sounds like you know her."

"Very slightly. Knew her husband much better. Went to high school with him. Excuse me, but I have to get moving on this. Call me in a couple of hours, I'll let you know."

"Couple hours?" Milliron said. "Wow, I thought it'd be a couple days at least."

"I don't have anything else right now," Grimes said. "So it will depend. Nothing unusual? Maybe forty-five minutes. Something comes up? Couple of hours. Don't expect the report for three days. Excuse me. Close the door on your way out, please."

As Grimes went to his locker and started to change clothes, Carlucci led Milliron out and to the elevator to the parking garage.

"He any good?" Milliron said once they were in the elevator.

"Grimes? My experience with him is, he's as good as you get around here. I don't recall him ever fuckin' up, if that's what you mean."

"He's actually a pathologist? A forensic pathologist?"

"Yup. And keeps gettin' reelected. Sometimes it actually works like it's supposed to."

Carlucci led the way to his car and gave Milliron a crash course in his voice-activated tape recorder. "Believe me," Carlucci said, "if *I* can work it, anybody can work it. An electronic genius I ain't. So now, after you get the warrant, you're bringin' him back to the county lockup, right? You're not takin' him back to Troop A, right?"

"Right, yes."

"Okay, so how long you think it'll take you?"

Milliron smiled. "I'll tell you, the one thing I miss about highway patrol is the chance to put a well-tuned automobile on a modern road. I'll say, oh, I don't know, fifty-five, sixty minutes from the time I pick up the warrant till I get to Sharon. I'm lookin' forward to it. I used to drive Go Karts. Actually, I was driving Go Karts about four years before I could drive on the road. Course now, the warrant, I can't control the speed of that. This duty DJ? She's in the Rocksburg Mall, is that right?"

Carlucci gave him the directions to the mall and to the district justice's office on the lower level and said he'd be looking for Milliron's return within three hours. They exchanged cards and wished each other luck.

Carlucci drove back to his station, circling City Hall once to make sure the mayor's Chrysler wasn't around, then went inside and checked in with Fischetti.

"Yo, Fish, you come up with anything on the remodelers?"

"Hey Rugs, it's Saturday, man."

"I know what day it is. You get anything or not?"

"All I got was answerin' machines except for a plumbin' contractor. McGann. Said he rebuilt their bathrooms. Here's his number, but I don't think you're gonna get him anymore today. Said he was gonna be on a job till four, four-thirty, then he was gonna go home'n get cleaned up and take his old lady out for dinner, it was her birthday or somethin'."

Carlucci copied the plumber's name and number into his notebook, thanked Fischetti, and went into Balzic's office and closed the door. He checked the Yellow Pages under accountants until he found the number for DeFelice Associates and found Angelo T. DeFelice, CPA, listed under that and then went through the White Pages until he found DeFelice's home number. He got an answering machine and left a message in his most official voice for DeFelice to call him.

Then he went through a Pittsburgh Yellow Pages looking for plastic surgeons before dropping his pen on the desk and rubbing his eyes and thinking, What am I doin' here, it's Saturday, none of these people're gonna be answerin' their phones. He sighed and leaned back in the chair and closed his eyes and rolled his neck five times in one direction and then five times the other way. He was in the middle of his third long exhale in a kind of meditation he'd been trying for some months to learn when the phone rang.

"Detective Carlucci? Angelo DeFelice returning your call. What can I do for you? Is this my business or yours? You need an accountant or, God forbid, do I need a lawyer?"

"Neither one, I don't think. Listen, uh, Mr. DeFelice—"

"Angelo, please. Call me Angelo."

"Okay. Angelo. You have clients named Picadio? Rocksburg Pre-Cast Concrete Company?"

"Oh yes. Sure. As long as I've had my own business, yes. Is there a problem?"

"Well I'm not sure. That's what I'm tryin' to find out."

"You mean with them personally? Or the business?"

"Well both actually. But start with the business. They okay there? They payin' their bills, stayin' ahead of the IRS, like that?"

"Well, Detective, uh, I'm sure you know that without a court order, I'm not going to discuss my clients with you. Not specifically. You do know that, right? Am I right in assuming you do?"

"Uh, Angelo, I'm not asking you for specifics. If I was, if I wanted to see the books, I'd be handin' you a warrant. That's not what I'm tryin' to do here. All I'm tryin' to do here is find out in general terms, you know, a sorta casual phone conversation, you know? Between you and me to find out maybe whether I need to get a warrant. I don't wanna have to go get a warrant. I don't wanna go creepin' and crawlin' through your books, Angelo, believe me. Not unless I absolutely have to. And right now I don't think I have to. But I don't think I'm bein' out of line if all I'm askin' is, you know, is the company in trouble? Are they payin' their bills, are they straight with the tax people, are they payin' their employees, that's all I'm askin'. I'm not askin' how much they're behind in their taxes, I'm just askin' if they are, that's all, you understand me now?"

"I think so."

"So?"

"So no. The company's not in any trouble with anybody."

Carlucci waited, but DeFelice added nothing else.

"So, Angelo? If the company's not in trouble, what's the rest? Is Mrs. Picadio Senior in trouble? Mr. Picadio Junior? Are they your clients as well—outside of the business I mean? You do their personal taxes?"

"Yes."

"Yes what? C'mon, Angelo, don't turn me into a hard-ass

here, I hate that. Just tell me, yes or no, you do personal work for them?"

"Yes I do."

"For the mother, for the son, for the wife, the daughter-in-law, which?"

"All."

"And? C'mon, Angelo, you're makin' this way harder'n it has to be."

"Uh, Detective, I'm thinking about my liability here. And I understand what you're trying to do, but I'm thinking that, uh, maybe it would be wiser for me if I called my attorney and talked to him before I continued to talk to you. So, uh, I'm going to hang up now and then I'm going to call him and then I'll get back to you, okay? Is that satisfactory? Well, it's gonna have to be, that was a stupid question. Good-bye, Detective." Then he hung up.

Way to go, Carlucci, took you less than two minutes to fuck that one up. How'd I fuck that up? I had him. The hook was in his mouth, he was in the boat, now he's swimmin' away, how the fuck'd that happen? That's ridiculous. What'd I say was so scary? Shit. Let him get away without even promisin' when he was gonna call back.

He flipped pages in his notebook looking for the number of the plumber Fischetti had talked to. He got a machine, but as soon as he identified himself after the tone, a woman picked up and said, "Frank's not here now. This is Gloria. What's this about? This is the second time you guys've called. What's goin' on with you guys? Somethin' goin' on? I'm startin' to get real nervous here."

"Mrs. McGann?"

"Yes, I'm Mrs. McGann. You gonna tell me what's goin' on?"

"I wanna talk to your husband about a job—"

"You mean for you? He did a job for you? Or you want him to do a job, what?"

"Oh no ma'am. Nothin' for me. A job he did for somebody else."

"He did a job for somebody else and the cops are callin'? Hey, it's not like we don't get complaints, but usually they go to the Better Business Bureau—"

"No no no, ma'am, no, no, gimme a second here, I'll explain." Jesus, what the fuck, can't I talk anymore or what? "Listen, let me start over here, okay? There's no problem here. Not with you, or your husband, or his business or any job he did, okay? All I wanna know is two things—three: I wanna confirm that your husband did a job for somebody and what the price was and that your husband got paid, that's all I wanna do, nothin' else, you follow me now?"

"Yeah. I follow you. But you're the police. Why do you wanna know that if there's nothin' wrong, that's what I don't get."

Carlucci swallowed and thought for a second. "Well, listen, ma'am, maybe I should be talkin' to your husband, you know, I mean, it's his business, right? He would know more about it than you—"

"Oh, wrong, wrong. What Frank does is take the old pipes out and put the new ones in. I do the rest. You wanna know whether we did a job and whether we got paid, you don't ask Frank. Frank, God bless him, I love him, but all Frank knows about money is he drives me to the bank every Friday. Believe me, if I died tomorrow? Frank would faint when he found out how much it'd cost to replace me."

"Oh right, sure, I see," Carlucci said, swallowing hard and feeling lucky that he hadn't alienated her. "I'm talkin' to the absolutely right person here. So, uh, Mrs. McGann, does the name Picadio ring any bells with you?"

"Picadio? Sure. Which one, Mrs.? Junior? Senior's dead you know."

"You had dealings with 'em all?"

"Oh sure. My dad and Mr. Picadio, the old man, they did a lotta jobs together, sure. And even Frank did some jobs with the old man. A lotta the plans out in the townships, back in the forties and fifties, after the war, when I was just a little girl, my mother used to take me out on the jobs almost every day, we'd eat lunch with my dad, oh my God yes, they had so much work then, I'll never forget that. And I would always see Mr. Picadio. His crew would be like five, six houses ahead of my dad, puttin' in the foundations and all the brickwork, and then they'd come back later and do all the rest, the patios and the wall stone around the driveways and the stepping-stones. And we always had their business, sure. They poured the cellar and built the foundation for this house and laid all the bricks, oh yeah. This was probably the last job he did before he died. He finished up here and he died, like, oh God, two weeks later. Was it two weeks? Yeah, two weeks, I'm sure. So you wanna know about a job we did for them? And whether they paid us? I can tell you right now, they don't owe us a cent."

"Always paid their bills?"

"Always. Within the month."

"All of them?"

"Every one. All of them."

"Your husband just remodeled the bathrooms in Junior's house, is that right?"

"Well not just. But yeah. That was, oh Jeez, a year ago last November I think Frank started that job. I could check if you wanna know exactly. But, yeah. He did all the bathrooms. Three. Yeah. And a powder room."

"You remember what the bill was?"

"If you wanna know exactly I have to go to the office—"

"No no no, don't do that. Just gimme a ballpark number, that's all."

"Oh, ballpark? Seventeen, seventeen-five."

"You're talkin' thousands, right?"

"Oh please," she said, laughing. "Three full baths? Five thousand apiece. Twenty-five hundred for the powder room. Good plumbin' ain't cheap, hon. He didn't get top of the line, by any means, but he was a long way from the bottom, I can tell you that."

"And you didn't have to chase him."

"Chase him? Oh absolutely not. No. He gave me a check for five when him and his wife picked out the fixtures'n hardware. We got the rest the week after I sent him the bill. Oh, hon, the whole family, they've always been like that. I don't know how they are with anybody else, but with us they're good as gold. And I never heard anything from anybody else about 'em. Is that what you wanna know?"

"And Junior paid you himself? He wrote the checks? Not his wife, not his mother. Him, right?"

"Yes, he did. He signed the contract, he signed the checks."

"Uh, did he ever say anything, hint around maybe, like he might wanna pay cash, huh?"

She didn't say anything for a long moment. "Listen, we're both adults here, right? I'm not gonna try to tell you we did-n't try to do some cash business when we were gettin' started, but, hon, believe me, somebody comes back com-plainin' about a job you did? And all you have is a buncha twenties in a drawer and no contract? Hon, believe me, you got a bigger headache than the one you were tryin' to avoid. We haven't been that young or that dumb for thirty years."

"Okay, Mrs. McGann, I understand. Thanks for takin'

time out to talk to me, I know it's Saturday, I really appreciate it."

"Well, you're very welcome, but listen, hon, as long as we're on the phone here, you know, we used to get a lotta city business when ol' Bellotti, when he was mayor before Strohn got in, you know? So do you ever, you know, have any conversations with the mayor about these things? Like maybe if the city needed some new toilets down at the ball fields or something, whatta ya think? You think you could mention we were still in business, drop a little hint? Couldn't hurt, right?"

"Uh, Mrs. McGann, believe me, I been talkin' to the mayor a lot lately, more than I want to sometimes, but, uh, usually plumbin' is not what we talk about, you know? But listen, if it ever comes up, you know, I'll be sure to mention your name, I will. Promise. Thanks again for your help."

He hung up before she could say anything else, and he sat there rubbing his temples and thinking, wondering how long he should wait for Angelo DeFelice to get back to him. He waited about a minute, then dialed DeFelice's number again, and after he got the tone on the message, he said, "Detective Carlucci again, Mr. DeFelice. I hope you got with your lawyer and I hope you're gettin' everything straight in your own mind about your liability and so on, but what I wanna say now is, I'm sure your lawyer reminded you what you already know—your communication with your clients is not protected, it's not privileged, so get back to me, okay? Soon."

He dropped the phone into the cradle, then sat there staring at it, his face screwed up so much that after a minute or so he had to remind himself to let his jaw drop and relax. He stood, walked in a small circle around the tiny office, which was hardly bigger than one of the interview rooms. He dropped back onto the chair and dialed Balzic's number. Balzic picked up, slightly out of breath on the ninth ring.

"It's Rugs, Mario. Hope I didn't get you outta the can."

"Naw, uh-uh, I was downstairs cleanin' out the cellar. Can't believe all the junk I been squirrelin' away, Christ. I came on a pile of *Life* magazines from 1944, can you believe it? My mother musta had 'em. They had me trapped for about two hours, yeah. So what's up?"

"Uh, you think Dom Muscotti'd talk to me?"

"Depends what you wanna talk about. You know he's retired, right? You do know that, right?"

"Yeah, I remember when you told me that, sure. But he didn't go deaf, right?"

"No, I'm sure he didn't."

"Well you think he'd talk to me? How would I approach him—I mean, how *should* I approach him, should I ask him to go in his back room? Should I give him a call first, what?"

"Nah nah, just go in, get him aside, you know—which may not always be easy, 'cause depends what time of day it is, you never know how much he had to drink, you know? So try to get him as early as you can—"

"Would now be okay?"

"Now? Sure. Should be all right. Sure, just go in there, just walk up to him, uh, lean over to his side, don't get in his face, and say, uh, Mr. Muscotti, I'm not sure you remember me, but then, introduce yourself, and then, uh, remind him when I first introduced ya. And tell him I said I thought it was okay for you to approach him, and tell him you got a problem that you think maybe he could help you with."

"So you think he'll help me?"

"Depends, Rugs. If he's half-shitface, forget it. He'll just bust your balls. But then, you gotta remember, he's still real pissed off about the way he got retired. They really jagged him off, so he's real touchy about that. My best advice to

you is, you know, treat him like he was still the goombah.
Besides which, you get to be chief, sooner or later, you're
gonna have to deal with who replaced him, so you might as
well start findin' out every fuckin' thing you can from him.
See, I made a mistake with you. I shoulda brought you
around more—"

"Yeah, Mario, I know, but I think you did the right thing
by tellin' me to keep my distance—"

"Yeah of course, but I did it for the wrong reason. I was
actin' like I was fuckin' bulletproof, you know? And that
was stupid, 'cause here I am, and there you are, and, uh—ah
what the fuck. Just one more mistake I made. So learn from
this, Rugs. You're never as fuckin' invulnerable as you think
you are. You're never bulletproof. The case is more important than you are, the job's more important. Remember? I
used to tell ya, if the case is worth prosecutin', then you
gotta assume that you're gonna be in a wreck or somethin'
and somebody else is gonna have to read your notes and take
it over, and if your notes are fucked up, if your case file's
fucked up, then how are they gonna prosecute the case? You
remember how many times I told you that?"

"Yeah, course I do."

"Well, see, with Muscotti, I kept everything in my head.
And now you gotta start over with him, and I didn't pay attention to what I was tellin' you, that's what I'm sayin'. I
didn't want anybody to say you might even look like you
were gettin' crumby around the edges, so I kept you outta
there—ah what the fuck. You'll make your own connection
with him. And with whoever took it away from him."

"You still don't know who that was, huh?"

"Somebody from New Kensington, that's all I'm sure of.
Probably one of Gerry Colella's guys, but I'm not sure.
Coulda been from another branch of the family up there. The
Masciolo side, I don't know. But you develop Muscotti the

best way you can, then see which way the bikers are leanin',
the Pagans? I know they got hurt real bad seven, eight years
ago. The feds did a job on 'em, but, uh, that doesn't mean
they dried up and blew away. Muscotti wouldn't touch 'em,
he wouldn't let those fuckers in his place. Which is probably
why he's retired, now that I think about it. He used to get on
me about bustin' 'em for violatin' the noise ordinance if he
heard 'em ridin' through town, so you know they were
makin' all that crank for somebody in New Ken. They
weren't doin' it for him, and they sure as hell weren't doin'
it on their own. They ain't smart enough, and the market's
too big.

"But to get back to your original question, whatta you
wanna see him about, maybe I can help ya."

"Nah, I already talked to you about it. Picadio, remember? Although, wait a minute, at that time, I was just askin'
if you knew 'em. I didn't ask you if the kid, Alfredo Junior,
if he had any problems with gamblin'—did I say anything
like that? I don't think I did. I'm sure I didn't. I think all we
talked about was the old man and his wife, the parents,
right?"

"No, right, that's all I remember. So what's with the son?
Junior."

"I don't know for sure. There's somethin' not addin' up
right. You ever hear of him havin' problems with his bookie?
Anything like that—that's what I wanna talk to Muscotti
about."

"Um, no. Nah, you're gonna have to talk to Muscotti. Just
do it the way I told ya. He gives you any shit, tell him I'll
vouch for ya, tell him to call me. But go in expectin' shit,
'cause he likes playin' with people."

"Okay, Mario. Thanks. Sorry to bother ya on Saturday."

"C'mon, Rugs, Christ, all I got is Saturdays, I thought I
told ya that. My life ain't nothin' but. Christ, I'm cleanin'

out the cellar, whatta you think? I'm drinkin' here at night, I'm sittin' around wonderin' maybe I should apply for a PI license, that's what I've come to. You know what women say about a woman's work is never done, huh? I used to laugh at that shit. But they're right. They are never done. And now I'm doin' it—all the stuff Ruthie couldn't do by herself. So for chrissake don't ever think twice about callin' me, you know? I don't give a fuck what it is, call me. I don't want you to think I'm beggin' here, Rugs, but fuck it, facts're facts, understand?"

"Sure, Mario, sure. Hey, you know, you don't have to tell me this, Christ, they make me chief I'll be callin' you every half hour."

"Okay, Rugs, okay. Thanks. I mean it. Thanks."

"For what?"

"For callin' me. I appreciate it."

Carlucci felt his brow going up. "Hey, Mario, thank you." Then he said good-bye and hung up. He leaned back in Balzic's chair and whistled softly and said, "Wow. Not even a month he's gone. Holy shit."

He looked at the phone for a long moment, but he knew that no matter how long he sat there looking at it, he was never going to know whether Angelo DeFelice was going to return his call. He put on his parka and headed out past Fischetti who, as near as Carlucci could determine, was trying to mollify a citizen who was complaining that her neighbor's teenage daughter was attracting at least four boys every afternoon after school who thought the best way to impress the girl was to smart off to her elderly neighbors. Carlucci offered Fischetti no consolation. He printed a note about where he was going and pushed it toward Fischetti and headed for his cruiser. The wind was whipping in hard swirls, and the clouds were spitting icy rain again. Carlucci lowered his face into the fake fur of his hood and turned his back to the wind and trotted to his cruiser, wondering how long he could make one beer last in Muscotti's.

"Mr. Muscotti," Carlucci said when he was within arm's reach of the burly old man sitting at the end of the bar. "You remember me? Rugs Carlucci. Chief Balzic introduced us." He extended his hand.

Muscotti took Carlucci's fingers and shook them once, weakly.

"You got a minute, Mr. Muscotti?"

"Do I got a minute? Kid, I got a cellar full of 'em. I rent 'em out. Fifty bucks apiece. How come you only want one? I ain't gonna make no money that way."

"You know what I mean," Carlucci said, feeling immediately stupid for having said it. He dropped his gaze and swallowed, remembering what Balzic had said about Muscotti wanting to play with him, wanting to bust his balls. Why'd I have to say that, you know what I mean. Christ.

"Do I know what you mean? How would I know that? Hey, Vinnie, you hearin' this?" Muscotti called out to his bartender. "I'm a mind reader now. I know what this guy means. Whatta ya think of that, huh? Holy crappola, I'm in the wrong business. I'm supposed to be in a carny. Dressed up like some friggin' Gypsy, whatta ya think, kid, huh? What's your name again? Rugs? Why they call you that, huh? People walk on you? People step all over you, huh, is 'at why they call you that? Rugs. I was you, Monday mornin' I'd be in the courthouse, I'd be changin' my name."

"Oh yeah?" Carlucci said, forcing himself to look directly into Muscotti's eyes, which were glinting with mean delight. "What would you change it to?"

"I'd change it to Mister. Then no matter how friggin' friendly people thought they was with me, they'd still have to call me Mister. And I wouldn't put up with no abbreviations either. They wouldn't be callin' me Miss, for instance. What're ya, ya gonna stand there all day, ya gonna drink somethin', what?"

"Uh. Beer. Draft beer's okay," Carlucci said quickly, adding even more quickly, "Can I get you one? Lemme get you one."

"Oh," Muscotti said, drawing his head back in mock surprise. "I mistook you. Not only am I gonna get rich, I'm gonna get drunk too. Sit right down here, young fella." Muscotti patted the stool beside him. "I can see our conversation is gonna be long and fruitful. Yessir. Hey, Vinnie, give my new best friend a beer here—what's it gonna be, Rugs, huh? Rollin' Rock? Iron City, what?"

"Rollin' Rock's fine, that's fine for me. What're you gonna have?" Oh God, Carlucci, what're you gonna have, is that what I said? Shut the fuck up.

"Well, I'll tell ya what I'm gonna have, Rugs," Muscotti said. "One you said you were gonna buy me, right? One? So I think what I'm gonna have is, uh, one bottle of Canadian Club. I'm just not gonna drink it all at once, you know what I mean? I'm gonna drink it one shot at a time. But just so you don't have to be reachin' in your pocket all the time, you can buy it for me all at once. Whatta ya think, huh? Two bucks a shot? Vinnie don't spill none, he'll get twenty-four, twenty-five shots outta there. You got forty-eight bucks, Rugs? Or do I needa cash your paycheck maybe?"

"Uh, Mr. Muscotti," Rugs said, clearing his throat and looking at his shoes, "I seem to, uh, I seem to have gotten off on the wrong foot with you here, and I don't know why—"

"Lemme stop you right there, kid," Muscotti said, standing and walking toward the back room. He turned and crooked his finger at Carlucci and said, "C'mon. Let's go in the back. Bring your beer. Vinnie, bring him his beer, c'mon." Muscotti set off through the kitchen, Carlucci suddenly hurrying to keep up, but then turning back when the bartender called out to him to wait for his glass of beer, which Vinnie handed to him with a bored smirk.

Muscotti was already sitting when Carlucci walked into the back room. There were three round tables identical to the ones out in the bar, but the finish on these tables had been worn away around the outside edge by all the elbows of all the card players from all the gin and poker games. Muscotti was sitting at the one farthest from the kitchen door. It was less than twenty feet from the door to the table, but Carlucci felt like he was slogging through ankle-deep mud to get to it. Muscotti's once red hair had long ago turned the color of concrete and his neck was loose with flesh, but his gaze was as blue-gray as the finish on a pistol, as hard as it had been the first time Carlucci had ever seen it, and it was aimed at him now.

Carlucci managed somehow to get across the room, saying to himself every step of the way, This is crazy. This old man's retired for crissake. He doesn't carry any weight with anybody anymore. And I'm queasy in my guts just lookin' at him. This is nuts.

Carlucci started to pull out a chair for himself, but Muscotti said, "I said we could talk back here, I didn't say nothin' about you sittin' down."

Carlucci froze. The hell with this, he thought, enough's enough. He started to protest, but before he could say anything, Muscotti said, "You walk in off the street, you introduce yourself to me, you think you gotta remind me who you are, you think you gotta remind me who introduced you to me. Then just 'cause you wanna know somethin', you're gonna buy me a drink. One drink. And that's all it's s'posed to take. The price of one shot of Canadian Club, I'm s'posed to throw my arms around you like I'm some hooker and you got a Popeye suit on. Maybe you didn't notice, Ruggiero, but I ain't wearin' a skirt. I'm a dinosaur, that's a fact. But I ain't gonna let nobody insult me the way you just did. I look stupid to you?"

"No sir, you don't," Carlucci said, trying his best to return Muscotti's hard gaze with his own. It wasn't working. He couldn't do it. "I, uh, I don't understand what I did that was so wrong. I talked to Chief Balzic before I came here. I asked him how I should approach you. He said if you gave me a hard time, I was, uh, I was supposed to tell you to give him a call. He would vouch for me—"

"Is that a fact? He's gonna vouch for you? Oh, so I'm s'posed to be impressed now, right? I'm s'posed to roll right over, is 'at it? I'm s'posed to split my skull open for ya and let you reach around in there till you find whatever you're lookin' for, is 'at it?"

"No sir. I didn't say anything about rollin' over. I didn't say anything about splittin' your skull. I didn't use any of those words. Maybe I said some stupid things, I'm not sayin' I didn't. But I didn't come in here and leave my manners outside like some jerk."

"Oh is 'at right? You didn't, huh? Lemme ask you somethin', Ruggiero. Detective. Detective Sergeant. You been a cop for twenty-some years. I don't know exactly how many, but I know it's at least twenty. You been a sergeant for at least ten years. You know how many times you been in my joint? Huh? I know how many times you been in here. I can count on both hands how many times you been in here. I can count on both hands and I wouldn't have to use my thumbs, that's how many times you been in here. And—"

"That was on Chief Balzic's orders, Mr. Muscotti. That wasn't me. That was his orders. I'm gettin' a bad rap here. He told me to stay outta here. That wasn't my idea. You call him. I mean it. You call him now. He'll tell you that himself. He told me that not fifteen minutes before I walked in here just now. He told me he made a mistake keepin' me outta here. He would've done it different he had it to do over again, so I really don't appreciate you talkin' to me like this. I'm also gettin' tired of standin' here. I don't deserve this."

Muscotti canted his head and lowered his eyelids halfway. He looked at Carlucci for a long time like that and said, "So have a seat. Drink your beer. I'll be right back." He got slowly to his feet and walked around Carlucci toward the kitchen. He was gone for about three minutes. When he returned, he was carrying another glass of beer as well as his own glass of Canadian Club and water. He set the beer in front of Carlucci and said, "Sit down, Rugs, I told ya sit down, whatta ya standin' for?"

"I was waitin' for you to sit down."

"Oh. Okay. So I'm gonna sit down now," Muscotti said, sitting heavily, with a noisy exhalation. "So whatta you wanna know?"

"You call Balzic?" Carlucci said, waiting until Muscotti was seated before sitting on the front two-thirds of the chair he'd pulled out earlier.

"What, you think I brought you back a beer just 'cause of how you started to talk? Lemme tell ya somethin' my father told me a long time ago when I was startin' to think I was a tough guy. He said never let your mouth write a check your body can't cash. In other words, all big talk does is tip your hand. It just shows everybody you're a fool 'cause the only people it impresses are the fools weaker than you are. 'Cause if that's all it took, hey, my bartender, he'd be the king of Sicily. But he ain't. He's a bartender. I ain't takin' nothin' away from him when I say that. He's a good bartender. But it don't matter how tough he talks, everybody knows the only reason he talks 'at way is 'cause of who I used to be, not 'cause of who he is. And nobody knows that better'n Vinnie. That's why I let him get away with his mouth.

"Course I called Balzic, you think I'm gonna give away

any part of what I know for the price of one ounce of booze? Now Balzic, hey, he bought me a lotta ounces. Over the years, all together, he probably paid for my kitchen. Just so you know, any conversation we're gonna have now, we're workin' on Balzic's credit here, understand?"

"I never doubted that for a minute. But even he had to buy you that first one once."

Muscotti nodded and smiled and raised his glass chest-high and said, "Salud. So? What's up?"

Carlucci nodded back and hoisted his beer and took a sip. Then he put it on the table and said, "I got a problem, maybe you heard about it. You know about Mrs. Picadio? Senior?"

Muscotti scowled and nodded. "That's a shame. Friggin' shame. I heard you were lookin' for some *tuzone*. Did I hear wrong?"

"No. You didn't hear wrong. I'm like ninety percent positive who did it. But he's dead himself—"

"He's dead? I didn't hear that."

"Yeah. Pittsburgh cops found him in her car."

"So?"

"So what I wanna know, if you can tell me, is about her son. Alfredo Junior. How much he gambles, who he books with. Can you help me out?"

Muscotti's scowl deepened. For a long moment he said nothing. Then he took a deep breath and said, "Far as I know, he books with Soup. You know Soup, right?"

"Yessir, I do."

"Well you ask Soup. He'll call me, but he'll tell ya. Course Junior goes to the tracks a lot. Soup won't know any more about that than I do. But anything else, he'll tell ya. So, uh, is that it?"

"Well, uh, where's Soup work out of? He wasn't in the bar when I came in."

"He don't work in here no more. Him and Vinnie had a, you know, a sorta difference of opinion last year. He's probably in his nephew's place. You know his nephew's place?"

"I don't even know his nephew. Oh, you mean Ronnie? The truck driver?"

"Yeah. It's up on Norwood. Used to be a barbershop. I forget what he calls it. Oh. Little Soup's. How the frig could I forget that, forgettin' everything anymore. Anything else?"

"That's it. I appreciate it very much. And from now on, I'll be stoppin' in, if that's okay with you."

Muscotti shrugged. "Unless you figure on just takin' up a stool and not buyin' nothin', why wouldn't it be?"

Carlucci stood, nodded by way of saying good-bye, and started toward the kitchen, but Muscotti called him back.

"Wait a minute. You asked me somethin', now I'm gonna ask you somethin'."

"Yeah, sure, go 'head."

"I don't like the sound of this."

Carlucci felt his brows going up. "Uh, what's the question?"

"That *is* the question. Why would I be sayin' I don't like the sound of this, you tell me."

"Mr. Muscotti, I'm just doin' my job, that's all. This job's no different from any other job I ever did. I have to get all the knots untied. This one's fulla knots, and they drive me crazy, that's all. That's all I'm doin'."

"A man's mother gets raped and robbed and she dies, and you're askin' me how much he gambles, and you're tellin' me you wanna untie all the knots 'cause they drive you crazy, and you don't understand why I say I don't like the sound of this, is 'at what you're tellin' me?"

"Somethin' like that, yessir."

"Oh. Yeah. Right. Everything's like glass now," Muscotti said. "See ya around."

"Yes, sir. You will. Thanks again for your help. I really appreciate it." Carlucci swallowed hard and hurried out through the kitchen before Muscotti could make another statement and call it a question. He stopped at the bar, brought out his money, and asked Vinnie how much he owed for Muscotti's drink.

"Put it away," Vinnie said. "Dom got that. Get outta here with your money. But don't be a fuckin' stranger no more, ya hear?"

Iron City Steve picked his head up off his forearms and said, "Hows come you never say that to me? All you ever tell me is familiarity breeds contempt. You're fulla contempt 'cause I'm so familiar, so hows come you never tell me don't be a stranger?"

"'Cause he don't owe me money yet. Speakin' of which, where's the five I loaned you yesterday?"

"I spent it in here!" Steve howled, sitting up, elbows sawing the air. "Whatta ya think? You borrow money just so you can pay it back? You borrow it so you can spend it! And after you spend it, you figure out whether it'd be cheaper to pay it back or file for bankruptcy. Why should I be any different than Wheeling Steel? If you're lucky, and you loan me another five? You might get back ten cents on the dollar. Fifty cents wouldn't be bad. A lotta Fortune 500 companies settle for less'n 'at. Whatta ya say? Got another five?"

Vinnie was smiling crookedly at Carlucci all the while Steve was talking. When Steve finished, Vinnie turned to him and said, "What I say is shut the fuck up'n go back to sleep, loan you another five, Jesus. For which I'd get to hear you bangin' the glass on the bar while you're pretendin' you're rich."

Steve lowered his chin to his forearms again and said, "Whose money you think I'm pretendin' with? Yours? You think I don't know it's Dom's? And anyway, you stole

more'n 'at outta the register before nine o'clock this
mornin', so whatta you hollerin' for? You lend me Dom's
five, I spend it in here, Dom makes a hundred percent on the
muscatel, and then you glom the five outta the register. And
you think it's easier for you to pretend you're smart than it
is for me to pretend I'm rich, sheesh. Wake me up if Louie
comes in. He owes me seven."

Carlucci shook his head, zippered up his parka, and hustled out to his cruiser, wondering if Soup Scalzo was really
in his nephew's bar. Little Soup's. On Norwood, is that
where Dom said it was? Except for the time Carlucci had
spent in the Army, he'd lived in Norwood all his life, in the
same house. He'd never noticed a place called Little Soup's.
Never even heard of it.

He left Muscotti's and drove across town to McCoy Road
and up to Norwood Hill to the confectionery store across the
street from the parking lot of Mother of Sorrows Church. He
parked in the church lot and hurried back across the street to
Oriolo's Confectionery.

Before the bell on the door quit ringing somebody was
calling out to him. "Hey, Rugsie, hi ya doin'? How's your
ma?"

"Mrs. Oriolo? What're you doin' here? I thought you quit
workin' here. Where's Tony?"

"Oh, Tony, he's in Ohio. He got a job there. He couldn't
work in here no more, Rugs, he couldn't stand it." She
shrugged. "I can't find nobody who wants to buy it, so what
am I s'posed to do? If I stay home, all I think about is what
hurts on me, you know? Least I come here, I get to talk to
somebody once in a while. So how's your mother, how you
doin', you doin' okay? I heard somebody say they're gettin'
ready to make you chief, is 'at right? Boy, that'd be wonderful, wouldn't it?"

Carlucci shrugged. "I don't know. Sometimes I think it

would, sometimes I'm not so sure. My head keeps goin' back and forth, you know? My mother's okay. The same, you know. Some days good, some days not so good. Like everybody else I guess."

"Well you tell her I said hello. Tell her I'm prayin' for her, okay?"

"Oh sure sure. Listen, you hear about a bar openin' up up here? Little Soup's? That ring any bells?"

"Oh yeah. Sure. Mary Scalzo's boy. Oh, what's his name. Ronnie? Yeah. Ronnie. He bought the barbershop, remember? Mr. Tarquinio's? Yeah. About five months ago I think. He just opened it couple weeks ago. I heard all they do in there is play cards. I don't know who goes in there. Soup's usin' it, you know, for whatever he does. You know what he does, what am I tellin' you? Can I get you somethin', Rugsie?"

"Huh? Oh, yeah. Give me a pack of those breath things there. The spearmint ones. Ronnie Scalzo, huh? I thought he drove a truck. He doesn't do that anymore, huh?"

"Oh I don't know, Rugsie. I guess not. But maybe he does, you never know who's doin' what anymore. God, used to be, people knew what they were doin', you know? Look at Tony, my God, three jobs in the last ten years. I think the longest one lasted maybe four years. And the pay kept gettin' worse. He's doin' pretty good now though. They make windows. I forget the name of that company out there. He comes back every weekend, you know, but they're havin' a terrible time sellin' their house. I told 'em, you know, I said, Rhonda, maybe it'd be better you just hold on to the house, you know? 'Cause you never know anymore. Here's your change, Rugsie. Thank you."

"Oh sure, you're welcome. Tell Tony I said hello. Haven't seen him, man, since I don't know when. Hey, good seein' you again, Mrs. Oriolo. Take care of yourself."

She smiled and waved and turned back to the small black-and-white TV she'd been watching when he'd come in.

He trotted across the street to his car and then drove about a quarter of a mile west on McCoy Road to where Mr. Tarquinio's barbershop had been. Except for his time in the Army, Carlucci had got every haircut in his life in the chair that sat in the middle of the tiny, square shop until Mr. Tarquinio had died last summer. Carlucci had been driving by right after the Fourth of July holiday, and some people milling around in front of the shop flagged him down. He'd found Mr. Tarquinio sitting in the barber chair, a *Rocksburg Gazette* spread across his chest, his mouth and eyes open, the ceiling fan gently rippling his white hair and the pages of the newspaper.

After Carlucci had called 911, he'd spent less than fifteen minutes searching for an address book and a will in the old man's sparsely furnished apartment behind the shop. The address book showed that all of the barber's relatives were in California. A metal box in the back of his clothes closet contained all the barber's bills for the last seven years, including ones for a safety-deposit box in Rocksburg First National Bank. Carlucci spent hours calling the relatives to arrange the funeral, but none of them called back—until they learned what was in the safety box.

Carlucci had watched one of the bank's officers open the box in the presence of the woman who ran the department, and their inventory showed twenty-five municipal bonds, all in denominations of five and ten thousand dollars. The woman who ran the department kept saying she didn't think it was possible to get that much paper into that little space. The paper that caused the relatives in California to start returning Carlucci's calls was the barber's will, crinkled under the bonds, which declared his intent to leave all his money to the Animal Rescue League of Western Pennsylvania. The relatives would howl and holler that the barber had never even had a pet dog, and Carlucci would listen just long enough for them to identify themselves, then he'd give them the switchboard number of the courthouse and hang up. . . .

While Carlucci was parking in the small gravel lot in front of the shop, which still had the words BARBER SHOP printed in red on a white wooden sign above the door, he thought Soup Scalzo must be losing it. When it was a barbershop, if all the chairs were occupied it became a gymnastics event just for somebody to want a different magazine, and now Soup was trying to turn it into a bar because he needed a phone number with somebody else's name on the bill? Carlucci couldn't help wondering whether Soup was hoping nobody would notice or whether he didn't care whether they noticed. Hell, Carlucci thought, Mrs. Oriolo had already noticed, and she wasn't even interested. On the other hand, Carlucci had driven past it at least a couple of times a week since Mr. Tarquinio's death and he hadn't noticed anything.

Carlucci found Soup reading the New York *Daily News* at a table where the barber chair had been. The table looked like the ones in Muscotti's back room: most of the finish around the outside edge had been rubbed off. Other newspapers were stacked haphazardly on the other side of the table on Soup's left. There was also an empty coffee cup between him and the papers. On his right was an ashtray filled with cigarette butts, a small squarish pad of white paper, and a number two pencil.

He dropped a corner of the paper to see who was coming in, then put it back up and started talking into it. "Hey, Rugsie. Long time no see. What's up? You want somethin'? Hey Ronnie! You got a customer. Sit down, Rugs, sit down."

Soup was short and thick with heavy lids and a thick lower lip. He always looked half-asleep. He got his nickname because he'd been a cook in the Army during World War II, but as far as anybody knew, he'd never cooked anything before or since.

Soup put the paper down after a moment and said, "So, uh, Rugs, I hear you're gonna be chief, is 'at right?"

"You probably know more about that than I do, Soup. Listen—"

"Hey, you want somethin'? Huh? Beer? Wine? Coffee? 'At's all we're allowed to sell. I couldn't get a liquor license. Just beer and wine. And coffee. Course, uh, my nephew don't learn how to make coffee better'n this, we ain't gonna make any money that way either." He nodded toward the empty cup. "So you want somethin'?"

"No thanks, Soup. Just information."

"Oh yeah? What about?"

"Guy name Picadio book with you? Alfredo Junior?"

"What's this about, Rugs?"

"Just wanna know if he booked with you, that's all. And how much? You wanna clear it with Mr. Muscotti, go ahead, call him. He sent me up here."

"Nah, I don't need to do that." He squirmed around in his chair and said over his shoulder, "Hey, Ronnie, that coffee ready yet?"

"Couple minutes, Uncle Soup," came a voice beyond a doorway in the wall opposite the front door. A heavy beige shower curtain hung from a pipe across the inside top of the door frame.

Soup turned back to Carlucci. "Did Junior book with me, huh? Is this about him or is this about me?"

"Him."

"Don't shit me now. I just paid the cocksuckers seven yards last week. I need a break here so don't shit me about this, okay?"

"I told ya, call Mr. Muscotti."

"And I told ya I don't have to do that." Soup leaned back

in his chair until it was on the back two legs. He rocked there for a moment, then settled forward again. "Yeah he booked with me. Course I ain't seen him for a while. Takes a vacation every year this time. He's down in the islands somewhere. Bahamas, someplace like 'at. What's this about, Rugs? Huh? You gonna tell me?"

"I told you. It's about him. So how much did he play?"

Soup thought that over. "A lot."

"C'mon, Soup. How much?"

Soup thought some more. "You know you're gonna owe me one for this, right?"

"No. I don't know that. I told ya, call Muscotti."

"And I told ya I wasn't gonna do that."

"And I told you this wasn't about you. So I'm not gonna owe you anything for anything that gets said here, okay? We straight on this? Or we gonna sit here'n keep goin' back and forth about who's gonna do what, like a couple junior high jagoffs?"

Soup thought some more. He twisted around and said over his shoulder, "Hey, Ronnie, what're you doin' in there? How long's it take to make coffee, Jesus."

"Comin' up, Uncle Soup. Almost ready. Comin' up here, just a second."

Carlucci put his elbows on the table and rested his chin on his knuckles.

Soup scratched the gray stubble on his neck and chin and turned back to Carlucci. "He was a pretty heavy hitter, yeah."

"Was he any good?"

Soup snorted. "Nobody's as smart as they think they are. Not me, not you, not Junior."

"So d'you ever have to chase him?"

"Rugsie, whatta you askin' me that for? They don't pay

me, that's their problem, I don't chase nobody and you know I don't, so whatta you askin' me that?"

"No exceptions? Ever?"

Soup leaned forward and said, "Hey listen. I don't do nothin' the state of Pennsylvania don't do. People make bets with me, they know the odds, and they know I pay and I pay better odds than the state on numbers and I don't ever have no tax man on my elbow like they got at the tracks, gettin' ready to put the arm on 'em when they win. And you beat me, I give you the whole ride. I don't keep back twenty percent for nobody, not Uncle Sugar, not Uncle Harris. So I don't want nobody lookin' down their nose at me, I don't care who you are. When I say I don't chase nobody, that's what I mean.

"But you don't wanna pay me, hey, sooner or later you're gonna wanna play with somebody, I don't care who. But I got a telephone just like everybody else. People call each other. That's what phones are for. So they all come back. And when they come back, what I tell 'em is exactly what you or anybody else would tell 'em. You wanna play now? Fine. Just settle up for back when. Simple as that. That's all I have to say."

"Okay. So did he ever try to get with another book?"

"Who doesn't? Some guys think, you know, change their book, change their luck. So he booked with one of Gerry Colella's nephews sometimes. Used to go to Wheeling and Waterford Park with him a lot. The one they call Pinhead, uh, what the hell's his name. Oh. Paulie, yeah. Real winner." Soup twisted around in his chair again and said, "Jesus Christ, Ronnie, what the hell're you doin'? I coulda been to the Giant Eagle'n back, bought a jar of instant in less time'n it's takin' you to make fresh." He turned back to Carlucci and said, "How long's it take to make a pot of coffee for crissake, huh?"

"I don't know," Carlucci said, shrugging. "I always make instant. So, uh, Soup, where you think he was gettin' the money, I mean if he was such a heavy hitter."

Soup shrugged his indifference. "My rule is, long as it spends, I don't care where it comes from."

"You never heard, you never asked, you never got curious?"

Soup's belly rose and fell several times in time with some guttural growlings that Carlucci guessed were supposed to be chuckling. "I think you're in the wrong place, askin' the wrong guy."

"Speakin' of places, Soup, don't you think this is a little obvious?"

"This? What this?"

"This place."

"Oh oh oh, yeah, I see what you mean now. No no, we're gonna knock this wall down here." He pointed with his thumb over his shoulder toward the wall behind him. "Turn this into one big room down here. I'm just waitin' for Tony Agnollo and his kid to finish up a job, then they're gonna come in here, rebuild this whole place, put a second floor on, oh yeah. I'm gonna live up there. Yeah, we're gonna have a terrace in the back, look down on the whole valley. Yeah, Tony's gonna build a bread oven out there. It's gonna be great. I been thinkin' about this place for so long I can't remember how long. Since I got outta the Army. Oh yeah. I tried to buy it from that barber half a dozen times. I mean, serious offers, not just chitchat. Serious.

"Listen to this," Soup said, suddenly very animated, "talk about goofy. He got all these relatives out in California and I found out none of 'em wanted this place. Yeah. All they wanted was his money, those assholes, they didn't even ask where he lived. How could you be that dumb? How do you like that? All I paid for it, you ain't gonna believe this—I got it for last year's taxes. He died before he paid his taxes last year. And last January, honest to God, last January, I offered him seventy-five for it. Swear to God. You know what I paid for it? Guess, go 'head, guess."

"I'm not even gonna try," Carlucci said.

"You're gonna shit. Eleven-fifty. Eleven hundred and fifty dollars! City, county, and school taxes. That's it. That's what I paid for it. I get the place of my dreams, the place I was willin' to go seventy-five large, I get it for less'n twelve hundred. On this whole hill, it's got the best view of the valley, I'm tellin' ya. When the sun sets on the river down there, it's like gold shinin' up at ya. When you leave now, go around the back and take a look, you'll see what I'm talkin' about. I can't wait, I can't. And you know what else? It goes all the way down to Tunnel Street in the back. Two hundred and eighty feet down to the sidewalk down there, yeah. I'm gonna terrace it. I can get three terraces in easy. Agnollo's other kid's a landscaper, he already told me we can get three in."

"Hey, Soup, what can I say, you look like a happy man."

"Happy?" Soup shrugged. "Happy don't cover it. Every time I start thinkin' about how it's gonna look, I get the way I was when I heard the fuckin' Nazis surrendered and I was still alive. And you know what else? I used to think anybody believed in luck was a sucker. All of a sudden I feel like the luckiest sonofabitch that ever lived. I mean, imagine. I wanted this place since 1946—since I got outta the Army! And I couldn't blast him outta here with dynamite. And he dies and it falls into my lap like a ripe cherry. It's almost enough to make me go to St. Malachy's, light some candles."

Carlucci, watching Scalzo's joy, wondered how much it would cost him to tweak Scalzo's nose by asking why the place was going to be named Little Soup's, after his nephew. Carlucci knew why, of course; Soup's reason for putting the place in his nephew's name wasn't any different from any-body else's reason for protecting his assets in the likelihood he was going to be arrested or sued. Soup had learned as well as any tax lawyer that the government cannot, in lieu of a cash fine, seize property from him that he did not own. Car-lucci was wondering how touchy Scalzo was about this, but the more he wondered the more he thought Scalzo wouldn't appreciate being tweaked about it, else why had he gone into such detail about how much he'd been willing to pay for this place and how lucky he felt over how it had actually come to be his. Carlucci kept his mouth shut, except to say thanks for the information about Alfredo Picadio Jr., and to say that he would go around back and check out the view. Scalzo had just opened his dreams. It would have been stupid, Carlucci knew, to tramp on something he'd been invited to share. Be-sides which, Soup was starting to really look pissed that his nephew still hadn't produced any coffee.

As Carlucci was going out the front door he heard Soup saying, "Hey, Ronnie, you pullin' your wang back 'ere or what? What the fuck're you doin'? What happened to the coffee? Jesus Christ . . ."

Carlucci turned right when he got outside and went scuf-fling across the gravel parking lot to the back of the one-story building until the view brought him up short. Soup was right. The Conemaugh River Valley was impressive from there. Mr. Tarquinio, or somebody he'd paid, had cut the trees and kept the brush low. The river was muddy brown from all the snow that had melted into it since New Year's, but Carlucci didn't have much trouble imagining what it would look like during a summer sunset. Like gold, Soup had said. Who knew what lurked in that bookie's heart? Who knew he had a heart? Carlucci hadn't. He'd never even sus-pected it.

Carlucci pulled into the parking lot of the Conemaugh County Jail. He'd been there only a half a dozen or so times since it had opened the second week of September, but each time he got out of his cruiser and looked around, he felt something rising in his chest, a buzzing, a humming, a beating like some winged insects had got trapped between his diaphragm and his lungs and were trying to get out but they were losing strength and they'd never been very strong to begin with. Then he'd get inside the lobby and push the button for the CO to open the gun box and he'd put his pistols inside, the 9mm Beretta from his belt and the .22 Smith & Wesson revolver from his ankle, and then he'd walk through the metal detector and the buzzing in his chest would be gone.

One day, years ago in the former county jail, he told Deputy Warden Richie Kerpinski about the feeling in his chest and Kerpinski had just laughed and said he used to get that way all the time himself when he'd first started, but he'd gotten used to it. "It's just knowin' in your secret heart how many stupid things you ever did in your life and how if it'd just gone maybe a coupla inches another direction one day you'd be a customer here 'stead of what you are. An asshole tryin' to pretend he's an avengin' angel." Kerpinski never talked like that when anybody else was around, but he liked Carlucci, so he enjoyed needling him.

"I'm supposed to see state police trooper Milliron," Carlucci said to the CO who'd exchanged his weapons and signature for a visitor's tag and processed him through the metal detector. "He on your sheet?"

The CO gave his sheet of sign-ins a quick scan and shook his head. "Not yet. He bringin' somebody in or you comin' in for an interview or arraignment or what?"

"He's bringin' somebody and we're gonna interview him after he gets him booked. Kerpinski around?"

The CO nodded and called Kerpinski on the intercom. "Detective Carlucci from Rocksburg PD's here. You want me to send him up or you wanna come down?"

Carlucci could hear Kerpinski over the static say he was coming down. Carlucci walked around the lobby, wondering where the buzzers inside his chest went when they left. Were they just taking a break? Or had they given up? Did they actually leave?

Kerpinski came bounding down the corridor, all nose, neck, shoulders, and arms, about six-two or three, two-forty or so, neck as thick as his biceps and his biceps bigger around than Carlucci's thighs, with the crookedest nose Carlucci had ever seen on a human being. The cartilage was bent so far to the left that Kerpinski's right nostril was barely a slit, and Kerpinski always sounded as though he had some chronic respiratory disease.

"Hey, Ski, no shit, you ever gonna get your nose fixed?"

"What the fuck you care what my nose looks like, you little dago prick. You queer for me or somethin'? C'mon, let's go outside, this place's drivin' me nuts."

"It's cold out there, man. It's like zero with the wind chill."

"Oh come on, you little pussy, it's cold, what the fuck. Whole time you were in Nam all you probably did was bitch about how hot it was, now it's winter you're bitchin' 'cause it's cold. It's winter, ya fuck, it's s'posed to be cold, c'mon, let's go, it'll get your blood movin', not that you got any." Kerpinski was wearing just a long-sleeved sweater over his shirt. He went bounding through the doors and out before Carlucci could protest again.

When Carlucci caught up with him, Kerpinski was doing jumping jacks and grinning like an idiot.

"What the fuck you so happy about?"

"I'm happy 'cause I'm finally gonna get a chance to bitch

at somebody personally responsible for makin' my life miserable, that's what I'm so happy about." Kerpinski stopped jumping and glared mischievously at Carlucci and advanced on him in a half-crouch, grinning and growling like some guard dog suddenly crazy with the idea that the joke really was on people. Carlucci started to back away but too late. Kerpinski caught up with him and hoisted him into the air by his armpits and held him aloft like he was weightless.

"C'mon, Ski, put me down, man—"

"Naw, fuck you, I ain't puttin' you down till you hear what I got to say."

"Aw c'mon, man—"

"Naw naw, just quit squirmin' around and listen. I got a really neat job here, man. Got my own office, got my own coffeepot, my own little fridge, my own computer, man, I even got carpets on the floor. Even my mother's proud of me, no shit. It's a fuckin' snap except for one thing. People like you keep arrestin' all these assholes and bringin' 'em out here and I gotta stop what I'm doin', you know, I gotta shut my Super Mario Brothers off and hide the disc and go try to figure out what to do with these fuckin' assholes guys like you keep bringin' out here. So I'm not gonna let you down till you promise you're gonna quit this shit."

"C'mon, ya goofy fuck, put me down."

"Promise, ya skinny little prick. 'Bout twenty more assholes and we're gonna have to start double-cellin' 'em and you know what the fuck that means. You know how nervous I get when I gotta double 'em in."

"C'mon, Richie, put me down, ya fuck."

Kerpinski dropped him and sent Carlucci staggering to catch his balance. "You ain't no fun," he said, hooking his thumbs in his belt and staring at the building behind Carlucci.

"You kiddin' me? Twenty more?"

"Yeah. Twenty. Who'da thunk it. Bunks and bedding already ordered. Probably gonna get 'em next coupla weeks. Fuckin' place ain't even four months old and it's about to be overcrowded. Man, I'm tellin' ya, somethin's wrong . . . and it's all your fault, you skinny little prick." He was growly and giggly again, sending Carlucci skittering backward.

"C'mon, Richie, don't do that, okay? One of these days you're gonna pick me up'n drop me I'm gonna bust a fuckin' ankle or somethin'. I'm too old for this shit, I'm tellin' ya."

"At ease for crissake, I'm not gonna hurt ya." He was staring at the building again. "Man, you'da told me five years ago I'd be thinkin' about retirin' after twenty-five I'da said you were smokin' bad shit. But I'm startin' to think about it, Rugs. More'n more. My old lady says I'm thinkin' about it way too much.

"But these people we're gettin' now? Man, they're from a different place, I'm tellin' ya. Says on their paper they're from Philadelphia and Scranton and Erie and Harrisburg and Pittsburgh, but don't believe it, man. I don't know whether it's the coke or what but these fuckers don't care. They do not care. About nothin', man. They're as empty behind the eyes as anybody I ever saw in Nam. You go in there right now, you'll see more thousand-yard stares in a half hour than you saw the whole time you were in Nam, I'm not shittin' ya.

"You know me, Rugs, takes a lot to shake my ass, you know that. But I'm tellin' ya, sometimes, more'n more lately, dealin' with these guys? I get the same squeezin' in my guts I got when I was tryin' to deal with the VC in their hootches, man. They were all scared and polite and bowin', but bigger'n shit, come nightfall, they'd be out there riggin' the trip wires, you know?

"We're holdin' all these federals for transfer, you know? All these ones got trapped in those fuckin' sentencin' guidelines? They give you that look, man, you know they got nothin' to lose and they know you know it, and don't you forget it for a second, hoss. The sonsabitches that passed that law oughta be puttin' in forty-eight hours every week for a couple months here just to see what their get-tough bullshit did. And now they wanna do this three-times-and-out shit? And the fuckin' state wantsa do it too?

"Man, where do these fuckin' people come from? I used to laugh at your boss, you know, when he'd be talkin' 'bout how the first thing any politician got elected had to do was spend three days in the joint right after he took the oath. I used to think ol' Balzic was just talkin' through his ass. More'n more, I'm tellin' ya, Rugs, that's exactly what oughta happen. These sentencing guidelines for dope? Man, the best thing that could ever happen is what Balzic said. Three days, three nights in the county jail not of their choice. Then let's see what kinda sentencing guidelines they wanna have. Want a coffee or somethin'?"

"Naw, no thanks."

"I wasn't gonna buy it for ya, ya little prick. I was just askin' ya if you wanted one. C'mon, let's go back in."

"Oh what, you're cold now?" Carlucci said, breaking into a trot to keep up with Kerpinski's long strides.

Kerpinski grinned down at Carlucci and said, holding the door for him, "You got a Thule parka on for crissake. That oughta be good for sixty below—'less it's some Taiwanese knockoff."

"Naw this is real. I traded some Air Force guy some VC shit when I was comin' through Seattle."

"You mean you had that coat since you come back from Nam? Twenty years?"

"Twenty-two actually. Yeah. Course I stay on top of it. Soon's I see somethin' comin' loose, I stitch it up."

"Well be careful where you step in here, hoss, they'll have it under a mattress 'fore you know it's gone."

"Detective Carlucci," came a voice over the PA system, "Trooper Milliron requests you report to the magistrate's office. Detective Carlucci please report to the magistrate's office."

"Ouu, sounds like a dangerous situation, Detective, had to go'n call in the Pennsylvania State Police. Probably some criminal activity involved. Listen, ya little prick, just try to remember, whatever the sonofabitch did, don't charge him with anything he can't make bail, okay? 'Cause if he can't, then I gotta find somethin' for him to do, okay? Think you can remember that?"

"That's your job, ya fuckin' Polack asshole. Ain't you the deputy warden of treatment?"

"No, ya little dago prick, that's not my job, that's my job title. My job is to convince my friends and relatives I'm advancing up the ladder of promotion in the Bureau of Corrections."

"I'm the only friend you got and I know that's a load of crap. If your old lady and your mother's still fallin' for it, you're in deep shit. I gotta go. See ya around."

"Think you can find your way down there, or would you like me to requisition you an escort?"

"Haw haw, very funny."

"How 'bout when you try to come back out? You want me to get ya a bag of crumbs or a big long string or somethin'?"

"Oh that's hilarious, that really is."

"And try to remember what I said, will ya? I don't care how many people he raped, robbed, or pillaged, I don't want him in here. Soon as you beat a confession outta him, get him the fuck back home where he belongs."

Carlucci walked away, shaking his head, and tried to go through the first set of doors on his way to the basement where the district justice's office and the booking station were. But when he pulled on the door, it didn't give, and when he turned around, there was Kerpinski grinning at him, his finger poised above the lock-release button.

"Patience, Detective, patience. Always a virtue at all times in all places, but especially in here. If I have learned anything in my years of service in correction, it's that patience is always what we're striving for. Otherwise you could hurt yourself jerkin' on a door like that. You could get a real bad boo-boo that way."

"Deputy Warden Kerpinski, report to the Alcoholics Anonymous meeting," came a voice over the PA. "Deputy Warden Kerpinski, please report to the AA meeting."

Carlucci howled. "What, they can't start the meetin' without ya? Hoo boy, hey, don't forget to take your name tag off and tell 'em don't look at that goofy suit you're wearin'. Otherwise they'll have to quit callin' it AA, you know? Anonymous? Have to call it, what? II maybe. Inebriates Identified, somethin' like that. Oh man, that's too much, c'mon, hit the button, I needa get movin'.'"

Kerpinski was grinning crookedly and scratching his throat when he hit the button allowing Carlucci to pass through.

Carlucci had to go through two more sets of doors till he reached the elevator that took him down to the booking station, the interview rooms, and District Justice Ralph Harmar's chambers. At each door, he had to wait for a CO to open the doors electronically, and as he entered each corridor, none of them longer than sixty feet, TV cameras at each end recorded his coming and going.

Carlucci was mulling over what Kerpinski had said about making preparations to start double-celling. This jail, completed less than four months earlier at a final construction cost of more than $47 million, was built to house a population of 386 prisoners, and it was already holding 366. If 20 more prisoners had to be housed there with no releases, double-celling was inevitable. Putting one human being inside an area five feet wide and nine feet long and locking the door was one thing; putting a second one in with the first was all the proof anyone ever needed to demonstrate that familiarity does indeed breed contempt. Carlucci vividly remembered interrogating a con in the former county jail about his aggravated assault of his cellmate because said cellmate refused to believe that lighting matches would dissipate the stench of his bowel movement.

In the elevator, Carlucci was also remembering that the county's previous jail had been overcrowded the day it opened in 1970. It had been a self-service laundry, and its intended capacity after remodeling was 96 cons, but the day it opened, it had 100. By 1980, the county had to buy three fifty-by twelve-foot trailers, park them in the exercise yard, and convert them into dormitories for the cons on work release. By the time the county commissioners had approved the building of this new jail, every cell in the old one was holding two cons, people awaiting trial were sleeping on tables in the library and on the floor in the corridors, and the county was farming out cons by the dozens to county jails in the rural south, west, and center of the state because a federal judge had ruled that the crowding in the former laundry was a violation of the Eighth Amendment's prohibition against cruel and unusual punishment.

Conemaugh County was paying as much as $60 a day to other counties to house their overflow cons; in no case was the county paying less than $45 a day. Since it was costing the county $35.62 a day to house cons in it own jail, the county solicitor's office had assigned one deputy full-time to do nothing else but bargain with other counties about how many prisoners they could accept and how much they would charge. Disregarding the overtime salaries of the deputy sheriffs, the county was also spending twenty-six cents a mile to transport the cons back and forth; and the commissioners, the district attorney, and the president judge had almost no opposition convincing taxpayers that a bond issue for a new jail would be far cheaper than the musical cells then going on. Only trouble was, the new jail was supposed to cost less than $50 million, but by the time all the change orders had been approved and by the time the bond issue was going to be retired, long after the millennium, the taxpayers were going to have paid more than $94 million for a jail that was close to being overcrowded four months after the first inmates walked through its doors. Welcome to incarceration in the nineties, Carlucci thought.

And if the get-tough-on-crime people went ahead with the three-times-and-out madness that had already started in California, it was going to be a long, ugly joke on everybody. Carlucci thought the country was getting collectively stupider. Every mistake that had been made regarding drinkable drugs from 1920 to 1933 was now being repeated with all the smokable, injectable, or ingestible drugs federal and state legislatures had decided to ban. And when guys like Kerpinski had to deal with all the people being crammed into his jail for possession with intent to sell illegal drugs or for driving under the influence, it was only a matter of time until the county started playing musical cells again.

Nobody won points standing around with his hands in his pockets when everybody else was applauding the state's DUI law decreeing that even first-time violators should do time, but those applauding the hardest apparently didn't want to think about what was going to happen to the state's jails as a result. *That* problem was left for people like Carlucci and Kerpinski to solve, people who had never been asked their opinion, not by state legislators, or reporters, or pollsters, about what was going to happen. People like Carlucci and Kerpinski were left to suck it up and deal with it. Any way they could.

"Hey, Rugs, over here," Trooper Milliron called out to Carlucci as he stepped into the booking area. Milliron did not look pleased.

"You get him? Any problems?"

"Oh no problem getting him, but we got a problem all right. He wants a lawyer. And all the way down here, like, every ten minutes, he kept repeating it, I want a lawyer, you got to get me a lawyer, that's my rights, you got to give me my rights, I ain't saying nothing."

"Where is he?"

"Over there," Milliron said, nodding in the direction of one of the interview rooms.

"You got my recorder?"

"Yeah, sure, here it is," Milliron said, taking it out of his breast pocket. "I shut it off after about the third time he gave me that routine. Figured there was no point."

"Sure, right," Carlucci said, adjusting the recorder so that it would start operating when he began talking to Givins. "You get a confirm on his prints? He is our guy, right?"

"Yeah, right. NCIC confirms him."

"Okay," Carlucci said, sighing and taking off his parka. He studied Milliron for a moment, trying to think how to say what he wanted to say, but he knew the only way was to just say it. All he had to do was keep his voice low and polite. "Listen, I know this is officially your case. I know I'm supposed to be here to offer whatever assistance I can and that's all I'm supposed to do, but, uh, I think I should do the talkin' in here."

Milliron looked relieved. "Actually, I was, uh, I was kind of hoping you were going to say that. I mean, you've done this a lot more than I have. Figure I can learn something. Already learned something about having a tape recorder. Nobody ever told me that before. So fine, I'll be glad to listen."

"Okay, good. Let's go give him somethin' to think about."

Carlucci led the way in and pulled one of the chairs around to the end of the table to which Luther Givins was handcuffed. Milliron closed the door and took a seat opposite Givins.

Carlucci put on his best stare and locked eyes with Givins. "Ruggiero Carlucci," he said softly, "detective sergeant Rocksburg PD, conducting first interview with Luther Alonzo Givins, age, uh, how old are you, Luther?"

"Twenty-nine."

"Age twenty-nine, last known address 103 Franklin Avenue, Rocksburg, Pa., uh, lemme see, sixteen-zero-five hours, January ninth, 1993, interview room—what room we in, Trooper? You know?"

"One, I'm pretty sure. Yeah, one."

"Interview room one, Conemaugh County Jail, Conemaugh County, Pa. State police trooper Claude Milliron also present.

"So Luther, just for the record here, you are Luther Alonzo Givins, is that correct?"

"Gimme a smoke, man, I wanna smoke. Gimme a cigarette."

Carlucci ignored that. "Well, Luther, for the record, Trooper Milliron and I know that you are in fact Luther Alonzo Givins 'cause the fingerprints that were taken from you when you were booked in here just a little while ago matched up with fingerprints on file with the FBI. That's been confirmed, Luther. We know who you are."

"I know who I am too."

"Good. So you look like you're doin' okay, right? No visible blood, no visible cuts or bruises, no swelling. No prob-

lems durin' your arrest or transfer here, Luther, whatta ya
say? Everything smooth?"

"Aw man, stop it. Gimme a cigarette. And no menthol neither."

"Interviewee Givins apparently concurs there was no
problem during his arrest or transfer by Trooper Milliron this
date from Sharon, Pa., PD. You know why you're here,
Luther?"

"I don't know, I guess I won a contest or somethin'. You
got this brand-new resort here, and, uh, and you want me to
check it out for y'all. C'mon, man, gimme a smoke."

"I'm not gonna do that, Luther. Try to concentrate on what
I'm askin' you."

"Aw man, shit." Luther turned away and leaned back
against the metal slats of his chair.

"I ask again, Luther, do you know why you're here?"

"Whyn't you tell me? What the fuck I know why I'm here.
Y'alls who brought me, I didn't bring myself. Fuck, why'm I
here. Like I'm 'posed to know that. Don't give a fuck why
I'm here anyway, I want a smoke. And I wanna see a lawyer.
And since I ain't got no money, you got to give me one.
That's my rights, so now whyn't you go on and do that, huh?
Get me a lawyer. And take these got-damn cuffs off me too,
man, they too fuckin' tight, cuttin' right through my skin
here'n shit, lookit here. C'mon look, I ain't lyin'.'"

Carlucci leaned forward to glance at Givins's wrists. Then
he leaned back and said, "Look all right to me. I could probably run a pencil between the cuffs and your wrist."

"Well go 'head and do it then. Go 'head, get you a damn
pencil out'n do it."

"Luther," Carlucci said, clearing his throat, "I think we're
gettin' off on the wrong foot here—"

"No shit."

"Yeah I do, I think we're startin' off all wrong. I think you need to put aside your desire for a smoke and start listenin' to me."

"Fuck you, man. Put aside my desire. Shit. Put your own fuckin' desire aside, man, gimme a got-damn cigarette."

Carlucci scootched forward on his chair until his face was about two hands' width away from Givins. "Luther, you know what you're askin' me to do? Huh?"

"Whatchu talkin' 'bout?"

"You mean to tell me you don't know that secondhand smoke has been declared a carcinogen? By the United States government? By the U.S. surgeon general? By the U.S. Department of Health? You know what a carcinogen is? Huh? That's somethin' that causes cancer. You don't know that if I gave you a cigarette, and you lit that cigarette, and you exhaled that smoke into this room in my presence, and I inhaled it 'cause I wouldn't have any choice about whether I wanted to inhale it or not—you mean to tell me you don't know that I would be conspiring with you to effectuate—you hear that word, Luther? Effectuate? I learned that from a lawyer once. Effectuate. It means to bring about. To cause to happen. It means if I gave you the smoke, Luther, I would be conspiring with you to bring about, to cause to happen, to effectuate a fatal disease upon myself. Lung cancer, Luther. If I gave you a smoke, I would be conspiring with you—you listenin' to me, Luther?—I would be conspiring with you to murder me. Do you seriously think I'm gonna conspire with you to commit murder? When the victim would be me? C'mon, Luther, I mean, I can see you conspirin' with somebody else to commit murder. But I find it real hard to believe you'd actually try to solicit me into a conspiracy to commit a capital felony against myself, I mean I really can't see that. But maybe I'm wrong. Maybe you got more balls than I think you do."

Givins said nothing. He looked at his hands and he crossed his ankles and his heels started bouncing.

"Luther, it's on the record here, 'cause I got a tape recorder in my pocket and I'm gettin' every word you're sayin', so it's on tape that you have requested an attorney to represent you, and Trooper Milliron witnessed your request, so everybody here, everybody in this room knows I can't be askin' you any more questions until after you been arraigned, and even then, if you don't have your lawyer present, I can't ask you another question. Not one. So I'm not gonna ask you any questions. I'm just gonna tell you some things. And I want you to think about 'em. And I want you to discuss 'em with your lawyer, whoever gets assigned to you. I want you to talk 'em over with him real good, 'cause this is gonna be real important to you. So now you listen up, Luther, you hear? You listenin'?"

Givins canted his head and glared at Carlucci. "Say what you got to say, man, get on with it."

"Good. That's good. 'Cause here's what I want you to think about. Mrs. Alfredo Picadio Senior, you remember her? Huh? Your aunt works for her. Worked. She doesn't work for her anymore. 'Cause Mrs. Picadio's dead. She's the victim of a homicide in the commission of at least one other felony, a robbery. And that makes it a capital felony. Now I know that the felonies you've committed in the past, Luther, they were all in Ohio, and I don't know that much about Ohio. But this is Pennsylvania, and in Pennsylvania, Luther, somebody gets murdered during the commission of another felony, that makes it a capital felony. That means that anybody who gets indicted for that murder, gets prosecuted, gets convicted, that person is by law gonna get sentenced to death. You with me so far?"

Luther's heels were bouncing faster. He continued to glare at Carlucci but he said nothing.

"I think you're with me. I think I have your attention. And that's good, Luther. 'Cause here's some other stuff you should talk over with your attorney. You should be sure and tell him about your felony convictions in Ohio. You tell him about those crimes you did with a gun, don't leave anything out. It's a bad thing to lie to your attorney. It's stupid. I don't know whether you know that, Luther, but it is, believe me.

"And also, and most important, Luther, you listenin'? Most important, you tell your attorney that at the time of Mrs. Picadio's homicide, you were livin' with your aunt who was employed as a cook by the victim. And you also tell him, that all the while you were livin' with your aunt you were drivin' her to and from her place of employment in Mrs. Picadio's house. And you also tell him that on the very day that Mrs. Picadio's body was discovered—did I tell you that she called 911 herself, Luther? Did I tell you that?"

Givins said nothing, continuing to glare stonily at Carlucci.

"Well doesn't matter whether I told you before, Luther, 'cause now we both know you know it. 'Cause she did. She plugged the phone back in and she hit the buttons herself. The asshole who did this to her, he didn't smash the phones or throw 'em away, no, he was too fuckin' stupid to do that. Or too scared. Or too excited. Maybe. But I think stupid. That's what he was. He just pulled the wires outta the box, that's all. So all she had to do was just plug one of 'em back in, which is what she did. And she was still conscious when the EMTs got there, Luther, whatta ya think of that, huh? That was one tough old lady, Luther. Have that happen to her that way, and she still had the guts and the presence of mind to plug the phone back in and call for help? Gotta respect her for that, I'm tellin' ya. I don't know whether I coulda done it.

"But she did it. And I want you to think about that, Luther.

And I also want you to tell your attorney what your aunt told me. You listenin' up, huh? Your aunt, in her own house, in her own words, without any prompting from me, told me herself that on the very day Mrs. Picadio was found, you, Luther, you failed to pick your aunt up from her place of employment, which you had been doin' all the while you were livin' with her. And not only that, Luther, when your aunt got home in a taxi that night? What she discovered was that you, Luther, you had taken all your personal belongings and had left. Gone. Without a word, without a note, without a call to your aunt tellin' her why you had failed to pick her up and why you were leavin', uh-uh, nothin' like that, no sir. You were just gone, Luther. And not only had you taken everything that belonged to you, you also took somethin' that didn't belong to you. You took all your aunt's money, out of a coffee can that she kept in a cupboard over the sink. Your aunt is accusin' you of that crime, Luther. She gave me the information. And she signed it. And we're gonna charge you with that crime in a little while. Your very own blood relative is accusin' you of committin' that theft by unlawful takin'. She's accusin' you of stealin' her entire life savings, Luther, and she wants you busted for that, man. She is pissed, Luther, I mean, she is seriously pissed. So if you were thinkin' about callin' her, I wouldn't do that if I were you. I mean if you're lookin' to have somebody come see you, hold your hand maybe, help you out in any way, if I were you, Luther, I wouldn't call my aunt. She would be the last person I would call. Maybe your attorney will have a different opinion about that, I don't know. You should probably ask him about that, you know, when you're talkin' to him about how you just happened to decide to leave your aunt's domicile on the very day this bad thing happened to Mrs. Picadio, remember? Maybe you're gonna wanna discuss with him the coincidence of those two things, you know? I'm not askin' you, Luther. These are not questions here. These are just speculations on my part about what you might wanna talk to your attorney about. After we get one for you.

"One more thing, Luther," Carlucci said, standing and reaching for the doorknob. "There's one more thing you might wanna discuss with your attorney. I'm not advising you here, Luther, I'm just suggesting this. I'm suggesting that you tell your attorney that I, me, Detective Carlucci of the Rocksburg PD, I would like to believe that you yourself had nothing to do with that bad thing that happened to Mrs. Picadio. I would like to believe that, Luther, but unfortunately, so far, I have not been able to find anybody, anybody at all, who was anywhere near that place where Mrs. Picadio was the night all the bad things happened to her. So maybe you and your attorney can come to your own conclusions about what that might mean, okay?

"You okay, Luther? You want me to repeat anything I said just now? You think you got everything I said? Not confused about anything? Huh? 'Cause I'll be happy to go over it again. Any part you want."

Givins turned away and shook his head, his heels continuing to bounce.

"No? Straight about everything? Fine. Okay, Luther, you take care, we'll be talkin' to you. We gotta go talk to the DJ now, set up your arraignment, get you charged and everything. It'll be a while, you just relax, okay? Maybe one of the COs'll get you a smoke."

Outside the interview room, on their way to the DJ's chambers, Milliron whispered, "Uh, I'm impressed. I mean, really. Doing that without notes, wow. And that part about the cigarette, Jeez, I almost started to smile once, I had to bite my lip 'cause he was looking right at me and I knew I couldn't let him see me smiling. I mean, Jeez, you laid the whole case right out there for him and yet—and yet you didn't. What made you think of that?"

"Uh, Claude, don't be too impressed, okay? I been usin' the cigarette thing for a long time now. It only gets tough if the sonofabitch doesn't smoke, 'cause I really don't have a very good backup. Just kinda wing it."

"Yeah, but you laid out the case against him without givin' away anything."

When they got into the DJ's chambers, Carlucci crooked his finger at Milliron to follow him to the unoccupied last row of seats. "Sit down, man, and listen. Don't go gettin' all gaga on me, okay? The thing I did is simple. Anytime you want to turn somebody, all you have to do is let 'em know one of the charges is gonna be conspiracy, and I don't care how you phrase that, accessory before, accessory after, involved with, complicity with, whatever words you feel comfortable sayin', you just have to say 'em, that's all. You just have to plant the seed that you know somebody else could take the fall—and the key word is *could*, understand? Not *would*, not *will*, but *could*. So since the only people who work alone are pros, everybody else, man, I mean, it's simple, everybody else has run his mouth, either before or after, to somebody else. I mean, that's their game. For the pros it's a job, and they wanna keep doin' it, so for them it's what they did. But for everybody else it's how much they get to brag about what they did. That's why the pros are tough, but everybody else? Shit, all you gotta do is let 'em know that you know that they couldn't keep their mouth shut. And if you say it the right way, they think, hey, this asshole just told me how I can beat him. So I don't care how you have to say it, I don't care what words you have to use, I'm tellin' ya that's what you have to think about goin' in. As far as the cigarette thing goes, God, I been usin' that ever since Balzic let me do my own interrogations."

"Who?"

"Guy that used to be my chief. Just got railroaded out. But I been usin' the cigarette thing long as I been a detective. 'Cause I never smoked myself, and I never liked people blowin' it in my face, so the first time, actually it just came out, I really didn't plan it, believe me. I just got pissed off because this smart-ass was blowin' it in my face just to irritate me. And it did. And I turned that fucker in five minutes. Five minutes he was practically bawlin' he was so happy to turn his buddies. He woulda turned his mother. Somethin' to think about, man, every time you hear some junior G-man running for governor or attorney general says he's gonna eliminate plea bargainin'. Fuck. We couldn't turn people, man, we'd have to go back to cattle prods. We'd have to go back to beatin' 'em on top of the head with a phone book."

Milliron's eyes went wide. "You're not telling me, uh . . ."

"No no, man, not me, Jesus, I never touch anybody, 'cept to make a collar. No, that's just what I heard from the old heads. You should talk to Balzic sometime, man. Guy's a walkin' encyclopedia about bad police work, man. He knows some shit'd make you squirm. So anyway, uh, let's get this Givins squared away here. I think, in addition to the theft against his aunt, all we should charge him with is strictly accessory to, before, during, and after, but not anything else. Lay the conspiracy thing on, just pile it on. That'll give his shyster, even if he's stupid—and believe me they got some beauties in the PD's office—that'll give him room to move."

Milliron looked puzzled. "Uh, I must be missing something here. I mean, if all we're going to do is charge him that way, what's his incentive? What happens if he doesn't turn anybody?"

"C'mon, Claude. You heard his heels shakin' and bouncin' in there just as well as I did. He knows we can

change the charges anytime we want. All we have to do is
claim new evidence. He can't wait to deal. Why you think he
was buggin' you for a lawyer all the way back? And you
can't ever blindfold guys like him. You gotta let 'em see the
way out. 'Cause don't forget, until we get the lab reports, we
don't have one piece of evidence that says he was even in the
fuckin' county when this thing went down. And I know better'n to hold my breath till either one of those labs gets
around to my evidence. I got this distinct feelin' I'm not
gonna see anything but pieces of paper from Pittsburgh. Not
that I'd blame 'em. I probably wouldn't get up offa any evidence either if things were reversed, but, uh, fuck, man, I
gotta do somethin' while I'm waitin'."

Milliron screwed up his face and sighed, his shoulders
slumping. "It's a felony homicide."

"Look, man," Carlucci said, "this is your case. You wanna
charge him with felony homicide, I can't stop you. But the
DJ's gonna ask you what ya got to back it up, man, and
you're gonna have to tell him, and when he hears what we
have, well, put yourself in his place. Ask yourself if you
would do it. I'm tellin' ya, he's gonna be a lot more open to
conspiracy on third-degree murder. You don't wanna go for
more'n that, really, there's no reason."

Milliron took some time thinking it over, but he nodded finally and began filling out the papers to present to the district
justice. The arraignment was over in an hour. Luther Alonzo
Givins was on his way to a cell with the promise that the
Commonwealth of Pennsylvania would provide him with the
services of the public defender's office to defend himself
against charges of violating the state's code Title 18 Section
3921 theft by unlawful taking or disposition; Section 2501
murder of the third degree; Section 3701 robbery; Section
3121 rape; and Section 903 criminal conspiracy to commit
all of the above except the theft by unlawful taking.

Now all Carlucci and Milliron had to do was let the walls
of the new county jail go to work on Givins, the steel-plat-
form bed on his back, the mostly unidentifiable food on his
stomach, the head counts on his spirit, the body-cavity
searches on his dignity, the charges against him on his mind.
But mostly what Carlucci was waiting to work on Givins
was the boredom. And to that end, before he left the jail, he
called his friend Deputy Warden of Treatment Richard Kerpinski and alerted him to the possibility that Luther Alonzo
Givins was a suicide risk.

Milliron was baffled by that one. "Man, I don't know,
Rugs. You ask me, if that guy was getting ready to kill somebody it wasn't himself. That was the last thing he looked
like."

"Yeah? Well, that's a difference of opinion we have. You
could be right, and I could be wrong. But the fact is, since I
expressed my opinion to the deputy warden here, he has no
choice but to put Givins under suicide watch. 'Cause the last
thing he wants to deal with is a black dude killin' himself in
his jail. That's mondo bad PR. So he's gonna do everything
he can to protect himself from that. Besides which, it's pol-
icy, man, he doesn't have any choice. All somebody has to
say is a guy is a risk, and they gotta put him on twenty-four
seven surveillance. Not only does Givins not get to watch
any TV, a TV camera's gonna be watchin' him all the time.
He can't move his bowels or masturbate without knowin'
somebody's watchin' him. And they also never turn the
lights out. He's locked in like that twenty-four seven until
somebody in county mental health gets around to evaluatin'
him. That could be two weeks, three, no tellin' how far
they're backed up. Meantime, you could be right, and I could
be wrong. I could just be, you know, overreactin' real bad.
But, all I'm doin', see, is the man has a history of violence
against other people. Who knows when he could turn that

against himself—it's happened before, plenty of times. So what am I, a bad guy for wantin' to make sure he doesn't hurt himself? So it also gives him a lotta time to think, so what? So all we gotta do is wait, see what he thinks about. C'mon, let's go, I'm starvin', I haven't had anything to eat since this mornin'."

Carlucci waited, and waited, and waited some more. On everybody. The Allegheny County coroner's reports on Wandoe Evon Best were the first to come in, and the people there were good to their word. They'd done all the blood work he'd asked them to do, and they'd done it in less than five working days. Carlucci hand-carried the reports to the Troop A crime lab, where he learned that the evidence he'd brought in was at least a week away from even the first stages of examination and analysis. When he called the Allegheny County crime lab to ask about hair, blood, fiber, and semen samples taken from Best's body, he got more or less the same answer on a time frame that he'd just heard from Troop A. And when he called Pittsburgh Major Crimes Unit detectives Tesari and Walls to see where they were in their investigation of Best's homicide, he was told by Walls they'd had to put it back because the mayor, the chief, the crimes unit commander, the papers, the TV stations, everybody was on their backs to clear the homicide of a woman who'd been shot through her kitchen window while she was putting dinner on the table for her family.

"What can I say," Detective Walls said, "she was a fine lady, you know, active in the community, foster mother in addition to takin' care of her own kids, leadin' drug marches through the 'hood and all like that, and she takes one in her kitchen and so far it looks like it wasn't even meant for her, you know? So everybody's pissed about it and you know as well as I do which direction piss falls. So happens, my partner lost his cool little bit last week so, uh, him and me's at the bottom of this particular pissfall, so right now, Detective, I hate to say it but you're the only person alive gives a shit about Wandoe. So I don't know when we're goin' get back to it. But somethin' come up, I told ya I'd call ya, and I will, but if you got somethin' else to do, my advice to you is to do it, okay? Sorry."

The something Carlucci tried to do was to find Alfredo Picadio Jr. through the local travel agencies, of which there were only five in or around Rocksburg, one in each of the malls on either side of town, and three in storefronts within two blocks of the courthouse on Main Street. He struck out in every one of them: Junior and his wife had not used any of them to arrange their vacation. Carlucci then called the airlines that had direct flights from Pittsburgh International Airport to the Bahamas and learned, after what seemed like unendurable delays on all the phone menus, that the Picadios had not booked travel that way either. So he called the airlines all back again and asked about connecting flights with stopovers from Washington, D.C., south to Florida. Who knew, maybe they didn't go direct, maybe they had friends somewhere. There were a whole lot of places in Virginia or the Carolinas or Georgia or Florida they could've gone to first.

When he was at the bottom of his list again, hours and hours after he'd begun, he found a reservations clerk from USAir who pulled up their names from the computer on a flight to Fort Lauderdale and then on Air Florida to Nassau. They'd bought open-ended round-trip tickets, which meant they could be coming back tomorrow, or five months from tomorrow. And since Carlucci had learned from looking through a *World Almanac* that the principal business in the Bahamas was tourism and since this was the middle of January in one of the coldest winters in recent memory, he guessed he could be on hold for days trying to find them.

And wouldn't Mayor Bellotti be thrilled when the city got *that* phone bill.

He went back to reading Coroner Wallace Grimes's report on the postmortem on Mrs. Alfredo Picadio Sr. And he learned again that she hadn't been just Mrs. Alfredo Picadio Sr. She had also been Angelina Marie Dipoli, born May 1, 1921, in Pittsburgh to Gregorio Dipoli and Marie Silvestri Dipoli. That was Grimes for you. He couldn't just do the post. He'd gone out to her house and found the family Bible, on his own. He certainly hadn't asked anybody in the city to do it for him. And when Carlucci had called him about it, all Grimes would say was that "she certainly wasn't a Jane Doe and she certainly wasn't just her husband's wife. If I thought it was going to be any big deal I wouldn't have done it. I just knew the family, that's all. I just thought all the names should be there, that's all. You have a problem with it, Detective?"

"No, sir." But there he was, staring at all her names again and thinking about how she'd spent the last conscious moments of her life. And then he stopped thinking about it because it was making him queasy, so he went downstairs and got himself a Diet Pepsi.

When he came back, Nowicki told him there was a call for him, and transferred it to the phone in Balzic's office.

"Carlucci here, what can I do for you?"

"You can get me the fuck out this suicide cell, motherfucker! Only time they let me out is to make phone calls and they done took all my money, man, I'm tired beggin' for quarters, man, so please, man, please please please get your ass down here and tell the motherfuckers let me out, man, I ain't gonna off my damn self no way!"

Carlucci said nothing. He just hung up, leaned back, and waited.

Five minutes later, Givins was back on the line again,

"Don't hang up, man, please don't hang up, please, you got to get me out, I can't sleep with these damn lights on all the time. I can't . . . I ain't shit in three days, man, I can't do that with that motherfuckin' camera lookin' at me all the time, don't hang up, please, please don't hang up. I can't get nobody in the PD's office, man, come down here and talk with me, you gotta come on down, man, no shit."

Carlucci counted out ten seconds silently, one thousand one, one thousand two, before he answered, with Givins talking nonstop through Carlucci's silence. "Yo, Detective! Yo, man, please! This ain't human, man, no shit, ain't nobody 'posed to be livin' with the lights on all the time, camera takin' your picture all the time, twenty-four seven, man, that ain't human, whatchu doin' this to me for, man, what the fuck I ever do to you, man? Tell me, I'll 'pologize, whatchu want? Please! You there? You still there? Yo? Detective? You there, man?"

Carlucci spoke as softly as he could without whispering. "I'm still here."

"Oh man you gotta talk up, I can barely hear you."

"I'm here," Carlucci said again, slightly louder.

"Say what?" There was a scraping and muffling as Givins called out to somebody on his end, "Say, man, this phone broke? This phone work, man, I can hardly hear this dude. Got-damn I got to talk to this man, you sure this phone ain't fucked up? Hello? Hello? You still there?"

"I'm here," Carlucci said, almost normally.

"I can hear ya better now, man, oh yeah. Listen, don't hang up, okay? Please? You gotta help me here, man. I mean, I ain't talked to my lawyer or nothin'. CO tell me could be two weeks before I gets to mental health, man, 'fore they gets around to me, you know?"

"Listen, Mr. Givins, you got a problem with the PD's office, you know their number as well as I do. I gave you their

number and you could get it right now from any one of the
COs or from any of the other inmates, so if you have a problem about your lawyer, you're talkin' to the wrong guy. I
can't help you with your lawyer. I did my job when I told the
DJ you had requested one. From then on, it wasn't on me. It
was on them and you."

"I know I know, don't hang up. Listen, uh, listen, Detective, I know I was talkin' trash'n everything little while ago,
you know, usin' wrong language'n everything, but that's just
'cause I'm so fucked up behind bein' in this cell and not gettin' no sleep and can't shit, see? I wants to 'pologize for that,
see, this place, these lights, man, they makin' me crazy—"

"Well then I guess I was right to alert the DWT, I guess he
put you in the right place—"

"Oh no man wait wait wait, that ain't the kinda crazy I'm
talkin' here. You know, I'm just talkin' shit here, that's all, I
don't mean crazy crazy like that. I just mean my jaw's gettin'
all tight, that's all, none of this super-crazy shit, you know,
thinkin' I'm goin' do somethin' to myself or nothin' like
that, that ain't what I'm talkin' 'bout—"

"All right, Mr. Givins, let's cut the crap. You got somethin' for me? You tryin' to tell me I should bring my tape
recorder down there, drive all the way down there, you tell
me, am I gonna get jagged off or what?"

"Uh-uh, no way, man. You come on down here, I got
somethin' for ya. You come on down, we get straight real
quick. No problem, man. You bring anybody you wants. Assistant DA, that dude from the state police, bring who you
wants, man, I got somethin' for ya, swear to God, man,
swear to God. I don't get out that cell, man, I'm goin' die a
constipation, I can't stand that, man, people be watchin' me
while I'm tryin' to do my thing. I can't stand it . . ."

Milliron was already there, reading over something when

Carlucci opened the door to the interview room. After they exchanged greetings, Milliron said, "You think he's ready?"

"I'm ready, I don't know about him. Fresh batteries, fresh tapes, I'm as ready as I can be."

A CO led Givins into the room and started to handcuff him to the table, but Carlucci waved him off. "That's okay," he said, "he doesn't need that, right, Luther?"

"Huh? Oh, right, man, right."

"You got cigarettes, Luther? You need some? What kind you smoke? Anything but menthol, right? How 'bout a Pepsi, Coke, coffee, whatta ya want?"

"Milk a magnesia, man. Ex-Lax. Gimme all ya got." He was not laughing. "My stomach hard as a rock, man, and it ain't from no sit-ups."

Carlucci started to hand the CO a five and to tell him to bring a pack of cigarettes, but Milliron said he'd get them and took off. In five minutes he was back, during which all Givins did was complain about his stomach and how he had never in his life gone that many days without moving his bowels. "I'm scared somethin' goin' bust, man, no shit, I am. I heard 'bout people bustin' a gut, everybody be laughin', but that ain't funny, man."

Milliron returned with three coffees and six packs of powdered cream and sugar and a pack of Winstons and matches.

"Oh man, coffee, it use to always work for me in the mornin', you know, but down there, don't even coffee work, I don't understand. But I'm glad you brought it, man, don't think I ain't grateful or nothin', I am, and I'm goin' to keep tryin' it, I know it goin' work sooner or later."

Carlucci turned on his recorder, identified everybody, stated the date, time, and place of the interview, and said, "Okay, Luther, you said you had somethin' for me. So what is it?"

"Well wait wait wait, ain't we goin' talk 'bout what you

goin' do for me first? Huh? Gettin' me out that mother-fuckin' suicide cell, man, c'mon now, that's what you said on the phone, man, you said—"

"C'mon, Luther, you're no cherry here, you know how this works, and you know we know how it works, so don't waste our time, whatta ya got?"

"Hey, right on. Cuttin' right to the chase, man, this is me cuttin' right to the chase, here I go. You got your box turned on? Yeah, I seen ya turn it on. Okay. Okay. Here we go. You ready?"

Carlucci sipped his coffee and said nothing. Milliron looked at his watch.

"Okay. Here's how it went down, man. I'm doin' my own thing, man, takin' care of business, man, ain't botherin' no-body. One day, man, I'm layin' up in the bed, listenin' to my man James Brown, here come Al Picadio, him and this other dude, Paul or Paulie somethin' I don't know who that dude was."

"He didn't introduce you? Or did he just tell you his first name."

"He didn't do no formal intro, man, if that's what you mean. He just said this is Paul or somethin'. He called him Paulie couple times."

"Okay, so this was in your aunt's house? On Franklin Avenue in Rocksburg, is that correct?"

"Yeah."

"When was this?"

"I don't know. October maybe. No. Yeah. October. 'Bout a month after I got here, yeah."

"After you got here this time, right? You've been here be-fore, right? Off and on? Right?"

"Oh yeah. Couple times."

"He ever talked to you before? Would you say you were

acquaintances, friends, drinkin' buddies, how would you describe your relationship with him?"

"Relation what? What the fuck you talkin' 'bout, man, he's a dago, I'm a nigger, my aunt cooks for his momma."

"And you're sayin' what, you never had anything to do with him before this conversation? When he appears out of nowhere at your aunt's house? With this Paulie person? To ask you what exactly? To rob his business?"

"Yeah that's right, that's exactly what he come for."

"Okay, run it down."

"Well, see, he shook me all up, man, 'cause he come boppin' on in his own self. Last thing in the world I'm thinkin' is the motherfucker have a key. I jumped up'n got my nine, man, I'm thinkin' I'm goin' have to deal with some motherfuckin' booster, man, and here he come, walkin' up the steps, man, I had my nine level on his ass when he come through the door. And when I see it's him I like to shit. I'm sayin' to myself, what the fuck he doin' here? And come in with a key? 'Cause all along, see, my aunt be thinkin' he don't know nothin' 'bout that house and there he was, man. I didn't never say nothin' to her 'bout him comin' on in like that 'cause I didn't wanna make her get all scared'n everything, you know? I still ain't never told her. She still don't know he know 'bout that, and musta been knowin' 'bout it all along, man. And see, that scared me right from the git-go too, I mean, this motherfucker knew 'bout this house, that mean he could put my aunt out anytime he want, and she don't even know nothin' 'bout it. She be thinkin' she be all safe'n shit, you know?"

"So what're you tellin' us?"

"I'm tellin' y'all I was scared, man."

"Scared because you thought you were gonna have to deal with a burglar or scared 'cause of what you thought he could do to your aunt?"

"Both, man, what the fuck you think? You hear somebody put a key in your lock and then you see somebody ain't even 'posed to know his momma did a deal with your aunt, and he be talkin' 'bout he goin' make you fat, what the fuck you think?"

"So were you scared of him personally? He ever lead you to believe he was a danger to you? He ever threaten you?"

"No . . . not exactly."

"Well obviously you didn't shoot him, right? You had your nine leveled on him, but you didn't shoot him so that tells me you had to recognize him, right? So that also tells me you have to've had some contact before, right? You're not gonna try'n tell us this was your first meeting? Or are you? Because if you are, this interview's over."

"Over? What the fuck you talkin' 'bout over? Wait wait, I didn't shoot him yeah, that's right, right, 'cause I seen who it was. That's right. We had done some business before, right, but this the first time I seen him this time, you know what I'm sayin'? In that house, man. I ain't never seen him before in that house, man, no way."

"And this was the first time you saw him anywhere since you moved back in with your aunt this time, is that what you're sayin', right?"

"Right, right."

"So what kinda business you do with him?"

"Oh man whatchu think? He want some weed, man. Everybody in the world in the coke business, man, people want weed they think all they gotta do is ask some nigger, niggers magic or somethin', all they gots to do is wave their dick around like it's a magic wand and they goin' come up with some fine Jamaican."

"So did you?"

"I didn't find no Jamaican, no. Found some other shit.

Didn't charge him too much, he was happy, I was happy, like that."

"Once, more than once, what?"

"More than once."

"A regular thing?"

"No man, it wasn't no regular thing."

"When he was doin' this, was this between just you and him or was he bringin' this Paulie around?"

"Nah this was just him, man."

"So you never saw this Paulie until he comes into your aunt's house—Al Picadio I'm talkin' about—with his own key? And comes upstairs where you're layin' in the bed listenin' to James Brown, and you get your pistol and you aim it but you don't shoot when you see it's him, am I right so far?"

"Right, right, you got it."

"And so after some chitchat in which he does not formally introduce this Paulie person, he then lays out a plan for you to rob his business?"

"Right, exactly. Say he got an idea we can all do some good for each other. He say his friend Paulie was connected up, and his boss be bustin' his balls and they was gonna get even, they was goin' do a number on him."

"Connected up? To the Italian mob? Is that what you took that to mean? That he was connected to the mob?"

"Well what else I'm 'posed to think?"

"And his boss in the mob—is that what they were sayin'? His boss, this Paulie's boss was bustin' his balls and he was tired of it and he and Al Picadio Jr. and you were gonna do a number on his boss, that's the way they approached you about this?"

"Swear to God, that's what they say, man."

"Okay, what'd they say, as close as you can remember it?"

"They say this Paulie was 'posed to go'n carry some bread to some dude from his boss, and they was goin' say some niggers ripped him off. Only what they was goin' do was put it in his office—"

"Whose office?"

"Picadio's."

"Okay, go 'head."

"And this the part, man, see, I just shook my head, 'cause I'm thinkin', these dudes is from Disney World, man. This Paulie say they goin' stash it in Picadio's place, and they goin' tell his uncle that his dumb-ass boss was the one give Paulie all this bread, see, it be *his* idea, see, so his uncle goin' come down on him for bein' so stupid to give the bread to Paulie in the first place. 'Cause his uncle don't want this jive motherfucker in the family business. 'Cause if he be my nephew I ain't goin' have him in my business neither, he even look stupid. And this motherfucker sittin' there tellin' me all he gots to do is talk his boss into lettin' him carry this bread for him, and then his uncle goin' come down on his boss's ass when he find out about it, but ain't goin' say shit to him, see, if you can b'lieve that."

"This was after they told you he was connected up?"

"Wait a second," Milliron said. "I'm not sure I'm following this. This Paulie tells you he's connected, but after he and Picadio lay out this ridiculous scheme, he tells you it's going to work precisely because his uncle is going to be pissed at his boss? Paulie's boss? For giving him this job? When he, Paulie, is not supposed to be involved in the business—why exactly was that, did he say? Why didn't his uncle want him involved in the business?"

"Hey I ain't his uncle, how the fuck I'm 'posed to know? But just listenin' to him, man, and watchin' him while he be talkin', shit, I wouldn't want him doin' nothin' for me neither. Look like a pinhead to me. Head come to a motherfuckin' point on top. Ack like one too. Be goin' huh huh'n shit to everything."

"What'd you say? What was that? Repeat that, about pinhead," Carlucci said.

"I said his motherfuckin' head come to a point on top, back here," Givins said, leaning forward and pointing to a spot on the back of his own head.

"Did Picadio ever call him that? Pinhead?"

"Call him that? Naw. I don't think so."

"Never told you his last name, never called him anything but Paul or Paulie?"

"Uh-uh."

"So did he ever say where he was from?"

"Whatchu be carin' 'bout him for, man, it was Picadio told me what to do. It was all him talkin', it wasn't that other dude. Goofy motherfucker just be goin', Huh, huh, like he humpin' or some shit."

"Okay okay, so tell us what Picadio said."

"He say there was goin' be fifty large, man, in his office. All I had to do was wait till he be gone on vacation, close his place up, man, all I had to do was just walk in and take it and walk out. I look at him and I say, man, whatchu take me for? You know I ain't goin' walk in there and touch nothin', man, 'cause who you think the cops goin' come lookin' for right from the git? My aunt work for your momma and I got two felony busts, man, what the fuck you thinkin' 'bout? And he said the cops ain't goin' know nothin' 'bout nothin' 'cause he ain't goin' tell 'em and what am I thinkin' about? 'Cause ain't nobody goin' know nothin' 'bout it but this Paulie dude's uncle and that was 'cause Paulie was goin' tell him his own damn self. Just to get heat on his boss for givin' him the bread in the first place."

"This is the damnedest thing I ever heard," Milliron said.

"Sorry. Didn't mean to get that on the tape, it just came out."

"That's okay," Carlucci said, frowning at Givins. "And you're tryin' to tell us now that you went for this? You agreed to do this?"

"Uh-uh, man, no fuckin' way I agreed to do nothin'! 'Cause all I could see was, hey, down the road when this thing get to the uncle? I mean, what the fuck he goin' say? Same thing any fool be sayin'—yeah, right, cool, okay, just tell me one thing, where the fifty large *now?* 'Cause that's what I be sayin'. So the next thing come to me, I mean, since they done already made up this bullshit, what was they goin' do but make up some more bullshit, which was goin' be, hey, we know where the nigger is. You just give us some time, we find that nigger ripped us off and we get your bread back. And then, you know what they goin' say next. Two, three days later, they goin' say, Hey, Unk, here the nigger's thumb. See, we done got him. But the fifty large be gone 'cause the nigger done put it up his nose 'fore we found his black ass. And what I seen next was a nigger with a tag on his toe, and these two motherfuckers standin' around sayin', See, Unk, this the nigger what fucked us over and we done took care of his black ass, only thing is we only got a li'l bit of the fifty large back."

Milliron couldn't contain himself. "Wait a second. You suspected this and you agreed to go along with it anyway?"

"I done tol' you, man, the dude had a key to my aunt's house! My aunt to this day don't know the dude know anything 'bout the deal she had with his momma. Right now I know my aunt be scared to death thinkin' what's goin' happen with her now. I ain't talk to her since I boogied, man, but I know she be sick she be so scared what they goin' do. I know she don't know what's goin' happen with her 'bout that motherfuckin' house. All she know is I done stole all her money, man. And when she find out I knew Picadio knew 'bout the house and I didn't say nothin' to her? What she goin' think? Y'all can't even bust me for that, but that's the wrongest thing I did. Fucked my own aunt over. I oughta be whipped."

"You trying to tell us that what you did to Mrs. Picadio wasn't in the same category as what you did to your aunt, is that what you're trying to say?" Milliron said.

"What I did? *What I did?* You outta your motherfuckin' mind? You ain't listenin' to me! You think I'm goin' go on in that office, man, my own self? You a crazy motherfucker. I just tol' you, the only way that bullshit goin' work is if they wind up with a nigger fulla bullet holes, man. That's the on-liest chance they got in the motherfuckin' world makin' this Mafia motherfucker b'lieve that bullshit. No motherfuckin' way in the world I'm gonna be *that* nigger. Shit no! I went to the city, man, East Liberty, man, found me a nigger, say, hey listen, bro, this a walk in the park, in and out, one minute, two tops, for two large, that's what I tol' the brother. I be lyin' my ass off to him."

"You got somebody from East Liberty to agree to burgle the place for two thousand dollars?"

"Hell yeah. They done offered me ten percent. Five large. So if I tell him I'm gonna give him two, what the fuck. I know what he be thinkin' anyway. Same thing anybody be thinkin'. He be thinkin' he goin' take all fifty and tell me, hey, motherfucker, get it if you can, it's mines now. Which be cool, 'cause when they come lookin' for me 'cause they need to turn me into a dead nigger, I say, hey, y'all don't think I'm goin' go on in there my own damn self, do you? You think I'm that stupid? I just give up the brother, that's all. The brother gots to go. It was the brother for my aunt's house, the way I sees it, and if they wants to give me three large, I ain't goin' argue. I'm goin' take it." Givins suddenly hung his head and sounded like he was choking back a sob.

"So what went wrong?"

"Whatchu mean what went wrong, man? You *know* what went wrong, you know how wrong it got. Motherfuckers lied. Everybody lies, man, I know that, everybody, I ain't no fool. But I'm thinkin' I got everything covered. Only thing is, I done forgot, man, how everybody lies. So I'm the biggest fool." He couldn't go on for a minute.

"You want more coffee, Luther?"

He shook his head. "Water. My throat's all dry. Just water's all I want, please?"

Milliron went and got some water in Luther's empty coffee cup.

"So what happened?"

"What happen, what happen, shit. What happen is the motherfucker come blowin' out the other end of the alley in her car, man. I'm 'posed to be pickin' him up at the other end of the alley, he 'posed to walk out, quiet, you know, like ain't shit goin' down, and here come the motherfucker 'round the bend on two wheels! In her motherfuckin' car! When he come out the alley, I see her car, I say aw no, can't be, but I know it's her car, and that fool, he got his arm out the window, the motherfucker be flippin' me the bird, man, and damn near hit a pole tryin' to make the turn. I tried to keep up with him but ain't no way I'm goin' catch him in her Pontiac, not in my Olds. I spent the whole motherfuckin' night lookin' all over East Liberty for that motherfucker. All next day, lookin' everywhere. It's almost like two, three o'-clock, man, the next day, I finally see the car in a alley, he be gettin' coffee or some damn thing, motor runnin', door wide open, I just be standin' there and here he come. Get in, start to shut the door, man, I jump in, stick my nine all up in his face, say slide over, motherfucker, we gots to talk. And he gives me this bullshit 'bout not only was there no money, there was this woman and I'm a lyin' motherfucker 'cause they ain't no money, he done tore the place upside down and didn't find nothin'! And he's screamin' at me how I done tol' him nobody was 'posed to be there, I'm a lie, I'm a lie, there was a woman, there wasn't no money, I'm a motherfuckin' lie, he be shoutin', carryin' on, I say shut up, man, you startin' to draw a crowd here, stupid motherfucker, lower your voice. And he just be gettin' louder and louder, man, and then the motherfucker tell me what he done done . . . aw Lord. Motherfucker tell me what he done to Miz Picadio. And I said aw shit, I'm sittin' in her car and my prints is all over the door and the roof and the steerin' wheel from when I jumped in and this motherfucker is screamin' at me and I just seen everything, man, just every motherfuckin' thing was just goin' to hell right in front of my eyes, man, and they ain't one got-damn thing I can do about it. I didn't know whether the motherfucker was lyin' to me 'bout the money or what. I kep' sayin' where's it at where's it at and he just kep' screamin' at me, man, you a lyin' motherfucker, you a lie, motherfucker, and I just burned him, man. Just burned the motherfucker. I started to wipe the steerin' wheel but there was this ol' motherfucker come in the alley to piss and was lookin' at me and I just said fuckit, and got on outta there. And then I come back home and got my clothes'n shit, took my aunt's money, and went on. Shoulda paid for that gas, that was stupid. If I'da paid for that gas like I was 'posed to, y'all wouldn't even be talkin' to me now."

Givins hung his head and shook it. After a long moment passed, he said, "I would appreciate y'alls doin' somethin' for me."

"What's that?"

"Did y'all carry my car on back here? You say you was goin' do that, did you do that?"

"Yes, I did," Milliron said.

"Well 'less somebody done copped it, it's in the trunk, my aunt's bread. I would appreciate y'alls gettin' it and givin' it to her, and tellin' her I'm a sorry-ass fool. She don't wan' talk to me. Hang up every time I call. She get her bread back, maybe she wan' talk to me. I know she don't deserve me, but, oh man, she all I got now. And I needs somebody, Lord Lord, I needs somebody."

"Where is it in the trunk?"

"Spare tire. Spare's flat, I stuck it up inside the tire. Three-fifty somethin', don't know exactly."

"Okay, Luther, if it's still there, we'll see that she gets it. And we'll get an ADA down here soon as we can to find out what everybody has to do. He's gonna have to talk to the DA in Allegheny County, find out what they want to go down. We can't cut you a deal here for what they wanna do, you know what I'm sayin'? You are gonna testify, right? I mean, you're not gonna stop here, right? You're not gonna get second thoughts about this, are ya?"

Luther shook his head. "Whatever, man. Just please tell me you goin' get me out that suicide cell, man, 'cause you know I done my part, man. Tol' ya what you needs to know. And what I needs is my privacy, man. Can't shit with no camera on me, it ain't right. It's humiliatin', man, gruntin' and twistin' up your face like that and you know some motherfucker be watchin' you, laughin'n shit."

"Consider it done, Luther," Carlucci said. "Don't worry about it anymore. Just one more thing I wanna know. I want you to think real hard. I want you to think about this Paulie person. You hear any town mentioned, any places, any bars, restaurants, clubs, anyplace where we might be able to find him?"

"Naw, uh-uh. I don't know, I don't wanna know. I hope the next time I see the motherfucker it's 'cause somebody want me to identify the body."

Carlucci turned off his recorder, and he stood and extended his hand to Luther. "I wanna thank you, Luther. You saved me a lotta work. I'm not gonna forget that. Everything I can do for you I'm gonna do. You hang in there. You might have to stay the rest of the day in your house, but I guarantee you'll be in another house by tonight, fair enough?"

Luther nodded and shook Carlucci's hand weakly.

Carlucci nodded for Milliron to follow him out and they conferred briefly about who was going to do what. Milliron agreed to contact the Conemaugh County DA's office to find out where and how they would proceed with Allegheny County, but they both agreed that since today was Saturday nothing much was going to happen until Monday, especially because Givins was already in custody. Milliron also agreed to ask around in Troop A CID to see if anybody working with organized crime could put another name with Paul or Paulie. Carlucci agreed to talk to Deputy Warden of Treatment Kerpinski to get Givins moved out of the suicide cell and back into the general population and also to see what he could come up with about this Paulie person. When Milliron asked him why he was so anxious to locate this Paulie, whoever he was, Carlucci said, "It's a loose end, that's all. Loose ends drive me nuts. I think we got Picadio tied up real tight with just what Givins gave us, but I'd really like to talk to this Paulie guy. The thing is, I just heard a name real similar to that. I swear a guy just talked to me about somebody named Paulie and he called him Pinhead, but I'll be damned if I can place it now."

At six-thirty Saturday evening, Carlucci was in Balzic's office, bringing the case file up to date, but his vision was starting to blur and his printing was getting wobbly. He had reached the point where he was starting to get a little frightened that something might be wrong with him physically, something other than normal exhaustion. He put down his pen and gave himself an earnest lecture that nothing was wrong, that all he needed was sleep.

Fischetti knocked on the door frame and stuck his head in and said, "Some guy from the U.S. attorney's office in Pittsburgh's on the phone, wants to know if anybody here's workin' anything involvin' somebody named Picadio."

"He ask for me specifically or just for whoever was workin' the case?"

"He didn't say workin' a particular case. Just said workin' anything 'involving'—that was his word—somebody named Picadio. None of my business, man, you look like you're gonna fall over."

"I'm just real tired, that's all." Carlucci picked up the phone and identified himself. "Who're you now?"

"I'm John Berkley. I'm an assistant here in the U.S. attorney's office, and believe me, I hate to be bothering you at this time on a Saturday night, but somebody bothered me, so I guess I'm within my rights to bother you. Does the name Picadio mean anything to you?"

"Uh, yeah, I'm familiar with the name. What's this in reference to?"

"This is in reference to a maniac who's been here since four o'clock this afternoon, came in demanding to be put in the Witness Protection Program, and I guess it was around an hour later when the powers that be decided I was the one whose weekend ought to be ruined, so that's when I came on board. Anyway, all this maniac keeps talking about is something that happened in Rocksburg—is that it? Rocksburg? I'm new to the area—"

"Yeah, Rocksburg. And he's sayin' somethin' about Picadio?"

"He's very hard to understand, he's very frightened, but yes, he keeps saying that name, Picadio, which doesn't mean anything to me."

"So, uh, who is he? And who does he say he wants to be protected from?"

"Name's Colella. Paul John. He's been stomping around here, ranting and raving about how his uncle wants to kill him. Says his uncle is big, big Mafia. Says I'm an asshole because I don't know that. I keep telling him I just got here Monday, and I'm not familiar with anything he's talking about, so I can't offer him a thing and I can't locate anybody who can, since apparently everybody from the Organized Crime Section decided to go into hiding at five o'clock yesterday. But since you seem to know something about this person, this Picadio, I'm open for suggestions. Believe me, you have anything to offer, I'll listen."

"You got transportation?"

"I'm sure I can locate some."

"Well, if he's who I think he is, you ask him to tell you what he knows about Gerry Colella, that's his uncle. You think any of that would interest your organized crime people, then I think you'll agree you gotta lock him up somewhere until somebody can make a decision about what he's worth to you. But I would definitely like to talk to him about Picadio, oh yeah. So if you can get him down here, I can sure as hell find a cell for him in the county lockup, if that's okay."

Berkley sighed. "Okay. How's this? I get him down there—wherever that is—and you talk to him, then Monday, the organized crime people can decide whether they want to talk to him. I really don't want to make this decision, I don't have anywhere near enough information, and if I don't get out of here by seven-thirty, my wife's going to be extremely unhappy with me. Just tell me where it is he's supposed to go."

"Fine. The new Conemaugh County Jail. You tell your driver he needs directions just call me back. Otherwise, I'll be down the jail waitin'."

Once inside the jail, Carlucci hunted down the CO supervisor and arranged for Paul Colella to be booked on a federal detainer, which Carlucci hoped that whoever was driving Colella would be bringing as well. "In the meantime, you got a table or a bench somewhere I can crap out on? I'm so goddamn tired, I'm gonna fall over I don't catch a little nap."

The CO supervisor told Carlucci to use the table in one of the interview rooms. "You're gonna wanna talk to this guy, right?"

"Oh yeah—if I can stay awake. Can't remember the last time I was this tired."

"So after we get him booked, I'll send him in and wake ya up, okay? Who's bringin' him?"

"I'm guessin' a U.S. marshal, but I don't know and I don't care. I gotta lay down, honest to God, my knees're shakin'."

The CO supervisor let Carlucci into one of the interview rooms and closed the door. Carlucci took off his parka and bundled it up for a pillow and stretched out on the table, feeling that luxurious relief that comes from getting off your feet when you're so tired your nerves are starting to jump. He knew he wouldn't actually fall asleep—he never could do that when he was as tired as he was now—he was just hoping to refresh himself by closing his eyes for twenty minutes or so and trying not to think about anything.

Balzic had been telling him for years that he had to learn how to nap. It made no difference how you did it, Balzic used to say, five or ten minutes here or there throughout the day, sitting or lying, you just had to find a way to do it that worked for you. Otherwise the weight of thinking not only what you should be thinking but also how other people were thinking—those who were cooperating with you as well as those who were doing everything they could to avoid cooperating with you—the weight of not being able to give your mind a rest would work against you in a way that was particularly dangerous to investigators. You would forget things, routine things, things any rookie would know to do. You had to find a way to refresh your mind, Balzic said, and nothing would do that like a nap.

Carlucci had no problem with the concept. He had a serious problem with putting it into practice, especially when he had reached this stage of feeling wired, like he had been drinking coffee all day to stay awake and then had drunk that one cup too many. So here he was, eyes closed, body relaxed, but instead of freeing his mind of thought, his mind was going into overdrive, one scene after another coming in a parade of images and words, his mother complaining about Balzic as though it was Balzic's fault Carlucci was working all these hours when Carlucci couldn't bring himself to make her understand that without all the overtime he couldn't afford to pay the women who sat with her every day, cooked for her, washed her, cleaned the house, laundered her clothes.

Then there was Mayor Bellotti, getting ready to do God knows what to manipulate Carlucci into thinking that being the next chief was the brightest idea anybody could possibly have, even though Carlucci knew that if new officers weren't hired and other officers weren't promoted, only two things were going to happen: he was going to get a small pile of new insignias to put on his uniform and a large pile of new responsibilities to add to the ones he already had.

Then there was Mrs. Alfredo Picadio Sr. and Luther Alonzo Givins and Wandoe Evon Best and Alfredo Picadio Jr. and now due to arrive at any minute Paulie John Colella, Jesus, Mary, and Joseph, did this thing happen the way Luther Givins was claiming it happened?

Oh Christ, Carlucci thought, sitting bolt upright with a gasp. Why didn't I ask him what happened to the gun? What'd he do with his nine? Milliron didn't say a goddamn word about it, where the fuck is it? Pittsburgh PD's gonna want that. Oh shit, this is what happens when you get tired, shit shit shit . . .

He fought the urge to go running around trying to locate Luther Givins. He bent forward and hugged his stomach and rocked for a few moments. He lay back down finally, growling at himself for conducting such a piss-poor imitation of an interview. A man tells you he shot the man who did the robbery, assault, and rape that led to a woman's death, and you can't even remember to ask him what he did with the gun. Oh Jesus, Milliron, I hope you ain't as tired as I am. I hope to fuck you have the sense to give that car a proper toss, Gawwwwwwd, how could I've been that fuckin' stupid! Oh easy, Ruggiero, it was easy. All you heard was what you wanted to hear and once you heard that, fuck, what was the point thinkin' about anything else?

Goddamn Balzic could just sit down, close his eyes, and ten seconds later, he'd be practically snorin', why the fuck can't I do that? And why didn't Milliron say anything about the gun? A guy just tells us he shot another guy in the woman's car in an alley in East Liberty, and neither one of you can think to say where's the weapon? Talk about your crack police investigators, Jesus. All you have to do to tie that one up for the Pittsburgh PD is find the nine, that's all you have to do, find the nine, find the nine. . . .

Then somebody was shaking him and his eyes didn't want to come open. He was licking his lips and trying to wipe the gummy corners of his mouth and saying, "Huh? What? Say what?"

"Your man Colella's here, Detective. You want a coupla minutes to get organized or you want me to bring him in now? He's booked."

"Oh yeah yeah," Carlucci said, swinging his legs off the table and stretching. "Where's the john, I keep forgettin', I needa go to the john, where is it?"

The CO led Carlucci out and down a short corridor and pointed out the door to the john for him. Carlucci hurried off, staggering slightly because he was trying to roll the kinks out of his neck. After he relieved himself and washed his hands, he splashed water on his face and dried himself with his hanky. He returned to the interview room to find a short, barrel-bellied man practically jumping out of his skin. He was jerking at the handcuffs and nearly sobbing with frustration.

The CO started to unlock the door, but Carlucci stopped him. "Listen, I know you got a pile of things you gotta do, but I really need a favor. You think you could make a call for me, give somebody a message, please?"

"Sure, Detective, I can do that. Who to?"

"Aw man, thanks. Call Troop A state police. Tell Trooper Claude Milliron he has to search the car, see if he can find that nine-millimeter pistol. He'll know what I'm talkin' about—"

"Christ, I almost forgot," the CO said. "He just called. Told me to tell you he found the pistol under the backseat."

"He found the nine?! Oh shit that's great! Great!" Carlucci shuddered and sighed with relief. "You can let me in now. Man, look at him, you think he's whacked out on somethin'? Christ, looks like he's gonna come right out of his skin."

"Nah, that's fear doin' that. His pupils're normal, I checked him out after we booked him 'cause I thought he was on somethin' too. But, you ask me, that's pure fear. That's his own chemicals doin' that."

The CO unlocked the door and stood aside as Carlucci went inside, hung his parka over the back of a chair, and set his tape recorder in the middle of the table. He sat in a chair at the end of the table, just around the corner from where Paulie Colella was handcuffed.

Colella's eyes were frantic, his breathing was shallow and

noisy, and his knees were jumping. He was tugging at the cuffs and cursing nonstop under his breath.

Carlucci identified himself, the day, date, time, and location of the interview, and the subject for the tape. Colella stopped cursing to listen. Everything else that he'd been moving continued to move.

"You're Paul John Colella, is that correct?"

"Get these fuckin' things off me 'kay? I can't stand these fuckin' things."

"You Paul John—"

"Yeah yeah yeah that's me. Take 'ese things off I'm tellin' ya."

"How old're you?"

"Forty-nine, c'mon, get these fuckin' things offa me."

"What's your address?"

"Harmarville."

"House number, street?"

"I'm stayin' in a motel. Valley somethin'."

"You don't have a permanent address?"

"Ain't nothin' permanent, buddy boy. You gonna take 'ese fuckin' things offa me or not? C'mon, man, Jesus Christ, huh?"

"The cuffs are for your own protection."

"My own what? You shittin' me? C'mon, man, stop fuckin' with me this way, this ain't right, I come in, I wanna help youse guys out, whatta youns do, huh? Youns treat me like I'm a fuckin' nigger or somethin'."

"Listen, Mr. Colella, I'll help you, but not until you help me, understand? So you gotta think about this. You gotta think about where you are and what you can do for yourself and how you have to go about it, you listenin' to me, huh? 'Cause doin' what you're doin', that's not helpin' anything. You're just workin' yourself up into a state where you're gonna pass out. You're hyperventilatin' right now, you know what I'm talkin' about?"

"Hyper what? You ain't shittin' I'm hyper! I walk in the fuckin' U.S. attorney's down there, they didn't have to come get me, they didn't have to send no-fuckin'-body for me, I come in on my own, I come in a fuckin' cab, I take a fuckin' taxi there, yeah. And whatta they do? Huh? The pricks, the assholes, the fucks, the stupid fucks, they bring me to this fuckin' place, like I'm some fuckin' *tuzone,* some fuckin' nigger, some fuckin' animal, I got all this information for them, you think they wanna hear what I got to say, huh? Fuck no they don't wanna hear what I got to say, the fuckin' assholes, they don't wanna know nothin'!"

Carlucci folded his arms and sighed. He swallowed and leaned back and crossed his legs and stared at Colella, whose face was bright pink. He was sweating, his spit was flying, he was jerking so hard on the cuffs his wrists were turning red.

Carlucci let him go on for another thirty seconds or so, then stood up, swept the tape recorder into his pocket, and reached for his parka.

"Hey hey, where you goin'? Whatta ya doin'?"

"I got better things to do than listen to some crazy man. Whenever you wanna talk to me—you hear what I said? Talk? Huh? Not scream, talk. Whenever you decide that's what you wanna do, you tell one of the COs, they'll give me a call. Meantime, see ya later."

"Wait! Whoa ho! Wait a minute! Jesus Christ, hey, sit down here, c'mon, what's your name again? Huh? Detective? Detective what? C'mon, sit down sit down."

"You gonna stop screamin'? Huh?"

"Yeah, right, course, sure, I'm gonna stop, yeah. Hey, c'mon, sit down, sit down. What's your name?"

"Carlucci. Detective Sergeant Ruggiero Carlucci. I'm with

the Rocksburg PD. When you wanna talk to me, you address me as Detective or Sergeant, I don't care which. But the most important thing for you to notice about me is this: I am in no way connected to or with anybody or anything in the United States Justice Department. I'm not with the U.S. attorney's office, I'm not with the U.S. marshals, so whatever happened down there or on the trip out here between you and them is not somethin' I can do anything about, you understand me? 'Cause I don't care what happened with you down there, you understand me? That's between you and them. What's between you and me is what you're willin' to tell me about Alfredo Picadio Junior and that's all I care about, you understand? Do you understand me? 'Cause if you can't separate me from the people you seem to think dicked you around in Pittsburgh, if you can't separate us, I'm walkin', understand? I'm not gonna sit here and listen to crazy screamin', that's out. So how we gonna do this, you tell me."

Colella rolled his eyes and sighed many times. He licked his lips and said, "Aw c'mon, sit down, huh? Detective, c'mon sit down, 'kay? I won't raise my voice no more, promise, c'mon, sit down. You gotta understand my situation here—"

"No I don't. I don't have to understand anything about your situation. All I have to understand is whether you're gonna tell me what I need to know about Picadio. Just focus on this, Mr. Colella. Alfredo Picadio Junior. Just put all your attention on that. I don't care about what you think your situation is. This is the only situation I'm interested in, right here, right now, because what I want you to know right now is this: there are two people dead because of this Picadio business. This bad Picadio business. And you know what bad Picadio business I'm talkin' about. A black male named Wandoe Evon Best—who I'm sure you don't know—he was shot to death in East Liberty, Pittsburgh. I do not have all the physical evidence I need, but that homicide isn't my case anyway. What I do have is a confession from the shooter which I'm gonna turn over to the Pittsburgh police and they can take it from there. I'm gonna tell you now the name of the shooter and it's a name you're gonna recognize. The shooter's name is Luther Alonzo Givins. You recognize that name, huh?"

Colella stopped moving. He grew very still. His eyes were all that was moving, darting from his hands to the table to the walls to Carlucci and back to his hands. "He confessed? What'd he confess to?"

"What do you think he confessed to, Mr. Colella? And why're you all of sudden gettin' coy? You were the one who took a cab in to the U.S. attorney, right? The assistant attorney you talked to down there, when he called me, he asked specifically for the officer who was workin' the Picadio case. Now all of a sudden you seem, uh, what? Mystified? Huh? That somebody confessed to their part in this business. What's the mystery here, Mr. Colella?"

Colella averted his eyes. "Well see, what I was gonna talk to them about down there, see that was somethin' else. That wasn't about this thing what you're talkin' about. What I was gonna talk to them about was, uh, my uncle. See? It wasn't about this. I don't know nothin' about no shootin' in East Liberty. Why the fuck would I know anything about that?"

Carlucci closed his eyes and turned his head and sighed. "Oh come on, man, cut the crap. Why would an assistant U.S. attorney call me on the phone and ask specifically for whoever was workin' this case? Why are you sittin' here right now? You think you got here by accident? Why would I even be talkin' to you—oh wait a minute. You didn't know anybody was dead. You haven't talked to anybody, have ya? You been so busy runnin' from your uncle—wait a minute.

Where you been for the last coupla weeks? Where you been since around Christmas?"

"Around. Here and there, you know."

"No no, I don't know. Where? Exactly."

"Uh, Lauderdale mostly. I was in Daytona Beach for a while. Then I went to Pompano Beach. But mostly Lauderdale."

"So you were what—the whole time Al Junior was in the Bahamas, you were in Florida?"

"Yeah. Mostly."

"Either you were or you weren't. What's mostly mean?"

"Yeah I was in Florida. So what?"

"When was the last time you talked to Picadio?"

Colella shrugged. "Christmas Eve."

"You had no contact with him since? No phone calls, no letter, no face-to-face, no nothin'?"

"I just said no. No means no. Don't it?"

Carlucci sat down and set the tape recorder in the middle of the table again. This was to impress Colella, because, being voice-activated, it had recorded everything that had been said so far. "So you think everything worked?"

"Huh? What worked, whatta you talkin' about, what everything? I don't know what you're talkin' about."

"I'll bet you don't. I'll just bet you don't. You're just runnin' from your uncle, ain't you?" Carlucci was incredulous. "Wait a minute, wait a second here. You been tryin', haven't ya? You been tryin' like crazy to get in touch with Alfredo and either you can't find him or else he don't wanna have nothin' to do with you, huh? That's it, am I right? Which is it—you can't find him or he don't wanna talk to you?"

"I ain't sayin' nothin' about this," Colella said. He was almost pouting.

"Then what the fuck you doin' here?" Carlucci said, standing and reaching for the tape recorder again.

"Wait wait wait! Wait a fuckin' second, where you goin'? Jesus Christ, you gotta stop doin' 'at, man, you're makin' me fuckin' crazy here, jumpin' up and down all the time, c'mon."

Carlucci sat down again and leaned close to Colella. "Hey, Paulie, this is simple. You don't wanna talk to me, there's not one reason in the world why I should be sittin' here. And there's not one reason in the world why you should be locked in here. You keep jaggin' me around, I'm gonna go find the supervisor and tell him there's been a mistake, we got no reason to hold you. And you know what he's gonna do? Huh? He's gonna take you to the front door and put you out and close it behind you. And then you know what I do, Paulie? Huh? Can you guess? Can't guess? No? I'll tell ya what I do. I turn into a real prick. I go find a phone and I drop a quarter on you, Paulie. I say, hey uncle, hey Mr. Colella, hey Gerry, your nephew needs a ride—"

"Oh shit shit shit," Colella sputtered, his round body bouncing off the chair with each burst of air. "Don't say that, don't say that, don't say that, Jesus Christ no, you can't do that, please please, honest to God, you can't do that . . ." He began to sob, tears streaming down his contorted face, round shoulders shaking. He fell forward on his fists and sobbed.

Carlucci leaned even closer. "Up to you, Paulie, up to you. It's all in your hands. You control your destiny here, not your uncle, not me. You. Whatever you do, I do. You treat me right, I treat you right. You fuck me around, I fuck you around, it's all up to you. So stop your bawlin' here and start actin' like a man. The simple fact is, you and your buddy Al, you were gonna fuck your boss around, get him in real heat with your uncle, but that ain't what happened. What happened is, what you and your buddy Al did, what you two real geniuses did, you set the wheels in motion that got his mother killed."

Colella reared up from the table, his red, rheumy eyes wild. "What? What did you say? His mother what?"

"Killed, Paulie. Murdered. Raped. Beaten so bad she died."

"Oh my God, oh my God," Paulie said. "I didn't do that. I was in Florida. I went to Florida. I didn't do that—"

"Oh but you did, Paulie. I know the whole story. Luther Givins told us the whole story. I got it on tape. And I'm gonna be talkin' to him, hey, three, four more times, whatever it takes to get all the details down, all the dates and the places and everything else I need. See, 'cause he's already talkin'. He's already up for murderin' the guy he hired, just like you and Al Jr. hired him, you get it? Huh? You startin' to get it now?"

"I didn't tell him to murder nobody! What the fuck you think I am?"

"I know what you are, Paulie. You are a coconspirator in a felony murder, that's what you are. And while it's factually true—I mean it isn't yet, but I'm sure you give us the names of all the places you stayed in Florida we can check to find out whether it's factually true you were in Florida when it went down—but that doesn't change anything, Paulie. 'Cause you started it. You and Al Junior. It all started with you two. I don't know why it started with you two, I mean, I can make a pretty good guess, but I do know you two started it. I don't have any doubt about that. He needed money and you figured a way you could both get some, isn't that right, huh? So if at the end of this whole chain reaction you two started, if the windup is a woman gets raped and murdered, what does that make you, huh? C'mon, Paulie, you can figure this out, what's that make you?"

Colella's head sank forward onto his fists again and rolled from side to side. What seemed like a minute passed. Then another. Finally, his head still on his fists, he said, "Jesus fuckin' Christ, how was I s'posed to know that was gonna happen, huh? How was I s'posed to know that, man, you tell me."

"The only thing I'm gonna tell you, Paulie, is if you don't start tellin' me what I need to know, and no games this time, no hesitation, you don't get right on it, you're gonna be in a whole lot more trouble with your uncle than you are with the state of Pennsylvania, you hear me? You hear what I just said?"

"My uncle, my uncle . . . you think you could hide me from him, you're wrong, you can't hide me from him. He'll find me, it won't fuckin' matter where youns guys put me, he'll find me. He will. 'At's what he does, man. He finds you, don't fuckin' matter where you go, he finds you."

"Hey, Paulie, listen up, Paulie. Yo, Paulie, you listenin'? Last chance. You don't start talkin' to me, I'm walkin', you hear? Either you talk or I walk."

"Oh man, she was s'posed to be in New York, man, she wasn't s'posed to be there. What the fuck was she doin' there, she wasn't s'posed to be there. Aw man, aw man, aw man . . ."

Sunday was the only day of the week that neither Mrs. Comito nor Mrs. Viola came in to stay with Mrs. Carlucci, so it was the one day of the week Carlucci had to spend all day in the house with his mother. Since she only left the house to see a doctor or a dentist, and since her main preoccupation was watching television, and since she wanted him right there beside her as much as possible when he was home, what he did every Sunday night after washing the dinner dishes and cleaning the kitchen was to sit with her while she watched her programs. But the only way he could do that, since he detested almost everything he'd ever seen on TV because of the background music, was to teach himself how to look at the screen without seeing it. His eyes would be pointed at the screen, but he would be tuned in to her and her reactions to what she was seeing. To him, it was just a variation of using peripheral vision to study somebody while pretending to look at something else. His only break from this came because by necessity he also had to use Sunday nights to wash his clothes, so he would be jumping up every half hour or so to go to the cellar to switch loads from the washer to the dryer and to put another load in the washer and then come back up and fold the clothes he'd just taken out of the dryer. This invariably annoyed his mother, who seemed unable to understand why he just couldn't sit still with her and enjoy her programs.

He hated her programs—not because they were hers, although the way she talked about them sometimes left him with the impression she believed they'd been made especially for her—he just hated them on principle. She watched *60 Minutes* and *Murder, She Wrote* and then she'd usually fall asleep sometime near the middle of the movie of the week that came on at nine. He associated most of the staff on *60 Minutes* with their reporting days during Vietnam. No matter what they were talking about or who they were talking to now, Carlucci simply could not separate Morley Safer, Ed Bradley, and Mike Wallace from his memory of them making their "war correspondent fashion statements," which is what he thought when he'd first seen them on the tube after he'd come back from Vietnam. It was when he'd first become intensely aware of background music and how it distorted everything for him, fading, as it did on TV, in and out from theme music to commercial jingles.

As for *Murder, She Wrote*, Carlucci had tried once to explain to his mother why it was nothing but Hollywood hokum, but she'd taken his criticism of the show as a criticism of her and had cried for nearly an hour after the show had signed off, alternately berating him for not understanding how much it meant to her to know that he liked what she liked and for spending so much time working that she could never find out what he liked on television. He'd gotten flip and told her he didn't like anything on television, which wasn't true, he did like some things on PBS, especially the cooking shows he sometimes got a chance to watch on Saturdays. She'd reacted by throwing a pillow at him, and when he bent over to pick it up, she'd rolled up the TV section from the *Rocksburg Gazette* and whacked him across the back of the head with it, nearly knocking him into the coffee table. Then she'd jumped up and cried out for him to watch himself or he'd get hurt and then she'd followed that up by hugging him and sobbing into his collarbone that only a terrible person would make her do that to him.

So Carlucci was constantly wary about how to respond to his mother's reactions to what she was watching. When the phone rang this Sunday night, he practically leaped to answer it. It was about ten minutes to nine, and his mother started yelling at him to quick answer it because Jessica Fletcher was just getting to the good part. "For Christ's sake hurry up'n answer it and don't talk so loud, I wanna hear!"

Carlucci took the phone off the hook in the kitchen into the stairway to the cellar and closed the cellar door before he spoke a simple yes into the phone.

It was Patrolman Harry Lynch at the station, working dispatcher duty.

"What're you doin' there, Harry? How come you're workin' this shift?"

"I owed Chubby Baker. He worked for me when my kid got married last month, and he wanted this weekend off, so I owed him, so I'm payin' him. Listen, I got two people here you been wantin' to see. They just walked in, like two minutes ago, and soon as they said who they were I told 'em I had to return a call to check on an officer and so now you're the officer I'm checkin' on. Mr. and Mrs. Picadio. What do you want me to tell 'em?"

"Well, uh, first thing you tell 'em is what happened to his mother. Listen, I can't get anybody in here to watch my mother or I'd come down and do it, Harry, believe me, I wouldn't stick you with this—"

"Forget about it, it ain't no big deal, I can do it. I mean after, what do you want me to tell 'em after, you know, about when you wanna see 'em?"

"Yeah, yeah. Okay. Listen, you tell 'em we got somebody in custody, don't tell 'em what for, no specific charges or anything like that, okay?"

"I'm listenin', go 'head."

"And you tell 'em I know this is a real bad time for 'em and everything, but I wanna talk to 'em as soon as possible, like tomorrow morning. I wanna talk to her first, okay? Say somethin' like, uh, lemme think, uh, like, uh, we're aware they have to make all the arrangements for the funeral and we know how difficult this can be for everybody and we wish to express our deepest sympathy for their loss, but, uh, a homicide was committed and we don't have any choice but to, uh, investigate it. It's our job and they have to understand that no matter how much we hate doin' it to them at this time, they have to understand it's our job and we have to do it, okay, how's that?"

"In pretty much that order?"

"Yeah, pretty much. But first, sit 'em down and tell 'em. If they freak out on ya and you need a hand, call me back, okay? I'll figure somethin' out about how to get out of here. But after you tell 'em, you know, be sure the next thing you say, you express condolences, you know, from the department and from the city, okay? And then tell 'em she's still up in the hospital, but they're not gonna be able to get in to see her, I don't think, unless you can get hold of Grimes and maybe he'll let 'em in. But I'm sure without his okay, nobody up there's gonna let 'em in, do you think? Whatta you think, Harry, huh? I wanna know what you think."

"I think you got it right. That's what I would've done, but I just wanted to make sure. Okay, lemme get to it."

"Harry? Just a second. Make sure she knows I wanna see her no later'n ten tomorrow morning, okay? And him no later than the afternoon. 'Cause Milliron and me are gonna be sittin' down with somebody in the DA's office at eight tomorrow, so we should be finished by ten easy and that's when I want her there, okay?"

"Okay, Rugs, you got it."

"Harry, wait, don't hang up."

"I'm still here. What?"

"Uh, one more thing. Whatta they look like? Worried, scared, nervous, what?"

"Not really, no. Just said he thought his mother was supposed to be back from New York yesterday or the day before yesterday, I don't think he knew when she was supposed to be back, but anyway she's not home and he was startin' to get a little antsy, that's all. Otherwise, they look like a coupla hot dogs on their way back from the beach, you know. Nothin' unusual otherwise. Not that I can tell."

"Okay. Just also don't forget to tell 'em we got somebody in custody, okay? Don't say who, don't say for what, okay?"

"Okay, Rugs. See ya."

Son of a bitch, Carlucci thought as he hung up. They're back. He's back. Carlucci shivered and felt an odd tingling in his scalp, felt his mouth go dry, felt his heart thumping.

"Rugsie, what're you doin', come in here, c'mon, you're missin' the end here, hurry up."

"Be right there, Ma. I'm comin'. Honest, just gotta get a drink of water here."

"Oh the hell with the water, c'mon, you're gonna miss how she solves it, hurry up, Jesus, you're slower'n dirt."

Carlucci filled a plastic tumbler with tap water and stood by the sink, drinking and thinking. Tomorrow was it. Tomorrow was the day. Tomorrow he was going to get them, he felt it as sure as he felt every swallow of water.

"Rugsie! Goddammit! What're you doin'?"

"Just drinkin' and thinkin', Ma, that's all. Be right there."

"Uh, Detective Sergeant Ruggiero Carlucci, Rocksburg PD, uh, first interview with Mrs. Alfredo Picadio Junior, ten-hundred-ten hours, 11 January 1993, interview room one, Rocksburg PD station, Rocksburg City Hall, Rocksburg, Conemaugh County, Pa. Present also is state police trooper Claude Milliron. Mrs. Picadio, would you please state your full name, age, address, and occupation?"

"I don't understand what's goin' on here," Mrs. Picadio said. "Last night when he said you wanted us—me—to come down here this morning, it was like, to clear some things up, I don't know what, but now here I am and you got that tape recorder goin', and I don't know what's going on. What's the tape recorder goin' for, I mean why's that have to be on?"

"Just state your name please? And age and address and so on, please?"

"This is really givin' me the creeps, I'm tellin' ya. I don't like that thing bein' on like that—"

Carlucci held up his hands. "It's simple, Mrs. Picadio. I don't trust my memory, the city can't afford a stenographer, and I can't take shorthand, so if I want to have an accurate record of a felony investigation, I have to have some way of doin' it, and this is the way I do that, that's all there is to it, there's nothin' else goin' on here."

"Oh so now you're gonna patronize me, for Christ's sake.

I get the message, you don't need to paint me a picture, I'm not stupid. You think we were involved with this, my God—"

"Just say what your name is, please? And your address—"

"Oh for Christ's sake, all right already. My name is Mrs. Alfredo Picadio Junior. My maiden name was Mary Dolores Gervase. Is. That's still my maiden name. Mary Dolores. My friends call me Dolly. Satisfied?"

"And your age, please, and your address and where you work, please."

"Oh for Christ's sake. I'm fifty-six. My address is number 12 Mercury Way, RD 9. We own Rocksburg Pre-Cast Concrete Company. I'm the sales manager. Do I have to give the address for the company or do you know where that is?"

"No, ma'am, we know where it is."

"Well it's a very prominent company in its field, but a lot of people don't know where it is."

Carlucci shot a glance at Milliron, but said nothing.

"So last night you said you had somebody in custody, so who is it?"

"Mrs. Picadio, I didn't talk to you last night, so just let me ask the questions, okay?"

"Well that cop that was here, he said! Not you, him!"

"I don't know what he said. I haven't talked to him—"

"Well either you have somebody arrested for this or you don't, which is it? Last night you guys're sayin' you have somebody—"

"Not me, Mrs. Picadio, I didn't say—"

"You know what I mean!"

"No, I don't."

"Oh sure. Today you don't know anything, you're singin' a different tune today, but what I want to know is what's goin' on here? You tellin' me I'm not allowed to ask any questions? Like who you got arrested? What, I don't have a right to know that? My God, it was my mother-in-law—"

"I didn't say I didn't have anybody in custody today," Carlucci said. "I didn't say anything like that. All I'm sayin' is, at this point, it wouldn't help either one of us for you to know who that is, that's all I'm sayin'. Uh, Mrs. Picadio, what I want to know, since you worked in the office, you said you were the sales manager, correct?"

"That's what I said, Jesus yes, I'm the sales manager."

"Didn't your mother-in-law also work in the office?"

"Well of course she did. I mean if she didn't work in the office it probably wouldn't've happened, would it? Course she worked in the office."

"So you worked with her, right?"

"I worked in the office, she worked in the office, it's a small office, of course I worked with her, what's your point?"

"Who took care of the books?"

"The books? Oh what, you think I did somethin' funny with the books? Jesus Christ I don't believe this."

"Who took care of the books, please, you or her?"

"She did. And our accountant. DeFelice. She did the day-to-day things, and then—on the computer she did it, some kind of spreadsheet somethin', I don't know what it's called. She got a computer two years ago, she took a class at the community college, she learned how to work the program and everything, I could never figure it out, but she would've never let me do it anyway and she wanted to do it, so I let her. I had enough to do anyway. And then, every three months, she'd go to DeFelice and they'd do the quarterly tax things, and then at the end of the year she'd get everything ready for him and then he'd do the annual tax things. That's why she was in the office, that's the only reason she'd be in the office—I still can't believe this, she said she was gonna go to New York, see some shows. If she'd of gone to New York the way she said she was goin' to, none of this would've ever happened. I don't know why she didn't go. She loved the theater. She went every year to New York, at least once. I used to go with her, but we got too busy. She loved Broadway. I can't believe this."

"Who took care of the money?"

"I just told you she took care of the books. Didn't I just say that?"

"I know you said that. I heard you. What I'm askin' you now is, who took care of the money? Who signed the checks, who tallied up the daily sales, you know?"

"Oh you mean the money every day. Why didn't you say so? Whoever felt like goin' to the bank. Sometimes I did, sometimes she did, sometimes Al."

"Who tallied it up?"

"She did. Listen, what're you sayin'—she was doin' somethin' funny with the books? Baloney. It was her business. What, she was diddlin' her own business? Puh-lease. She didn't have any reason to, my God, she had everything she wanted. Anytime she wanted anything, she just bought it, what—you think she was dippin' into the cash drawer? Oh please. Believe me, the only thing she wanted she couldn't have was grandchildren."

"Uh, you're older than your husband, aren't you?"

Mrs. Picadio stiffened, her chin pulling back into her neck. Her neck right above her collarbone gave her away. Her deeply tanned face was smooth, artificially taut, but the skin right above the collar of her blouse was a crosshatch of wrinkles and mottled with liver spots. As were her hands. She'd kept her hands on the table ever since she'd sat down, the better, Carlucci guessed, to display all the rings, eight of them, as well as her perfect crimson nails. But when she pulled back, the wrinkling on her neck intensified.

"What's that have to do with anything?"

"Well, you were just sayin' how your mother-in-law wanted grandchildren and she couldn't have 'em. Which I took to mean you couldn't have 'em, and I was just askin' if it was because you were older than your husband, that's all. How old were you when you got married? Was this your first marriage? His first?"

She pulled back even further. "I don't see what you're asking all these questions for. What kind of questions are these? Whatta you wanna know these things for? Whatta they have to do with her, uh, with what happened to her? I don't understand and I don't like it. And if these're the kinda questions you asked me to come in here for, I'm walking out of here right now 'cause I'm not gonna answer personal questions like this."

Carlucci never hesitated. "Mrs. Picadio, you and your husband spent a lot of money in the last couple of years—"

"Oh that's it!" she said, jumping up and sending her chair scraping backward until it hit the wall.

"Sit down, Mrs. Picadio."

"You kiss my rosy red ass and get outta my way, I'm not gonna say another goddamn word to you. Who the hell do you think you are, we spent a lotta money in the last couple of years, you little twerp. You got any idea who Al is? You know how prominent we are in this community? Huh? You know Angelo Bellotti?"

"I know the mayor, Mrs. Picadio. He's my boss, sit down, please."

"Oh he's my boss," she mimicked him. "Well, *my* husband gave *your* boss twelve hundred dollars for his campaign last summer, Charlie Brown, which just happened to be the biggest single contribution he got from anybody, buster, and when I tell him how you been talkin' to me in here, you little pisspot, you're gonna be lucky they let you clean toilets—"

"Sit down, Mrs. Picadio."

"You get outta my way, I'm not gonna tell you again. My mother-in-law's not even in her casket yet, never mind in the ground, and you're talkin' to me like I'm some baby machine on welfare, some teenage welfare whore, oh this's gonna cost you, you little shit, you just wait and see. Get outta my way!"

"I'm not gettin' outta your way, Mrs. Picadio, and you're not leavin' till I understand some things—"

"I don't give a shit from a snake what you don't understand, you little prick—"

"Sit down, Mrs. Picadio, I'm not gonna tell you again. If we have to, we'll handcuff you to the table and the worst thing right now for you to think is we can't do it. 'Cause believe me, we can. So sit down."

She tried to bluff it out, but the longer she looked at Milliron, the more she seemed to sense that Carlucci would do what he'd said. After she lifted her chin several times, each time exhaling noisily through her mouth, she sat back down. Carlucci guessed that gesture was supposed to mean she thought she was still in charge, but it struck him as being so childish he nearly got the giggles.

Instead, he said softly, "Thank you, Mrs. Picadio. I appreciate that. Now what I wanna ask you again is, just to clarify this in my own mind, you didn't ever tally the daily take, is that what you're sayin'?"

"Yes. That's what I'm saying."

"Was this ever a problem for you? With your husband?"

She snorted and laughed. "What're you talking about, what kinda problem?"

"Well, did you ever think you should be learning how to do what she did? Ever say to your husband, one day somethin' could happen to her, and you'd have to keep the books, take over—"

"I used to keep the books! Before she got the computer! I did it for years, then one day she decides she wants this computer and she wants to do the books on the computer, so I said, hey, you wanna do it, do it, I don't care. You wanna know the truth, that stuff bores me. She said fine. I said fine."

"Oh. I see. So you never concerned yourself with what might happen if, say, she would become incapacitated in some way. Or maybe die? People get old. They die—"

"Listen, I don't know where you're goin' with this, but I already told you, I don't know how many ways you want me to say it. I didn't care nothin' about keepin' the books. That was her job, and far as I'm concerned, she could have it."

"So, uh, you just spent the money, is that it?"

"What kinda thing is that to say—I just spent the money. I told you, I worked! I did everything else there that needed to be done, I licked stamps, I licked envelopes, I answered the phones, I made coffee, I don't just spend money, I earn it! I don't have to apologize to anybody for what I do, least of all you, you little twerp."

"Well, Mrs. Picadio, that may be true you earned your money, you don't just spend it, but the facts are, you have spent a whole lot of money in the last couple of years. You and your husband. I have here, for example, the names of all the plastic surgeons who, uh, performed, uh, elective surgery on you." Carlucci opened a manila folder and took out a sheet of paper on which he'd hand-printed the names of all the surgeons who'd operated on her. He slid it across the table to her.

She bent over to read it and gasped. "Where did you get this? You little bastard, how did you get this? These people can't tell you this, this is confidential—"

"All it is, Mrs. Picadio, is a list of surgeons' names and the procedures they performed on you and how much they charged. And down at the bottom is a list of all the hospitals' charges. And since it was all elective surgery, you and your husband paid for that—"

"It was not all elective surgery! That's baloney. Two of them were not elective surgery. I had to have those done—"

"The fact is, whether you had to have a couple of those particular procedures done is beside the point. Which point is that no insurance company covered those charges or reimbursed you for them later, even though you tried to claim that those two procedures were necessary—"

"I don't believe you! Snoopin' around in my life like this, I don't believe this!"

"As you can see, Mrs. Picadio, that's a considerable amount of money you and your husband paid—"

"So what? So what? What's this have to do with anything?"

"Uh, here's another list I think you might wanna take a look at," Carlucci said, opening the manila folder again and sliding another sheet of paper toward her. "As you can see, those are the names of the remodelers you and your husband contracted with over the past two years to do work in your home. New kitchen, new bathrooms, stuff like that. Look it over, go ahead, I want you to know what I'm talkin' about."

"I don't have to look it over," she said, scrunching up the sheet and pushing it back at him. "I know what we did. I was there. I wasn't asleep. Al and me were right there the whole time. I know what we got."

"I'm sure you know what you got, Mrs. Picadio, but what I'm also sure about is you don't have a clue what it cost—"

"And you know what I'm sure about? So what? That's what I'm sure about. What difference does it make what it cost, we paid for it! We don't owe nobody a cent!"

"Very true. That's part true. Not now you don't. But for a while there, you and your husband were gettin' a lot of registered mail. Yes ma'am, you don't owe anybody anything now, but for a while there you were gettin' a whole lot of dunning letters. I have talked to several people, doctors, hospital credit people, remodelers, they've all said they sent you registered mail, and if we have to, we can check with the post office. They keep a record of registered mail for a year, did you know that? They do. And we can check it. And even though you paid all these people off, that doesn't change the fact, ma'am, you and your husband've spent a pile of money in the last couple of years, rebuildin' your house. Rebuildin' you."

"Oh ain't you the smart-mouth cutie? 'Rebuildin' your house. Rebuildin' you.' Ain't you just too goddamn cute for words."

"Uh ha. Now the bad news, Mrs. Picadio. We got a court order for your mother-in-law's accountant, DeFelice? We got a court order so we could have our own accountant look over the books. And guess what?"

"I'm sure you're gonna tell me," she said, her jaw tight.

"This is just a preliminary finding right now, but I'm sure the rest of our accountant's report is gonna show the same thing," Carlucci lied. There was no court order, no preliminary finding by any accountant hired by the city. Carlucci was making it up as he went. "The preliminary finding is that there's no way your husband's business made anywhere near the amount of money you two spent in the last two years on the house and yourself. Couldn't happen."

"Izzat so," she said, teeth clenched. "Like I just said to you before, which if you would of been payin' attention like you should of, you would of heard me say I don't have nothin' to do with the books so I wouldn't know whether we had enough money to buy gas for the trucks never mind what else we paid for anything, what do you think of that, ya little cutie pie you? You know what I think? Huh? I think you couldn't get laid in a women's prison with both your hands fulla hundred-dollar bills, that's what I think. I think you spend too much time all by yourself, that's what I think. Can I leave now? What am I askin' you, I'm leavin'."

Carlucci stood up casually, pulled his chair aside and held out his right hand toward the door. "Feel free, Mrs. Picadio. The mayor's office, uh, in case you still wanna see him, once you get outta here, just turn right, go to the end of the hall, that's where his office—"

"I know where his office is, I been there plenty of times before."

She started to stomp out, but Carlucci put his arm out shoulder-high. She pushed against it, but was very surprised when she couldn't move it aside.

"Tell your husband don't forget," Carlucci said. "We got an appointment, soon as he gets things squared away with the funeral director. This afternoon, no later, you hear me? Tell him, don't make the mistake of tryin' to screw me around, I won't tolerate that, I promise you. He ain't here by two o'clock, I'll have every cop in the county lookin' for him."

"I'm not tellin' him anything. You want him to know somethin' you tell him. Now leave me outta here."

Carlucci dropped his arm and stepped back. She huffed out of the office, her spike-heel boots rapping the floor down the hall to the mayor's office. Carlucci didn't know whether the mayor was in, but it didn't matter. He'd accomplished what he'd set out to do.

But when Carlucci turned around, he saw Milliron's mouth hanging open. Milliron was looking sorely confused. "Man, Rugs, what was that about? You just lost me. Completely. What was that?"

"Well, you tell me. Whatta ya think it was about? Wait a minute. Gotta make sure this recorder's off. Okay. Go 'head."

Milliron shook his head. "Don't get me wrong, I know you know way more about interviewing people than I do, but I really, uh, I mean, don't take this wrong, but, uh, that looked like a total waste."

Carlucci cleared his throat. "Well, to tell ya the truth, I didn't intend for it to go that way, but soon as she brought up the thing about the grandchildren, I figured, hey, here's a nerve that's been exposed for a long time, might as well touch it and see what happens. So I touched it, and you saw what happened."

"Well yeah. But what happened? I mean that's any use to us?"

"Well, you may not agree with this, but what I learned is she thinks she's somebody special. She'll lick stamps, she'll answer the phone, she'll even take money to the bank. She'll spend the money—hey, will she ever spend it, I mean, she kept those rings out there the whole time, except when she got all huffy and jumped up. That's the only time she didn't care whether the rings were out there for us to see. She'll spend the hell out of the money, but she ain't gonna be bothered with all the little details, like countin' it to make sure it's right."

"And so, what's admissible about that?" Milliron said, his mouth dropping open again after he finished talking.

"Admissible? C'mon, Claude, you don't think it's worth somethin' to find that out about Dolly, who, if nothin' bad happened and life went on like she thinks it's supposed to—I mean, sooner or later, her husband was gonna inherit the business, right? But Dolly doesn't wanna take the trouble to count the money? She'll lick stamps and envelopes, she'll take the cash bag to the bank, but she can't be bothered with that one little detail?

"I think that was real important to learn, Claude, I'm not sayin' you have to agree with me, but I'm glad I learned that. 'Cause what that tells me is she didn't have a fuckin' clue what was goin' on. She thinks her old man's a money tree. So I think I saved us a whole lotta time just pissin' her off like that. I'm not sayin' you have to agree, of course, but that's what I got out of it. I mean, far as I'm concerned, I think we can zip this one up real fast. Especially since you found that pistol. Man, I'm so glad you found that. 'Cause, now, I don't think we have to think about her at all. Dolly. Imagine. Some people got the right names, no shit. Anyway, I mean, I think this was all him."

Carlucci turned the tape recorder on and identified himself, the case number, the time, the date, the location, and the identities of the others in the room, Milliron and Alfredo Picadio Jr.

Before Carlucci could say anything else, Picadio, leaning forward toward the tape recorder, said loudly, "I ain't answerin' nothin' till my attorney gets here. I don't care who you are or where we are, this is an outrage. This is a goddamn outrage to treat me and my wife like this, to treat us like this . . . and my mother . . . my mother is not . . . God rest her soul . . ." He couldn't continue. His shoulders began to shake, he flung his head forward onto his arms, and he began to sob.

Carlucci turned and looked at Milliron. Milliron looked back. They shrugged at each other and sat back in their chairs and waited.

When Picadio picked his head up finally, his eyes were nearly puffed shut and his nose was dribbling clear mucus onto his upper lip. He struggled to get a hanky out of his back pocket, bouncing up once to let it come clear of his pocket, and he wiped his eyes and face and blew his nose. He cleared his throat several times, trying to talk, but just shook his head and fought back more sobs.

Carlucci cleared his own throat, and said softly, "For the record, Mr. Picadio, you have asked for your attorney to be present and we know he's on his way, but I want you to know that you are a suspect in a conspiracy to commit a felony, namely robbery—"

"What?" Picadio's eyes rolled and he blinked ponderously twice. "What did you say?"

"You heard me, Mr. Picadio, I said it very clearly. And you know why I said it. What I'm telling you now is—and I want you to be very clear about this, I don't want there to be any doubt later on about when you were informed that you were—are—a suspect in a felony, you understand? I'm telling you now, that as of this minute, the minute this interrogation began I am informing you that you are a suspect. You hear me now?"

"I heard you! I just don't believe you! My wife said you were a little bastard, but I didn't believe her either. How the fuck could you believe this about me? That was my mother for crissake! You sonofabitch you, we weren't in this room I'd beat your fuckin' head in, I'd bust your fuckin' skull, you said this to me anywhere else!" He was on his feet, veins bulging in his neck and forehead, hands doubled into fists.

Milliron said quietly, "Sit down. Sit down or I'm going to put you down, put handcuffs on you, and lock them to the table. I'm not going to say it again."

Picadio's eyes shot wildly for an instant from Milliron to Carlucci and back. His breathing was getting louder and faster, and his nose was running again. He looked down at his fists and then back at Milliron and eased back down onto the chair. He kept his hands in his lap.

"All I've said to you, Mr. Picadio, is that you are a suspect in a felony and in a conspiracy to commit a felony. And I'm saying it again, Mr. Picadio: you are a suspect in a conspiracy to commit a felony, namely robbery. I'm also gonna tell you that I'm very confident that between us, between Trooper Milliron and myself, we have all the evidence we need to make the case against you. You hear what I said? I said I'm very confident about this. And you wanna know why, Mr. Picadio? Huh? I'm gonna tell you why. 'Cause what happened to your mother shouldn't't've happened to a rabid rat. Nobody deserved what happened to your mother. Nobody."

"Shut up!" Picadio said, clamping his hands over his ears. His head sank onto his chest and he shook it from side to side many times.

"Aw no, I'm not gonna shut up, Mr. Picadio. And neither is Trooper Milliron. And neither are the EMTs who found your mother. And neither are the doctors and nurses that tried to keep her alive, in the emergency room. And neither are the doctors and nurses in the ICU who tried to do the same thing. And neither is the coroner, who knows *exactly* how your mother died. And we're all gonna be testifyin', Mr. Picadio. Against you, in court, for the whole world to hear. There's gonna be reporters there, photographers, they're gonna be takin' your picture every time you walk in and outta that courthouse—"

"Shut up!"

"Oh no, Mr. Picadio, I'm not gonna shut up about this. I'm not ever gonna shut up about this, 'cause this is the most disgusting thing I have ever seen in twenty-two years as a police officer. The only time I ever saw things more disgusting than this was when I was in Vietnam. And, Mr. Picadio, you were the one got the ball rollin' on this disgusting thing, sir. You. Nobody else. You and your buddy Pinhead, remember him? Huh? Paulie? You two planned it out, and you hired a person to carry it out, only what you didn't know is, that person you hired, he hired another person to actually do the burglary, 'cause he knew what kind of man you are, Mr. Picadio. He didn't know at the beginning what you were, but he figured it out soon enough, oh yeah. He figured you were lyin' to everybody. Isn't that right, Mr. Picadio, you were tryin' to trick everybody, weren't ya?"

Picadio's hands were still clamped tightly over his ears.

Somebody knocked on the door and Milliron opened it and leaned around it to see who it was. He came back and closed it, but kept his hand on the knob, and he said, "His lawyer's here. Want me to let him in now or we going to wait for whoever the DA's sending, what? What do you think's holding up the DA?"

Carlucci shrugged. "Hey, they don't wanna keep their appointments, what're we s'posed to do? We told 'em for two hours this morning. How many ways we gotta tell 'em? How many times?"

Milliron shrugged, opened the door, and backed away to allow a paunchy balding man to come in. He draped his gray herringbone topcoat over the back of the fourth chair in the room and set his briefcase on the table.

"Detective Carlucci," the paunchy man said, extending his right hand, "always a pleasure." He turned to Milliron, extended his hand and said, "F. Louis Feinberg, attorney-at-law, and you are?"

Milliron introduced himself, then everybody sat down.

"Alfred? I'm here, Alfred, you feeling all right? Is there something I can do for you right at this moment? You look terribly distressed. Can I be of immediate assistance?"

Picadio shook his head, still slumped forward, his hands still over his ears, but at least the tips of his fingers were no longer white.

Feinberg looked at Carlucci and shrugged. "Where's the ADA? I understood somebody was going to be here."

Carlucci splayed his hands and shook his head. "I don't know where he is, Mr. Feinberg. He said he'd be here, that's all I know. When we were layin' out the case for him, he said he'd be here. You wanna call the DA and ask him where his guy is, be my guest. You don't, that's fine. You wanna start, you don't wanna start, whatever you wanna do is okay with me."

"Well, no sense wasting time, let's get started. They'll get here when they get here. Time flies as we all know, and sooner or later we're all going to get to look at what you have, so why make me go through all the motions, we're all adults here, right? So what do we have here, Detective?"

"Hey, you wanna start, fine with me. DA got a problem with that, you two can fight it out, but I'm tellin' you right now, don't you come back on me about this. I'm not gonna listen to that, understood?"

Feinberg nodded and waved his fingers dismissively. "Don't worry about it, just tell me what we have here."

"Okay, just remember. There's the two of you there and the two of us here and the tape recorder's on, okay? Understood?"

"Understood, fine, okay, get on with it."

"Okay, so what we have here is a homicide at the end of three other felonies, a robbery, an aggravated assault which led to the death of the victim, and a rape. I cannot tell you for certain in which order these things happened. I don't think anybody can, I don't know. All I'm sayin' right now is, that's beyond my knowledge at this time."

"Go on."

"Obviously, the coroner's gonna testify to the cause, mechanism, and means. His report's right here. We have interviews with several people, namely one Luther Alonzo

Givins, who will testify—in exchange for less time naturally—that he was hired by Mr. Picadio here to rob his place of business. Mr. Givins, who is the nephew of the woman who was employed as a cook by the victim, Mr. Picadio's mother, will testify that Mr. Picadio told him that because of the, uh, the outrageous expenses his wife had run up as a result of her, uh, desire I guess is the word to use, uh, to rebuild herself and her house, Mr. Picadio had no choice but to get some money fast. A large amount of money. People were startin' to dun the hell out of him. We haven't done it yet, but if we have to, we can go check the postal records on registered mail to verify what they've said.

"And we have also interviewed, we being Trooper Milliron and myself, separately and together, a certain Paul John Colella, whose name I'm sure you're familiar with, Counselor. Girardo Colella, remember? I think you used to represent him, didn't ya?"

"Still do," Feinberg sniffed. "Make your point."

"You know his nephew, Paul? The one they call Pinhead?"

"I'm familiar with him, yes, go on."

"Well Mr. Paul Colella, it turns out, used to be good buddies with your client here. Seems they spent a lotta time hangin' out together over the last few years, you know, goin' to the tracks, Waterford Park, the Meadows, you know. And it also seems that Mr. Colella is in fear for his life and he will do damn near anything not to get his uncle any more pissed off at him than he already is. But I think you would maybe know more about this than we would, Counselor, I could be wrong."

"I'm listening. Go on. Where is Paulie, by the way?"

Carlucci's eyebrows went up. " 'By the way? Where is Paulie by the way'? You kiddin' me? Where do you think?"

Feinberg cleared his throat. "Had to ask. You know that. So get on with it."

"Had to ask, yeah, right. Well, since Pinhead is convinced Uncle Gerry's gonna cut his nuts off and nail 'em to his chest, and since he has also managed to convince the U.S. attorney of the same thing, where do you think he is? Actually, where he is isn't really important far as we're concerned. On the other hand, the tapes of his conversations with us, now they're right here." Carlucci took three sixty-minute tapes out of his briefcase and pushed them across the table to Feinberg. "And you're welcome to play them for yourself and anybody else who wants to listen. We got the originals. U.S. attorney's got copies, and I'm sure they're makin' more, but if you want me to give you a quick summary of what's on 'em, I'll be glad to do that."

"If you would, please, yes."

"Okay. What you're gonna hear on these tapes, is, uh, Paulie, contrary to Uncle Gerry's wishes, he got himself involved in some family business, namely the sale and distribution of illegal drugs, namely amphetamines, PCP, and cocaine. Had a nice little sideline goin' with one of his uncle's soldiers, one Joseph Gambelini, also known as Joey Gambels, you know him?"

Feinberg said nothing.

"Well, this is all unbeknownst to his uncle, of course, and as things will happen, his boss in this sideline, Joey Gambels, for some reason or other, he started to bust Paulie's balls over something, exactly what, Paulie won't say. But, uh, also as things will happen, his buddy Al Junior here, is also havin' serious money problems, so he starts, uh, Al here, he starts lettin' Paulie start usin' his place of business, the Rocksburg Pre-Cast Concrete Company, as a stash. For both illegal drugs and cash. In return for which, of course, Al Junior takes a certain percentage, I think the amount was usually ten percent, but sometimes more, sometimes less. You with me so far?"

Feinberg was rolling his tongue back and forth on the inside of his lower lip. "Go on."

"Well, as these things will happen, it seems the faster your client makes money from this little scheme, which of course Uncle Gerry isn't supposed to know anything about, the faster he makes the money, the faster his wife can dream up new ways to spend it. And he, being the good husband that he is, but the big stupido, he can't think of new ways to make it. So I don't know at this point exactly whose idea it was, whether it was Paulie's or your client's, but one of them schemes out this little plan to get Paulie's boss, Joey Gambels, to advance him, Paulie, a large amount of cash, apparently much larger than he'd ever handled before, so the two of them can then set up a phony robbery—burglary, whatever you wanna call it, 'cause they sure weren't gonna report it to us—that will not only make them both a pile of money but will also get Gambels in a lot of heat with Paulie's uncle, apparently in payback for all the shit Gambels has been givin' him, you follow me?"

"I follow you," Feinberg said.

"There's more."

"Let's hear it."

"Well the part I already told you is on tape, but this part, what I'm gonna say now, this is all surmisin' on my part, 'cause I don't have any evidence. It's just that there isn't any other logical explanation. So maybe when you talk to him about how he wants to proceed, you'll discuss it with him."

"Less melodrama, Detective, if you don't mind. What's your surmise?"

"Okay. Paulie was just tryin' to trick his uncle and Gambels. But your client here, he was tryin' to trick everybody. What I figure is, he probably told Paulie they'd split it after they got it back from Luther Givins. After they killed Mr. Givins. Because that was what they were gonna tell Paulie's uncle about what happened to the money. Only thing was, the guy they hired to do the burglary, Givins, he figured that out for himself. So since he had his own problem with your client—he was afraid your client was gonna screw up a housing arrangement your client's mother had with Mr. Givins's aunt—because he was afraid of that happening, Mr. Givins in turn hired somebody else to do the actual burglary. Only two problems with that—where there was supposed to be fifty thousand cash, there was no money. And where there was supposed to be nobody, there was your client's mother. And the person Mr. Givins hired, one Wandoe Evon Best, when he ran into that situation, where there was a person and no money where there was supposed to be no person and lots of money, he went nuts and did the terrible thing we all know about. All because your client here needed the whole fifty thousand, real bad. 'Cause he'd been gettin' registered mail from all over the place, doctors, hospitals, contractors, everybody was on his ass. The only people he paid off in full were the plumbers. But by the time Wandoe Evon Best shows up lookin' for the fifty large, all the rest of the people had already been paid. In full—"

"Shuddup! Shuddup!" Picadio screamed, lunging across the table at Carlucci.

Carlucci pulled back so quickly he tipped his chair over backward, but kept himself from going over with it only to slam into the wall with his shoulder. He needn't have ducked. Milliron was on Picadio in a blur, pulling him across the table and slamming him to the floor in one motion, dropping his right knee on the back of Picadio's neck and twisting Picadio's left arm down and around to the small of his back. He had Picadio's right hand stretched out and pinned to the floor with his own right hand. "Want to give me a hand here?" Milliron grunted to Carlucci.

Carlucci reached around behind his own belt and got his handcuffs and knelt beside Picadio, still squirming around on the floor while Feinberg was saying, "Alfred! Alfred, this is not a good move, Alfred. Alfred! You hear me? You're making everything worse for yourself."

"Fuck you too," Picadio said, his face twisted against the concrete floor. His squirming was growing weaker by the moment, mostly because Milliron was bearing down on his knee onto Picadio's neck.

Carlucci secured the cuffs finally and Milliron hauled Picadio up off the floor and into a chair opposite where he had been sitting. Milliron, stretching his neck, smoothing out his shirtsleeves, and tucking in his shirt, stood directly behind Picadio.

Carlucci tucked in his own shirt and twisted his belt around so that the buckle was back where it was before Picadio lunged at him. He looked at Picadio, but spoke to Feinberg. "I, uh, I don't think there's any point in chargin' him with assault on a police officer, Counselor, 'cause I think he's already got enough problems, but you better tell him not to do that again."

"Alfred? Did you hear what the detective said. I caution you, Alfred, I'm advising you as a friend as well as your attorney, please don't do anything like that again, please."

"Aw go fuck yourself," Picadio snarled, his head rolling from side to side, his gaze fixed on the floor. "My mother's dead, I'm s'posed to worry what he says, huh? Fuck him too. Who cares . . . fuckin' bathrooms. You know how many fuckin' bathrooms we got? Huh? Three! Three and a half! We got a fuckin' half a bathroom! How can you have a half a bathroom? I'm askin' myself, how many places can you piss at one time, huh? How many places you need to have so you can shit, huh? We got to have three . . . and a half! That's four toilets! Four! My wife got one hole to piss out of, I got one hole to piss out of, but we got four holes to piss into! Yeah. Four! And they're all new! Fuckin'-A. Five thousand dollars apiece for the three full baths, oh yeah! Oh yes, bet your ass! And for the little half bathroom? Huh? The cutesy-poo little fuckin' powder room we got to have for our guests, huh? That we got to have all foo-fooed up for these fuckin' guests we're always havin' only they never come back, huh? Or they never show up in the first place, huh? Twenty-five yards for that fuckin' powder room! Oh yeah. You know who shows up at my house, huh? These parties my wife's always havin', she sends out these fuckin' invitations. Yeah. The fuckers are engraved! Engraved fuckin' invitations to people I don't know, people she wants to get to know better, people who never show up! Oh they used to show up. Oh yeah. They show up once, twice, then fuckit, you never see 'em again! You know who shows up, huh? The mayor showed up one time. Yeah. My wife paid some fuckin' caterer about four hundred bucks for food, we wind up takin' it down the Salvation Army. The mayor didn't even bring his wife. He shows up, half shitface, stays about half a fuckin' hour, he don't eat nothin', just drinks, till I gotta drive the fucker home. I told her, I say, these people don't wanna know you, why the fuck you keep askin' 'em to come around, they don't know you, they don't wanna know you, who are these people, they wouldn't give a fuck you dropped dead on their lawn, what the fuck you invitin' 'em here for? You know what she says, huh? She says—get this—she says we're prominent in the community, we gotta act like it. Prominent in the fuckin' community! We make fuckin' burial vaults, we ain't prominent! We make fuckin' patio stones! Splash blocks, tongue-and-groove wall blocks, we ain't fuckin' prominent in nothin' 'cept the concrete business!

"You know who else shows up? Paulie the Pinhead shows up, that's who! Paulie! He don't get an invitation but he shows up, bet your ass, he got fuckin' radar or somethin', I don't know how he hears about this shit, but open the door and there he is! Oh yeah. And who does he bring with him? His whores, that's who. That's who winds up pissin' in my brand-new toilets! Whores! Niggers! Some of 'em are niggers, he brings 'em to my house, he thinks it's funny! I say to him, who the fuck knows where they been, who they been with, this fuckin' asshole, he laughs, he thinks it's a big goddamn joke, he brings 'em to my house! I'm schemin' with this fuckin' asshole so I can pay for toilets 'cause my wife thinks we're gonna have parties for these people who never come back—and who winds up pissin' in 'em? Nigger whores! And my mother's dead! Jesus Christ . . . my mother's dead . . . this is what I was put here for? To make a burial vault for my mother? Jesus Christ . . . Jesus Christ . . ."

Carlucci looked at Feinberg and said, after a moment, "I think you oughta hear these." He reached into his briefcase again and brought out four cassettes and stacked them in front of Feinberg.

"These are what, now, that you're giving me?"

"Those are copies of the interviews I had with Luther Givins. I'm sure you'll see I wasn't exaggeratin' anything I said. There's one more thing I want you to know, Counselor, before you decide how you wanna go with this. The physical evidence is a lock."

"Indulge me. How so?"

"The Allegheny County lab is gonna tie the bullets they took out of Wandoe Best to the nine-millimeter pistol Trooper Milliron found in Luther Givins's Oldsmobile. So the physical evidence there is gonna back up Givins's confession to that shooting. Which shooting took place inside your client's mother's Pontiac. The physical evidence taken from the victim in that homicide, by the Allegheny coroner, blood, semen, hair, and fiber, that all ties him to your client's mother, which also backs up Luther Givins. We got the report from Troop A crime lab on that yesterday morning, so everything Givins says is backed up. Which all goes to back up everything Paulie Colella says. Haven't had time to make copies of the lab reports, but I can do that real fast, coupla minutes, just gotta go down the hall to the secretary's office."

Feinberg nodded and said, "I'd like to talk to Alfred now."

"Fine. I'll make these copies for you, I'll be back in a coupla minutes."

Outside, before Carlucci headed for the copier in the city secretary's office, he said to Milliron, "Hey, Claude, you get a chance to get up to Miss Brown's place? Give her the money, huh?"

"Oh yeah, didn't I tell you that?"

"If you did I musta been thinkin' about somethin'. So what'd she say?"

"Oh she was very very happy, very excited. Kept saying, 'Oh thank you, Mr. State Trooper Man, oh thank you Mr. State Trooper Man.' She was pretty excited. That was neat. Uh, I want to thank you, Rugs."

"For what?"

"For letting me do that. I know you could've done that yourself."

"Hey," Carlucci said shrugging. "Every once in a while you need to, uh, you know, look into somebody's eyes and see they don't hate ya. Even for a coupla seconds. Does ya good, believe me. Listen, long as I'm makin' copies for the shyster, you want some?"

"Just the ones from Allegheny County. I already go copies from our lab." Milliron ran his tongue around the inside of his mouth. "Hey, Rugs, I wanna say something."

"Sure. Go 'head."

"Uh, just want to say it's been a pleasure working with you. I mean it."

"Hey, same here, man. Thanks. I appreciate that."

Balzic finished pouring the Rolling Rock for Carlucci and poured himself half a glass of French merlot. He took a seat across the kitchen table and then stood back up. "You want some provolone? Huh? Some gorgonzola? How about some calamata olives? C'mon, it'll give me an excuse to have some. It's all fresh as hell. Just got it this mornin', me and Ruthie were in the Strip all morning. God, I love that place."

"Nah, Mario, thanks anyway. Just the beer's fine. I'm not hungry, really, but you go ahead, you know."

"Rugs, shit man, you look like you got a world on each shoulder." Balzic sat back down and held the merlot aloft to study the color against the ceiling light. "Can't be that bad. You get offered the job, hell, I thought you wanted it. Get to put those scrambled eggs on your cap. Don't you want it now, what's the problem?" He sipped the merlot and held it in his mouth, sloshing it from side to side before swallowing.

"What's the problem, Cheezo man. My mother . . . oh, man, all I did was, Mario, honest to God, all I did was just start to talk about it, you know, just—just barely get started. Just said, 'Hey, Ma, I just want you to think about somethin', okay? Just give it some thought, you know, you don't have to go gettin' upset about it or nothin' 'cause nothin's set, all we're gonna do right now is I want ya to think about it maybe, you know? Just think about goin' to the county home, you know, just roll it around in your mind a little bit,' that's all I said, and, man! You'da thought I was—Jesus Christ, I don't know what she thought I was tryin' to do, but, man, it was, shit, I couldn'ta done anything worse to her if I'da thrown a hand grenade in her lap. Man, she come outta that chair at me, Jeeeez-us, screamin', swingin', 'Whatta you

tryin' to do, you ungrateful little bastard, I turn my back fo
five minutes you wanna put me in the goddamn county
home, I changed your diapers for ya, I fed ya, I clothed ya,
kept a roof over your head, me and your father, who do ya
think did all those things for ya, ya-ta-ta ya-ta-ta,' didn't
know who did that for me all those years I couldn't take care
of myself, oh man. I'm tellin' ya, Mario, I been called a
sonofabitch and a bastard by a lotta people in my life, but
man, when she said—holy shit, I mean when she called me
those things, God, I got such a chill, I'm tellin' ya, it went
right up my guts, up my esophagus, I thought, man, she's
gonna kill me. Honest to God, all I could think of was, no
shit, keep her outta the kitchen, man, don't let her get near
the knives, she's freaked. Completely."

Listening to Carlucci, Balzic just kept shaking his head.
"Hey, Rugs, I'm sure I don't have to tell you, but that's the
hardest thing—I think anyway—nah, not the hardest, but one
of the hardest things, any kids and parents have to deal with.
Christ, I can't imagine, you know, what I'm gonna feel
like—what the hell, I live long enough, it's gonna happen.
You know, Marie and Emily, one day, they're gonna come to
me, they're gonna say, hey, you know—who knows what
they're gonna say—Hey, ya old geezer, this is the second
time you wrecked the car, or whatever. Or the second time
you set the kitchen on fire, or whatever. Believe me, I can
imagine how your mother felt. I mean, sittin' around here, all
the time, much as I do, you know, I don't feel real real useful
myself, you know what I mean?"

"Yeah, but what am I s'posed to say, Mario? I mean I
don't know what to say. How'm I s'posed to say it? I mean
Bellotti, hey, he's about as subtle as gravel in your roller
oats, you know? 'You want the job? Fine. We want you to
have the job. We think you're gonna make a fine chief, an
outstanding chief. Blah blah blah, look at the way you han

dled this Picadio case. Brilliant police work, brilliant. I know people in the county, I can get your mother moved to the top of the list at the home. Next opening, she's in, no problem, just say the word, she goes right to the top of the list.' Like what am I supposed to say? No, I don't want the job anymore? No, I want the job, but you can't use that on me to get me to take the job? No, I want the job but you're gonna have to figure out some other way to get me to feel grateful for the promotion? I mean what, what'm I supposed to say to them both? Christ, I don't know what to say to either one of them. But see, if there was just them, that'd be one thing. But it's not just them. There's another problem."

"Well, not that you need another one, but what?" Balzic said, going to the refrigerator to get some provolone and the calamata olives. He got a knife and a couple of plates, just in case Carlucci changed his mind.

"Okay, listen to this," Carlucci said, scooching around on his chair and putting his elbows on the table and his chin on his hands. "Suppose, just suppose—'cause it's the longest shot in the world far as I can see right now—just suppose my mother agrees to go in. So I brought it up with Mrs. Comito and Mrs. Viola, you know—the women who watch her? You know who they are, right?"

"Right right, I remember, go ahead," Balzic said, slicing some provolone and offering it to Carlucci, who closed his eyes, shook his head, and sighed. "So what about the women? What, you're worried 'cause they're gonna lose their job?"

"Yeah, of course, exactly. I mean, Christ, when I told Mrs. Comito, she started gettin' all bleary-eyed, you know, right away. She's sixty-one, she can't apply for Social Security for another year, and who knows, Christ, what she'll get, not much, you know, peanuts probably. Probably three hundred a month or somethin'. So she really needs this money. Same

with Mrs. Viola. So now all of sudden, it's not just about my
mother—who thinks I'm the biggest prick in the world for
even suggestin' it, you know. Now there's two other old
ladies—she goes in the home, they're screwed outta what I
been payin' 'em. And there's fuckin' Bellotti, he thinks he
just made me the greatest offer in the world. I'm tellin' ya,
Mario, I don't know what the fuck to do. I need some help,
man."

Balzic leaned forward and made a circle in the air with his
paring knife. "Rugsie, first thing I'm gonna tell ya, listen to
me now, I know about this stuff. First thing, you gotta quit
drinkin' beer. Beer's okay for when you just got a thirst, you
know? But when you need to think, man, ya gotta have the
wine. *In vino veritas,* that's what the old Romans used to
say, and they knew what they were talkin' about. In wine,
truth, Rugs. In wine, truth. Now, most people, what they
think that means is, you know, people start drinkin' they say
what's on their mind, they speak the truth. And that's true, I
don't doubt that for a minute. But there's another side to it,
which is what I'm tryin' to tell you now. Wine always
helped me think. You know why? Huh? It made me slow
down. I'd sip the wine, I'd look at it, I'd smell it, you know,
I'd taste it, I'd get into it. It'd slow me right down, make me
understand, remind me, you know, that I wasn't gonna get
anyplace gettin' in a big rush to get somethin' worked out.
Ya gotta switch to wine, Rugs. Beer's okay for when you're
hot, thirsty, but it doesn't do enough to slow ya down."

"C'mon, Mario, this isn't what I need to hear. And, uh,
don't take this the wrong way, okay? I mean, I understand
what you're tryin' to say, Mario, but what I need more than I
need a lecture about wine, is what am I gonna tell Bellotti?
I mean, what do I say to him? How do I say it? 'Cause for
sure, my mother's not goin' for it, I know she ain't. I bring it
up again about her goin' to the home, I don't know what

she's gonna do. I mean it. She hasn't talked to me since. She just glares at me. I keep tellin' her, you know, hey, Ma, it was just a thought, you know, you don't have to go, I was just checkin' to see how you felt about it, that's all, now I know, and, man, all she does is, wow, she just gives me this look. Jesus, scares the shit outta me, I mean, one thing's sure, that's the one thing I am not gonna be bringin' up with her again. So what do I say to him?"

Balzic shrugged. "I wish you'd let me pour you a glass of this merlot, Rugs, really. You need to slow down. Sittin' here lookin' at you, man, you're practically frantic for crissake."

Carlucci threw up his hands. "Oh go 'head, pour me one, Christ." He stood up, hitched up his pants, and took a couple of steps around the kitchen. "You're relentless."

Balzic smiled and went to a cabinet over the sink and got another glass. He rinsed it under the faucet and dried it and held it aloft to make sure there was no water or spots on it. Then he set it on the table and poured it half full of the merlot. "Here ya go, Rugs. Now don't just gulp it down. First, you slosh it around in the glass, get the smell goin', see? Then you smell it, get your nose right down in it. Take it all in. Everything it has to give ya. Then hold it up to the light, see what it has to give ya there. Take your time. Look at the edges, look at the middle, it's different. Then take a mouthful. But don't drink it. Slosh it around in your mouth, side to side, coupla times, let it get all over the roof of your mouth, your cheeks, your tongue. Then—then you swallow. And you follow it all the way down. All the way. C'mon, sit down here, c'mon. Go 'head, pick up the glass, go 'head. That's it, that's it, ain't gonna bite ya. Then, when you do that a coupla times? After you do that, then, that's right, go 'head, that's when we'll figure out what you need to say to that prick Bellotti."

Carlucci had the wine in his mouth and was moving i from side to side very tentatively, his cheeks barely bulging on each side. At last he swallowed. He licked his lips, looking as though he knew he was expected to say something bu not knowing what, so he tried to convey something through a half-grimace, half-smile, his eyebrows going up, the corners of his mouth going down, his shoulders going up, his lef hand turning over in the air and making vague ovals. "Is this good wine, huh? I don't know, is it?"

"What do you think?"

"Yeah, but what I think, I mean, I don't know whether it's any good or not, you know? I say it's good and it ain't you'll think I'm a jerk. I say it stinks and it's good, you'l think I'm a jerk."

"Rugsie, Rugsie, Jesus Christ, no wonder you're al fucked up about Bellotti. This ain't about whether I'm gonna think you're a jerk 'cause of what you say or don't say abou what's in the glass and what's in your stomach. First place of course it's good or I wouldn't be drinkin' it and if it was bad would I be givin' it to you? C'mon. But if you don't like what happens inside your nose and your mouth and your throat, it doesn't matter whether I say it's good. It just so happens I think this wine is very good. But that may also be because it was a gift from my daughters, for Christmas. So you know, maybe my taste buds are all screwed up because I'm thinkin' about who bought it for me, you know?"

"Oh man, this is all gettin' too complicated for me, really I just, I don't know, I mean, this ain't helpin' me deal with Bellotti, Mario. I understand you're tryin' to teach me some thin' here, and maybe I'm too much of a stonehead to get it but I just can't get my mind off what I'm supposed to do about him."

"You really want me to tell you what to do about him?"

"Yeah. Really. Yes. That's what I really want, Mario."

"Okay, it's real simple. You just invite Bellotti home with you."

"What? You kiddin' me?"

"No no, listen. You go to him, you say, Mr. Mayor, please, *you* have to tell my mother what you have in mind for me. You have to explain it to her, sir, *you*. *You* have to explain it to her 'cause she don't wanna hear it from me. Only you gotta be careful how you say it to him. You can't be the least bit like a smart-ass, like I was just soundin' there. You gotta go to him, you got to let him see on your face what kinda shape you're all bent out of because of this. You say it like this. You say, Mr. Mayor, I understand what you're tryin' to do for me, get my mother into the county home. Believe me, I appreciate it, but my mother, Mr. Mayor, my mother does not appreciate it. She thinks I'm tryin' to abandon her. She thinks I'm betrayin' her. She thinks I'm nothin' but an ungrateful little prick who's tryin' to get rid of his mother who worked so hard all her life, all the while I was growin' up, to bring me up right and to take care of me, and now all I wanna do is get her outta the house so I don't have to think about her no more. And you say to him as sincerely as you can, you say, Mr. Mayor, you have to help me out here. I wanna accept your offer. I wanna be chief. You still wanna be chief, right? You didn't change your mind?"

"Huh? Oh no. Course I want it. Yeah, absolutely."

"Well then, what you have to say to him is you believe his offer was made in absolute good faith. But you say, my mother thinks I'm tryin' to hurt her. So if you can find the time, Mr. Mayor, I would appreciate it if you would come home with me tonight, or whenever, and if you would talk to her, if you would tell her what you had in mind, so she would know I wasn't lyin' about this, makin' it all up. Because she doesn't believe that you made this offer to me. I think it would make all the difference in the world if she heard it straight from your mouth, then she'd know I wasn't just tryin' to dump her. You think you can take the time to do that, Mr. Mayor?

"See, Rugs, you approach him that way, you're not turnin' his offer down. You're turnin' it around on him, see? Whether he goes home with you or whether he just thinks about goin' home with you, it won't make any difference. He'll know he made you this offer and you think it was a good offer and you really want to accept it. 'Cause, see, you know when they say, it's not the gift, it's the thought that counts? Well, you turn that around, in Bellotti's mind, it won't be that you didn't accept the gift, it's that you wanted to accept his gift, see? Because, believe me, knowin' Bellotti the way I do? If you don't let Bellotti think you're still grateful for him tryin' to get your mother at the top of the list, man, trust me, it's very important you make him think he's done something wonderful for you. You can't deny him that or he'll become a real pain in the ass. He'll make trouble for you every chance he gets. He will."

"Oh Mario, I don't know, man, I don't know if I could bring that off."

"Sure you can. Here, c'mon, have some more wine. And forget about it for a while. Tell me about this Picadio thing. All I know is what I been readin' in the *Gazette* and you know what they tell ya. Nothin'. C'mon, I wanna hear how you got this good son, this member of what—what'd his wife say? They were a prominent family? Is 'at what she said, no shit? A prominent family?"

"Oh yeah. That ain't all she said. Kept callin' me a little twerp. Kept tellin' me how much money her old man gave Bellotti last election. Oh man—you wanna hear the tape, huh? I got it right here, you wanna hear it? It's hilarious. Besides, maybe I listen to it again, who knows, maybe I'll be able to stop thinkin' about Bellotti for a little while. And my mother, God."

"Course I wanna hear it, you kiddin'? Play it, play it, go 'head. But don't forget the wine, Rugs, really. Remember the wine. You need to do that."

"Yeah," Carlucci said, sighing, putting the tape into his recorder and turning it on. "Maybe you're right."

Welcome to the Island of Morada—getting there is easy, leaving . . . is murder.

Embark on the ultimate, on-line, fantasy vacation with
MODUS OPERANDI.

Join fellow mystery lovers in the murderously fun MODUS OPERANDI, unique on-line, multi-player, multi-service, interactive, mystery game launched by The Mysterious Press, Time Warner Electronic Publishing and Simutronics Corporation.

Featuring never-ending foul play by your favorite Mysterious Press authors and editors, MODUS OPERANDI is set on the fictional Caribbean island Morada. Forget packing, passports and planes, entry to Morada easy—all you need is a vivid imagination.

Simutronics GameMasters are available in MODUS OPERANDI around the clock, adding new mysteries and puzzles, offering helpful hints, and tak-ing you virtually by the hand through the killer gaming environment you come in contact with players from on-line services the world over Mysterious Press writers and editors will also be there to participate real-time on-line special events or just to throw a few back with you the pub.

MODUS OPERANDI is available on-line now.

Join the mystery and mayhem on:
- America Online® at keyword MODUS
- Genie® at keyword MODUS
- PRODIGY® at jumpword MODUS

Or call toll-free for sign-up information:
- America Online® 1 (800) 768-5577
- Genie® 1 (800) 638-9636, use offer code DAF52
- PRODIGY® 1 (800) PRODIGY, use offer code MOD

Or take a tour on the Internet at
http://www. pathfinder.com/twep/games/modop

MODUS OPERANDI—It's to die for.